About the Author

Neil Coley resides in the Staffordshire City of Lichfield with his wife. He has written several books about its rich histroy. They are:

NON-FICTION
The Lichfield Book of Days
The Beauty and the Spy
Lichfield Pubs
Lichfield People
Secret Lichfield

FICTION
Lichfield Stories

An Alien Autumn is his first novel.

An
Alien
Autumn

Neil Coley

Matador
9 Priory Business Park,
Wistow Road, Kibworth Beauchamp,
Leicestershire. LE8 0RX
Tel: 0116 279 2299
Email: books@troubador.co.uk
Web: www.troubador.co.uk/matador
Twitter: @matadorbooks

ISBN 978 1800464 063

British Library Cataloguing in Publication Data.
A catalogue record for this book is available from the British Library.

Printed and bound in Great Britain by 4edge Limited
Typeset in 11pt Adobe Garamond Pro by Troubador Publishing Ltd, Leicester, UK

Matador is an imprint of Troubador Publishing Ltd

For

Martha, Polly, Annie, Elizabeth, Catherine and Mary

Now he was calm. Now he was satisfied. The great frenzy of hate and revenge that had consumed him had passed and, for the time being, he was himself again. He stood in the dark, deserted street and looked up at the night sky; it was extraordinarily clear. It had been a cold and wet day; the damp, yellow-tinged fog had been swirling around the grimy streets for most of the dull, daylight hours. But now the rain had stopped and there was no smoke, mist or clouds to obscure his view of the stars. With his keen eyesight he could see thousands of them, some brighter, some twinkling more than others, but all were beautiful - all were holy. There could be no mistake they were the work of God. Their bright magnificence convinced him that He had been pleased with what had been achieved tonight. 'My reward for doing God's work,' he whispered to himself.

But he had not been able to complete what he had set out to do. He frowned. He had silenced the woman with his knife; he had plunged it into her many times - but had been interrupted before he could use it to cut away the source of her evil and corruption. He had heard the sound of footsteps further down the street and he had been forced to abandon his work. He suddenly felt his rage return. Not now! Not now! He relaxed again. There would be other occasions. He would have more time. He would give himself more time. He would plan his work carefully from now on. He would need the dark. He would need the alleyways and dank, dismal back yards. He would need the shadows. Next time he would be more successful in fulfilling God's work. He would strike at the purple and scarlet clad Whore of Babylon when she turned her back on him – when she offered herself to him. He would grab her by her hair, lay her on the ground, slice through her neck and he would make sure that he had plenty of time to rip out all that was unholy inside her – all that was unclean. And then, when his work was done, God would smile upon him and make him calm again and dispel the pains in his head. But would his work ever be finished? There was so much to do. Would he ever have enough time? He frowned again. He didn't know. His time might be shorter than he thought; he did not have any to waste; he would act again soon - as soon as God directed him.

And then he noticed in the night sky immediately above where he stood that one of the stars was moving from left to right across the heavens. He had seen shooting stars before but this one remained bright and didn't fizzle out after a second or two. As he watched the star sped in its diamond brightness across the sky and he was suddenly sure that this was the sign he had prayed for. It was without doubt a clear signal from God that told him he was right to want to clear up the filth that surrounded him in this iniquitous place. He dropped his gaze from the sky to the street. 'Soon,' he said aloud. 'Soon I will begin to clear up. Soon I will rid this city of all its abominations.' He tapped his knife, which was tucked into his belt, lovingly cradled inside his coat, and walked on. The only sound he could hear was the click, click of his own boots echoing in the dirty, damp, deserted street.

1

Arrival

'Are you sure these garments are what the inhabitants of this place called London are wearing, Apprentice Commander?'

First Commander Treve Pacton Ashto looked at himself in the reflective screen. It showed him to be attired in the most ridiculous clothing he had ever seen. Black, comparatively baggy leggings covered his long legs and an equally dark tunic, made of heavy material of an animal origin hung around the top half of his body. Underneath the tunic he wore a plain white linen shirt with a stiff collar that already chaffed his neck, a tightly buttoned, grey coloured, sleeveless garment that Apprentice Commander Atia had informed him was called a waistcoat and round his neck a long, pointless piece of blue and white striped material tied in a complicated knot that had taken Atia several minutes to arrange for him. On his head he wore a black, silky and ludicrously tall item of headwear with a curled brim that he, after staring at it for a long time, could not even begin to fathom its practical purpose.

'Yes, First Commander, I am completely certain that this mode of attire is how a male member of the ruling class of this area called London is dressed at the moment.'

'And what exactly is this for?'

Ashto picked up the silver topped walking stick that was leaning against the console of the ship's replicator.

'Well, from what I can gather, this stick or baton may convey authority in the highly stratified society of London and informs those of a lower caste or class as to the importance of the individual who wields it.'

'So it's a weapon of some sort then?'

'Partly perhaps but mostly it seems to have a more symbolic societal function as well as a practical one in helping an individual negotiate the byways of the London conurbation in a more efficient manner.'

First Commander Ashto nodded causing his hat to fall down over his eyes. Annoyed, he glanced at the replicator accusingly, considered for a brief moment giving it a kick for getting the measurement of his head size wrong, and took the top hat off and brushed back his short dark hair with his hand. He looked at the walking cane and nodded again. He understood symbols of hierarchy and seniority, as did all Jarans. In the egalitarian society that had been created over the centuries across the Jaran Federation, where patronage and unearned privilege had been long been abolished, power and influence was dependent on gathered experience, wisdom and, in particular, age. He had always been taught to defer to those elders who wore their merited trappings of seniority: the painted face-markings of the philosopher class; the skin-tattoos of the political officials and the various colours, hues and stripes of the military caste's clothing. As a young and comparatively junior member of the Exploration Executive he had worn the usual bright yellow, tightly fitting uniform to mark out his position in the overall structure of his profession but he was not without ambition and hoped that one day he might graduate to the next level of the Explorer class and command a bigger crew on a much more important mission. Then he would be entitled to wear a green uniform and would be assigned far more interesting tasks than the evaluation of this small blue planet in this insignificant and usually ignored sector of the galaxy.

First Commander Ashto hobbled across the replicating room after having a last skeptical look at himself and his outlandish outfit. The black shiny footwear the ship's replicator had supplied him with felt uncomfortable and heavy, nothing like the soft but highly serviceable shoes he normally wore. He sat down gladly at a computer console and skimmed through the many images showing Earth males and what they wore. The pictures showed them dressed more or less like he was now but he still found it difficult to believe that those individuals below on the planet they called Earth could be happy to be clad in the heavy, ugly and impractical clothes shown in the images. According to Atia's researches Earth's humans could tell what social caste their fellow inhabitants belonged to from the type, quality and age of the clothes worn. This puzzled Ashto as the people in the pictures displayed on the computer screen all looked exactly the same to his eyes. He was staring intently at the images, trying hard to ascertain the subtle differences when Atia interrupted his thoughts.

'So how do I look, First Commander?'

Ashto switched his attention from the computer screen to the Apprentice Commander. She too was wearing the clothes that had been produced for her by the ship's replicator and Ashto's first inclination was to laugh out loud but he stopped himself from doing so on the grounds that it would be rather rude and not very professional for him to do so.

Atia was dressed in a long, incredibly fussy, dark blue gown with many pleats and flounces that almost reached to the floor. At its rear was a padded section that made the gown protrude at the back in an utterly preposterous way and seemed to be specifically designed to hinder the Apprentice Commander's overall speed and movement. On top of this she wore an almost equally long outer covering and on her head was a strange looking device that seemed to be mostly made from feathers plucked from unfortunate avian creatures. In her hand was a long stick-like instrument covered in a material that opened out into a kind of cover, maybe to be used as some sort of protection against falling debris from the strange, rather ramshackle buildings this London seemed to be full of if the computer images could be trusted, something that Ashto had come to doubt after seeing the strange clothes he, and now Atia, were having to wear. He looked with sadness at the Apprentice Commander. He had grown used on their mission so far to seeing his fellow crewmember dressed in her light blue service uniform as she moved effortlessly and freely about the ship efficiently carrying out her duties. Now she was completely covered up by what seemed to be unnecessary layers of loosely hanging skirts and folds. He noticed that she too wore heavy and uncomfortable looking boots as she bent down with great difficulty to secure the large number of awkward looking buttons with which they were adorned.

Ashto felt a great amount of sympathy for Atia who was going to be so encumbered by the strange clothes she would be forced to wear down on the planet's surface. His attire would be bad enough but hers seemed so much more difficult to cope with and manage. During the two-year journey from Jara to this little-known planet on the edge of the galaxy, Ashto and his Apprentice Commander had proved to be an effective and hard-working team as they planned how they would go about assessing its viability for a meaningful intervention by the Jaran Galactic Federation. He had not met her until the first time they had trained together for the mission when they seemed to mesh straight away. During their time together so far Ashto had been duly impressed with the work ethic, intelligence and professionalism of his Apprentice Commander. During their voyage across the galaxy in their two-person Initial Explorer-class spacecraft they had got to know each other well and gradually realised that as a team they could work together in a mutually respectful and commendably professional way. Their relationship had developed slowly and by the time the ship had gone into orbit around the planet its inhabitants called Earth they had become firm friends as well as devoted colleagues. Ashto and Atia had, as was usual on such long journeys, indulged in recreational sex, but only on those occasions when they were both off duty and there was little else to do with regard to their mission. Now that they had arrived at their destination they had both been very busy in their preparations and had had no time for such frivolity.

Ashto suddenly realised he had been staring fixedly at Atia as she continued to adjust her clothing and attempt to make it more comfortable and so he turned his attention to the medikit that Atia had assembled earlier. This would travel with them on their journey to the planet's surface and contained the usual emergency antiseptic field dressings and skin sealant, antibiotic hypodermics, analgesics and of course a portable diagnostic and assessment console. They already had the medical computer administer preventative vaccinations that would protect the two of them from the many rampant viral and bacterial pathogens they would come into contact with on the Earth's surface. Ashto had to admit that he was quite staggered at just how many biological hazards assailed the humanoid population of this large conurbation called London, the biggest city in the most important state on the planet. How any of the people on the planet actually survived for any length of time was quite beyond his understanding and it came as no surprise that their average life expectancy was far shorter than those of Jarans. The computer had even suggested that First Commander Ashto and Apprentice Commander Atia should consider wearing breathing masks while in London due to the high level of carbon-based carcinogenic particulates present in the atmosphere but Atia had, quite sensibly, said that it would be difficult to explain such devices to the individuals they would meet as there was little understanding of the dangers caused by such airborne pollution amongst the general populace. Atia had therefore suggested they should have additional vaccinations of anti-carcinogen nanites. These would greatly reduce the chances that the polluted air would render them seriously ill during their proposed five-year stay on the planet Earth or cause them to suffer any long-term damage to their internal organs.

In a strange way Ashto was looking forward to the extended trip he and Atia were going to undertake. As well as being more than happy to spend time with his Apprentice Commander he had to admit that he had limited knowledge of fieldwork so far in his career. His only similar experience up to now had been as Apprentice Commander to First Commander Roma during their exploration of planet 1508/55-8, a mission that had been relatively short and fruitless. The planet, it turned out, had no dominant sapient life form, few natural resources and limited plant life that had, however, caused him to sneeze uncontrollably for most of the time he was on its surface. Despite this, First Commander Roma had been pleased with his efforts and she had forwarded a very favourable evaluation report about him to the Sub-Committee at the end of their time together. He had also, he believed, provided his First Commander with an interesting and inventive sexual companion during downtime periods. His current mission, one in which he was senior officer, would now provide him with a chance to prove that he was worthy of future promotion. He considered himself lucky too to have Apprentice Commander Atia as his assistant. In the two years since they had been travelling to this sector of the galaxy she had proved herself to be a more than competent crewmember and consistently came up with very useful suggestions. She was also an amiable companion in their off duty periods too and a more than adequate recreational sexual partner.

Again Ashto found himself staring at Apprentice Commander Atia as she stood in front of the reflective screen adjusting the strange headwear she wore that hid most of her attractive long dark hair now tied up in the, presumably, current Earth fashion. Stirring himself out of his reverie for a second time Ashto walked over to a computer console. His boots, while he was still aware of their oddness, were becoming more comfortable as he got used to them. He decided to do a final check on the details they would need to know when down on the planet's surface.

The computer scans had shown that the population of the London conurbation was around the 5.5 million mark, a sizable settlement by any standards. The city was the prime administrative capital of the state called Britain, which controlled a large, planet wide empire. Although theoretically a queen ruled Britain, and indeed the whole empire, the actual government of the country consisted exclusively of high-caste males who were selected by a limited number of other property owning males. Females it seemed did not have the right to cast votes in the selection of the government, a state of affairs that Ashto found extremely odd and thought would inevitably lead to some degree of gender conflict in the future. The main language of Britain was, for some reason, called English but in London as a whole the scans had shown that several other languages were also regularly spoken but often only in certain limited enclaves within the city. The computer had suggested that this situation was the result of migration to London from other states in different parts of the world due to economic and in some cases philosophical pressures. Ashto found this latter reason difficult to understand but concluded that when or if Jaran officials enrolled the Earth into the Galactic Federation and Jaran language and laws eventually became used universally across the planet, its inhabitants would no doubt be thankful to the Federation for its thoughtful benevolence in ending this piecemeal and confusing political and linguistic situation. In the meantime, to allow them to communicate when on the planet, both he and Atia had downloaded the Standard English, currently in use there, directly into their neural implants and had been conversing in this unfamiliar language since going into orbit. Also loaded onto their implanted chips were some basic geopolitical details about the planet Earth that they might need to refer to quickly without having to consult their hand-held computer terminals that were linked to the main ship's computer.

Apprentice Commander Atia again interrupted Ashto's thoughts.

'First Commander, I believe it's time for us to proceed to the planet's surface.'

'If everything is in order, Apprentice Commander, then we shall make our way to the shuttle craft and begin our exploration and assessment of this place called London.'

Ashto picked up one of the two large leather bags in which the pair had placed spare clothes, the medikit, a large supply of desiccated food sachets, two miniature drones disguised as small flying insects, a couple of hand-held computer terminals, a portable replicator and various other pieces of equipment they would need on the planet. He patted the security belt he wore under the ridiculous outfit he was clad in to ensure that it was still there. In the belt was a large supply of newly replicated gold coins that the computer had informed the Jaran pair they would be able to used as exchangeable units of currency at their destination, the place they would be spending the next five years.

Apprentice Commander Atia bent down to pick up the second leather bag, smiled to herself, flashed her dark brown eyes and twirled her parasol as she noticed that the First Commander was still hobbling in his newly replicated boots as he led the way to the shuttle.

My utmost greetings and felicitations to the esteemed members of the Sub-Committee.

I, along with Apprentice Commander Atia Mo Margo, arrived at planet 2007/52-3 as instructed and entered planetary orbit after employing the ship's cloaking procedure as per regulation 613/49. We have also launched the requisite number of scanning satellites into geostationary orbit around the planet, known locally as Earth, and these will, of course, provide us with all the planetary analysis and ground communications we will require in our future explorations.

Initial sensor scans have so far indicated that some of the inhabited regions of the planet are partially industrialised up to a relatively primitive, pre-digital technological level. There are no indications that any of the civilisations native to the planet have the slightest capability to detect vessels in orbit and so I have instructed Apprentice Commander Atia to turn off the cloaking measures in order to conserve energy on the ship.

Our scans have also revealed the dominant sentient species of the planet to be bipedal humanoids. First indications have shown these inhabitants to have an outward physical appearance remarkably similar to that of Jaran physiology. However, on average the males and females of the planet are somewhat smaller in height than those of the Jaran Federation humanoid population by some 12.23% and also have a much shorter overall lifespan than those of the population of Jara Prime.

Approximately 71% of the planet is made up of liquid water and its landmasses range from large continental areas to islands of varying sizes. The atmosphere is almost identical to that of Jara and therefore breathing apparatus will not be required by the initial orientation and exploration team or by personnel on any subsequent diplomatic or trade mission in the future.

The land areas of the planet seem to be sub-divided geopolitically into a large number of disparate states of various sizes and configurations. Evidence seems to show that many of these states are frequently involved in armed conflict with one another. Indeed from what we can glean from the planet's archives, via our scanning systems, the history of this small planet is one of almost continual warfare precipitated by economic, territorial or philosophical disagreements.

From the planet's records we have scanned so far there appears to be no consolidated single authority that represents the entire planet as a whole, a state of affairs that could help as well as hinder any communication with its inhabitants during potential future interventions and negotiations by the Jaran Federation.

In light of all of this, Apprentice Commander Atia and I have chosen, in our initial analysis, to focus on the largest populated conurbation on the planet, which is the main city of the most technically advanced state of the world. This state holds sway over many other areas across the planet and according to initial examinations of its historical records has established a long standing tradition of waterborne exploration, territorial conquest and imperial ambition. Surprisingly perhaps the state occupies a relatively small group of islands situated in close proximity to a large continental landmass. In the local language the state is referred to as the United Kingdom of Great Britain and Ireland. However some sources refer to the state simply as Britain or England and others call it Albion, or even, in a seemingly more pejorative way, Perfidious Albion. The reason for this rather complicated nomenclature is not yet entirely clear.

Most of the power sources available on the planet seem to be based on steam and coal gas although there is some evidence of electrical experimentation. Fossil fuel, such as coal, is used universally and there is no evidence of the use of solar, wind, fission or fusion technology – the development of which seems to be some way into the future as far as the inhabitants of the planet are concerned. Excavations designed to exploit petroleum products have begun in some areas of the planet and there is evidence that research into internal combustion technology is reasonably well advanced. Until that particular research comes to a practical fruition (I would estimate within the next five to ten Earth years – a standard Earth year being the equivalent of 0.9 of a standard year on Jara Prime) then most of the transportation in the developed states of this world, and in many of the less developed ones, will continue to rely on steam-powered land and sea-going locomotion as well as animal-powered surface vehicles.

The reliance on fossil fuels over the previous one hundred years since some of the states on the planet underwent a comparatively rapid and comprehensive industrialisation process is causing a significant rise in carbon dioxide levels in the atmosphere. Calculations carried out by Apprentice Commander Atia seem to suggest that the planet will begin to experience quite serious changes in its climatic conditions in approximately one hundred years time due to the atmospheric accumulation of carbon. This will lead to significant changes in the planet's overall ambient temperature and would consequently result in the eventual melting of the planet's polar water ice caps and a potentially catastrophic rise in sea levels throughout the planet. This is obviously an area that would be incumbent on us to mitigate if the planet Earth is to be bought into the Jaran Galactic Federation and may be an argument against any possible incorporation when, or if, any decision is made on the matter by the Sub-Committee.

Initial Conclusions

There seems to be no doubt that the planet Earth, on an initial analysis, seems potentially ripe for a meaningful interaction with the Jaran Galactic Federation. Our initial action plan therefore is for Apprentice Commander Atia and myself to spend the next five Earth years in an intensive study of the planet. This would then enable the Sub-Committee to draw up a detailed action plan for a potential integration process to take place with the possibility of bringing the planet Earth into the Jaran Galactic Federation at the earliest convenient time.

To achieve this detailed study I am proposing that Apprentice Commander Atia and I will travel to the Earth's largest metropolitan area, locally called London, and there for the two of us to carefully and surreptitiously integrate ourselves into the local population. This will enable us to conduct an in-depth analysis of the region, its inhabitants and social mores, with a view to eventually providing a definitive conclusion on the planet's viability, in terms of its potential future integration into the Jaran Federation.

I will make my next report to the Sub-Committee after Apprentice Commander Atia and I have arrived on the planet's surface and have made initial preparations for our integration into the local community.

With my utmost loyalty to the Glorious
Jaran Galactic Federation,

First Commander Treve Pacton Ashto.

2

A Journey to London

First Commander Ashto was feeling extremely miserable as he walked in the heavy rain along the tree-lined Woking street that was fringed with houses of various styles. The leather holdall he was carrying was extremely heavy and he was very aware that the thick woollen clothes he wore were soaking up the rainwater at an alarming rate making him feel more uncomfortable than he had ever felt before. He voiced his wish that he would like to discard some of the very wet garments he was wearing.

'I do not think that that would be a sensible idea First Commander. According to my studies the local inhabitants have certain social mores that would seem to strongly discourage any such disrobing in public.' Apprentice Commander Atia also carried a large leather bag and she too was wearing heavy and extremely unfamiliar attire but seemed to be coping with her exertions and the adverse weather conditions rather better than the First Commander.

'It wouldn't be quite so bad if the temperature was not so cold. Are you sure that we have not landed somewhat nearer to the polar region of this planet than you originally calculated?' As he spoke Ashto could feel rainwater dripping from his ludicrous headwear and rolling down his cheeks. He stopped to put down his luggage and dab his face with the end of the blue tie thing that for some ridiculous reason he wore around his neck.

Atia frowned at his action and quickly looked around to see if any of the local human habitants had noticed. 'No, First Commander, I am quite sure that we have arrived at the exact place we had planned to be. At present it is summer in the Northern hemisphere of this planet and the temperature, although somewhat lower than the average for this time of the year, which the local populace refer to as August, is nevertheless within normal climatic parameters for the region. It appears that this particular summer in this part of the world has had much higher than average precipitation levels, but at least it is not far now to the place designated as the locomotive vehicle interface.'

Ashto sighed and picked up his bag and followed Atia as she led the way to Woking Railway Station.

It was a relief to both when they reached the porticoed entrance to the station building and they were able to put down their bags they had been carrying. Ashto approached a small window just inside the strange brick built building. The window had the word *Tickets* printed over it. Ashto and Atia had already found out from the computer database on board their ship that they would need to obtain something called a 'ticket', which apparently was a printed pass that would allow them to access the mass transit system that would take them into the centre of this large city called London. Behind the bars of the low window was an elderly Earth male wearing a dark blue uniform seemingly made from the same thick material that Ashto found so uncomfortable. He also had a blue peaked cap on his head and large grey whiskers on either side of his face. Ashto found this arrangement of facial hair extremely strange and the sight caused him to stare with curiosity at the man's face.

'Yes sir, what can I do you for?' said the man impatiently.

Ashto was puzzled by the man's words but nevertheless forged ahead with the request in the unfamiliar language he had been practising in his head on the way to the station.

'Er yes... I would like to obtain tickets for myself and my assistant which will enable us to access the locomotive transport that will subsequently convey us to the central area of the conurbation known as London,' he said as he bent down to speak to the man behind the barred window.

'Please,' whispered Atia from behind him.

'Please,' said a smiling Ashto to the man behind the window who was looking extremely puzzled.

'You want a ticket to London Waterloo?' said the man as he took off his hat and ran his fingers through his greying hair. He'd already had a hard day and the cold temperature and wind blowing in from the outside wasn't helping. If only he could put on his overcoat and scarf while he continued to serve people but the Station Master, a right tyrant and a stickler for the rules, would never allow such a lessening of standards, even on a very cold and drafty so-called summer's day like today.

Ashto was flummoxed. He thought that he had expressed himself in this English language very clearly. He searched his neural implant to see if there was an alternative way of asking for these 'tickets'.

'Yes, we would like to travel to London Waterloo,' said Apprentice Commander Atia moving to the window so that the Earth individual behind it could see her.

'Right you are, miss,' replied the man. 'That will be a total of eight shillings and sixpence for a single journey for two in a first-class compartment.' The man smiled warmly at Atia. She was the prettiest looking thing he had seen in many a day. Beautiful eyes. Nice and tall too.

'Is this an adequate amount?' said First Commander Ashto handing over one of the newly minted gold sovereign coins.

Bloody foreigners, thought the man behind the window as he sorted out the large amount of change, which he then passed to the First Commander. Ashto looked puzzled at the handful of silver coloured coins he had been given and was just about to ask a number of questions of the ticket seller when an impatient cough from a man in the queue behind him caused Atia to grab his arm and gently lead him away from the ticket window.

Ashto dropped the coins into the integral pouch on the side of the heavy coat he wore feeling that his first contact with one of the inhabitants of this planet, whilst not entirely perfect, had gone quite well. He had been accepted as a fellow denizen of this planet Earth without any problem and felt sure that he would be able to continue his deception without the slightest fear of being discovered.

The pair walked through to the station's platform handing their tickets to another human in a blue suit and peaked cap, carefully copying what everyone else seemed to be doing. The man clipped their tickets that had been proffered by Ashto and handed them back to him. Ashto looked at the holes that had been made in the thick cardboard railway tickets and smiled with understanding. A primitive way of designating those who had obtained the correct means by which to travel on this vehicle but not without a certain degree of logic, thought Ashto. He and Atia continued onto an area designated as Platform 1 according to a sign that hung on chains from the canopy that jutted out from the building from which they had just emerged. As they stepped onto the platform that was open to the elements they discovered that the rain had stopped and a bright, watery sunshine lit up Woking railway station.

Ashto and Atia found a place along the platform where they could talk quietly to each other. As they moved along past many other individuals and couples who were also obviously waiting for this 'railway' vehicle to appear Ashto noticed that most of the other male persons who were wearing similar attire to his own and who were also holding metal topped walking sticks, made to remove their headwear ever so slightly and nodded their heads whilst smiling at Apprentice Commander Atia as she passed by. Atia also noticed that she seemed to be earning quite a number of what appeared to be admiring glances and smiles from these Earth males. While smiling back in what she hoped was an appropriate way she thought about this phenomenon and decided that it was because she was rather taller than all of the other females standing on the station platform. It was logical, she thought, that within a highly stratified caste structure such as that which seemed to exist in this part of the planet that those individuals who were taller than the norm would attract a greater degree of kudos as a result.

'Well, Apprentice Commander, our first encounter with these Earth humans seemed to go quite well,' said Ashto.

'Yes it did, First Commander but we will need to concentrate hard to ensure that we are as accurate as possible in the terminology we employ in our conversations with the people of this world,' replied Atia. She suddenly realised that she had failed to utilise her parasol in the same fashion that most of the females on the station platform had already done. As she quickly worked the mechanism causing the beige and blue parasol to open she turned to Ashto to speak.

'I do believe I have discovered what this implement is used for First Commander.'

'Please inform me, Apprentice Commander.'

'Well it appears that this item, this 'parasol' as it is called, provides protection from the rays of the nearby star, which is referred to as the Sun.'

Ashto looked concerned by this news. 'I was under the impression that our analysis of possible dangers on this planet precluded the need for wearing any covering to protect us against harmful levels of gamma radiation prevalent in the atmosphere.'

'Our readings were correct, First Commander, and we are in no danger. I believe that many of the females carry these parasols firstly as an item of fashion and secondly for cosmetic purposes to avoid exposure to ultra-violet light and the consequent darkening of their skin, which presumably is not a fashionable accoutrement to have if you are a member of a particular caste in this human society.'

Ashto had a number of related questions that he thought needed to be discussed by Atia and himself but before he could speak he noticed that people on the platform had begun to edge forward. And then he saw the reason for the general movement. Coming along a track made from steel rails, seemingly kept apart at a designated distance by large pieces of timber, was the locomotive vehicle, smoke and steam issuing forth from various parts of its mechanism.

As the railway engine slowed to a stop at the platform, hissing and steaming close to where the pair stood, Ashto and Atia marveled at the nature of this alien machine, which, while fundamentally quite primitive, certainly appeared complicated and impressive.

'An interesting piece of indigenous technology, Apprentice Commander Atia.'

'Indeed, First Commander, a machine that exhibits some of the attributes of a living and breathing creature; I am actually rather looking forward to this journey on this railway.' Atia smiled. She was getting used to this strange language that the neural implant, which had been inserted directly into the cerebral cortex of her brain, was enabling her to speak and communicate in. She felt that she was quickly mastering the various idiomatic phrases and curious linguistic constructions that the people of this part of the planet utilised in their speech.

A young station porter examined the tickets the pair continued to hold and directed them to a compartment in a particular carriage. He picked up the large holdall that Atia had placed on the floor while she had been waiting for the train to appear and seemed to look slightly askance at Ashto for expecting her to carry such a very heavy piece of luggage. As Atia stepped onto the carriage the porter smiled at her and held her elbow helping her into the compartment. Atia at first was alarmed at the physical contact proffered by this human and almost instinctively delivered a swift blow to the young man's throat area in order to incapacitate him but stopped herself just in time and smiled back at the young man. It seems that the males of this planet are both patronising and indulgent towards females in this society – I must remember not to take offence at such actions, she thought as the young porter, with difficulty, lifted her bag onto the luggage rack inside the compartment.

Ashto and Atia settled down into the backward facing seats of the first class compartment. Opposite them was a male and female couple dressed in more or less similar attire to what they were wearing. The man, who also wore a neatly trimmed grey beard, stood up from his seat as Atia entered and doffed his top hat. Noticing this Ashto likewise raised his hat to the female who sat opposite to him. Ashto now realised the importance of wearing the strange and seemingly idiotic headwear the ship's computer had replicated. It was obvious to him now that the hat, being part of the way certain males dressed on this planet, existed for mainly symbolic reasons allowing them to acknowledge and defer to females in this non-verbal way. He felt satisfied to have solved this mystery and was confident that he could cope with the many similar cultural situations that would occur in the future as he interacted with these Earth humans. Whilst he was mulling this over he noticed that the man seated opposite Atia was smiling profusely at the Apprentice

Commander. Ah, thought Ashto the symbolic interaction continues and he smiled in the same way to the woman who sat across from him.

'Ahem...' the man in the seat opposite gave a strange grunt. 'May I enquire whether you are both travelling to Waterloo?'

'No, we are going to London and...' began Ashto.

The First Commander was cut short by Atia who addressed the man, 'Yes, indeed we are going to London. Are you travelling to the same ultimate destination?'

The man frowned. 'Er ... yes we are. I intend to do some business transactions in the city and my wife will doubtless be visiting a large number of shops in Oxford Street. By the way my name is Bennett and this is my wife Catherine.'

'We are pleased to meet you Bennett and Catherine. My name is Treve Pacton Ashto and this is my assistant Atia Mo Margo.' Ashto inwardly congratulated himself on remembering to leave out their Jaran rank designations, which, no doubt, would have sounded somewhat strange to human ears.

Atia thought that she must have a word with the First Commander about the nomenclature they should use whilst on this planet.

'Foreigners eh?' said Mr Bennett somewhat disdainfully. 'American?'

Ashto quickly searched his neural implant for the meaning of the words.

'Yes, Bennett, we are indeed foreigners from a different state to the one we currently find ourselves in. We are, as you have guessed from the continent of America which is situated across the Atlantic ocean and we have travelled to this particular state, which is known as Britain, by sea because powered flight has not yet been developed anywhere on this planet.' Ashto smiled. He had, he believed, come up with a very good and plausible answer to the question that this Earth person called Bennett had posed.

Atia, who had also been searching her language implant quickly decided to speak before First Commander Ashto could say anything else. She had noticed that Mr Bennett and his wife were staring at the First Commander in a strange way and that their mouths were slightly open in what she assumed was a look of surprise.

'Ah, of course my husband is employing humour in his conversation with you,' she said. 'We are, as you have so correctly deduced, visitors from the United States of America here to see the sights of Britain. We are starting our visit in London and we are very much anticipating that it will be most enjoyable, enervating and fruitful.'

The surprise on the Bennett's faces lessened a little but they still seemed rather dumbfounded.

'He called you his assistant?' said Mrs Bennett

'That is correct. I am both his wife and his assistant. My husband, you see, is a writer and he is hoping to compile a treatise about London and the rest of Britain that will greatly appeal to those others in our home country who will subsequently follow in our footsteps and visit this small but highly influential state in which you live. I am here to assist him in that process.' Atia smiled and both of the Bennetts smiled back looking relieved that they were not, as they had momentarily thought, in the presence of some foreign and potentially dangerous maniacs.

'The United States must be so very different to Great

Britain,' said Mrs Bennett, 'are you going to be in our country for long?'

'We will be here for five of your years at which point our mission will hopefully be complete and we can return to our home state – this United States of America, as you call it,' said First Commander Ashto.

'Well don't you also call it that?' said Mr Bennett looking confused again.

'We do indeed,' interjected Atia, 'but it has been a long journey and First … my husband is feeling rather tired.'

'Of course you both must be exhausted, my dear lady,' said Mr Bennett smiling indulgently at Atia and seemingly unable to take his attention away from her. 'Where are you staying in London if I may be so bold as to inquire.'

Atia had prepared herself for this sort of question and had spent a great deal of time studying maps and data regarding the London conurbation on the ship's computer. She believed that she knew a great deal about the geography, the layout and the sort of society of the city into which they could quietly infiltrate with a view to garnering much information about the local people and how they would react when faced with any future intervention by Federation officials and possibly military personnel. She believed that she had discovered which particular area of the conurbation would be the easiest and most suitable for her and the First Commander to integrate into as seamlessly as possible.

'We are planning to base ourselves somewhere in the Whitechapel or Spitlefields area of London. Then my husband can get on with his researches and write about the places he sees and the social mores of the people who reside in the area.'

Both Mr and Mrs Bennett looked horrified. 'You are planning to spend five years in such a place?' said Mrs Bennett.

'I would strongly advise you not to even venture into the East End of London for five minutes, let alone actually live there for five years,' said Mr Bennett, 'the place is a den of scoundrels, foreigners and thieves not to mention many women of a very dubious nature indeed. Er … when I say foreigners I mean those sorts of foreigners one wouldn't want to meet – lowlifes, degenerates, disreputable Jews and darkies of all shades! Your dear wife sir would be in very grave danger!'

It was Ashto and Atia's turn to look confused. They had not considered the possibility that any particular part of this city the Earth people called London would be any more dangerous than any other part. They had of course realised that their mission would not necessarily be easy or completely straightforward. Indigenous wild animals could always pose a threat to planetary explorers for example, but they believed, as long as they kept their true origin a secret and did not take any untoward risks they would face few significant dangers from the actual humanoid inhabitants of Earth. They had no idea who these individuals that Mr Bennett had mentioned were exactly and had begun to feel that perhaps their preparations for their mission had not been quite as thorough or as comprehensive as they might have been.

Whilst Ashto was considering what Mr Bennett had said there was a great hissing noise from outside followed by a loud chuff, chuff sound, as the train pulled out of Woking station. Suddenly the air smelt of sulpher and Ashto noticed steam, bits of ash and grey clouds of smoke sweep past the carriage's window.

'We will take your words and reflect upon them,' said Ashto, 'but I do not think that I, or my assistant, who is also my wife of course, will be in any danger. We have come to this London fully prepared to carry out our researches and interact on a peaceful basis with the inhabitants of the city.'

'Well your interactions, as you describe them, may not be as peaceful as you think. Surely you have criminals and ne'er-do-wells in America too. If I were you I would obtain a firearm at the earliest possible time in order to make sure that you and your extremely pretty wife are safe. I would certainly countenance against going outside of your abode during the hours of darkness.'

Ashto understood most of what Mr Bennett had said. Searching his neural implant again he discovered that a 'firearm' was a primitive hand-held projectile weapon and this knowledge caused him to look at his leather holdall that was currently sitting on the seat beside him. Inside the bag was the disrupter device that Federation regulations insisted should always be carried covertly on planetary exploration and orientation missions. Ashto inwardly shivered at the thought that one day he might actually have to use the disrupter to reduce one of these Earth humanoids to their component atoms. He was naturally against violence and believed strongly in the credo that was embedded at a very early point in Explorer Executive training that violence towards other life forms, particularly sapient life forms, was something that was only to be used when all other methods of defensive tactics had been completely exhausted. He had not expected the inhabitants of this planet to be anything other than benign, friendly and compliant and was shocked by Bennett's suggestion that he and Apprentice Commander Atia might be putting themselves into some degree of danger.

The next part of the journey continued quietly with both Ashto and Atia deep in thought as they reflected on what Mr Bennett had said. They looked out of the carriage windows at the very green but unfamiliar alien landscape passing by. At one point Ashto was disturbed from his pensive reverie by Mr Bennett offering him a cigar.

'They are very good. My company imports them directly from the Caribbean island of Cuba,' said Mr Bennett as he held one of the thick brown and pungently smelling tubes towards Ashto.

Atia was a little alarmed when she saw First Commander Ashto look carefully at the cigar he had been offered and hesitate as though he couldn't quite work out what the object was. Would he accept it and start eating it? Even humans from this far off United States of America would surely not be so lacking in knowledge as to fail to recognise the true purpose of a cigar. She had hoped that her First Commander would have remembered the in-depth briefing they had both received from the ship's computer, which mentioned many of the idiosyncrasies that these Earth humans had. Among the things that the computer had informed them about, during the hours of their pre-journey briefing, was data regarding the strange habit that many of the inhabitants of this planet had, whereby they lit tubes made from a cultivated plant product and then sucked into their mouth and lungs the resultant smoke that was filled with carcinogenic properties. Atia had doubted this information when she first heard it and thought that there may have been a glitch in the computer's programming. Surely no individuals on any planet in the known galaxy would be quite so stupid as to do such a thing but here in front of her was the evidence. Atia breathed a sigh of relief when she heard the First Commander's reply to the offer of one of these cigars.

'No thank you Bennett,' said Ashto, 'I do not partake in this ubiquitous but highly damaging tobacco smoking addiction that is indulged in by large numbers of humans on this planet.'

Mr Bennett looked at Ashto and frowned trying to decide if the strange foreigner opposite was joking again – employing humour in his conversation as his wife had indicated earlier.

'Well I would have thought that an American would appreciate a fine cigar since I believe they grow a lot of tobacco out there!' said Mr Bennett shrugging.

He struck a match and held it to the cigar and soon great clouds of smoke issued forth from it and filled the train compartment with an acrid and pungent haze. Within a minute Ashto and Atia were coughing uncontrollably and both were wishing they had brought the breathing apparatus mentioned by the ship's computer.

'Charles, please put the cigar out. Can you not see that our two American friends are obviously not used to such things?' said Mrs Bennett.

Charles Bennett looked horrified at the prospect of stubbing out his recently lit finest Havana cigar but the stern stare from his wife convinced him that it was best not to argue with her about the matter and so he lowered the carriage window and reluctantly threw the expensive cigar outside.

Humphing ostentatiously he sat sulking for the rest of the journey.

Atia still spluttering from the effects of the smoke thanked Mrs Bennett and was much happier now that the frosty atmosphere in the compartment had resulted in no more awkward conversations for her to have to deal with.

After a total journey time of 35 minutes the railway train pulled into London Waterloo station. Ashto and Atia were impressed at the number of people waiting on the platform as the train came to a halt – it would obviously take them a while to get used to the multitude of humans residing in the London conurbation. They were also thankful to be able to say a quick farewell to Mr and Mrs Bennett and quickly alighted from the carriage. Following the mass of people that had also got off the train they soon found themselves in the station's booking hall and the exit to the street outside.

Using a small hand held terminal that was linked to the ship's computer via the satellites in orbit around the planet, Atia was able to lead the way from the station to Waterloo Bridge and across the River Thames. Halfway over the bridge Ashto and Atia stopped to take in their first sight of the city of London. What they saw both impressed and horrified the Jaran pair in equal measure. Before them they saw the large number of grand buildings, the crowded streets and the vastness of the river Thames full of water-going vessels of all sorts and sizes. They also could see at a glance how polluted the river was and Atia remembered how the computer had informed them that it was only within the last twenty years or so that any sort of sewerage system had been constructed in order to carry away the waste that was produced by the humans of this city. It had not been many years ago, according to the computer, that the Thames River had literally been an open sewer running though London. An outbreak of the water borne disease cholera, some twenty years before, had caused many of the inhabitants to die of the malady and Atia shivered to think that people would actually drink water drawn from this river. Even now, despite the recently built sewers, when the tide turned the river would often be filled with the excrement of millions. Atia would no more drink from this brown, scummy, polluted mess of a river than point a fully charged disrupter device at her own head.

Atia and Ashto looked at each other in disbelief. Atia checked her small computer terminal and ascertained that at one time this river would have had been comprised of clean water and would have been teeming with all sorts of native water-dependent life forms. Now hardly anything lived in it. How difficult would it be for the authorities to introduce a regulatory system that would dissuade individuals and manufacturing organisations from polluting this river? The pair walked on from the centre of Waterloo Bridge feeling that a full understanding of this city called London, with its obvious contradictions, would take a very long time for them to develop.

My greetings and utmost felicitations to the esteemed members of the Sub-Committee.

Several hours ago Apprentice Commander Atia and I arrived on the surface of the planet 2007/52-3, known locally as 'Earth'.

Our shuttle vessel landed to the south of the large conurbation known as London and as per regulation 613/55 we returned the craft back to the main ship, currently in orbit around the planet and set the recall instructions so that we are able to call for the shuttle to return should we need to visit the ship for some reason in the future or in the unlikely event that we might need to make a hasty escape from the planet.

The area where in which we landed is known locally as Horsell Common and is a large area of open land, mineral quarries and woodland, which provided us with an extensive amount of concealment while we conducted our landing procedures and disembarkment from the shuttle.

Utilising our scanners we made our way to a settlement a little less than one kilometre away, a small town by the name of Woking, where we used a surface based steam powered locomotive vehicle to convey us to the central area of the London conurbation.

The journey to London on this primitive, but surprisingly efficient, vehicle was of particular interest as during it we made our first significant contact with two of the inhabitants of Earth. In our conversations with the pair, Atia and I were, I believe, totally convincing in our adopted undercover guise as bone fide book researchers from a place called the United States of America. We seemed to be completely accepted in that role by the Earth humans we conversed with.

Having arrived in London our next task will be to secure a living space where we can base ourselves and which will enable us to continue our mission of study and evaluation. Having done that I will make my next report to the Sub-committee as soon as possible.

With my utmost loyalty to the Glorious
Jaran Galactic Federation,

First Commander Treve Pacton Ashto.

3

London

Hailing the two-wheeled animal-drawn vehicle that Atia informed her First Commander was called a hansom cab was relatively straightforward. The pair had stood to one side whilst observing others perform the hailing process before they had attempted to do the same thing. Ashto was pleased that he didn't have to walk the streets again wearing his uncomfortable Earth footwear and carrying his heavy holdall. After they had seated themselves inside the small vehicle the driver opened up the trap door in the roof of the two-seater vehicle and asked the pair where they wanted to go. Atia was fully prepared for this and answered him confidently: 'The corner of Whitechapel High Street and Commercial Street please driver.'

'Righto, Miss,' replied the unseen cabbie from his elevated position at the rear of the hansom.

Atia and Ashto sat back and although they were jolted around inside the vehicle they found the journey through the alien streets of London, crowded with people and animal-drawn traffic, interesting and informative. The creature pulling the hansom particularly fascinated First Commander Ashto. This quadruped animal was, according to their earlier computer briefing, called a horse and there were some 50,000 of these animals in London most of which were utilised in pulling vehicles of various types. As the cab travelled the byways of London he noticed that the horse occasionally produced waste, which simply fell onto the street and was left lying there. The streets through which the cab travelled were littered with piles of such material and Ashto did a quick calculation in his head as to the total amount of this substance produced over a whole year; it was an immense total. Ashto hoped the governing authorities in this city had found a way to deal with this issue before it drowned in a morass of this animal by-product.

The Jaran couple observed the passing buildings, people and street scenes as the hansom cab travelled from the Strand where they had hailed the vehicle. They watched as crowded street followed crowded street – up Fleet Street and Ludgate Hill and past the great edifice of St Paul's Cathedral; along Cornhill, Leadenhall Street, Aldgate Street and finally into Whitechapel High Street. At the corner of Commercial Street the cabbie stopped the hansom and opened the little trap door. 'That'll be two bob Guv'nor,' said the cabbie.

Apart from knowing that the driver of this vehicle now needed paying in the local currency Ashto had no idea what his actual words meant. He reached into the pouch on the side of his coat – a pocket the computer had called it –

scooped up the handful of metal coins he had been given at the railway station and from his great height passed them through the trap door to the driver. 'An extremely interesting journey sir; many thanks to you for driving this primitive animal-drawn vehicle with such skill.'

Atia climbed down from the cab, carefully holding her skirts out of the way of her boots and Ashto followed her.

The cabbie touched his whip to his head, smoothed his mustache and drove off thinking that, after being given the biggest tip in all the years he had been a cab driver, he could now go to a nearby cabmen's shelter, have a good meal, a nice cup of tea and a bit of a rest.

As the hansom cab clattered away Ashto and Atia looked around at the scene before them. Whitechapel Road and Commercial Street were crowded thoroughfares swarming with people and horse-drawn traffic of all kinds. Ashto noted that only a few of the males in the streets of this area were attired like he was, wearing top hats and carrying canes. Most individuals, he noted, were dressed somewhat differently and he began to appreciate the ship's computer's information on the way the various social classes in London could be differentiated by what they wore. Although many of their clothes had a passing resemblance to the garments that had been provided for Ashto by the replicator back on the ship, the First Commander's garments were new, neatly pressed, made of good if rather heavy organic material, whereas many of the male humans who were now passing by intent on their own business were dressed in clothes that were worn, threadbare, spattered with mud or were dusty and marked. Many wore soft caps that Ashto thought looked far more comfortable than the top hat he had on his head but which were so obviously of an overall cheaper design, harder wearing perhaps and indicative of the fact that these were working males engaged in a variety of physical tasks that Ashto could only guess at. One human male who walked past the Jaran pair had large wooden boards attached to the front and back of his body. On the boards were the words 'Pavilion Refreshment Rooms, 191 Whitechapel Road,' a sight which baffled Atia and Ashto at first but after consulting their implant data they were able to ascertain that this constituted a method of advertising a certain product or service in a comparatively inexpensive way. Other workmen drove wagons containing piles of bricks, tiles, planks of wood, assorted pieces of metal. Some wagons were piled high with unfamiliar fruit or vegetables, one or two even had live creatures in them. Ashto looked with regret at these large eyed and forlorn looking animals, which, no doubt, were soon destined to end up as food sources for the local populace.

'This way I believe, First Commander,' said Atia briskly, having realised that standing on the street looking with interest at everyone and everything that passed by could draw unwanted attention to themselves.

Apprentice Commander Atia led the way back along Whitechapel High Street. As she and First Commander Ashto wound their way along the crowded street Atia again drew a certain amount of attention from the individuals she passed. Some simply stared at the unusually tall and attractive dark haired woman in her fine clothes, while some men doffed their caps in the way that Atia was now becoming quite used to. Some of these Earth males even made verbal comments directed at her loudly enough for her to hear.

'La-di-da!' said one.

'You're a jammer and no mistake!' said another.

'Nice klobber!' 'Proper bit of frock!' 'Giv us a warm bit darlin!' said others.

Atia had no idea what these comments actually meant but those she could hear clearly she carefully stored away in her implanted linguistic memory bank for later defining. She just smiled at the men in what she hoped was an appropriate way.

After a short while Atia, using her handheld computer terminal as surreptitiously as possible, turned right into another road. A sign high up on the wall of one of the buildings proclaimed it to be Goulston Street.

Atia stopped to talk to the First Commander: 'According to my researches along this particular byway is a building, part of which I believe will be suitable for us to use as a base for our mission. It will have provision for sleep periods as well as sanitary arrangements and will provide us with a well-situated abode while we carry out our mission in this London conurbation.

Ashto nodded in assent and looked forward to being able to put down his heavy holdall and relax in comfortable surroundings.

The pair walked along Goulston Street until they reached an austere brick built, five-storey edifice on the right hand side of the street. As they stood looking at the building Atia wondered what they should do now. What was the procedure for procuring a place in this building where she and the First Commander could put their belongings and use as a base of operations for their five-year study of this planet?

'First Commander, my researches prior to coming to this planet did not include instructions on how to actually access living spaces in this Wentworth Model Dwellings as it is called.' Atia kept her voice low so that Earth inhabitants passing by could not hear what she was saying.

'Perhaps we could ask this female?' said Ashto, walking towards an elderly lady on the nearby street corner who was seated on the ground and who appeared to be selling what looked to be a type of fruit out of a large wicker basket.

'Yes dearie, what would you like?' said the old woman, looking up at Ashto who towered above her.

'Greetings,' said Ashto, 'My assistant and I would like to procure a room in this building," Ashto pointed to the Wentworth Model Dwellings, 'do you happen to know how I would proceed in order to fulfill this particular desire?'

'Aaw, ain't yer lardy-da! You want to move into the Jew house?' replied the woman. 'Yer'll need to see the landlord. He lives at 108. Mr Cohen his name is – buys an apple off me everyday – nice fella, not like some of the others I could mention – most of 'em don't even speak the Queen's English. Would you like an apple for yourself and your good lady?'

Ashto took in most of what the elderly woman had said to him and agreed to buy two apples. In exchange he gave the female one of the gold coins from his belt.

'I can't change that!' she screeched, snatching the sovereign from Ashto and looking at it dumbfounded. 'I ain't never seen one o' them afore. Is it real?'

'It is decidedly real,' replied Ashto somewhat confused by the female's attitude. 'Please keep the currency in return for the information and fruit you have furnished to me and my assistant ... my good lady, as you refer to her. I thank you most profusely, esteemed elderly female.'

The woman quickly tucked the coin into a small pouch that she wore on a belt around her waist. She was extremely pleased. In all the years she had been scraping a living in this area selling apples, pears and oranges this was the best day she had ever had. Tonight she would have a nice slap up meal of pie and mash and perhaps treat herself to a port and lemonade or two. It had been ages since she had been able to have such nice things to look forward to.

Ashto walked back down the street to where Atia had been waiting. He gave her one of the apples.

'It is a fruit called an apple apparently,' he said rather proudly.

Both of the members of the Jaran exploratory mission realised that they were hungry and in need of sustenance. It had been quite a while since they had last eaten. They both bit into their respective apples and were surprised at how tasty this Earth fruit was. They stood outside the entrance to the building that had a sign on it indicating that it was the way to get to apartments 108 to 119 whilst they finished their impromptu meal. A passer by was intrigued by how Ashto and Atia finished off their apples, cores, pips and all.

They managed to locate apartment number 108 but they were rather amazed at how damp, dismal and dirty the entry vestibule to the building was. A great amount of litter and dust had blown into the entrance and nobody had bothered to tidy up the resulting detritus lying there. Jarans were, on the whole, very fastidious when it came to tidiness. Young Jaran children were taught at an early age that one's living space should always be clean and well kept. Woe betide any adolescent Jaran who left their clothes lying about on the floor of their sleeping area or who left hairs in the bodily cleansing pods. The dirty, dusty and horse-excrement filled streets of this great conurbation called London had been off-putting enough for the two Jaran explorers but this lack of cleanliness so near to living areas was very disturbing.

First Commander Ashto knocked on the door of number 108 and after a short wait a small dark-haired man, who had to adjust his somewhat myopic gaze to peer up at the two tall Jarans standing in his doorway, opened the door.

'Good afternoon, my dear sir and madam, now what can I do for you?'

The man wore the curious metal and glass sight correcting instruments attached to his nose and ears that Ashto and Atia had seen occasionally being worn by some of the humans in this city.

'Mister Cohen I presume. I and my assistant and wife would like to occupy one of your living spaces for the next five of your years. We would be very quietly engaged in our studies, being residents of another state, the United States of America in fact, and we would be particularly assiduous in the maintenance of the living space's cleanliness and neatness over that period of time,' said Ashto, pleased that he was able to sum up his and Atia's requirements so succinctly.

The man took off his spectacles, cleaned them on his shirt that hung over his trousers, put them back on his nose and squinted up at Ashto.

'If I might presume to suggest to you my dear sir, that you and your charming missus don't appear to be the sort of clientele we would normally expect to hinquire about our dwellings. While I would thank you for your said query

I would not be being truthful if I was not to suggest that you pair, as not exactly of the Jewish persuasion, would be somewhat out of place in these model dwellings. I would therefore 'umbly suggest that you do not insist, my dear sir, on persuwing your intention to seek residence here but instead it would be more fittin' for you and your good lady wife to walk up the street a little way, cross the road into Bell Lane and call at Missus Smith's Guest 'ouse – an accomerdation that will, I wholeheartedly believe, suit you far better that an apartment in this 'ere building.'

Ashto understood few of the words that this man, Mister Cohen had uttered but certainly was left with the impression that this particular building was not suitable for them. He was about to continue the conversation with the diminutive man when Apprentice Commander Atia tugged at his arm and led him away.

Back outside in the street the conditions had started to change and large spots of rain had begun to fall and splashed onto the dirty road. A chill wind began to blow down Goulston Street. It was the moment that the weather again started to deteriorate and the rest of the summer of that particularly benighted year would continue to be one of the coldest and wettest in living memory.

'Let us do what that human male suggested, First Commander and find this Mrs Smith's Guest House quickly before this precipitation worsens.' Atia did not like the idea of her heavy and voluminous clothing becoming sodden by the rain for the second time that day.

An old and rust streaked sign attached to the wall proclaimed the location of Mrs Smith's Select Guest House in Bell Lane. Ashto pulled on a thin rope that was situated near to the door and which had a sign next to it that read 'pull for entry'. Almost immediately an elderly woman dressed in black opened it.

'Oh do come in sir and madam, out of this very narsty weather.'

'Thank you,' said Atia who had decided to take the lead in this next conversation before the First Commander could open his mouth.

'An' what can I do for you?' said the woman, rubbing her hands together, looking like she was already beginning to feel the discomfiture of the sudden cold snap in the weather.

'We would like some accommodation for the foreseeable future please.'

'Of course my dear madam, I'm Mrs Smith an' I would be only too pleased to provide you with the same. I 'ave a very nice room that would do nicely for a lovely couple such as yourselves.' At this point Mrs Smith glanced at Atia's left hand, noticed the lack of a wedding ring and winked at the Apprentice Commander. Atia nearly asked the woman if she had something wrong with her eye but decided that she would consult her neural implant later to find if there was any information regarding the symbolism denoted by such a strange eye movement.

Mrs Smith led the pair of Jaran explorers to some stairs. As the three climbed the two flights, Atia noticed that the landlady had trouble negotiating the steep steps and huffed and puffed with the effort. When they reached the second floor landing she stopped and informed the Jaran pair that the sudden change in the weather had: 'brought on my hartheritis something rotten.' Neither Atia nor Ashto fully understood what the woman meant apart from the obvious fact that she had some malady of the hip or her leg that was causing her to experience pain in that region. They watched her as she fiddled with her bunch of keys and unlocked the door leading them into a darkened room. Mrs Smith limped across to the window and opened the curtains allowing a weak and watery sunlight to enter the room.

The room was the most basic living space the Ashto and Atia had ever seen. A metal-framed double bed was placed on one side of the room. On the bed were two pillows, a bolster, a thin mattress and coarse woollen blankets covered by a counterpane that had obviously seen better days. A battered looking writing desk and chair stood beneath the window next to a dark wood dressing table equipped with a dusty mirror. On the dressing table stood a large ceramic bowl, a chipped jug with a rose pattern on its side, a piece of flannel material and a small towel. On the opposite wall was an equally dark and rather dismal looking wardrobe and next to it was a fireplace. On the mantelpiece shelf over the fireplace was a gas lamp and a clock that had stopped working; it and everything else in the room was covered with a thick patina of dust. The walls were covered in ancient looking dark blue wallpaper that was blotched with indeterminate grey swirls. On the wall over the head of the bed was a single black and white print depicting a flock of sheep grazing in a field.

'If you would like the room I'll send my girl in later to make up a nice fire in the grate,' said Mrs Smith.

'Excuse me, Mrs Smith, but where are the sanitary arrangements?' said Atia looking around mystified at the lack of a cleansing pod.

The woman looked puzzled before she suddenly worked out what Atia meant.

'Oh the water closet and bathroom you mean. The recently installed Joule's latest patent water closet and the shared bathing facilities are just down the corridor,' she announced proudly. A chamber pot is of course in the usual place,' she whispered, pointing at the space beneath the bed. Let me know what day of the week you require a bath and I will supply you with a large and very nice towel,' she said smiling, pleased with the largess that she was able to bestow on the tall and rather handsome couple.

The woman let the two Jarans look round the room in silence for a minute before broaching the cost of the rent.

'Well,' she said, 'if you would like the room it costs five shillings a week, payment in advance of course.'

Ashto looked at Apprentice Commander Atia, who seemed totally taken aback by the state of the room and its lack of sanitary arrangements, but when she didn't offer any objection he took out two of the gold coins from his security belt and gave them to Mrs Smith.

'Will this be adequate?' said First Commander Ashto.

Mrs Smith looked at the two sovereigns that now nestled in her arthritic hand.

'That will do very nicely indeed sir, thank you kindly. Er ... would it be possible to have your names? Just for my paperwork you understand.'

'Certainly, madam; my name is Treve Pacton Ashto and this is my wife and assistant Atia Mo Margo.' Again the First Commander was pleased that he had not, out of habit, mentioned their Jaran titles. He repeated to Mrs Smith the writer and assistant cover story the pair had developed since arriving on the planet.

'Pleased to meet you both and no mistake … Mr and Mrs Ashton, I hope you will be very comfortable.' A slight smirking smile lingered on the lips of Mrs Smith as she turned and hobbled out of the room.

First Commander Ashto and Apprentice Commander Atia sat on the bed and looked around the room.

'Do you believe, First Commander, that we will be able to stay in this awful room for the next five Earth years?' Ashto had never seen Atia look quite so miserable.

'It is not so bad Apprentice Commander. True it is basic in the extreme but we seem to have everything that we will need.'

'First Commander, there are not even any sanitary arrangements available to us in this living space. We have no cleansing pod and we will have to make do with a weekly bathe in a shared sanitary space. I really cannot imagine anything much worse.'

Ashto had never heard Atia speak in such negative terms before. As far as he was concerned she had always been, up to this point, the most optimistic of colleagues, someone who he had indeed admired for her fortitude and determination to get their task completed.

'Apprentice Commander Atia, I believe that we should come to terms with the somewhat uncomfortable position that we find ourselves in and begin the job we came to this planet to undertake. Perhaps in the near future we could look for more salubrious living quarters but in the meantime we should start on the task we have before us.' Ashto was happy with the way he was dealing with the situation; showing leadership without autocracy was his immediate aim in attempting to motivate his crewmember.

Apprentice Commander Atia stood up and almost visibly shook herself.

'You are completely correct First Commander. This may be the worst living space imaginable – a living space that makes the sleeping arrangements on the ship for the past two years seem like the best vacation hostel on Jara Prime but our task is to complete that which the Jaran High Command has instructed us to do. I apologise profusely for my show of weakness in the face of adversity. It will not happen again.'

And with that the Apprentice Commander rearranged her voluminous dress, dabbed her face with a handkerchief she had found in the computer replicated reticule she had been holding and sat down at the writing desk her handheld computer terminal at the ready.

My greetings and utmost felicitations to the esteemed members of the Sub-Committee.

I am pleased to be able to report a one hundred percent success rate so far in the mission. Apprentice Commander Atia and I have negotiated the first task of infiltrating ourselves into the society of the conurbation known locally as London, the main city on planet 2007/52-3, known hereafter, for ease of communication, as the Earth. We have managed to find a living space (called a lodging in the local terminology) in the very heart of London alongside a large number of the Earth humans who live and work in the area. The living conditions we have submitted ourselves to are decidedly primitive but endurable.

So far we have confirmed that the Earth's social structure is organised on a rigid caste or class basis with a relatively small number of wealthy and well-nourished individuals exercising power over the great mass of other individuals in this city. We have not as yet fully discovered the reasoning behind this palpably unequal state of affairs or the power structures involved that support such a society but we are well on the way to shedding some light on such details. The regularly produced daily newssheets, referred to as newspapers in the local parlance, are invaluable in discovering more about the various societal interactions that are going on around us.

Most of the Earth humans living in the area we have based ourselves belong to the lower castes of society and are manual workers for the main part or retail operatives of one type or another. There also seems to be a sub-strata of individuals who are without regular means of support and either live on the street or beg for a few coins to enable them to purchase temporary accommodation for the night-time hours. In our initial perambulations around the local area, Apprentice Commander Atia and I have been surprised at the signs of poverty that exist in this city, which is the richest city in the planet's foremost and wealthiest state. There appears to be little official provision for the poorer members of this society – amazingly there is no universal pension system provided for elderly individuals in evidence and there seems to be very few childcare or health care institutions to provide help and assistance to people of this caste. It is a situation that Apprentice Commander Atia and I have found difficult to come to terms with.

The geographic layout of the area does little to mitigate the amount of privation suffered by much of the local populace. The many alleyways, passages and backyards, that are hardly touched by daylight even on a bright day in the planet's summer months, lead to a myriad of small living spaces that are so overcrowded it is difficult to understand how any sapient creature could exist in such conditions. Nicknamed 'rookeries' in the local vernacular these spaces are very often home to whole families living in conditions that on Jaran Prime would not be considered suitable for wild animals. Children, in particular, suffer greatly.

Apprentice Commander Atia and I have been astounded to discover that very little education is provided for children beyond an extremely elementary provision. There is nothing that prepares the young of this area for a worthwhile existence as adults or provides any escape from the crushing poverty that will be their lot for life and as a consequence social mobility in this society is virtually non-existent. What employment there is often of the repetitious, mind-numbing variety that is poorly paid and offers little hope for any sort of advancement. Criminal behaviour of all sorts is, by all accounts, rampant.

Health care is minimal and most of the residents distrust medial practitioners to such a degree that the last place they will go to in the event of illness is to the few and poorly funded local health centres, called hospitals in the local language, and which seem to most humans to be simply places where one goes to die.

As a result of this situation it is little wonder that many in the local adult population spend much of their disposable currency on alcoholic refreshment, which is comparatively inexpensive and which no doubt temporarily dulls the reality of their miserable and forlorn lives. Late at night and even sometimes in the daylight hours it is not unusual to find males or females insensible with alcoholic drink lying at the side of walkways. These sad individuals are usually ignored by other residents who simply walk around them and who seem to accept that this state of affairs is one of normality.

This reliance on alcohol along with the extreme poverty of the area has led many individuals to enter into a life of permanent or casual sexual prostitution. This phenomenon does not exist on Jara Prime although I have heard that similar habits have existed on the more outlying regions of the Galactic Federation. In this area of London these sexual transactions usually take place between males and females on the streets, in the back alleys and yards of the rookeries, with the female providing sexual favours for a minimal amount of the local currency. Often the few low value coins they earn from these sexual encounters can be used to purchase a sleeping space, often shared with a stranger, in a dilapidated common lodging house usually referred to, in the local parlance, as a doss house.

The conditions in which much of the local populace exist make Apprentice Commander Atia's and my living space seem almost salubrious in comparison and as a result we have stopped complaining to each other about our situation. We spend much of our day walking around the local area observing, listening and gathering information via our recording devices. We are becoming more skilled at understanding the local dialects and accents and communicating with members of the human population. No one suspects that we are not from the planet Earth. We are aided in this regard by the fact that many of those living in the area are from other places outside of this state called Britain. Many of these alien migrants appear to come from places situated on the large landmass adjacent to the islands that make up the country of Great Britain. These migrants have come here from other states where many of them have suffered persecution the reasons for which are extremely difficult for us to fathom. Sometimes there seems to have existed philosophical differences between people on such a scale as to cause some groupings to leave their home states and head for the London conurbation. Sometimes this persecution can be put down to racial differences between humans although Apprentice Commander Atia and I have found it quite baffling, to try to identify any actual racial differentiation between Earth humans. The human species on the planet Earth in fact seems to display a great deal of homogeneity. The situation is certainly nothing like that which exists on planet 2101/88-1. In my Explorer Executive training I remember graphically how that particular planet famously was the home of two sapient species, humanoid and insectoid, who were involved in a armed conflicts that lasted many centuries prior to the intervention by the Jaran Federation. Today both of those races live in complete harmony and indeed I believe that members of both species have represented the Galactic Federation via both the Diplomatic and Explorer services.

That is all I am able to report for the time being. I will send my next report when we have succeeded in gathering more data and intelligence relevant to our mission.

With my utmost loyalty, etcetera,
First Commander Treve Pacton Ashto.

4

Whitechapel oysters

'Are you feeling completely well, Apprentice Commander?'

'Quite well, First Commander, but I seem to have developed a series of itches on various locations of my epidermis, brought on, apparently by small insectoid life-forms known by Earth humans as fleas, or possibly lice, that exist on my person and is most probably due to the lack of a proper cleansing pod in our living quarters.' Atia grimaced as she tried to scratch a region of her groin area and failed due to her efforts being hampered by the preponderance of material that made up her many layers of outerwear, skirts and petticoats.

The pair sat in an oyster bar in Whitechapel High Street deciding whether to actually eat from the plate of cooked, marine bivalve creatures that had been placed between them. So far they had decided to make do with nibbling pieces of the coarse bread that had also been provided by a rather grubby looking young waitress. This had been their first attempt at finding palatable Earth food since arriving in London some two weeks before. Since their arrival they had been eating from the supply of reconstituted Jaran vegetable meals they had brought with them from the ship but had decided it was now time to sample some of the local food varieties.

'This seafood is considered to be a staple of the poor of London,' said First Commander Ashto pointing at the plate of oysters that steamed pungently on the plate before him. He reluctantly picked up one of the warm shells and was almost going to scoop out the contents when Atia cautioned him against his action. She clutched her small computer terminal just below the level of the table so as to avoid others in the crowded eating-place seeing what she was doing.

'First Commander, it would be unwise to swallow that creature of the seabed. According to the information just provided by the ship's computer the coastal shallows where these bivalves are harvested are often in close proximity to sites where sewage pipes emit untreated excremental waste into the sea. The chances of becoming ill from eating one of these creatures are relatively high. I suggest that we just make do with this bread and tea.'

Ashto frowned, dropped the oyster back on the metal plate and slid it along the rough wooden trestle table to where an elderly man sat. He was dressed in worn and tattered clothes, nursed a tin mug of tea and had been casting envious eyes on the plate of cooked oysters. He nodded his gratitude and began tucking into the oysters with gusto.

'It is just as well, First Commander, that we bought with us from the ship plenty of vegetable based, nutritional food sachets to provide our sustenance until we can find Earth food that suits our systems. It may be difficult for us to find palatable food in this region of London called Whitechapel.'

'That is true, Apprentice Commander, although we do need to adopt as many of the local habits as possible in order to provide cover for our mission and convince others that I am an author from the United States of America here to write about what I experience in London in order to pass relevant data on to my presumed, if mythical, home audience,' Ashto said before taking a sip from his mug of tea.

'You are quite correct of course, First Commander. Actually First Commander, I was wondering if we should dispense with our Explorer Executive honorifics when we are conversing with each other in public on the basis that what we say may be overheard by local Earth humans and cause them to think that we may not be exactly who we say we are.'

'I understand, Apprentice Commander Atia, the success of our mission should outweigh every other consideration, but how would we address each other in that case?'

'Well, First Commander, as you know, since meeting our landlady, the rather hard-of-hearing Mrs Smith, she has come to refer to us as Mr and Mrs Ashton. What I suggest, purely in case of us being overheard by others, is that we refer to each other in the same way that an actual married couple here on Earth might do.'

'I see, Apprentice Commander, so I would call you wife and you could call me husband? That would seem to be a most sensible idea.' Ashto had another drink of his tea, which he had grown to appreciate since first arriving on the planet.

'Yes, First Commander, that is one possibility. However I would like to suggest that we utilise one of our given names and alter it slightly so that it becomes similar to an Earth style name in the same way that your patronymic name Ashto became, via Mrs Smith's dysfunctional hearing, the name Ashton, which is, so my research reveals, a relatively common family name in some of the states on this planet.'

'Please explain further, Apprentice Commander.'

'Certainly, First Commander, as you know one of my given names is Margo which, coincidentally sounds exactly the same as a name sometimes given to Earth females, although it is spelt slightly differently employing an unspoken or silent letter "t" at the end of the word.'

'That is interesting, Apprentice Commander. What would my Earth name be?'

'Well, First Commander, one of your given names is Treve which is not too far away from the reasonably common male Earth name of Trevor. So I would propose, with your agreement of course, that from now on, whilst we are on this planet and in this city that we refer to each other as Margot and Trevor, two very Earth sounding personal names that will not in any way arouse suspicion in any one overhearing our conversations.'

'I concur with your analysis and your proposal, Apprentice Commander ... I mean, Margot.'

'Thank you ...er Trevor, I am sure that this will help us in our mission as we attempt to gather more information about the Earth and its people. We will of course, once we have completed our orientation task and are back on board the ship, revert to using out official Jaran titles.'

'Of course, that goes without any need of explanation.' Ashto smiled at Atia and had an overwhelming desire to hold her hand across the table but decided that, on balance that action would not be appropriate or very professional.'

'There is one more thing, First Comm ... Trevor.'

'Please go ahead and explain ... Margot.'

'I have begun to notice that whenever we introduce ourselves as Mr and Mrs Ashton, Earth humans invariably look at my hand, my left hand in fact, and notice that I am not wearing a wedding ring there. This then causes them to display a rather enigmatic smile as a result and some even momentarily close one of their eyes in what is known in this language as a "wink." I believe that this reaction occurs because they suspect that we are not actually married to each other and that we have embarked on a relationship that is considered to be, in London at least, one of an illicit nature.'

'I see. This wedding ring is therefore symbolic of an Earth couple's nuptial commitment to each other.'

'That is correct First Commander ... I apologise, Trevor. Apparently during a wedding ceremony in this particular culture the female usually receives a gold ring from the male, which then provides confirmation to others that she is from that time forward a married woman. In some cases the male also wears a gold ring on his left hand although that is far from being a universal trait.'

'Well In that case, ... Margot, we will immediately find a retail establishment at which we can purchase one of these wedding rings.'

First Commander Ashto smiled at Apprentice Commander Atia. He had begun to realise that his relationship with her was becoming more than that which usually exists between a mission commander and a crewmember. He felt pleased to be able to make Apprentice Commander Atia content and happy. If she felt it was necessary to wear one of these marriage symbols then that is what she should do.

As the two stood up and walked out of the eating-house heading for the jewelry stores of the West End a man who had watched Ashto pay for his oysters with a gold sovereign followed them.

5

Flower and Dean Street

'This particular street, according to the ship's computer data bank, is the lodging house, or doss house, centre of the Whitechapel area, ... Trevor,' said Atia.

'Even by the standards of Whitechapel, it is certainly a very down-at-heel place,' said Ashto, pleased to be able to draw an idiomatic phrase from the language area of his neural implant and employ it in his conversation.

It had been dull, cold and raining for most of the day. A low mist had now descended on the city, the smell of coal fires hung in the evening air and some of the gaslights in the street had already been lit. Autumn had seemed to come early to London in this year of 1888. After their abortive attempt to eat a meal of oysters, Ashto and Atia were taking their usual early evening stroll around the district in their quest to gain more knowledge about the humans who lived in the area. During the next five years they aimed to visit most parts of the London conurbation as well as other regions in this state called Britain in order to build up a detailed picture of the inhabitants and how they would respond to a diplomatic visit by Jaran officials and any military personnel that might accompany them.

On the corner of Dales Place the couple stopped and Ashto bought a small flower to wear as a buttonhole from an emaciated looking young female selling flowers. He had seen other well-dressed men wearing a small piece of local flora on the lapel of their jackets and thought it a delightful tradition. He gave the young woman, who was really no more than a child, a shilling coin and she in return smiled broadly at him. She had never been given so much money before for a single bloom. Atia looked down at the young woman's oversized, battered and mismatched boots she was wearing.

'Do you not own a proper pair of shoes my dear child?' said Atia.

The young woman looked up at Atia who towered above her diminutive figure. 'No, miss – me mum pawned 'em las' week to buy some food – she said me plates'd be fine in these'n as long as I didn't step on any broke bottles.'

She held up her left leg and displayed the sole of the boot that consisted mostly of a large hole that showed her unprotected and grubby foot inside.

'Well child, take this coin and buy yourself some new footwear as soon as possible.' Atia passed a gold sovereign to the young woman who looked at it with unbelieving eyes.

'A thick 'un! Ain't never seen one of 'em before. Is it real?' She bit the coin in the manner she'd seen adults do on the rare occasions they had come into contact with large denomination coins, smiled broadly again and ran off in the direction of Brick Lane.

'She will almost certainly have the coin taken from her by her mother before she is able to purchase any footwear,' said Ashto.

'I know, but at least it may provide her family with some nourishing food in the near future, just as long as the mother and father, if she has one, do not spend it all on alcohol, which is what is most likely going to happen.' Atia looked at Ashto. The pair had experienced feelings of sympathy many times for the humans of Whitechapel they had met in the two weeks they had been living in the area. The levels of overcrowding and poverty that existed in the district had frankly amazed them. They realised quite early on that the region of London they had chosen to reside in was an area of great privation and neglect but the extent and depth of Whitechapel's poverty never failed to move them. They knew they could never hope to alleviate the extremes of deprivation that they came across but found it impossible not to give some high value coinage to the street vendors and ragamuffin children they met on their travels. However, despite the deep levels of poverty they had seen in the short time they had been on the planet they were also impressed by the resilience and forbearance of the Earth humans in what was obviously a daily battle to survive in the horrible and overcrowded rookeries where most of those in the area lived.

Atia and Ashto watched as the young flower seller, still clutching her basket of blooms skipped happily down the street and disappeared into the mist that was becoming thicker as the murky daylight began to fade still further.

They were about to turn around to head back to their guest house in Bell Lane when a man, large by Earth standards, appeared in front of them, pulled a small knife from his pocket, grabbed Ashto by his coat collar and held the weapon against the First Commander's throat.

'Righto Mary Ann, give me all yer money afore I stick you!' said the man.

Ashto looked at the man with interest. He and Atia had yet to personally experience any obvious criminality in Whitechapel although they knew the area was rife with such activity.

'You must be one of the individuals the ship's computer refers to as a footpad or street robber and whose professed aim is to relieve unwary citizens of their valuables. Fascinating.'

'Sharrup la di da boy before I snuff out yer candle. Give me yer bunce, all of it. Now!'

'Apprentice ... sorry... Margot. I hope that you are recording details about this interesting incident for our records.'

'Indeed I am ... Trevor, and I now seem to have enough data on this particular individual.'

At which point Atia swiftly delivered a sharp blow to the man's throat with the side of her hand, an action that caused him to drop the knife and stagger backwards, gasping for air, a confused look on his face. He tried to speak but found that he couldn't, which increased his confusion even more. He fell to his knees and Atia stood over him.

'I suggest to you my good sir, that you think very carefully about mending your ways. Carrying a sharp bladed implement in order to steal personal belongings from peaceful individuals is not the way one should comport oneself if a civilized society is to be maintained. You are lucky on this occasion that we do not conduct you to the nearest law-enforcement authorities. Now be off with you and think carefully about what I have said.'

With considerable effort the man rose to his feet, rubbing his neck and throat. He considered saying something but the look on the tall and imposing looking Apprentice Commander's face made him think better of it and he walked stiffly away.

'It was inevitable that this sort of incident would happen at some point,' said Ashto brushing off his jacket and straightening the flower in his buttonhole.

'Agreed … Trevor,' replied Atia, 'although we should now consider whether it would be wise to carry the disrupter weapon on our journeys around the area in the future. Had there been more than one of these ruffians we might have found it a greater problem with which to deal.'

'You may be right … Margot; I will certainly consider the point before we venture out tomorrow. Shall we now return to Mrs Smith's guesthouse establishment? Please take my arm.'

Atia took Ashto's arm in the manner they had observed other couples do and walked back down Flower and Dean Street and then turned left into Commercial Street. Although the August weather had improved slightly from the unusual cold and wet of the previous month there was a definite Autumnal feel about this last day of the month of August and the streets were damp and greasy with the low lying drizzly mist that had descended wholesale on the city.

The Jaran pair's journey back to Bell Lane only took five minutes but on the way they witnessed many examples of the extreme poverty of an area they had now started to get to know better each day. The many hungry looking young children in the street, some playing in a desultory fashion, others staring open-mouthed at the couple as they passed, often with open hands begging for money. Some were shoeless, most looked neglected and waiflike, with clothes that were threadbare, patched and ragged. Homeless individuals sat huddled in doorways, hardly clothed at all and shivering with a look of helplessness in their eyes.

A few adult humans were standing outside their houses, looking enviously at the well-dressed young couple walking down their street. It was unusual to see such obviously wealthy persons walking around the area. Occasionally toffs from the West End might visit the local music halls and pubs of the area in the evening. Often these were dissolute young men in search of cheap thrills or 'tot hunting' as they called it – scouring the streets for pretty young girls who would be compliant and grateful for their attention. A married couple in the fine clothes walking around the streets of Whitechapel seemingly taking an interest in the sights and sounds around them was a much rarer sight, however.

As the Jaran pair continued their journey an acrid smell of smoke hung in the air making each lungful they took seem thick and cloying. Some of this came from the coal fires in people's dwellings, the resultant grey clouds swirling from every chimney. However, much of it still lingered in the atmosphere from the large warehouse fire that had taken place at the Thames' South Quay dock on the previous evening and which had lit up the whole of the East End of London for many hours during the night.

In Commercial Street the horse drawn traffic still clogged the busy thoroughfare even though it was late in the day, and a crowd of people spilled out of the Princess Alice public house on the corner of Wentworth Street, many drunk on cheap ale and gin and some already incapable of standing. Ashto and Atia had both realised that at some point they would have to venture into one or more of the public houses in Whitechapel, a prospect neither were particularly looking forward to. As well as the chance of getting involved in some sort of altercation with a drunken local, alcohol did not suit Jaran physiology very well and until they were more confident about keeping their true identities secret they had shied away from entering such places.

After a few minutes Ashto and Atia reached Mrs Smith's guesthouse just as the persistent drizzle was turning into heavy rain and rolls of thunder could be heard rumbling around in the distance. They were both feeling somewhat depressed as they often did after their daily perambulations around the poverty stricken area that was Whitechapel. Using the key they had been given to the side entrance they made their way up the stairs and to their room – a living space that they were gradually getting used to but they still found almost as equally depressing as their recent walk around the local area.

'I would very much like to bathe,' said Atia, but unfortunately I had my weekly allowance of bathwater two days ago.' Atia, like all Jarans was used to utilising a proper bodily cleansing pod every day and Mrs Smith's rule about only having one bath each week had made her feel particularly woebegone. She constantly felt grubby and itchy and was fairly convinced that the odour she was emitting from her body was extremely unwholesome. The smell of most of the humans she had met so far in the last two weeks was far stronger and more pungent than anything she had so far experienced in her life and although she was gradually growing used to the perpetual bodily odours of others she was not at all happy that she probably smelt as bad as they did.

'First Commander, have you noticed any particular odour exuding from my body?'

Ashto had been occupied looking out of the window onto the street below. 'No, Apprentice Commander, not at all and I wouldn't let it worry you. When I was on my previous exploratory mission on planet 1508/55-8 under First Commander Roma we had to spend several months sheltering in a cavern and due to the high levels of hydrochloric acid in the planet's water supply we could not wash at all. It is simply a matter of getting used to being unclean. And, by the way, would it be acceptable to you, Apprentice Commander, if we continued to refer to each other by our adopted Earth names even when we are alone in each other's company? Just so we do not accidently use to our Jaran titles and names when we are out amongst the humans.'

Atia smiled. 'Of course... Trevor, that is an eminently sensible point.'

'Then it is agreed ... Margot.'

Atia continued to smile as she looked down somewhat shyly at her newly acquired and shiny gold wedding ring that she now wore on her left hand. Looking up at Ashto and still smiling she said: 'Trevor ... as we are now, for all intents and purposes, off duty for the rest of this twenty-four hour Earth cycle would it be appropriate, do you think, to amuse ourselves this evening by indulging in some recreational sexual activity?'

Ashto's face, which had been looking rather serious, brightened. 'I think that that is a splendid idea ...Margot.'

Ashto walked from the window, where he had been watching the electrical storm brewing in the leaden skies above Whitechapel, over to Atia who sat, still smiling, on the edge of the bed and helped her to begin the long process of removing the many layers of her female Earth garments.

There had been a ferocious storm earlier. Thunder roared and lightning had flashed across the skies above London – a definite sign that God had wanted him to continue his work this night. And this time it had been different and more satisfying. He had carried out what he had hoped to do and had consigned a whore straight to the pits of hell. However, he did not feel that this particular achievement had brought his work to a close – no, not by any means. This woman of the streets was just one of many and it was clear he still had much to do. He had brought his long, sharp knife to her throat and sliced though the whiteness of her corrupted flesh before she had time to scream. He had felt the thrill as the sharpness of his blade bit through the tendons, arteries and windpipe of her neck. She had been totally in his power like a calf waiting for slaughter.

He had noticed that her front teeth were missing. He had commented on how pretty her bonnet was and she had smiled at him. 'It's jolly isn't it, do you like it?' she had said with a toothless grin. And then she had turned her back to him and pulled up her skirts. 'Come on,' she had said, 'stick it in. You'll find it nice and warm and wet.' Then she had laughed drunkenly – she stank of drink and almost fell over even before he had touched her. She had laughed again and that's when he grabbed her hair, pulled her head back and sliced her throat to the bone. Her neck made a gurgling sound as he lay her down on her back on the wet ground where heavy rain had been falling most of the evening. Her eyes were open and she stared at him in her last few dying moments as he knelt down, pulled up her skirts and plunged his knife into her *stomach and drew it down her abdomen. He felt a great pleasure to know that she wouldn't be using those filth-ridden parts ever again. No longer would she be asking for a few pennies to allow men to spill their life force into her.*

He had stood up and looked down at his work – his sacred work. There she lay, her legs spread wide apart, her intestines poking bloodily out of the long jagged rip his knife had made. The blood had now stopped oozing out of her slashed neck. 'Now she will be reaping her just deserts in hell,' he whispered aloud, smiling, pleased at what he saw. 'It was God's work,' he said.

He took a cloth from his pocket, wiped his hands and the bloody blade on it before tucking the knife back inside his coat. He backed away, reluctant to cease admiring his night's handiwork and then turned on his heel and walked quickly back down Bucks Row and onto Whitechapel Road where he turned right towards the place where he lived. He looked around to make sure that no one was watching him and then threw the bloodied cloth over a wooden fence onto some waste ground where it landed in a puddle of rainwater that quickly turned a deep red.

6

The Britannia Public house

First Commander Ashto entered the Britannia pub, which was situated on the corner of Dorset Street and Commercial Street, with some trepidation. He had decided to visit the drinking establishment on his own despite Apprentice Commander Atia's protestations. As First Commander he had insisted on carrying out this next unpredictable part of their mission alone, although he eventually agreed to Atia's suggestion that he should put the small disrupter weapon in the pocket of his coat. Ashto also carried the micro recording device the computer had incorporated, via the ship's replicator, into one of his coat buttons. This would allow him to record visual and audio information and enable it to be sent directly back to the ship's computer database for future analysis. Atia had researched the data held by the ship's computer on London's East End public houses and had warned Ashto that he could quite easily encounter aggressively intoxicated and possibly dangerous individuals there and should be prepared to deal with any incidents caused by such humans without drawing too much attention to himself.

With Atia's help Ashto had studied carefully the parameters of behaviour that would be considered appropriate when he was inside the Britannia public house and also what sort of beverage would be best for him to consume whilst he was there. Alcohol of any sort was generally detrimental to Jaran physiology in a number of ways but the Jaran pair also realised that for the First Commander to fit into the drinking establishment's usual clientele without raising any suspicions he would need to imbibe a certain amount of alcoholic drink. Atia, therefore, using her link to the ship's computer, had ascertained that the best sort of liquid of an alcohol-based nature that the First Commander should consume was something called bitter ale. This substance, Atia had informed First Commander Ashto was a beverage made from fermented grain along with other plant based additives and was lower in alcoholic content than a number of other liquids that would be readily available at the public house such as wine, gin, whisky or brandy.

Ashto's plan was to engage with others in the Britannia, perhaps offer to buy individuals alcoholic refreshment and then, when he had succeeded in gaining their trust, ask apposite questions that would help towards his and Atia's assessment of the humans in London. This, they hoped, would give them a valuable insight into the psychological make-up of Earth humans and provide the pair with the sort of information that might help them to decide the best approaches for any Jaran diplomatic, colonial or military personnel to take in the future.

The atmosphere in the dark and low-ceilinged Britannia was thick with smoke from many cigarettes and pipes as Ashto walked to the bar where his researches had indicated he must go to purchase his beverage. The smoky murk made him cough almost immediately but he was pleased to note that, as he entered the public house, only one or two of its occupants had stared at him and they had soon returned to whatever they had been doing beforehand. Ashto failed to hear a number of muted comments about 'posh geezers from the West End coming into our boozers,' made by one or two of the customers in the Britannia. As Ashto reached the bar he noticed that, according to a large clock hanging on the wall behind, it was 15 minutes past 7 o'clock in the evening.

A few men stood at the bar some smoking and talking in loud voices while others were glumly looking at the amber coloured liquid fast disappearing in the large glasses in front of them. Ashto took off his top hat and waited patiently until the human behind the bar came over to him and asked, in a gruff voice, what he wanted.

'I would like to purchase a pint glass of bitter ale please my good sir,' said Ashto. His voice was loud enough to be heard over the general din of the pub and he was aware that as he spoke the noise of conversation in the pub died down slightly as though a number of those present had stopped to listen to what he was saying.

The waistcoated barman grabbed a pint glass and pulled down on a beer pump handle. The beer came gushing out of the tap filling the glass. It was, Ashto thought, one of the least appetising sights he had seen on his brief stay on the planet Earth so far. The muddy colour of the beverage and its foamy top surface reminded Ashto of how the river Thames looked when he and Atia had first arrived in London. The barman informed Ashto how many pennies he needed to pay in return for the pint of beer and Ashto took a handful of coins from his coat pocket and sorted through them. In the last two weeks Ashto had become better acquainted with the complicated monetary system used by the people of London. He now was able to identify the copper coloured metal coins known locally as pennies, emblazoned as they were with the head of the local Queen called Victoria. He was also able to recognise the copper halfpennies and farthings and also the silver coloured threepenny and sixpenny pieces, shillings, florins and half-crowns. Ashto paid the barman the four penny coins that covered the cost of the drink and took a sip of the unpleasant looking liquid in the large glass. The taste of the beer wasn't quite as bad as he had anticipated but his grimace on swallowing the sour liquid had been noticed by a pipe smoking male sitting at a nearby table. The man who wore a battered and dusty bowler hat and well-worn suit of clothes had previously been engrossed in a newspaper.

'Not used to the proper stuff, hey Guv'nor?' said the man putting the newspaper down.

'On the contrary,' replied Ashto as he took a further sip of the brown liquid, 'I am very used to a large range of alcoholic beverages in this area of London.' He tried hard to overcome the gag reflex he felt in his throat.

'Well Guv'nor, I'll take yer word for that! Come over here and sit down. Take the weight off yer trots, as it were.'

Ashto was glad to be invited to sit. Although he was now fairly used to the boots he wore he still found their basic design uncomfortably flawed as they persisted in painfully rubbing various parts of his feet. The middle-aged man, who had a friendly whiskery face, raised his glass of beer to Ashto.

'Cheers – down the hatch!' said the man finishing off his pint and by nodding at Ashto's drink indicating that he should do the same.

Ashto, wanting to fit in with the local humans as much as possible, picked up his beer and drank deeply from it. He was quite surprised to notice that this time the liquid, whilst still fairly sour tasting, did not seem quite as bad as before and he was even more surprised to find that in next to no time he had completely finished the pint of frothy brown beverage.

Ashto had come into the Britannia with the express purpose of talking to and befriending some of the humans and therefore asked the man if he would like another drink.

'That's very decent of yer me ole china, I'll have another bitter ... and a whisky chaser if that's all right by yer good self?"

Ashto, slightly nonplussed by the man's terminology, said it was and went to the bar to ask for the drinks deciding that he too should also have a pint of bitter with one of these whisky chasers. Soon returning he placed the drinks on the table.

'Thankee most kindly, Guv'nor.' The man took a deep draught of the bitter ale and Ashto followed suit. The man drank about half of his beer before then picking up his glass of whisky and swallowing it in one. Ashto did the same and spent the next few seconds spluttering. He struggled to get his breath as his throat felt like someone had set fire to it.

The man stifled a laugh. 'So Guv'nor, yer not from around here; what are yer doin' in this benighted corner of our fair city? By the way I'm Sadler, Tom Sadler.' He held out his hand and Ashto shook it.

'You are correct in your analysis Mr Sadler,' said Ashto his throat still feeling somewhat raw from the fiery liquid he had just consumed. 'My name is Trevor Ashton and I do not originate from London. I am, in fact, from the United States of America and am here with my wife to write about the city of London and its inhabitants so that a greater understanding and appreciation of it will be evident in the minds of my fellow citizens of the aforesaid United States of America.'

'Well Guv'nor you Americans certainly have got a gift for words but if I didn't know any better I'd 'ave thought you was one o' 'em haw-haw toffs who come down the East End looking for thrills and a bit of cheap tot, if you catch me meaning.'

Ashto didn't really know what this human called Tom Sadler actually meant but covered up his discomfiture by taking another large swig of his drink. Strangely, thought Ashto, he was actually starting to enjoy this alcoholic beverage called bitter ale and had soon finished his pint and offered to get some more for himself and Mr Sadler.

'Don't forget them whisky chasers me ole pal.'

'Yes, of course,' said Ashto as he wound his way to the bar, his Earth-style footwear causing him to feel a bit unsteady on his feet.

Ashto soon returned to the table with the drinks, flopping down gratefully into his seat. He was surprised to find that he was enjoying his visit to the public house far more than he had anticipated, despite its smoky atmosphere and the alcoholic beverages he was imbibing, which were not as unpleasant as he had presumed they would be.

'I 'spose yer've 'eard about the murder in Bucks Row las' night?' said Sadler tapping his newspaper before having a deep swig of his beer.

'Murder, last night in this locality? No, indeed, Mr Sadler I have not heard anything about that event,' said Ashto, slightly slurring his words.

'Yes, my friend, bloomin' big hullabaloo last night. Woman foun' with 'er throat cut from ear to ear. Insides were all 'angin' out too they say.'

'That is terrible! Who was this unfortunate female? Why would she be killed in such a way?'

'Who's to say? Work of some loony bloke no doubt. 'Er was a street tart by all accounts so she probably didn't give him 'is money's worth an' he took offence an' decided to put 'er lights out for good an' all.'

Ashto took a large drink of his beer as he searched his implant for the meaning of the phrase 'street tart.' He was shocked at this news. Of course he knew that Whitechapel was a lawless place in some regards but the murder of one Earth human by a fellow human in this area where he had decided to live was something he had not been fully prepared for. The fact that the murder victim was a female killed, according to Mr Sadler, in the course of her work as a prostitute was even more shocking. Ashto had known ever since he had arrived in the Whitechapel area of this vast city of London that a large number of poverty stricken females were prepared to sell themselves on the street for the sexual pleasure of others, but the news that one of these poor, desperate and unfortunate women had been killed in such a horrible way was totally appalling.

Another man also in his middle years, wearing a peaked cloth-cap and scarf around his neck despite the warm atmosphere inside the crowded pub and who was seated nearby had been listening to the men's conversation. 'I knew 'er. Nice gal – no side to 'er. Poll 'er name were. Liked 'er booze – used to get elephants in the Frying Pan on Brick Lane most nights so she'd let yer do 'er for the price of a gin or two. Did 'er once or twice meself to save botherin' the missus when I got 'ome.'

Without thinking Ashto drained his beer glass and then picked up his whisky and drank that down too. Although he had not immediately understood all of the words the man in the cap had used he had picked up the general gist of what he had said and shivered at the thought of what this woman had gone through just to get a small amount of money for alcoholic drink.

'Do the policing authorities know who has perpetrated this heinous crime?' said Ashto to the man in the cap.

'Eh?' said the man.

''Ave the mutton shunters copped anyone for doin' her in?' said Tom Sadler to the man.

'No, course they ain't. Crushers 'ave bin all over the place but they ain't got a clue as usual. If it were some proper bit 'o frock in the West End they'd 'ave catched 'im by now but they ain't bothered.'

'Can I get you another alcoholic drink, sir?' said Ashto to the man.

'Why thankee, Guv'nor, much obliged, I'll have …'

'A pint of bitter ale with a whisky chaser?' said Ashto

'That'd be just right Guv'nor. Ta.'

Once Ashto had returned from the bar with drinks for himself and the two men he continued the conversation about the previous night's murder.

'Could I ask you two gentlemen whether the killing of one person by another human is a common occurrence in this part of London or was last evening's tragic event somewhat of a piece of aberrant behaviour?'

The man in the nearby chair scratched his head and looked confused. Mr Sadler however responded to Ashto's question: 'Well, Guv'nor ... Mr Ashton,' Sadler smiled, 'it is, as you say, a fairly common occurrence. Usually involves some bloke doing in 'is missus because of somethin' she's said or cos she ain't cooked 'is spuds the way 'e likes 'em. He usually regrets it too – right up to the time they march 'im to the gallows and stretch 'is neck for 'im.'

Ashto looked horrified and took a large gulp of his beer.

'And then there's them that should be in Colney 'atch who 'ave a grudge against the workingwomen. Prossies quite often get bashed or cut up by some 'o their clients who are frustrated that they can't get it up 'cos they're full as a goat or they've been stung by one of 'em and given a dose of somethin' that's caused them to piss pins and needles. Lots o' dark alleyways roun' 'ere to wainwright someone if you've a mind to.'

Ashto hoped that his recording device was registering all of this useful if rather confusing information that he and Atia, along with the ship's computer, would no doubt be able to decipher at a later date. At the moment it was all that Ashto could do to stop his eyes from seeing a double image of this Earth human called Tom Sadler. Perhaps another round of drinks would make everything a bit clearer thought Ashto. The man in the nearby chair and Mr Sadler were all too willing for Ashto to fetch them some more beer and whiskies from the bar which strangely seemed to Ashto to be somewhat further away than it was before.

Once Ashto had shakily ferried all the drinks from the bar to the tables he was keen to hear more from the two men about the inherent violence in the Whitechapel area.

'Gentlemen,' said Ashto finding it increasingly difficult to stay focused on the matter in hand and with a inappropriate desire to want to start giggling, 'I would like to hear more about the local area and the fact that it is, as you say, a place where the murder of females is a commonplace occurrence.'

'Well it's like this, Mr Ashton,' said Tom Sadler, 'you may have noticed in that in this area of the 'Chapel there ain't a great deal of money about to say the least. What money there is to be 'ad 'as to be worked for, whether it's in the factories, markets, the slaughter 'ouses or out on the streets. Therefore when some people become angry they takes it out on others, usually thems they're closest to at the time, the missus or the kids or a street wagtail or even the cat if there ain't no one else around. Others just take it out on those they meet about the place or in local boozers.' Sadler smiled at Ashto and winked.

'I blame all the forriners I do,' said the other man. 'It's getting' so that yer can't 'ear the English language being spoke proper no more – people blatherin' away in Jewish or Rushin. I reckon that when they catch the one that did Poll in he'll turn out to be a Jew or a Pole or some'n else who shouldn't be 'ere.' The man leant back in his seat and took a large gulp of his beer.

First Commander Ashto looked at the man through bleary eyes. It was getting to be increasingly difficult to keep his vision from splitting things into two of everything and he began to worry that the alcoholic drinks he had been imbibing might be having a deleterious effect on him. He was also suddenly aware of his need to urinate quite badly and stood up, somewhat unsteadily, and began to wonder aloud where the pub's sanitary arrangements were.

'You mean the pisser?' said Tom Sadler. 'It's out in the back yard, through that door over there,' he said, pointing at a doorway.

Ashto headed off in the general direction of the door at first not quite sure which one of the three identical doorways he could see was the correct one that would lead to the sanitary facilities in the outside yard of the public house. He decided to head for the middle one, a hunch that luckily turned out to be accurate.

Having used the primitive urinal, which consisted of a basic black cast-iron screen behind which was a gutter that emptied directly into the adjoining drainage system, Ashto buttoned up his trousers and set off to walk back into the pub and resume his interesting conversation with the two Earth males. However, he found his way was blocked by two other men who stood in the doorway, one of whom responded to Ashto's, 'Excuse me my good sirs,' by grabbing him by his lapels with his left hand and pushing him backwards across the yard so that Ashto's back was forced against the urinal screen. In his other hand the man held a compact leather cosh weighted with lead balls.

'All right me old cock, we'll take that money what you've bin flashin' about,' said the first man whose large beefy hand held Ashto's coat in a firm grip. Ashto felt a little spittle from the man's mouth land on his nose. The man, although considerably shorter than Ashto was nevertheless fairly powerful looking and had a old, deep scar running diagonally across his face from his left eyebrow to below his lip on the right side of his face.

'Sir', said Ashto smiling at the man, 'I would very much appreciate you loosening your grip on my coat and letting me return to my new found friends back in the public ho ...'

Ashto's words were cut short by a sharp punch to his midriff delivered by the man.

Winded Ashto considered reaching for the disrupter device in his coat pocket but decided against doing so. He did not feel it appropriate at this stage to atomize this individual without trying to utilise other methods first.

While Ashto recovered his breath he noticed that the second man, as equally rough looking as the first, had moved to a position immediately to the side of him. He too held a cosh looped around his right wrist.

'Gentlemen" said Ashto trying to regain his breath, 'I'm very sure that we can resolve this issue peacefully without resorting to further violent behaviour.'

'Shurrup! Give us yer money before we lay yer out permanent like.'

Ashto noticed that the first man had raised his right hand ready to deliver a blow with the rather nasty looking weapon he held. Ashto quickly calculated that any blow the man made to his head might cause him to lose consciousness and if the second individual also struck him irreparable damage could be sustained to his cerebral functions. That was something to be avoided at all costs. At the very least it would require himself and Atia to return to the ship for some urgent medical repairs. Ashto made another instant calculation of how much force was needed to render the two men insensible without doing them any serious or permanent damage. He shifted his stance somewhat to ensure he was well balanced, factoring in that, for some unknown reason, he had recently been experiencing balance problems and then simultaneously, using both of his open hands, struck the two men squarely in the nasal area of their faces. The heels of both of Ashto's hands hit the men's noses firmly enough so that their necks snapped back causing them to fall to the damp ground instantly unconscious. Ashto knelt down to check that both men were still breathing and that he had hit them with force enough only to break their noses and cause the occipital and phrenic nerves in their necks to be disrupted and cause insensibility. Once he was satisfied that he had not shoved their nasal bones back into the frontal lobes of their brains and that the men would survive and eventually regain consciousness, he turned them both over into a recovery position, to ensure that the blood running from their noses didn't end up in their throats and cause them to choke, picked up their coshes and dropped them down the drain next to the urinal screen. Ashto then dusted himself down and returned to the smoky atmosphere of the inside of the pub. After this temporary piece of excitement in the back yard of the Britannia he was actually looking forward to drinking some more bitter ale and whisky chasers.

Ashto went straight to the bar and ordered another round of drinks for himself and his two new human friends. He carefully carried them back to the tables managing to spill only a little of the liquid on the way. He was quite surprised to find that a human female had joined the man with the peaked cap and was happily perched on his knee.

'How about treatin' me to a drink too darlin?' said the woman in a loud, gruff voice.

'Of course my dear madam,' said Ashto, 'what sort of beverage would you like me to obtain for you?'

'Oo ain't he a proper gent? Ta, I'll have a large rum if it's all the same to yer, I'm not feelin' too well today so need a bit of rum to warm up me insides.'

Ashto made another unsteady trek to the bar and soon returned with a glass containing a strong smelling dark coloured liquid.

'Oo thank you darlin, I've bin out on the street working tonight an' I was feelin' a bit down so I need this med'cine,' said the woman before she swallowed the rum in one gulp.

'You are most welcome my dear madam. Can I be forward enough to enquire as to the nature of the work you've been engaged in?' Ashto looked the woman up and down. She was dressed almost entirely in black clothes that had obviously seen better days, although he did notice that she wore red and white stockings and well-worn brown boots. He estimated her age to be about forty-five years old and noticed that as well as being somewhat overweight she was looking rather pale and ill with a persistent cough punctuating some of her words as she spoke. Her dark brown hair contrasted with her deep blue eyes and she had an equally blue bruise over her right eye.

'Oo, ain't he the one!' said the woman turning to wink at the man in the cap. The two human men laughed out loud leaving Ashto looking puzzled as he tried to work out what the joke was that had so amused them all.

'Well ducky yer've only to come round the back with me and I'll show yer the nature of me work,' she said, 'an' I'll only charge you sixpence seein' as you've treated me to a drink.'

Ashto's puzzlement faded as he realised what it was the human female was implying. There was no doubt that she was one of the street prostitutes who operated in this part of London.

Ashto, as politely as he could, declined the woman's offer.

'That's all right dearie, not to worry. No doubt a big 'andsome bloke such as yourself is never lacking in female company so to speak,' said the woman winking at Ashto, 'but anytime you fancy a quick one just ask someone to direct you to Dark Annie – they all know me round 'ere. Well gents, I must be on me way. Got to get some money for me bed tonight an' I ain't goin' be getting it sittin' around here talking to you lot.' With that she gave the face of the man in the cap a quick squeeze and staggered out of the pub, coughing and obviously slightly the worse for drink.

Ashto turned to Tom Sadler: 'Isn't that female in grave danger out on the streets if there is someone out there killing street prostitutes?'

It was the man in the cap who answered him: 'There's no need to bother worryin' about Annie. She can look after herself' – tough as nails she is. I've known her for years. Always willin' to let you have 'er if yer get the need if you know what I'm sayin'. I knew 'er 'usband – 'e was a coachman to some toff in the West End afore 'e went an' died a few years back leavin' 'er without no money an' nowhere to kip. That's when she started to go tartin' on the street to earn a few coins for a bed in the doss 'ouse.'

Ashto was thoughtful for a moment and then, noticing that the men's glasses were empty, he finished is own pint of bitter ale, downed his whisky and weaved his way to the bar to get another round. The clock behind the bar said twenty minutes past eight o'clock.

Atia sat at the desk reading the previous day's copy of the Times newspaper. Ashto lay on the bed, still dressed in his clothes; Atia had placed his uncomfortable boots neatly underneath the bed. When the First Commander woke up and started to groan Atia put down the paper and walked over to where he lay.

'Ah, First Commander, you are back in the land of the living!'

'Please, Margot, do not speak quite so loudly.'

'My apologies ... Trevor, I did not realise that an over-indulgence in alcoholic drink caused hyper-sensitivity in one's hearing capability.'

Ashto groaned again and held the side of his head. 'Margot would you please administer to me some of those strong analgesic capsules we brought with us from the ship? I feel like my head is about to split open. How do these Earth humans put up with these symptoms? It is beyond imagining how they would ever drink alcohol more than once!'

'Perhaps, Trevor, they do not imbibe quite as much as you managed!'

Atia walked over to the wardrobe where the Jaran medikit was kept and removed from it two of the analgesic pills. She let the wardrobe door slam shut on purpose.

'Ahh! Please Margot could you be just a little quieter?' Ashto whispered.

'I will try my best, Trevor.' Atia smiled as she handed the First Commander the painkillers and a glass of water.

'Never again,' said Ashto as he sat up, swallowed the capsules with some of the water. 'I will never have another one of those alcoholic beverages ever again. The bitter ale was quite palatable but I should not have tried to keep up with the humans and the whisky chasers were positively lethal.'

'Well thankfully not quite, but I did warn you against drinking any of the distilled alcohol known locally as whisky. It is far too strong for Jaran physiology. I will have to run some diagnostics on you to ascertain if you have sustained any long-term organic damage due to your prolonged exposure to the alcoholic substances you imbibed last evening before you came banging on the door in the early hours of this morning. If it had not been for your express orders not to do so I would have left here and looked for you last night as I was extremely concerned about your welfare.'

First Commander Ashto looked up at Atia with bleary eyes. 'I am truly sorry for awakening you so abruptly last evening … er this morning. It will not happen again. If I ever venture into one of the human's public houses at some point in the future I will eschew all forms of alcoholic drinks, especially that which is known as a whisky chaser. I am convinced that humans would live for many more years if they did not abuse their bodies in such a self-destructive way.'

Ashto sat up and perched on the side of the bed. His groans were now not quite as heartfelt.

'How are you feeling now Trevor?' said Atia.

'Slightly better, thank you Margot, I am going to attempt to stand up soon.'

'Well, before you do that, Trevor, perhaps I could read you something from yesterday's Times newspaper that may provide our studies of this planet with a certain degree of focus over the next week or so.'

'Yes, by all means, Margot, please do just so long as you keep the volume of your voice at a quietly modulated level.'

'Of course, Trevor,' said Margot smiling again as she stepped across the room and fetched her copy of the Times.

Atia returned to the bed and sat down next to the First Commander. In a soft voice she read from the newspaper: 'The sensation that is the theatrical production of Dr Jekyll and Mr Hyde continues at the Lyceum Theatre in London's Wellington Street. The play which began its run on August 4th and which is still attracting enthusiastic reviews stars the American thespian and theatre manager, Richard Mansfield, whose acting skills have been lauded by both the press and the theatre-going public. Mr Mansfield's portrayal of the decent doctor who is transformed into a murderous monster by the self-administration of a bespoke mixture of chemical and biological substances is masterful. His transformation from the good doctor into the grotesque creature that is Mr Hyde is almost unbelievable to observe and has thrilled and shocked audiences in equal measure. Indeed it is important to state that the production could well be too strong for certain ladies of a nervous disposition and there have been several instances of female patrons of the said theatrical presentation swooning at Mr Mansfield's transformation scenes and thereby having to be carried out of the auditorium to enable smelling salts to be administered.'

'This newspaper feature is extremely interesting, Margot, but could you explain why you think it is relevant to our mission? And could you continue to employ your very considerate low-level volume?'

'Indeed I can, Trevor,' Atia continued in a stage whisper. 'The newspaper article goes on to further extol the virtues of this theatrical production which is an adaptation of a recently published extended story, or novel as it is called by Earth humans, of a similar title. It would seem to me that one way of helping us to fully understand the psychological make-up of the humans on this planet is to examine a number of their art forms, such as this play, as it is referred to in the local idiom. It seems to me that the production sounds very similar to the portrayals of Jaran figurative puppetry displays that are popular in our summer and winter festivals of cyclical revival.'

'That is true, Margot, although those tales are told to entertain the children of Jaran Prime in particular. This Earth theatrical production is, according to what you have just read out, definitely designed for adults and seems to encompass themes of a very serious nature. Why would Earth humans want to present such matters as entertainment?'

'I am at a loss to explain that, Trevor, but that is my point. If we can examine the reasons why such fictional narratives of such seriousness appeal to the people of this planet as entertainment then we will be much closer to a fuller understanding of the way in which Earth people are psychologically motivated and how their way of thinking is shaped by external events. That, I believe, will provide us with a substantial insight into Earth humans and will help us to provide advice pertaining to any possible action taken in the future by the Jaran High Command and their decisions regarding this planet.'

'You may well be correct, Margot. That is an interesting thesis you have put forward. Do you propose therefore that we should purchase tickets to enable us to witness this theatrical performance?'

I do indeed, Trevor. I suggest that we visit the Lyceum theatre this afternoon and buy the tickets. I believe too that a long walk will also be therapeutic for you with regard to your present fragile condition. An extended perambulation will, as the Earth humans say, enable you to get some fresh air, although our experiences so far have demonstrated that the air in London is anything but fresh.'

Ashto smiled weakly at his fellow Jaran operative and nodded, immediately regretting the movement. Atia smiled back and patted Ashto on his thigh.

My greetings and utmost felicitations to the esteemed members of the Sub-Committee.

Since arriving in the large London conurbation Apprentice Commander Atia and I have continued to assiduously collect information on the local inhabitants of this, the largest city in the most important state on the planet known as Earth. I would say that to date our mission has been a great success and the data we have gathered so far will doubtless be of invaluable use to the personnel tasked with any future diplomatic actions with regard to the planet Earth.

However, there are certain aspects that any Jaran officials that follow in the footsteps of Apprentice Commander Atia and myself need to be fully aware of. I will obviously detail all possible problems we have encountered in my final summative report to the Sub-Committee but for now let me just mention one particular pitfall. It has long been realised that the consumption of alcoholic substances tends to have a deleterious effect on Jaran physiology, which is the main reason why alcohol is a restricted narcotic substance in most regions of the Jaran Galactic Federation. As part of our researches into the psychological make-up of the Earth humans I recently made the bold decision to venture into one of the local alcoholic refreshment establishments known in the vernacular as public houses or often, just pubs. It is to be understood that I did so with great reluctance and took the precaution of instructing Apprentice Commander Atia not to accompany me but to be on hand to intervene if anything untoward should arise.

My visit to the particular public house called the Britannia, one of the drinking establishments in the Whitechapel area of the city, was not without a certain amount of peril, as I shall describe. (Incidentally for some reason as yet unknown the public houses in London, and presumably elsewhere in the state called Great Britain, all have individual names that are drawn apparently from historical, cultural or allegorical sources).

The Britannia public house was crowded and noisy even at a relatively early hour in the evening. The smoky atmosphere, caused by the humans almost universal habit of inhaling the gases from lighted items made from a local plant substance called tobacco, took a good deal of getting used to but I did eventually manage to put up with the situation as any real Earth human would have done. My visit soon bore fruit, however, as I was able to initiate conversations with some of the humans in the public house. Some of these initial contacts were extremely convivial and helpful others were less so. Certainly I was able to learn a lot about Earth humans' approach to life generally and was surprised at the sanguinity of many of those to whom I spoke, even the ones who live in day-to-day conditions of poverty. Most humans seem to face up to the privations of life with a good deal of humour, perseverance and determination although some fall rather quickly into a life of crime and many more seem to try and hide from the realities of their existence by imbibing large amounts of alcohol on a regular basis. The lesson appears to be that if Jaran officials want to obtain the support of the poorer castes of Earth humans then all that needs to be done is to provide them with plenty of access to cheap alcoholic liquids.

Unfortunately to ensure that I did not stand out too much in the public house and cause any of the humans there to suspect my own origins I also found it necessary to drink a certain amount of the alcoholic beverages that were on sale. It was a distasteful thing to have to do but because our mission is of such vital importance I felt it only fair that I should undergo such an ordeal. I sampled two sorts of alcoholic substance. The first is known by the humans as bitter ale or beer, a fermented grain based liquid that in small quantities is relatively harmless to Jaran physiology. It is, however, a sour tasting and rather unpleasant liquid that it would be best for future Jaran officials visiting the Earth to avoid. The second substance is more harmful I would say and is called a whisky chaser. This is a strong alcoholic beverage that is consumed in small quantities and is also made from grain but goes through a distilling process as well as a fermentation one. To gain the trust of some of the humans I encountered in the public house I found it necessary to imbibe these two substances but luckily I was able to keep my consumption of them to a minimum and suffered only limited deleterious effects as a result.

It will be necessary in the future no doubt for me to visit such establishments again but having discussed the issue with Apprentice Commander Atia it has been agreed between us both that she will accompany me on any future excursions to such places. This is due to the possibility of problems that may arise in relation to criminal activity inside the public house. I was able to witness such activity at close quarters on my visit to the Britannia but was able to deal with the matter in a swift and surreptitious manner.

Our regular journeys around the London conurbation have begun to take us further afield from our base in Whitechapel. On the day after my visit to the public house, a day that is designated as Sunday on the local human calendar, Apprentice Commander Atia and I visited, for only the second time, an area of London known locally as the West End. Our main purpose was to purchase tickets to allow us to attend a dramatic theatrical event that is to be held in one of the buildings in that area. We were only able to buy tickets for a presentation that takes place in several days' time so we spent much of the afternoon looking around the area.

At a place called Covent Garden we stopped to watch a puppetry display. This entertainment was called a 'Punch and Judy Show' and on the surface it was similar to puppetry entertainments on Jaran Prime and like those are also designed primarily for children to observe. However, Apprentice Commander Atia and I were quite disturbed by the narrative set out in the show. The main character, Punch, was a strange parody of an Earth human whose main preoccupation seems is to inflict physical punishment on his connubial partner, Judy and their young child and then to beat to death other puppets that represent authority figures such as the local law official. The display ended with a representation of capital punishment and the appearance of a curious figure that seemed to personify the concept of evil. It was all very strange and unsettling. What added to the discomfiture felt by Apprentice Commander Atia and I was the fact that throughout the show the children watching seemed to find the brutality of the story hilariously funny. Every time Punch inflicted harm on one of the other characters the children laughed, clapped and cheered. Apprentice Commander Atia and I are still discussing the full ramifications of this experience and have yet to come up with an explanation as to what it tells us about the psychological make-up of humans. I will be able to say more about this in a future report perhaps.

Finally, on a lighter note, Apprentice Commander Atia and I have managed to aid our attempts to fit in with the local population by temporarily adopting Earth style names. The Apprentice Commander and I are now known as Mr and Mrs Ashton. The title Mr and Mrs denotes that we are a married couple in Earth terminology and the name Ashton of course derives from my own patronymic. This subterfuge seems to enable the two of us to proceed in our gathering of data without having to constantly explain that we are from another state on this planet or that our living arrangements are outside the normal social norms adhered to by most humans in this particular region of Earth.

That concludes my report to the Sub-Committee at this time. I shall report again when we have gathered more relevant information about the Earth humans.

With my utmost loyalty, etcetera,
First Commander Treve Pacton Ashto.

A thick yellow mist had descended on the city again, another sign that he was safe to continue doing God's work. He had been unable to sleep and so had left his home to walk the streets for hours deciding where and when to carry on his labours. By the time he had found her the sky was beginning to lighten and already some people were out of their beds and on their way to work at the nearby Spitalfields market. He saw the drunken whore stagger out of the Ten Bells pub and so he followed her keeping to the shadows as she veered from side to side, sometimes in the horse road and sometimes on the pavement. He saw her speak to a number of men who were on their way to work – all rebuffed her, one had shouted insults at her. And then he saw his chance – he knew that this was the right place for his work to carry on. He caught up with her; it wasn't difficult, sodden with drink as she was.

'Dearie,' she had slurred, 'would you like to treat me to the price of a bed? I'm not feelin' terribly well this mornin' and I need to lie me head down.'

He had pointed to the narrow entrance that led to the back yard of the building. 'Will you?' he had said.

She had shrugged, said, 'yes,' her face looking pale in the early morning light.

A woman walked by on the other side of the road. It didn't matter; he was immune from harm while he carried out his holy mission – God saw to that. He followed the whore down the passageway – they emerged into a dark back yard where she leant against a wooden fence for support and coughed.

'Come on then there's a dear, be quick as I really need to lie down and get some kip,' she said as she hoisted up her skirts, turned around and stuck out her rear to make it easy for him.

'I think you are going to have plenty of time to sleep,' he said as he grabbed her by the throat. His strong hands stopped her from making any sound at all as he held her throat in a vice like grip until he felt her go limp. He then laid her on the ground, turned her head to face away from him and brought his knife to her neck.

'So die all filthy whores!' he said aloud.

God would be pleased at the sharpness of his knife as it sliced through her neck. A spurt of blood, looking almost black in the half-light of the shadowy yard, spattered against the base of the wooden fence. But he was only halfway there. Killing her is not nearly enough – God wanted more from him, he was certain of that. He pulled up her clothes and opened her legs in a parody of the carnal activity she had offered to anyone willing to give her a few copper coins. He felt a thrill as he plunged his knife into her stomach and dragged it downwards. He then lifted her innards out of her body and placed them over her left shoulder. He had gutted animals many times before, pigs, lambs, even rabbits – this was no different. He noticed that in her hand she held a piece of paper. He opened her hand – it was easy to do so – it was still warm. The paper was a crumpled up envelope. Inside were two pills. He lay the envelope at her feet, 'she can take it with her to hell,' he said aloud. He searched her. In a pocket he found two farthings, a bit of cloth and two combs – he put these items at her feet too. He wiped his bloodied knife and hands on her skirts and then stood up. He looked at his handiwork and liked what he saw. He felt fulfilled. Again he had carried out God's work and felt blessed as a result. Then *he heard some noise from inside the building. A light was lit in an upstairs room. It was time to go. He had one last look at the body that lay on the ground and then walked back up the passageway and out onto the street. He walked up Hanbury Street and then turned left into Commercial Street and on to his workplace. He glanced at his pocket-watch, a present from his mother so long ago. It is almost six o'clock on the morning of Saturday 8th September.*

7

Dr Jekyll and Mr Hyde

The foyer of the Lyceum theatre was crowded as Ashto and Atia made their way to their seats in the stalls of the auditorium. They were surrounded by male and female humans in fine clothes with some of the woman wearing bright, obviously expensive jewelry.

'This is very different to Whitechapel, Margot. Going to a theatrical presentation is obviously not something the humans in that area would seem to aspire to.'

'I agree, Trevor, although the cost of the tickets would doubtless be an economic impediment to most of the humans in the area we reside.'

The tall figure of Apprentice Commander Atia dressed in a long, elegant, dark blue dress again drew plenty of attention from the men present. There were many doffed top hats and smiles directed at her as she walked by arm-in-arm with First Commander Ashto. Atia, by now very much used to the attention she received in public, smiled back politely.

Once the Jaran pair had found their seats several rows back from the stage they settled into their chairs, looked around and took in their surroundings. Ashto was impressed by the ornate nature of the decoration of the ceiling and walls of the auditorium. In many ways it reminded him of the grandeur of the interiors of many of the public buildings of Jara Prime. It was evident that the humans considered these theatrical presentations of some importance if the architecture of this theatre was anything to go by.

Atia, however, looked at the humans around her. She was interested in noting particularly the wealth on display just in this small corner of London's West End and how it contrasted so vividly with most humans' everyday existence in Whitechapel. Surely, she thought, there was something intrinsically wrong with a system in which such a vast disparity of wealth could exist between two areas that were so comparatively close to each other geographically. Here most of the women she could see wore jewelry studded with diamonds and other valuable and rare gemstones. Just one of the necklaces or bracelets on display would be worth more than a workingman or workingwoman in the East End of the city would see in their entire lifetime. How could it be that a society that was so heavily weighted in favour of one group of people over another could continue in such a way? Surely there were enough humans around who also saw the terrible unfairness of a system that allowed such inequality to exist? On one hand there was the extreme poverty of Whitechapel with its overcrowded hovels, poor sanitation, prostitution and doss houses and on the other hand was the sort of ostentatious wealth she saw around her in this West End theatre. Atia shook her head and Ashto was just about to ask her what the problem was when the orchestra in front of the stage began to play some dramatic music.

After a few minutes of the overture the curtain rose displaying a mock-up of the drawing room of the home of a well-to-do person. After another minute a dark-haired man dressed in a double-breasted jacket and dark tie walked on to the stage and many in the audience applauded. This man, thought Atia, must be the American actor, Richard Mansfield, who in this summer of 1888 had taken London's theatre-land by storm and was, at the moment, one of the most famous people in the city. The individual he was portraying in this opening scene was Doctor Jekyll, a respected London physician who seemingly was an upstanding member of society and who had devoted his life to his vocation and to the betterment of the health of the people of the society in which he lived. However, his friends and fiancée had become concerned about Jekyll's relationship with a mysterious individual called Edward Hyde.

Ashto and Atia were able to follow the plot of the drama quite easily. To them it seemed that the story was about the universal theme of good versus evil and also postulated that the personality of an individual could demonstrate both such extremes at various times.

Richard Mansfield was, thought Atia, an attractive looking human male with a great deal of presence. His occupation as an actor, she surmised, was mostly dependent on the way he could project his personality, or at least that of the character he was portraying, out to those watching in the audience. Atia could see the logic in these theatrical presentations. Unlike the children's puppetry shows on Jara prime having real people playing these fictional characters made a good deal of sense not only from the point of view that the narrative seemed more realistic but also for its intrinsic entertainment value. She was enjoying this 'play' as the Earth humans called this type of presentation and soon found that she became wrapped up in the plot as the story progressed.

And then it came to the lauded transformation scene that Atia was particularly looking forward to. It began with Mansfield, as Doctor Jekyll, holding up a glass vial so that the audience could see it clearly before he swallowed the vivid green liquid it held. The transformation started slowly. Mansfield began to twitch ever so slightly before he then started to convulse violently. The audience including Atia and Ashto watched transfixed as Mansfield doubled up and seemed to shrink into himself with his head almost tucked between his legs. And then gradually with his body seeming to twist in an unnatural posture he lifted his face to the audience, which issued a collective gasp, as they were able to see the change that had come about in Mansfield's features. Gone was the demeanour of the benevolent and thoughtful Doctor of medicine and in its place, staring out at the audience, was a twisted and grotesque mask of malevolence. Here was the face of Mr Hyde, a face that was full of cruelty, malice and evil.

As the curtain came down for the interval and the audience clapped enthusiastically, Atia and Ashto turned to each other both wide eyed with appreciation and a certain amount of shock.

'Trevor, that was truly impressive. I do not think I have ever been so taken with excitement as I was with the first part of this theatrical presentation.'

'You are completely correct, Margot. I am certainly very much looking forward to the second part and the denouement of this fictional narrative,' said Ashto who then looked down at the programme open on his lap. 'It appears that there is now an interval of twenty minutes to allow the audience to buy some liquid refreshment; can I purchase something for you?'

'No thank you very much, Trevor. I think that as most of the liquid refreshments on offer would contain alcohol so it would be best if we avoided them.'

First Commander Ashto smiled at his Apprentice Commander and gently squeezed her hand. 'I believe you are correct, Margot.'

'Trevor,' said Atia in a whisper, 'what is your assessment so far of this theatrical presentation, this 'play'. Do you believe that it holds any relevance with regard to our mission?'

'We will have to send all the material we are gathering about it to the ship's computer for analysis obviously. By the way I take it that you are recording all that we observe this evening?' Atia patted the front of her black felt, feathered hat, where her micro-camera was concealed, to indicate that she was. 'I do believe,' continued the First Commander again in a whisper, 'that this presentation does contain some important lessons for us with regard to the complicated psychological make-up of Earth humans.' Ashto looked around to ensure that he was not being overheard. 'Along with the Punch and Judy show we observed recently we are, I believe, obtaining a number of insights into the minds of the people of this planet.'

'I agree, Trevor. We are seeing in this presentation, as well as in the recent puppetry display, that humans are able to process discussions about basic concepts such as good and evil, right and wrong, conformity and aberrant behaviour in ways that also can be regarded as entertainment. If we look around this auditorium we see Earth humans here for an evening's entertainment and not to take part in a philosophical discussions about important issues but, nevertheless, those conversations will doubtless take place during this interval and after the presentation is over in much the same way as we are discussing its ramifications at present.'

'I agree with you, Margot. It is a presentation that raises some vitally important questions and I am sure that when this particular narrative concludes there will be a number of judgements that those present here today will make. However, I am not quite so sure whether we can draw similar conclusions about the Punch and Judy show as that seemed merely to depict interpersonal violence in a purely comedic way. It will be difficult for us to draw any profound conclusions from it I would have thought.'

'You are possibly correct, Trevor but do you not think that the parodic nature of the violent incidents that are perpetrated by the Punch character tell us something about the Earth humans' attitude to the world at large. For example, when Punch hits the Policeman with his wooden stick is he not demonstrating Earth humans' inherent dislike for authority figures generally. As he says himself when he carries out such an action – *that's the way to do it!*' Atia spoke the last few words in the nasally style of the Punch puppet causing Ashto to laugh loudly and several of the people around them, who had returned to their seats from the theatre bar, to turn around and stare at him. One man in the row in front of the Jaran pair tutted in a rather pointed and ostentatious manner. Atia smiled at her First Commander and then winked at him. She was rather taken with this Earth human eye gesture she had learned about and Ashto smiled back broadly and reached out and squeezed her hand again.

The pair then turned to look at the stage as the orchestra had begun to play again heralding the start of the second half of the drama.

As the Jaran couple left the auditorium at the end of the play the thunderous applause of the audience still rang in their ears. The actors had received a standing ovation but the loudest applause was reserved for Richard Mansfield himself as the American stood at the front of the stage and bowed graciously to the audience. Ashto and Atia had followed the lead of the rest of the spectators present and stood and applauded as loudly as anyone else. At first this human trait of clapping hands together to signify enjoyment and appreciation had seemed strange to the Jaran pair but they were now used to the habit and had been pleased to participate in the collective response.

The Jaran couple walked out of the theatre after Atia had retrieved her coat from the cloakroom attendant. Ashto had decided not to bring his outerwear and as soon as he stepped outside onto the crowded street outside the theatre he regretted his decision as despite it being only the 8th of September there was a definite chill in the air.

'It will be difficult to hail a hansom cab here, shall we walk on a little?' said Atia.

'Certainly,' said Ashto rubbing his hands together to warm them.

The pair walked down Wellington Street to the Strand, an area where they knew it would be easier to find a hansom to take them back to Whitechapel. On the way they passed a young boy selling newspapers. He wore a flat cap and held a large bundle of newspapers almost as big as himself as he shouted: 'Evenin' News – another 'orrible murder in the East End – read all about it 'ere!'

Ashto sorted in his pocket to find a threepenny coin and gave it to the young lad to pay for the halfpenny paper, ' keep the change,' he said.

'Thanks Guv'nor, 'said the lad smiling broadly and tucking the coin in his pocket.

Ashto quickly read through the article about the murder before passing the newspaper to Atia.

'The poor woman,' said Atia after reading the story. 'There is not yet any indication of who the unfortunate female was,' she continued, 'but I would not be at all surprised if the victim was again a poverty stricken person forced out on the streets by economic necessity.'

'You are doubtless correct, Margot. It is one of the many consequences for having a social system where there is such a huge gap between the lives of the rich and the poor and there is little provision made for the latter group. Unfortunately there is nothing that we as individuals can do about it'

The Jaran couple looked at each other. Atia nodded with

sadness in her eyes and walked with Ashto to the edge of the pavement in order to flag down a passing hansom cab.

As the cab trundled from the West End to the East of the city Atia and Ashto sat in silence looking out at the passing crowded and busy streets. As they approached the corner of Whitechapel High Street and Goulston Street Ashto shouted out to the driver to stop. He paid the cabman and the Jaran pair exited the hansom.

As they walked up Goulston Street Atia suddenly turned to Ashto saying 'Trevor I think that we should find out more about these murders that are occurring in this area of London. I believe that if we can discover why these terrible deeds are taking place it will help us in our assessment of Earth humans and how they would react if in future representatives from the Jaran Galactic Federation should one day appear among them.'

'You may be correct, Margot, but how would we go about the task?

'I haven't quite worked out exactly what methods we would use to discover more about the person responsible for such crimes but I believe that a visit to another of the local public houses might be necessary. There we might be able to hear theories put forward by those most affected by the murders.'

'Who exactly did you have in mind, Margot?'

'It is quite simple, Trevor. We need to listen to and to talk to those females who are most at risk.'

'You mean the women who spend all of their money on alcohol and then go out on the street to prostitute themselves to earn more?'

'That's exactly who I mean, Trevor.'

'Well it may be a viable course of action, Margot, but I would doubt very much that those females would open up their innermost feelings to me. I would imagine that all they would tell me is which dark alleyway I should go to engage in some sort of sexual activity with them.'

'You are correct, Trevor which is why I should be the one to venture into a public house and talk to these women.'

'What? No, Margot you cannot be serious. Dressed up in your fine clothes you would be an immediate target for all the criminals around. I cannot allow you to put yourself in such danger.'

Atia frowned at her First Commander, 'Are you forgetting... Trevor that I am fully capable of looking after myself. I have passed examinations in all forms of Jaran martial arts and in some of those from other regions of the Federation. Besides,' she smiled at Ashto, 'I will not be wearing this type of attire.'

Ashto looked puzzled as Atia smiled enigmatically at him.

8

Atia Goes Further Under Cover.

'Do you think you should wash these before actually wearing them?' First Commander Ashto looked with distaste at the garments that Apprentice Commander Atia had laid out as neatly as she could on the bed in their room in Mrs Smith's Select Guest House.

'With respect, Trevor, I believe that that would somewhat defeat the purpose of wearing them in the first place.'

Atia had been out that morning and had visited a dingy pawnshop, Spearman's on Commercial Street, purchasing a set of female clothes for her to wear when she was to go undercover. 'They are for a local woman who has lost most of her clothes in a fire,' she had told the male behind the counter of the musty smelling shop. He had shrugged suggesting that it was none of his business why a well-to-do looking lady should be buying cheap second hand clothes in his Whitechapel shove-in shop.

Atia looked with quiet satisfaction at her purchases. No doubt they were swarming with lice and other vermin but that, reasoned Atia, would only add to their authenticity. They were old, threadbare and splattered with various kinds of filth but they were just what she needed if she was to blend in seamlessly with the women in the local drinking establishment she planned to visit later in the day. She picked up the boots from the floor next to the bed. They too had seen better days but she was pleased to note that the soles, while well worn, were intact and would not let any water in to soak her feet. In the pawnshop she had held her own shoe against a number of women's boots but all were far too small for her long feet. In the end she had to settle for a pair of elastic sided men's boots that seemed to fit her perfectly.

'Margot, I have just thought of a possible impediment that will make your disguise potentially unsuccessful.'

The Apprentice Commander looked quizzically at her Commanding Officer. 'What is that, Trevor?'

'Well it is to do with the way in which the people of the East End vocalise, in particular the local dialect words, phrases and verbal mannerisms they employ in their speech. When I was in the Britannia public house it was difficult at times for me to fully understand what was being said. However, as I was perceived to be a West End toff, as they referred to me, it was logical that I would experience some difficulty in understanding the local vernacular. Your disguise as a member of the poorer class will be undermined by you inability to communicate with the locals in their own particular brand of the English language.' Ashto looked quite smug as he thought he had presented a final reason as to why Atia should not undertake this difficult and hazardous mission herself.

''Ere what yer sayin,' me ole cock sparrer? I ain't no normal bit o' jam, me. I'll walk into that pub, shake me prize faggots a bit an' if any toe rag tries anythin' on I'll toast their bloomin' eyebrows so I will! Any bugger who wants to argol bargol with me will get an earful, gor blimey if they don't. So have a horse and cart an' let me go an' natter to those sozzled and leaky bits o' frock in the boozer!' Atia smiled broadly at the First Commander who stared open mouthed in surprise.

'Margot, I have no idea what you have just said but it sounded amazingly authentic. The customers in the Britannia were all talking exactly like that. How have you come to terms with the local dialect so quickly?'

Well, Trevor I have been researching using my implanted neural chip in conjunction with its interface with the ship's computer to compile a list of useful terms and phrases as well as practising in order to perfect a suitable accented speech pattern that would not seem out of place among the members of the lower echelons of society – the sort of humans that inhabit the Whitechapel area and its local public houses. My only concern is that I may overdo the use of dialect words but if I do I am assuming that since I will be feigning drunkenness brought on by an overindulgence in alcoholic drink I will be excused any slight divergence from the general norm.'

Ashto looked puzzled. 'Margot how are you going to consume alcoholic drinks yourself without being adversely affected by them? In my experience it is very difficult to avoid drinking to excess in these public houses and do you have enough knowledge of what drunken behaviour actually looks like?'

'Trevor, I have had plenty of recent experience of witnessing drunkenness.' Atia smiled at the First Commander who suddenly realised that she was referring to his own behaviour on his return from the Britannia in the early hours of the morning several days before. He blushed as the memory returned while Atia continued: 'besides, I am confident that I can find ways of disposing of any alcoholic beverage I am offered without actually drinking it.'

Ashto nodded. He did not doubt that the Apprentice Commander was completely capable of carrying through with her deception but he was still concerned about her being on her own in what could turn out, for any number of reasons, to be a hostile environment. As each day went by he had felt a greater emotional attachment to Apprentice Commander Atia and could not countenance anything that could put her safety in jeopardy.

'Do you have a plan of how you are going to extract useful information from the local females in whichever public house you decide to visit, Margot?'

'Yes I have, Trevor. By the way I have decided to use the pseudonym of Maggie when I am dressed in my recently purchased attire. The name Margot might seem a little out of place in those particular environs ... a bit on the lardy-dardy side as the locals might say.'

'I'm sure you are correct in your assessment, Margot, or should I now call you Maggie?'

'Not quite yet, Trevor, wait until I am wearin' me new klobber!' she said with a broad smile.

Apprentice Commander Atia continued to smile as she noticed the look of admiration on the face of her First Commander. She went across to the desk and picked up that morning's newspaper.

'I have been reading the details of the latest murder and the information about the poor victim and what the police are intending to do to track down the perpetrator.'

'So what does the newspaper report say, Margot?'

'Well, it appears that the victim's name was Annie Chapman. It is assumed by the police that she was involved in casual prostitution and was well known in the public houses of the Whitechapel area. She used to live in Dorset Street with an individual called Jack Sievey but of late had been residing at Crossingham's lodging house also in Dorset Street. It seems, according to the Times reporter present at yesterday's inquest, that she was in the habit of occasionally prostituting herself to gain enough money to afford the few pence she needed to stay at the common lodging house. She was killed in the back yard of another lodging house at 29, Hanbury Street where her body was found early on last Saturday morning. She had died due to loss of blood from a severed throat and had been strangled beforehand. Her body was then mutilated with her intestines removed from her abdomen and placed over her left shoulder and her uterus was completely removed. The inquest heard from the police surgeon, Dr George Philips, who suggested that the murderer might have some anatomical skill and also that Annie Chapman was seriously ill with tuberculosis before her untimely demise. The police are conducting investigations and have held interviews with certain suspects according to the newspaper report and may be close to arresting the killer.'

'Margot, does the newspaper report say anything about what this unfortunate human female looked like?'

'Hmm…yes it does, apparently she was wearing a black skirt, a long black jacket, an apron, red and white woollen stockings, a black wool scarf and lace up boots. Oh yes … she had brown hair and often referred to herself as Dark Annie.'

Ashto stood up from the side of the bed where he had sat listening to Atia reading from the newspaper. He looked shocked as he walked over to the room's one window. 'My goodness,' he said, 'I do believe that I met this particular female in the Britannia public house.'

'Really, Trevor, are you certain?'

'I think so, Margot. She was dressed in the way described in the newspaper and she called herself Dark Annie. She was not very well … she coughed a great deal … and she was very intoxicated as she left the Britannia.' Ashto screwed up his eyes as he sought to remember his evening in the Britannia pub trying to recall the woman … the woman who now lay dead in a local morgue, her wretched life ended in the most violent of ways.

'That would very much fit in with the newspaper's assertion that the unfortunate Annie Chapman visited the local public houses on a regular basis, Trevor.'

'Yes it does, Margot, so does this mean that you will be visiting the Britannia this evening?'

'I may do, Trevor but I was thinking that I would start at the Queens Head public house which is on the opposite side of Commercial Street to the Britannia and thus is also near to where the murder of Annie Chapman took place. There I may be able to ascertain what some of the local inhabitants of the Whitechapel area are saying about the murder and their attitude to the terrible event. I will be particularly interested in what females in the pub might be saying, particularly those casual prostitutes who may frequent the drinking establishment, bearing in mind that they would seem to be at a greater risk than anyone else.'

'Margot,' said Ashto, with a look of concern, 'are you intending to assume the role of one of these female prostitutes and if so how do you propose to convince others in that regard.'

'Please Trevor, do not worry, I have thought this through in great detail. If anyone asks me I will say that I am newly arrived in Whitechapel from another area of London and am looking for some sort of gainful employment to enable me to afford some inexpensive accommodation. In the meantime I am, like so many others in this area, sleeping out on the streets in whatever sheltered nook I can find that is out of the rain and cold. No doubt someone will suggest that I should try my luck at selling my sexual favours, as the humans put it, for a few pennies in order to afford to stay in one of the local common lodging houses. However, again like many of the others, I will demonstrate my willingness to spend what little money I have on alcoholic drink.'

'I have accepted that you are determined to carry out this excursion into one of the Earth humans' drinking establishments this evening, Margot, but as your First Commander I am going to insist on two safety measures. First, you must take with you the disrupter weapon, which you must use if your life is threatened in any way, regardless of whether your true identity would then become obvious and second, you must also carry about your person a communications device so that if necessary you can summon me to the public house to assist you should you face any difficulty you cannot deal with yourself.'

Atia smiled and touched the hand of Ashto and gently and fondly squeezed it.

'I understand, Trevor, I will follow your orders to the letter.' She leant across and kissed him.

First Commander Ashto watched from the window of the Jaran couple's room as Atia left Mrs Smith's Guest House and sauntered down Bell Lane on her way to the Queens Head pub. She had changed into the dirty and somewhat smelly pawnshop clothes a little earlier and Ashto had to admit that she certainly looked the part. She would be considerably taller than all of the women and probably most of the men in the public house but other than that she was indistinguishable from the many poor females who inhabited the streets and the common lodging houses of Whitechapel. Ashto was still nervous about the whole endeavour but at least Atia had agreed to his two instructions and was carrying the disrupter device and a communicator in a pocket that she wore in her skirt. If anything went wrong she could contact Ashto who was ready to run the short distance to whichever public house location Atia found herself in and assist her. In a very last resort Atia could use the disrupter to atomise any human who posed an existential threat to her although that would almost certainly mean an end to their mission on Earth and would also entail an inevitable and abject admission of failure to be delivered by First Commander Ashto to the members of the Sub-Committee.

Atia felt confident as she strolled along the streets of Whitechapel heading for the Queens Head public house on the corner of Commercial Street and Fashion Street. True the clothes she wore did not smell too good although thankfully her keen Jaran olfactory sense had been much blunted by several weeks of living in Whitechapel. The pawnshop bought clothes also made her itch in her most intimate places but she had also learned to co-exist with the many lice, fleas and other assorted bodily vermin that seemed to be an everyday fact of life in this, one of the poorest areas of London. A suitable smearing of soot on her face obtained from the grate in Atia and Ashto's room made it look as though she had not washed for many weeks. Her long dark hair, now unkempt and frizzy, completed her disguise. At the last moment she had removed her 'wedding ring' from her finger knowing that it would be far too much of a temptation for any local thief who would fancy their chances of taking it for themselves.

Atia practised her slightly drunken walk as she headed along White's Row toward Commercial Street and the Queens Head, occasionally swaying from one side of the pavement to the other and smiling broadly at any individuals she passed. Most of the humans ignored her, some males swore at her or belligerently pushed her away but one man stopped and talked to her suggesting they could go somewhere quiet to transact some business of a sexual nature. In character now she rejected his suggestion in no uncertain terms, using a few of the choicest swear words she had learned and carried on to the Queens Head feeling pleased with herself that her disguise had, so far, proved successful.

9

The Queens Head

The Queens Head public house was a little less crowded and noisy than Atia had anticipated. It was a large corner pub where only about half of the tables were occupied by groups of human males and females, drinking, talking and occasionally laughing raucously. Many more men and women stood at the bar in various states of inebriation. The smoke, from cigarettes and pipes hung heavily in the air but Apprentice Commander Atia tried her hardest to stifle any cough she felt coming on; immunity to smoky air must develop very early on in the life of London based humans, she thought, and she didn't want to appear out of place in any way. The acrid atmosphere couldn't quite blot out the smell of the pub's interior, which to Atia seemed to be a mixture of sour beer and human waste. The Jaran Apprentice Commander dreaded to think what the sanitary arrangements in a place like this would be.

The main room of the Queens Head had a number of alcoves where people could sit in relative privacy. Around the room tables and chairs were placed close together on a bare wooden floor that was badly in need of sweeping.

Atia weaved her way around the pub as though she was searching for someone in particular. What she was actually doing was looking at where the best means of escape would be should she need to depart from the pub quickly and she was also weighing up with which of the humans it might be best to strike up some sort of conversation. Atia had decided that her best strategy would be to simply march up to some individuals and start talking. Seeing a group of four females sitting at a table having an animated conversation she went over to them and wiping her nose on the sleeve of her jacket and sniffing loudly confidently said: 'Any of you lot seen me ole man roun' 'ere? 'Es a short bloke with a beer belly an' a rovin' eye. Wears a billycock 'at to cover 'is bald 'ead.'

The four turned to Atia and looked her up and down.

'An' who are you comin' in 'ere an' demandin?' said a women with curly chestnut coloured hair held back with a dirty yellow bow. As she spoke she puffed on a thin cheroot.

'Beg pardon,' said Atia, 'but I'm just out of the bonehouse and 'e said 'e'd meet me 'ere. Prob'ly been picked up by the coppers for somethin' or other I shouldn't be surprised.'

'You're not from round 'ere are yer?' said another of the women. This one had fair hair and was dressed in a purple bodice, black jacket and skirt.

'Naw, south of the river – the ole man and me thought we'd see if there's any work round 'ere but 'e's obviously done a bunk to somewhere else, with some little tart if I knows 'im,' replied Atia.

'What's yer name?' said a third woman.

'I'm Maggie, Mag me friends call me. Can I sit and rest me plates o' meat, I've done a lot of walkin' about today lookin' for the toe rag. I'd stand you all to a drink if I had enough,' said Atia looking with studied care at the farthings and halfpenny coins she had retrieved from her skirt pocket.

'Fourpence,' Atia announced, 'an' that was for me doss tonight. Aw blow it! I'll get a drink an' I'll hav' to sleep under the stars again getting' wet in the rain.'

Atia went to the bar and purchased a glass of gin. She had wondered if she could get away with just asking for water but she reasoned that that request would be so out of place, bearing in mind the person she now pretended to be, that the bar staff would almost certainly let everyone in the pub know and her impersonation would be revealed.

'I'm goin' to make this last,' she said to the women at the table as she returned from the bar, 'ain't got no more tom and funny now.' Atia took a little sip of the gin trying her best not to gag at the taste of the strong drink.

'So what workhouse were you in?' said the fair-haired woman who seemed to be the most friendly of the group.

'Lambeth bonehouse in Renfrew Road. It was all right for a bit but I got sick of the skilly ev'ry day so me an' me ole man left an' we come 'ere to Whitechapel. Didn't know 'ee was goin' to bugger off else I'd 'ave stayed where I was. Still, no point mopin' about is there?' Atia raised her glass to the others and sipped a bit more of the gin. It took an effort of will for her not to grimace at the taste of the alcohol. 'So what are your names and do you know if any of the doss 'ouses round 'ere will let me 'ave a night on the slate?' Atia looked at the four women and smiled.

'Well I'm Ada, this is Liz;' said the fair haired woman, indicating the curly haired female who scowled at Atia, 'an' this is Nell;' she said pointing at a young woman with auburn hair who if she had cleaned herself up would have looked almost beautiful Atia thought. 'An' this is Jane, who don't ever say much' – a nervous looking young woman who could have only been in her twenties smiled at Atia and then looked down as if embarrassed. Atia noticed that she had a clay pipe in her hand and she would occasionally suck on it even though the tobacco in it had all gone.

'Pleased to meet yer all,' said Atia raising her glass again. She had managed to spill a little of the clear liquid onto the floorboards underneath the table while Ada was introducing the women to her. 'So what about the doss 'ouses round 'ere?

'Naw, they won't give yer nothin' on tick. They always wants yer to pay up front – fourpence for a bed at Crossingham's in Dorset Street, which is the best of 'em round 'ere, eightpence if yer want a bed on yer own,' said Liz with a scowl.

'Ain't that where poor old Annie used to doss?' said Nell.

'Yeah that's the one, it's not too bad – I've bin to worse I can tell yer,' said Liz, scratching her arm as she spoke.

'Who's poor old Annie?' inquired Atia, feigning ignorance as she took another sip of her gin and surreptitiously poured what remained in the glass onto the floor.

'Didn't you hear about the murder las' Sat'day?' said Ada, 'woman who used to drink in 'ere was killed. 'Er throat was cut from ear to ear an' then she was split open down the middle an' all 'er insides was taken out. Awful it were.'

'They're all callin' the killer The Knife and some people

roun' 'ere are sayin' he might be a doctor from up West,' said Nell, her eyes wide with excitement.

'Yeah, now yer come to mention it I did 'ear about that down in Lambeth. Ain't the coppers got nobody for it yet?' said Atia.

'Naw,' said Liz taking another puff of her cheroot, 'too busy scratchin' their arses an' drinkin' tea I shouldn't wonder.'

'No,' said Jane in a quiet voice, 'I heard that they got some bloke for it an' they've locked 'im up in Leman Street nick. There was a big crowd of people outside shoutin' for 'im to be 'ung.'

'I 'eard that too,' said Liz, 'it's that Jew called Pizer, who always 'angs about outside the Britannia. 'Es a cobbler an' the police 'ave said that 'e calls 'imself Leather Apron.'

'Good riddance, that's what I says,' said Ada, 'it's not bin safe for a girl to go out on 'er own lately. Never know who's out there waitin' to do yer in. Is there anyone around who'll treat us to a drink do you think?' Ada looked around at the other customers in the pub, grimaced and shook her head.

'So is there any work goin' roun' 'ere do any of yer know?' said Atia.

'Naw not much,' said Liz, 'I do a bit o' cleanin' at a doss 'ouse when the fancy takes me. It's enough to get me a bed for the night. One or two women sell flowers or matches on the Whitechapel High Street but it don't earn you much an' it's miserable when it rains 'eavy like today – almost as bad as tuggin' on some bloke's smelly john thomas round the back yard of the pub.'

The women laughed but before Atia was able to ask another question three men who had just walked into the Queens Head interrupted the group.

'Well, well, well, who'd 'ave thought we'd 'ave bumped into these lovely ladies in 'ere, an' all of yer so jolly too,' said one of them who appeared to be the leader of the three. Atia quickly examined the man and his two companions. They were youngish, late twenties she estimated and dressed in clothes that were slightly better than the Whitechapel norm. The male who spoke wore a black bowler hat over his longish fair hair and a light grey suit with black edging around the lapels and cuffs of his jacket. He had a false smile on his face and Atia, who by now could recognise irony and sarcasm in human speech, at once realised he was there to cause some sort of trouble. The man's two thickset and thuggish looking companions glared at the women with undisguised and menacing contempt. Undoubtedly, thought Atia, these men were there to act as support to the first man and they were almost certainly carrying weapons of some sort.

'Well ladies,' said the man, 'I 'ave bin lookin' for yer lot for some time now but 'aven't been able been able to find 'ide nor 'air of any of yer.' As he spoke he sidled up to the young woman called Nell and started to run his fingers through her hair. 'Anyone 'ud think yer'd been avoidin' me for some reason.' He smiled a smile that Atia thought carried more menace than anything she'd seen so far in her brief stay on planet Earth.

'Look,' said Liz, 'we ain't bin workin' on the streets, not since these murders 'ave bin 'appenin' – it's too dangerous – we 'ave to stay together. Any girl what goes off with some bloke on 'er own can end up with 'er throat cut and 'er guts ripped out.'

'Oh yeh, The Knife, 'eard about 'im. But, I'm very pleased to tell you ladies that 'es now been caught and is currently languishin' in a police lock-up so ladies of yer ilk can all get back out there an' start earnin' a bit of money – cos the next time we meet I'll expect to collect our fair share from yer. Let's face it there ain't much else yer lot can do is there?' The young woman Nell grimaced and gave a yelp as the man who had been winding a knot of her long, dark red hair around his finger gave it a swift pull.

''Ang on a bit, what 'ave we 'ere?' said the man, noticing Atia for the first time. The man let go of Nell's hair, and walked over to where Atia sat. Standing next to her he looked her up and down and stroked her cheek with the back of his hand. Atia decided, for the time being, against powering her fist into the man's groin. 'Well ain't you the pretty un? Hey lads,' he said to the other two men, 'how would yer like to get some of 'er eh? Very nice indeed! If I weren't in a 'urry I'd take 'er round the back meself, if you know what I mean!' He winked at his two friends who guffawed at his joke. 'But unfortunately, time is of the essence an' I must depart this den of inequity an' get on with me more important business.' He smiled again, tipped his hat to the women and gestured to his two scowling lieutenants that they should head for the front door of the pub with him following on.

'Who the bleedin' 'ell was that?' said Atia who glared at the men as they left the pub.

'That was Squibby,' said Ada, 'one of the Old Nichol gang. They all live in the Old Nichol, a street at the top of Brick Lane and when they ain't 'avin fisticuffs or knife fights with the Hoxton High Rips, they go about collectin' money from local women. It don't matter to them 'ow us girls are gettin' their money, whether we're gettin' it from johns on the street or doin' other stuff, they still want a share of it.'

'Can't you tell the coppers about 'em?' said Atia.

'What! Where you bin livin' – in a convent?' said Liz, 'Anyone who went to the crushers and dobbed 'em in would end up with their face slashed with a razor blade, or summat worse.'

'Yeh, remember what happened to that Emma Smith earlier in the year in Brick Lane, that was 'orrible what they done to 'er, she ended up dyin' in agony,' said the woman called Jane in a quiet voice.

'Yeah, unless you got a great big bloke to protect you from the likes of one of the gangs round here you ain't safe,' said Ada, 'so you ave' to keep out of their way, or if yer don't yer 'ave to 'and over any money yer've made.'

'That really is the height of unfairness,' said Atia, who was so shocked by what the women had said that she forgot momentarily to use her East End accent causing Ada and Liz in particular to give her a strange look.

'Naw it' ain't bleedin' fair an' that's the truth,' said Ada still looking a little oddly at Atia, 'but what can we do?'

Atia was at a loss as to what to suggest to the four women. They were just four individuals out of so many such women in the same position. Either try to find honest work when there was hardly any around or go out on the streets and try to earn a living by prostituting themselves – that seems to be the Whitechapel choice, thought Atia. And if that were not difficult enough tonight she had learned that there were gangs of men operating in the area that were in the habit of extorting money from the poverty stricken women of the area taking whatever little they could raise when often it was a struggle to get enough to afford a bed for the night in some run down doss house. It was little wonder Atia considered why poor women like these round this table should attempt to forget about their miserable lot in life by drinking themselves into oblivion. She wondered if she would she do anything differently if she were in their position? One thing that the Apprentice Commander was convinced about, however, was that if she ever saw this Squibby again it would take a huge effort of will on her part not to use the disrupter device on him and reduce him to his component atoms, particularly if he was in the process of extorting money from women such as these.

Atia was so deep in her thoughts that she had to be nudged by Ada to make her respond to something she had been asked. ' Mag, Liz said she's getting' another round of drinks in an' do yer fancy one?'

'Er, no ta, I've got to go and find me ole man – 'e'll prob'ly be in the Britannia over the road promisin' the earth to some poor woman.'

'Please yerself,' shrugged Liz as she went off to the bar for the drinks.

Atia smiled at the women, wiped her nose on her sleeve for good effect and headed off to the Britannia public house.

My greetings and utmost felicitations to the esteemed members of the Sub-Committee.

The humans who live in the part of the London conurbation are a strange mixture and it is difficult to draw any generalized conclusions about the inhabitants of this planet based on our interactions with them so far. Both Apprentice Commander Atia and I are glad that we have given ourselves a reasonably extended orientation period of five Earth years to complete our assessment of the humans on the planet. Let me try to explain to the Sub-Committee what I mean exactly.

The other day, the Apprentice Commander and I were walking along one of the busy main thoroughfares of the Whitechapel area when we witnessed an act of extreme bravery and humility. The roadways in this part of London, indeed in most parts of London, are extremely busy. There is a great deal of traffic – carts, wagons, private hire cabs and public transport vehicles called omnibuses. As I have mentioned before all the road traffic here is horse-drawn, the horse being the main beast of burden evident in the conurbation. On this particular day, during our perambulations around the area we suddenly noticed that a human female child, aged about four years we estimated, ran out in front of one of these omnibuses, which are pulled by two very large beasts. She ran into the road in order to gather her small rubber ball (a human toy that is bounced and thrown to be caught by others) completely unaware of the danger she had put herself in. The girl's mother screamed loudly but did nothing to retrieve her daughter, being paralysed with grief or fear. Just before the young child would have been trampled to death by the horses' hooves she was grabbed by a human male who, at considerable risk to himself, dashed in front of the omnibus and pulled the young girl clear of the vehicle and delivered her back to her mother who was overcome with gratitude. When Atia and I obtained a closer look at the man we could see that he was undoubtedly one of the vagrants who tramp the area looking for casual work and who sometimes beg for money on street corners. Quite often the local inhabitants of the area shun this type of person, but here was such a man who had put his own life at risk in order to save the child of a poor woman. The woman tried to give the vagrant some money as a reward, but he refused, I believe because he realised that the woman probably had as little money as he did. He just accepted her thanks and walked on. Apprentice Commander Atia and I have seen other acts of generosity and selflessness in the area since we have abided here but this was the most conspicuous.

On the other hand we have also become aware of the egregious acts of violence and threatening behaviour that have occurred in Whitechapel. Foremost among these are a number of murders that have taken place in the area in recent weeks. It appears that a madman (some have called this person simply 'The Knife') has taken to slaughtering poor, homeless women on the streets late at night. In some ways it is not surprising as there are many dark alleyways and deserted yards where murders can be committed with impunity. There are also many woman out on the streets in the dark, usually because they have not got the very small amount of money needed for a bed in one of the common lodging houses, or else they are letting human males engage in some variation of sexual activity with themselves in order to raise the money for a bed for the night. These women are, of course, extremely soft targets as generally they have no way of defending themselves and naturally their lifestyles tend to ensure that they are often alone in the small hours of the evening. At the time of writing this report the local law enforcement authorities seem to have arrested a human male who most people in the Whitechapel area believe is responsible for the killings. Atia and I are hoping that this is true and that these murders will now cease.

There are other sorts of violent criminals, however. Two days ago Apprentice Commander Atia went undercover, or should I say even more undercover than she already was and took on the role of a poor female who had just left a workhouse (a building where poor homeless individuals and families can obtain a modicum of subsistence in return for some menial and physical labour. It is really one of the few safety-net features apparent in this society and prevents too many poor individuals actually perishing on the streets).

In this role, Atia visited two of the many public houses that abound in this area, places where many of the poverty stricken locals can buy cheap alcoholic drinks and attempt, temporarily at least, to forget about the sad and seemingly hopeless lives they lead. While in one of the public houses Atia discovered that many of the poor women of the area are being threatened and forced to hand over what is ironically referred to as protection money by organised gangs of men who have no qualms about inflicting violence and significant injury on any of the females who refuse to hand over at least some of their money to them. I have to say I have rarely seen the Apprentice Commander so angrily animated, as she was when she returned from her visit to the public houses. She was all for attempting to locate the individuals responsible for this extortion and very forcibly demonstrating to them the error of their ways. However, I pointed out to Atia that we were here to observe and it was not our role to intervene into the everyday lives of the humans in this city. Apprentice Commander Atia quickly agreed that our mission was of the utmost importance and unless she was personally threatened would do her best to stay out of any disagreements between humans in the locality.

And so our observations and data gathering continue apace. We are learning so much about Earth humans and it is clear to us that after our five-year analysis we will be able to provide advice to any future Jaran diplomatic intervention in great and pertinent detail.

With my utmost loyalty, etcetera,
First Commander Treve Pacton Ashto.

10

Atia has a Plan

'Mr Ashton, would it be quite conven'ent to 'ave a little word with you do you think?'

Mrs Smith had intercepted First Commander Ashto as he was in the process of leaving the water closet and heading back to his room.

'Of course,' said the First Commander, 'in what way may I assist you, Mrs Smith?'

'Well, Mr Ashton, it is somewhat of a delicate matter I wish to raise with you.'

'Really, Mrs Smith, and what is it exactly?'

'Well Mr Ashton, as you are very aware I run a decent guest 'ouse and I do not allow any unchristian practices to take place under my roof.'

Ashto felt puzzled by Mrs Smith's words and thought hard to try to ascertain what the elderly Earth woman was alluding to. He stared blankly at Mrs Smith who saw that as a sign to continue with her point.

'You must understand, Mr Ashton, that I 'ave 'ad to struggle 'ard over the years to maintain the decency of this 'ouse, what with me being a widow of many years standin' an' all and I 'ave carefully selected my lodgers in order to ensure that they do not bring ... unwanted nocturnal activities to this establishment.'

'I'm very sorry, Mrs Smith, but I do not quite understand what you mean?'

'Well, Mr Ashton, in that case let me speak quite plain to you. The other day I saw you, with open arms indeed, welcome a dubious, unwholesome and dishevelled looking young female person back to your room. She entered your room and appeared to stay there throughout the entire evening. I'm not sure where your good lady, Mrs Ashton, was at the time but I doubt whether you would want her to be appraised of the situation.'

'Ah, I see, Mrs Smith,' said Ashto quickly realising what his elderly landlady was after. 'I apologise most profusely to you, Mrs Smith; I should have known that you would not treat such a situation lightly. Would some financial recompense smooth over the matter and prevent you from mentioning the unfortunate incident to my dear wife?' The First Commander reached into his pocket and produced a gold sovereign, which he placed in Mrs Smith's slightly twisted arthritic hand.

Mrs Smith smiled in a conspiratorial way and touched the side of her nose in what Ashto knew to be a signal that his landlady would, for now at least, keep the matter to herself.

'Oh, and by the way, Mr Ashton, if in the future you would be desirous of using another room on a temporary basis please inform me. It will be at your disposal for a 'alf-a-crown each 'our that you avail yourself of it.'

Ashto, assured Mrs Smith that he would let her know if in future he would be in need of the extra facility and ushered her away as he made his way back to his and Atia's room. There, with a large smile on his face, he told Atia about his confrontation with Mrs Smith.

'The old, money-grubbing witch!' said Atia whose grasp of the English language was progressing well, 'she must be watching all our comings and goings!'

'Yes, indeed, Margot, when she was talking it was extremely difficult for me not to break out into laughter and in the process give away our little secret.

'Well, we have more important matters to see to than to placate the strange imaginings of Mrs Smith,' said the Apprentice Commander. It had been several days since Atia had been in the Queens Head and Britannia public houses and her innate sense of injustice at the actions of the Old Nichol gang had grown. 'If the poor women of the local area hadn't got enough to cope with in trying to find money for a bed for the night, deal with their over-reliance on alcoholic substances and avoid having their throats cut by a madman stalking the streets at night they also had to deal with gang members trying to take away what little money they had managed to gather in the first place,' said Atia.

'You are completely correct, Margot, but we must ensure that we do not lose sight of our main objective of gathering information for the benefit of the Galactic Federation. Certainly if we can in some small way we can help with any of the problems faced by certain individuals in Whitechapel we should do as much as we can but we cannot jeopardise our main role here on this planet in the process.'

'You are, of course, totally accurate, Trevor. However, if I … if we can alleviate some of the misery experienced by individuals we come across during our observations then I strongly feel that it is our duty as fellow sapient creatures to take some sort of affirmative action on behalf of the downtrodden humans of this area. As a fully-fledged member of the Exploration Executive you surely must feel sympathy for the poor females I was talking to a few evenings ago as they try to survive in a hostile environment. It appears to me that Earth humans have a great capacity to achieve good things if they are given a chance and are not hampered by a social system that condemns them as worthless and puts more and more obstacles in front of them. Is it any wonder that many of the humans simply give up and succumb to the temporary expedient of drunkenness?'

There were many reasons why First Commander Ashto felt so attracted to his Apprentice Commander. There was the efficient, professional and no-nonsense way she approached her tasks as part of the Exploration Executive of course, but he had also got to know her on a more personal level in the two years or so they had been engaged on their mission, both in the confines of the ship and much more so of late on the planet Earth. In that time he had come to know the 'real' Atia. She was, without doubt, a female of great compassion as well as great intelligence; a person who was capable of real empathy – a trait that was not one of those that was usually foremost in Jaran mental make-up. Jarans were logical, efficient, determined, loyal and painstaking but sometimes, in Ashto's view lacked a certain amount of fellow feeling and sympathy for other species they came across in their explorations. It is made quite clear in the Jaran Explorer Executive credo that explorations of other planets should be accomplished with as little interference as possible into the internal affairs and conflicts that take place among the indigenous population of those planets with the one proviso that members of Jaran exploration personnel are given absolute licence to protect themselves should the situation arise. As far as First Commander Ashto was concerned, in light of Atia's recent encounter with the Old Nichol Gang, it would seem that she, in her guise as Maggie, along with many of the other woman of the area, were in constant danger from such organised crime and that any pre-emptive action taken against such lawless individuals could be seen as self-preservation in line with the codes and conventions of the Jaran Galactic Federation Explorer Executive.

First Commander Ashto smiled fondly at Atia. She had discarded her disguise as Maggie and was now dressed in her more usual human attire, a day outfit of brown worsted she had purchased in Oxford Street the day before as the Jaran pair had explored the West End of the city. She sat at the desk, pouring through the newspaper that was laid out in front of her.

'The police authorities at Leman Street are still detaining the individual called John Pizer in relation to the murder of Emily Annie Sievey although the newspaper seems to suggest that they know the man is actually innocent of the crime and are keeping him in gaol simply for his own protection from the rather belligerent crowd outside the police station. It seems very clear that they have no other leads to go on.'

'Do you think that it is likely that the men you saw in the public house the other evening might actually be the perpetrators of these crimes against the homeless women, Margot?'

'It is possible, Trevor, they definitely seem to have been responsible for the murder of a woman called Emma Smith earlier this year. She was found with terrible internal injuries probably caused by the forcible insertion of a bottle into her vagina and who, after a number of days in a coma, eventually died from peritonitis. Using our link to the Ship's computer I have been able to scan some of the police records pertaining to the incident and although there is little doubt that her murder was the responsibility of an extortion gang – if not the Old Nichol Gang then one of their rival organisations – the Police have been unable or unwilling to arrest the perpetrators.'

'Do the policing authorities see any similarities between the murder you have just described and the more recent ones in the local area?'

'Not really, Trevor, there have been three murders of women in Whitechapel since the beginning of the month of August. The first was a woman called Martha Tabram, who was stabbed thirty-nine times with a small bladed implement. The second woman, Mary Anne Nichols, who was known as Polly, was killed by a deep incision to her neck, inflicted with a long bladed knife, which caused her to bleed to death. The third poor victim, Emily Annie Sievey, often known by the family name of Chapman, was also killed by a deep cut to her throat before her abdominal area was then mutilated in a grotesque fashion with some of her internal organs removed and placed beside her body.'

Ashto grimaced at the description of the last killing; he found it difficult to believe that any sapient being could commit such actions. 'Margot, what would motivate an individual to carry out such awful murders?'

'Well, Trevor, if the killings are perpetrated by the Old Nichol Gang or another such group then they would have been carried out as a blatant warning to all poor women in this area that they should continue to hand over some of their earnings as a form of protection against such atrocities being carried out on them. However, it seems to me that the methods of these recent crimes are substantially different to the Emma Smith killing and perhaps point to the murders being carried out by one unbalanced individual acting alone for some unknown motive. It certainly seems that the local police are a long way from solving these unfortunate incidents and would have doubtless arrested the Old Nichol Gang if there was any evidence at all that members of it were responsible for them. Such has been the amount of public unrest in the Whitechapel area because of the murders, with the local police station being besieged by worried residents, that that authorities are very anxious to solve the murders and placate the local community as soon as possible.'

'So, Margot, in light of what you have just said are we going to intervene in any way with regard to the Old Nichol Gang or just let matters evolve naturally and hope that the authorities will eventually deal with them?'

'Well, Trevor, even if the Old Nichol Gang have not been involved in the latest murders it is certain that they have been extorting money from the poor women of the area and quite possibly were responsible for the brutal killing of Emma Smith. So my plan, with your permission of course, is to adopt the guise of poor, homeless woman Maggie again, seek out the leader of the gang, whose name appears to be Squibby, and warn him and his compatriots that the women of Whitechapel are no longer in need of their so-called protection and they would do well to stay away the area.'

'And do you think, Margot, that the Old Nichol Gang will heed your warning? Also I am extremely worried that you are placing yourself in grave danger. These male human Gang members seem to be extremely ruthless and unforgiving and will undoubtedly outnumber you if you confront them at some point. Do you not think that I should accompany you on any mission to undermine the position of these humans?'

Atia smiled fondly at the First Commander. She was touched that Ashto felt so protective towards her and as each day went by she grew closer to him. However, she needed to demonstrate to him, and to herself for that matter, that she could deal with such issues on her own without having to rely on her superior officer to protect her. She would do her best to ensure her own safety but was determined that she was going to carry out this mission of her own devising herself and make this little part of London safer for women who had already fallen on hard times and, in her opinion, should not be plagued by other humans for financial gain.

'No, Trevor, I am determined to deal with these particular unpleasant individuals myself, but I will, as per your previous instructions, ensure that I carry a communications device on my person as well as the disrupter weapon which I will not fail to use if I am in any danger at all.'

'Margot, on this occasion I want you to keep in constant

touch with me at all times so that I can assist you if you need help. I hope that is quite clear.'

'It is Trevor, I will use an earpiece and microphone switched on throughout my mission in order to keep you fully informed of my situation.' Atia smiled again at her First Commander, grateful again that he was so concerned about her. She was determined, however, that she was going to carry out this mission of hers decisively and with as little outside help as possible. It was her chance to prove herself and ensure that her First Commander, who she knew was always scrupulously fair in such matters, would be recommending her for promotion as soon as their mission on planet Earth was completed. Nervous but excited she took off her normal Earth clothes and replaced them with her 'Maggie' attire. She was ready to go and give Squibby, the leader of the Old Nichol Gang, the biggest shock of his life.

11

The Old Nichol Gang

That evening Atia toured the grimy streets and crowded public houses of Whitechapel in the hope of tracking down the gang leader known as Squibby. After visiting the Britannia, The Queens Head, The Alma and The Ten Bells, always with the pretext if asked, that she was looking for 'me ole man', she headed towards the Princess Alice on the corner of Wentworth Street and Commercial Street. As she weaved along the busy streets she tested the small communications device that nestled in her ear, covered up by her long, dark and suitably unkempt hair. She spoke into her sleeve where she had concealed an equally small microphone attached to a cheap bracelet she wore on her wrist and hoped that passers-by would assume that she was having a drunken conversation with herself.

'Trevor, I have been to a number of local public houses but haven't as yet managed to find the members of the Old Nichol Gang who were in the Queens Head the other evening. I am now heading toward the Princess Alice. If they are not there I will return to the guesthouse and try again tomorrow.'

'Message received, Margot. Take care in the Princess Alice.' First Commander Ashto sat at the desk in the couple's room at Mrs Smith's guesthouse a worried look on his face. He peered out of the window to the street below, gloomy in the half-light of this overcast late summer evening. He had been transferring some information to the ship's computer database but found it difficult to concentrate on the task in hand. He was very concerned about Atia and what could befall her at the hands of the Old Nichol Gang if they reacted badly at being confronted by the Apprentice Commander. He didn't know exactly what Atia's plan was and doubted that she did herself apart from her general desire to warn Squibby to keep away from the women of Whitechapel. In any case he was ready to leave the guesthouse in Bell Lane and dash as quickly as possible to wherever Atia was in order to help her out.

'Margot, where are you at this moment?' said Ashto into his microphone.

'Just about to enter the Princess Alice so I will not speak to you when I'm inside but I will make sure that my microphone is switched on so that you can hear everything that takes place. I will speak to you later.'

Ashto sighed deeply and sat back in his chair, adjusting his earpiece so that he was absolutely sure he wouldn't miss anything important that was being said inside the Princess Alice.

As Atia entered the large and crowded public house the first thing she noticed was a woman standing on a chair beginning to regale a group of beer drinking men with a song. 'C'mon Kate give us one of yer songs!' one of the men had shouted. The woman sang a plaintive and highly sentimental song that seemed to end every few lines with a chorus of: 'For I can't find Brummagem,' to which many of the men joined in. The female, though obviously roaring drunk, had a good and tuneful voice, thought Atia, and she wouldn't have been surprised to learn that she had sung for her living at sometime in the past. She was a handsome enough looking woman although obviously ground down by years of living in poverty and an over-reliance on alcohol. Atia watched the petite dark-haired woman as she finished the song. The men cheered and one of them gave the woman a large glass of gin as a reward.

And then Atia, peering hard through the cigarette and pipe smoke saw Squibby. There he was standing at the bar drinking, sticking out somewhat in his smart, light grey suit. He wore no bowler hat this time and his fair hair looked dirty and ruffled. His two 'helpers' were there too standing protectively close to him and laughing at his jokes. Seeing her chance Atia marched confidently to the bar deliberately nudging one of Squibby's henchmen in the back as she forced her way through the crowd and ordered a gin. The henchman grunted and looked around menacingly at Atia; Squibby had noticed her too.

'Let me buy that drink for yer my love,' said Squibby, slurring his words, obviously intoxicated noted Atia.

'No ta, I'm very choosy who I drink wiv,' replied Atia.

Squibby looked at Atia with his head slightly tilted to one side and with a smile of recognition on his face. 'Hey,

I know you,' he said, 'you're that dollymop what was in the Queens Head the other night.' He pushed one of his henchmen aside and moved up close to Atia who looked down her nose at him. 'You're a tall un and no mistake,' said Squibby looking up at Atia who was several inches taller than the he was. 'New roun' 'ere are yer? Well, it's high time you an' me got acquainted wiv one another. What's your name then darlin'?'

'Mind yer own business,' replied Atia with a sneer as she then proceeded to take a small sip of her gin. Although she still objected to the awful taste of the clear alcoholic drink she found that it was helpful in settling the nervousness that she was feeling deep inside her stomach.

'Well, that's not very nice is it lads?' Squibby's two henchmen gave a low chuckle as they continued to stare in threatening fashion at Atia. 'Ere I am being all polite and just 'opin' for a friendly chat with this 'ere young lady and she turns all nasty like – won't even tell me 'er name.'

'It's Maggie, if you need to know, now sling yer 'ook an' leave me in peace.' Atia took another sip of her gin.

Squibby's expression changed. His mouth took on a cruel sneer and his two henchmen moved ever so slightly nearer to where Atia stood with her back to the bar.

'Yer *must* be very new roun' 'ere obviously or yer would know that yer need to talk a bit more polite to me otherwise I'll 'ave to teach you a lesson like, an' it'd be a lesson yer would not enjoy one little bit, let me assure yer of that.' Squibby's sneer turned into a smile. Atia thought to herself that this gang leader was obviously in a good mood after doing a fair bit of drinking and so she would need to provoke him a little more directly.

'Don't need no lessons from the likes of you, ta. Now can I carry on drinking in peace? I 'ate being bothered by such a trumped up little streak o' yellow piss such as yerself.' With that Atia turned round to face the bar and indicated that she wanted another gin.

Back in the guesthouse Ashto grimaced at the words Atia had just used. He stood up, put on his coat and prepared to dash out to the Princess Alice public house.

Out of the corner of her eye Atia could see Squibby turn an angry shade of red and nod to his two compatriots who proceeded to grab her by both arms and quickly bundled her toward the side door of the pub that led out on to Wentworth Street. Atia swore loudly at the men as they took her out but was not too voluble in her defence as this was exactly what she had wanted to happen. No one in the pub offered to help her. One or two watched with interest as she was unceremoniously bundled out into the street but most simply ignored what was happening, obviously used to such incidents regularly taking place. Atia knew nobody would intervene, the reputation of the Old Nichol Gang was obviously well known and people were not going to risk their own safety by helping a complete stranger. That was good. She wanted to deal with Squibby herself without putting the lives of any other Earth humans in danger.

The two large and muscular men both about the same height as Atia quickly dragged her a few metres down the street and took her into a damp and fetid alley that opened out into a small court that smelled strongly of drains, urine and vomit. Atia's mind was now clear and focused. One of

Squibby's henchmen pinioned her arms behind her back while the other stood by ready to warn off any passer-by else who had decided to use the alleyway to access one of the nearby buildings or to urinate up against one of the walls. Squibby stood in front of Atia close enough for her to smell his foul beer breath.

'Well, well, yer don't seem to be quite so mouthy out 'ere do you – yer lanky bitch?'

Atia looked down at Squibby, so much distain and anger in her eyes that he instinctively slightly backed away from her.

'Yer definitely need to be taught a bit of a lesson, that's for certain. Right lads – yer can bend her over for me 'cos I'm planning see if her pokehole is any warmer and more welcoming than her mouth. Yer two can have a go after me – don't think I'll be too long.'

Squibby's henchmen laughed and then each grabbed one of Atia's arms forcing her to bend forward so that her rear end stuck out. Squibby was undoing his fly buttons and obviously looking forward to the coming encounter. Atia bided her time until all three men were in striking distance.

Ashto was almost frantic with worry at the turn of events and was standing by the door of the guesthouse room undecided whether or not to leave now and make a rescue dash to Wentworth Street. Against his better judgment he decided to stay where he was for the time being. He was aware that Atia was skilled in the defensive arts but three to one were not good odds as far as he was concerned.

In the dank courtyard Atia was ready. She felt Squibby behind her begin to pull up her skirts and mustering all of her strength quickly pulled her strong arms inwards. Squibby's two henchmen were taken by surprise and crashed into each other, their foreheads coming together with a loud and resounding crack. While the two were dazed she quickly used both of her hands, with practised skill, to find the pressure points in their necks and, seconds later, both were insensible and lying on the foul, muddy, litter strewn floor of the court.

Surprised at the swift turn of events Squibby stood where he was and frantically tried to stuff his erect penis back inside his trousers at the same time as reaching down to his right boot and grabbing the long thin knife he kept there. Unfortunately for him Atia had by now turned around to face him and aimed a sharp, accurate and very satisfying kick to his groin. Squibby doubled up and howled loudly, dropping his knife and clutching his now extremely painful testicles with both hands.

Atia now knew what she wanted to do and reached inside the deep pocket in her skirt for the disrupter she carried. She was sorely tempted to click the weapon on to full power, aim it at Squibby and get rid of him totally, knowing that she would feel happy to see the little extortionist reduced to his component atoms and disappear into the air forever. However, taking the life of any sapient being was anathema to Atia as it was to all Jarans and as much as she thought it would be doing the humans of this planet a big favour by getting rid of the vicious young criminal she found that in the final analysis she couldn't bring herself to kill Squibby. She was, though, determined to give him a warning that in future he would need to keep well away from the females of Whitechapel. Therefore, she reasoned, something drastic would be needed to ensure he did just that.

In the guesthouse Ashto, who had listened to the scuffling noises had taken place in the courtyard and who had heard the painful cry issued by Squibby, could contain himself no longer. 'Margot, are you all right? Are you hurt? Please speak to me.'

'Trevor I am fine, thank you. I have incapacitated Squibby's two henchmen and am just deciding what salutary lesson to inflict on Squibby to ensure that he and his gang stay away from Whitechapel in the future.'

''Ere – who yer talkin' to? What are yer going to do to me?' whined Squibby in a slightly higher vocal register than he had been using earlier. As he backed away from Atia he tripped over a drain cover and fell onto his rear looking scared.

Atia had decided what to do. She wasn't going to dispose of Squibby, her ingrained ethics would simply not allow her to do such a thing but she did know that she needed to be ruthless in teaching the young gang leader a drastic lesson that would make him think several times before coming back to Whitechapel and threatening any more local women.

Atia bent down and grabbed Squibby's left arm holding it steady in her firm grip.

''Ere, what are yer doin?' Squibby sounded so pathetic that Atia almost felt sorry for him but she knew what she was going to do. 'You will not feel any pain,' said Atia. Taking her disrupter and ensuring that it was only on 10% power she held it against Squibby's left hand and pressed the activator. Instantly the young man's left hand disappeared as the atoms that comprised it were dispersed into the surrounding atmosphere. Atia rolled up Squibby's sleeve to make sure that the wrist was properly cauterized examining it carefully. She knew that one of the main medical issues on this planet was the lack of any effective antiseptics and having taken care to preserve Squibby's life she did not want him to expire with sepsis in a few days' time due to bacteria entering the wound. Squibby looked open-mouthed with shock as she examined his wrist with its missing hand and as Atia let go of his arm he held it up in front of his face disbelieving what he saw.

'What 'ave yer done with me hand?' he asked in tears.

'Compared to what I could have done you are an extremely lucky human,' answered Atia. 'Now listen carefully to me – I have taken away your left hand and if I ever see you in Whitechapel again or if you send any of your compatriots to threaten any of the women of this area I will personally hunt you down and I will cause your entire body to disappear in the way I have just done to your hand. Look at me! Do you understand what I am saying to you?'

Squibby, through shock and tears, nodded and mumbled a 'yes miss'.

Atia then stood up and looked down at the man she had just maimed. She felt some sort of pity for him but not too much. He would be able to manage fairly well with one hand in the future, manage far better in fact than the poor women he had been all to keen to threaten and terrorise with rape and worse.

Atia stepped across to Squibby's two henchmen who were still lying unconscious in the mud and filth of the court. After satisfying herself that they were still alive she maneuvered both men into a recovery position, put her disrupter back into the pocket in her skirt, dusted herself off and went back along the alleyway into Wentworth Street and stopped outside the pub. From inside she could hear the woman singer was performing another song, cheered on by her drunken audience.

She now felt able to speak into her sleeve to the waiting First Commander.

'Mission accomplished, Trevor. I have dealt with Squibby and warned him about returning to Whitechapel. I believe I will have impressed on him the foolishness of going against my wishes.'

Ashto breathed a sigh of relief. 'Well done, Margot, I am extremely impressed. Did you suffer any injury yourself?' he asked, trying hard to sound nonchalant.

'None whatsoever, Trevor, thank you for inquiring. One thing that I learned about humans like Squibby this evening is that they are very predictable and rarely do anything that is unexpected.'

'Are you coming back to the guest house now?' said the First Commander.

'I am on my way, Trevor and am looking forward to seeing you.' Atia smiled. She really was glad to be going to see someone who she cared for and who appeared to care for her. Remembering to weave her way from one side of the pavement to the other in the usual drunken fashion, she made her way back to Mrs Smith's guesthouse in Bell Lane still smiling and feeling extremely happy.

He smoked his pipe as he watched the man fawn over her. He saw him pin a red flower onto her bodice. He had then followed the two of them for some time, waiting for his chance. Now the man and the whore were talking and he would have to wait even longer. He didn't mind. The doorway where he stood was out of the rain, which had been falling for much of this Saturday evening and moreover it was dark and shadowy enough so he could not be seen by anyone.

He had woken up in the morning knowing that this day was the day he would carry on with his good work. He had been itching to begin again. God had then brought him to this place and pointed out the whore he was going to deal with next; he didn't mind waiting a little longer.

He followed the pair to Berner Street where they stopped and then appeared to argue. The man had then hit the whore, pushed her into the wall of the nearby three-storey building and then had walked off in an obvious huff. Putting his pipe in his pocket he had crossed the street to where she stood. The whore was obviously drunk and swaying from side to side, holding the side of her face where she had been struck. By the entrance to Dutfield's Yard he spoke to her: 'how are you?' he had said in a soft voice.

She had turned and smiled as though she expected to know the person who had spoken. She stopped smiling as he grabbed her by her long chestnut coloured curly hair that was tied back with a dirty yellow ribbon and dragged her down to the ground just inside the open gates of the cobbled open space. If she had screamed it wouldn't have mattered; she wouldn't have been heard, as there was the sound of loud communal singing coming from the tall building that backed onto the yard. As it turned out she didn't utter a sound before he bought his knife to her throat and with his practised hand cut deeply into her neck.

He was now ready to begin his work. He began by raising both her legs up into the position that the whore would have been very used to when conducting her vile trade. But what was that? The clip clop of a horse's hooves and the grinding and crunching of wheels on the damp and gritty street; and then the horse, wagon and driver slowly pulled into the yard through the narrow opening and he was forced to quickly retreat into a dark corner. The horse whinnied loudly as it came to the woman's body lying in its path. The cart stopped and the driver tutted and climbed down patting the horse's flank to calm him. The raucous sound of singing from the building behind him continued as the wagon driver examined what it was that lay on the ground and had so disturbed his beast. The wagon driver uttered a Yiddish oath and ran into the tall building to fetch help.

He had to leave his work lying there untouched and unfinished. He swore aloud; God would not be pleased. Frustrated, he walked quickly back up Berner Street where he turned left into Commercial Road East. At Whitechapel High Street he turned left again and soon found himself outside Aldgate railway station. That was when he saw her. She was drunk and singing to herself as she weaved erratically along the street. He followed her as she crossed into the City from Whitechapel, walked up Mitre Street and turned right into a deserted Mitre Square. He watched as she headed towards a dark corner of the Square, well away from the only nearby gas-lamp, and settled herself against the wall of an empty house, pulling up the fur collar of her jacket against the chill of the night and rearranging her black straw bonnet so that it provided some padding for her head against the rough bricks of the building. The woman was obviously planning to sleep there tonight. She did not yet realise that she would never leave this spot alive and would sleep for a very long time.

As he approached her, his knife already in his hand, he heard her continuing to sing softly and mournfully a final song to herself.

12

The Double Murder

'Oh, Mrs Ashton, ain't it just so awful?' Mrs Smith collared Atia as she returned from her regular weekday morning trip to buy a newspaper. She had been glad to get out as, for the last two days, she and First Commander Ashto had been closeted in their room working hard compiling information and uploading it to the ship's database. They had eaten frugally from the supplies they had bought from the ship and Atia, for one was looking forward to walking out in the local area again and perhaps eating some of the human food they had grown to enjoy – fried potatoes and fried fish being among their favourites.

'Good morning, Mrs Smith, to what exactly are you referring?'

'Oh, Mrs Ashton, 'aven't you 'eard? There have bin two more 'orrible murders! Two unfortunate women with their throats cut and with all their insides left lying around. I really don't know what is becoming of this world we live in I really don't.'

Atia was suddenly interested. 'When exactly did these murders take place, Mrs Smith?'

'Both of the poor benighted women were found early on Sunday morning by all accounts, Mrs Ashton. It's gettin' so that a woman can't go out in the street these days without havin' her throat slit from ear to ear – I don't know what's to become of us all … I shall 'ave to take another one of me Cockles' Antibilious Pills to settle me poor stomach down so I will … Mrs Ashton?' Mrs Smith was left talking aloud to herself while she searched in her bag for her pills and Atia had rushed off to her room in order to read about the latest murders in the newspaper.

In their room First Commander Ashto was lying on the bed engrossed in a thick magazine he had recently purchased. As Atia entered the room he smiled at her and pronounced on what he was reading. 'This story … this novel, A Study in Scarlet by a writer called Arthur Conan Doyle, is absolutely splendid, Margot. You must read it after I have finished. It's all about a man called Sherlock Holmes, who describes himself as a consulting detective and who operates in present day London – he's tremendously clever – although the story is fictional it says a great deal about Earth humans and … Margot, what is the matter?' Ashto had suddenly noticed the look of anger on the Apprentice Commander's face as she had stormed across the room, flung her hat onto the bed and quickly sat down at the desk opening up the newspaper in front of her.

'Two more women have been murdered in Whitechapel, Trevor, both killings happened early on Sunday morning!'

'You don't think the Old Nichol Gang were responsible do you, Margot?' said Ashto looking worried, putting his magazine down, raising himself up and sitting on the edge of the bed.

'No, Trevor I do not think so. The two murders seem to bear some of the hallmarks of the three previous killings that have taken place in Whitechapel since the beginning of August. According to the newspaper the perpetrator of the murders has been seen by no one and after killing his victims appears to vanish without leaving a trace.

Atia concentrated on the newspaper article becoming more animated the more she read. 'This is outrageous!' exclaimed Atia.

'What does it say, Margot?' said Ashto.

"It describes the murdered women as "the very lowest types of humanity" and says that they were "outcasts of the pavements!" I cannot believe that the humans writing in these newspapers can refer to other humans in such disparaging terms. It is as though there were two species of humans on this planet and not one. Jarans have much more so called humanity in one of their fingers than some Earth humans have in their entire bodies!'

'Margot, does the newspaper give any details about where the murders took place?'

'Yes Trevor, let me just find what it says,' said Atia still obviously brimming with anger. 'Ah here it is. The first murder took place in Dutfield's Yard, just off Berner Street. The victim's name was Elizabeth Stride. She had been staying at a lodging house in Flower and Dean Street and by all accounts was known as a hardworking woman. Her usual occupation was that of a charwoman and only when she was driven to extremities did she resort to prostitution. The second murder took place in Mitre Square, which is just outside Whitechapel. The victim has not yet been identified although unconfirmed sources say that she might have been called May Kelly. Crowds have gathered in Berner Street demanding that the police do more to find the killer and the Whitechapel Vigilance Committee, set up in the wake of the first three murders, have urged the Home Office to offer a large financial reward for the arrest of the murderer.'

'Two murders in one evening,' said Ashto, 'it's almost beyond belief. Just as we are starting to come to some early conclusions about the psychological make-up of Earth humans, something takes place that seems to defy any form of logical pattern we have so far ascertained. What do you propose, Margot? Should we look into these crimes in the hope of adding to our sum knowledge about humans or just ignore them as aberrational details?'

Atia's dark eyes fired at Ashto. The look on Atia's face was one that the First Commander had not seen before today. She was full of rage; there was no doubt of that. This business of these Whitechapel murders had had a profound effect on the Apprentice Commander and she was obviously deeply concerned about the plight of the poor women of the area, her attitude to the Old Nichol Gang had shown that. Even before she spoke therefore Ashto knew what Atia's answer to his question was going to be.

'First Commander ... I'm sorry, Trevor ... there is no doubt in my mind whatsoever that we should use our resources to help the local policing authorities find the perpetrator of these atrocious killings. We should do so, in my opinion, because if we can develop an understanding of the motivation of the murderer and also the mindset of those searching for the male or female responsible we will discover a great deal more about Earth humans. That surely will only be of help to us in the compiling of your substantive concluding report to the Sub-Committee.

'I agree, Margot. We must draw up a plan of action that will hopefully lead us to this seemingly heartless and irrational killer.'

Atia smiled. 'I am so pleased that you agree we should take action. I would further propose that as from today we should split our resources and follow up any leads separately, allowing us to cover more ground so to speak. We can then report back to each other in the evening in order to compare our findings.'

Ashto wasn't quite so sure as Atia that the approach she had just outlined would be the most sensible but since the Apprentice Commander had proved herself to be more than adequate at protecting herself in the recent past he could only go along with her suggestion. 'Yes Margot, I agree, but as with your recent mission regarding the Old Nichol Gang I think it will be important again that we have the capacity to keep in touch should the need arise.'

'Agreed, Trevor.'

'Good.' replied Ashto, somewhat relieved at Atia's compliance. 'What do you suggest should be our action plan?'

'Well, Trevor with your permission as head of our mission I will attempt to attend the inquests into the two recent killings. It is the custom in this part of the planet for violent or unexplained deaths to be examined by an official called a coroner who hears evidence from witnesses and who then requests a jury of selected individuals to return a decision on how the death came about. According to the newspaper the inquest into the first victim is due to begin today at 11 a.m. at the Vestry Hall in Cable Street. The second victim's inquest is due to take place on Thursday at the Coroner's Court in Golden Lane in the City of London. By attending the inquests I may be able to pick up pertinent information, which I will then supplement by computer scans of records compiled by the police both in the Whitechapel and City of London areas. I will also hope to interview a number of the relevant participants in the inquests to gain further insight into the killings.'

'That sounds extremely comprehensive, Margot. However, I am a little puzzled how you will be able to speak to individuals involved in the investigations without raising suspicions about your motives.'

'I have thought about that, Trevor. I intend to pose as a reporter for an American newspaper – I will need to do some research on which publication would be appropriate for my purposes and will need to forge some documentation but both matters should be easily dealt with using a link to the ship's computer and its satellite scans.'

'You have my permission as First Commander to carry out your plan, Margot. In the meantime I will visit the locations of both murders and see what information I can glean from local residents. If there is any organic material remaining at the murder sites then I will endeavour to collect it and using the medical diagnostic console and ship's computer it may be possible to isolate the perpetrator's DNA signature.'

'Then, Trevor we have a plan and we shall meet back here to compare notes on our day's findings.'

'Agreed, Margot.'

And with that Atia set about her research and the forging of documents and Ashto put on his coat and prepared to leave the room. Ashto half thought that he might give Atia a kiss before he left but decided that it would not be the professional thing to do. Atia watched Ashto leave and felt slightly disappointed that he had left the room without giving her a kiss.

The walk to the Vestry Hall was a fairly long one for Atia as she strolled down Goulston Street, Whitechapel High Street and Leman Street, past Wilton's Music Hall and onto Cable Street. She wore her brown suit and a small brimmed hat of a similar colour, which sported a single feather attached to it. Over her shoulder she carried a businesslike brown leather bag containing a notebook and several pencils. She would, she reasoned, need to look as professional as possible if she were be convincing in her new role as a foreign journalist in Britain there to report to her American newspaper on the subject of the Whitechapel murders. As usual she attracted a number of ribald comments from local young men as she made her way down the streets, but she was used to these by now and simply smiled benignly at them. When she got to the hall she showed her newly produced press pass to the policeman on the door who simply waved her in. She knew that a woman newspaper reporter would be a rarity in this overwhelmingly male dominated society but had reasoned that in the United States of America, where she purported to originate from, the attitude to females in the workplace might be a little more enlightened than in Britain. In any case her documents revealed her to be a journalist from the

New York Times newspaper and she doubted if anyone in London would be able to contradict her right to be there and ask questions in that capacity.

The inquest had already started by the time Atia took her seat in the reporters' section of the seating area. The other occupants of the seats, all men, glanced at her with some interest and one smiled warmly at her and nodded. The inquest was presided over by Coroner Mr Wynne E. Baxter, who had also been in charge of the inquests into two of the previous Whitechapel murder victims. Atia, who sat with a notebook on her lap and a pencil poised in her hand, listened attentively as the Coroner questioned the first few witnesses.

Atia was particularly interested in the evidence provided by a man called Louis Diemschutz who had discovered the body of Elizabeth Stride. He was a steward at the International Workingmen's Educational Club, the back door of which led out into Dutfield's Yard where the murder had been committed. He had been returning home in a cart pulled by his pony when he had come across the body of the victim lying in the yard. At first he thought it was simply a bundle of clothes on the ground but when he realised that it was the body of a woman who had had her throat cut, he and another member of the club, who he had summoned help from, went off to find a policeman. Atia was especially interested to hear whether he or anyone else had seen the perpetrator in the yard as he had been disturbed by Mr Diemschutz driving into the yard before he could mutilate the woman's body. That meant the murderer must have been forced to make a hasty escape, but in spite of that nobody had seen him in the yard. It seemed that the murderer had fled once Mr Diemschutz had gone inside the club to fetch help. It appeared again that the Whitechapel murderer had an almost uncanny ability to slip away from the scene of a murder without being seen by anyone at all.

After Louis Diemschutz had given his evidence, closely questioned by Mr Baxter, the Coroner, there were many other witnesses called including the policeman, Constable Henry Lamb, who was the first law official on the scene, Frederick Blackwell, a doctor who was the first to examine the body of the victim and a woman called Mary Malcolm who claimed that the dead woman was her sister, an assertion that appeared to be wrong according to many others who were questioned after her. The witness that Atia found the most interesting was a man called Michael Kidney who testified that he had lived with Elizabeth Stride in Dorset Street for much of the last three years. He had a history of being drunk and disorderly and of assaulting Elizabeth Stride in the past because he thought she had been seeing other men. Atia made a note of his name and details as someone that might have a motive for murder and could be responsible at least for this particular killing.

When the inquest was adjourned for the day Atia did not feel that she had made very much progress. As she sat reviewing and adding to her notes the man who had smiled at her earlier in the day sat down next to her.

'Apologies for interrupting your thoughts but can I introduce myself? My name is Rogers of the Evening Standard ... and you are?'

'Margot Ashton, of the New York Times,' said Atia shaking Mr Rogers' hand.

'American – you are a long way from home, Miss Ashton.'

'I'm a very long way from home,' said Atia, 'but it is *Mrs* Ashton,' she continued pointing to the wedding ring she wore on her left hand.

Rogers smiled at Atia a somewhat disappointed look on his face. 'Is there a lot of interest in our little murders in America then Mrs Ashton?'

'Indeed there is, Mr Rogers, hence me being sent here to London to cover the events for our readers.'

'Quite,' said the Evening Standard reporter smiling.

Atia thought he had something of a pleasant face only marred, in her view by a small gingery moustache perched above his upper lip. He was young, mid twenties she guessed, about the same height as Atia and dressed in a dark suit that had perhaps seen better days. Atia wasn't sure how much remuneration newspaper reporters in London received but Mr Rogers didn't seem to be overtly affluent.

'Are there many lady journalists in America, Mrs Ashton?'

'I wouldn't really know, Mr Rogers, I just concentrate on doing the best job I can do without worrying overmuch about the gender balance in my chosen profession.'

'Of course not,' said Rogers, 'as with many such things I imagine that you Americans have much to teach us here in the old country where our views are not as progressive as they are there.'

Atia smiled and nodded putting her notebook and pencil into her large leather bag that she wore on her shoulder. 'Well, Mr Rogers, it has been very pleasant meeting you but I must now be on my way and carry on with my work.'

'Of course, Mrs Ashton; could I possibly give you one of my cards? It includes my business and private addresses if ever you feel in need of any help or advice in finding your way round London.'

Atia smiled and took the card, glancing at it before slipping it inside her bag and silently reminding herself that she should get similar business cards made for herself in her guise as an American newspaper reporter. 'Thank you Mr Rogers, I am sure that our paths will be likely to cross once again at some juncture in the future.'

'I do hope so, Mrs Ashton,' he replied still smiling.

Mr Rogers watched Atia as she left the Vestry Hall and sighed. He had rarely, he believed, seen any woman quite so beautiful as the lovely Mrs Ashton. Her husband, he reasoned, must be the luckiest man on planet Earth.

Ashto had left the guesthouse in Bell Lane and headed towards Berner Street, just off Commercial Road East. As he walked down Goulston Street he noticed a group of people gathered outside one of the entrances to Wentworth Model Dwellings on the left side of the narrow street. When he got to the group he saw that a policeman stood in the alleyway stopping people going into the passage that led to numbers 108 to 119. Maneuvering his way to where the policeman stood he asked the officer what the trouble was. The policeman looked Ashto up and down and obviously deciding that he was harmless enough answered in an officious and no nonsense way: 'Police investigation in progress sir, now if you'd like to move along there is nothing at all to see here now.'

Ashto smiled at the policeman, tipping his hat before continuing down Goulston Street. Before he left he had made sure that he had taken a picture of the inside of the entrance to the building the policeman had been guarding. He had done so by utilizing the miniaturised visual recording device that was concealed in one of the buttons of his coat. There was little doubt that evidence, connected to the recent murders, had been found by the police in the very entryway where he had stood several weeks before fruitlessly inquiring after the possibility of renting an apartment in the building. When he returned to the guesthouse he would be sure to link up with the ship's computer and get it to scan for whatever new evidence the police had discovered in Goulston Street.

A few minutes later Ashto found himself in the narrow thoroughfare of Berner Street where a number of local residents along with a few sightseers from other parts of London were staring with interest at the gateway to Dutfield's Yard. At one side of the Yard stood the three-storey building where the eighty or so members of the International Workingmen's Educational Club met each Saturday evening. However, the gates to the Yard were now padlocked and peering through it Ashto could see that there would be no way that he would be able to examine in detail the scene of the murder that was situated a few feet beyond the gates. He could also see quite clearly, however, that there would no longer be any relevant evidence left at the scene. The yard had obviously been washed down and scrubbed clean and only the faintest bloodstain could be seen where the poor woman, Elizabeth Stride, had been so brutally killed just the day before. After ensuring that he had a visual record of the scene there was nothing else to do but continue with his plan and make his way to Mitre Square and the site of the second murder.

Ashto walked back along Berner Street and then along Commercial Road East to Whitechapel High Street and past Aldgate station and Aldgate Street soon arriving at Mitre Square, which was just across the boundary of the City of London. Again Ashto noticed the police presence guarding the entrance to the Square. After briefly speaking to the City of London policeman who was stopping people entering the area where the murder had been committed Ashto stood for a while among the crowd of interested bystanders deciding what to do next. After having brief conversations with a couple of those present he decided that there was nothing tangible he was going to learn standing in the small crowd and that he would walk across to the coffee shop opposite the Square's entrance and reassess his strategy. It may be that he would have to return this evening when the police had left the Square and he would be able to examine the site of the murder properly.

The coffee shop was dark, smoky and pungent with the smell of ground coffee beans. Ashto gratefully sat down in a seat by a window where he could keep an eye on the situation across the street and ordered a coffee from the young female waitress. Ashto had developed a fondness for the Earth drink during the last few weeks and particularly liked it with a little cream stirred into the dark, rich smelling liquid.

The waitress soon bought his coffee, which he gratefully sipped, after adding his cream from a little jug, as he watched the small gathering at the entrance of Mitre Square. People came and drifted away and the lone policeman keeping people out of the Square looked decidedly bored. And then Ashto noticed that two official looking men in civilian clothes arrived, walked up to and spoke to the uniformed man guarding the Square. The policeman proceeded to point in the direction of the coffee shop where Ashto sat watching. The two then walked purposefully across the narrow street towards the shop and, instinctively knowing that the men were coming to see him, the First Commander quickly finished his coffee, looked around to see if there was an alternate way out of the small coffee shop, decided there wasn't and made for the door in the somewhat irrational hope that he could slip away unnoticed by the two approaching individuals.

Ashto only just managed to get out of the door before the two men blocked his way. Both were burly looking and one of them sported an impressive array of facial whiskers, a male human trait that had fascinated Ashto right from his first day on the planet Earth. The other man, middle-aged, short, blond, mustachioed, dressed in a checked suit and with a bowler hat perched on his head put his hand firmly on Ashto's shoulder. 'Excuse me sir, do you have a minute or two? This is Sergeant Thick and my name is Inspector Reid of H Division, Metropolitan Police. We would like you to accompany us to Leman Street police station where we would wish to ask you some questions.' Ashto smiled weakly and nodded. As usual this action caused his top hat to fall over his eyes.

The two men didn't say anything to Ashto as they walked to Leman Street. At the police station they took him to a small, whitewashed room furnished with just a table and two chairs and he was asked to sit down. Inspector Reid sat down opposite Ashto and Sergeant Thick stood by the door his notebook and pencil in his hand.

'Can you tell more your name please?' began the Inspector.

'My name is Trevor Ashton, Inspector.'

'And can I ask what your business is?

'I am a writer from the United States of America. I am in London writing a book about the city in the hope that it will be of use to others from my country who plan to visit London in the future.'

'Where about in the United States do you hail from?'

Luckily the First Commander did not need to hesitate while he searched his neural implant for some relevant information as he had discussed this very point with Atia recently. 'I am from the City of New York, Inspector.'

'I see, Mr Ashton. Can I now ask you what you were doing today?' Inspector Reid stared deeply and unblinkingly into Ashto's eyes. Ashto decided he would need to be careful with this Earth human who he thought seemed more formidable than most.

'I do not quite understand what you mean, Inspector.'

'You were seen talking to a police officer in Goulston Street at the site of a current police investigation, you were then followed by myself and Sergeant Thick to Berner Street where we saw you peering with a great deal of interest through the gateway of Dutfield's Yard, the site of the one of the murders last Sunday. We then followed you all the way to Mitre Square where you again spoke to the officer on duty who got the distinct impression that you wanted to see the exact place where the second murder took place. What exactly was the reason, or reasons, for your interest in these sites, Mr Ashton?'

'Inspector, it is of the utmost importance that I provide for my potential readers a true and comprehensive word picture of the present day city of London including details of any recent events that may or may not interest them in their future visits to this great city. I would be letting that readership down quite badly if I did not include something about the awful, violent crimes that have recently taken place in the Whitechapel area.'

Inspector Reid sat back in his chair and looked at the First Commander with his piercing blue eyes. 'Mr Ashton, does the name Jack the Ripper mean anything to you?'

Ashto quickly searched his implant for the name thinking that it might be something an American should know. He found nothing that was immediately obvious and slowly shook his head. 'I'm sorry Inspector but that name means nothing to me at all. Who is the gentlemen to whom you refer?'

'Four days ago the Central News Agency in London received correspondence from a person who signed himself Jack the Ripper and who claimed to be the Whitechapel murderer.'

'That is interesting, Inspector but I fail to see how such information would have any relevance to me.'

'Well Mr Ashton, according to our language experts at Scotland Yard, graphologists and suchlike, the letter contained some words and phrases that might have been written by someone with American antecedents or who had spent some time living in the United States. Since you say that you are an American who is evidently very interested in the recent murders that have taken place in Whitechapel, to the extent that you have endeavoured to visit the scenes of the two latest killings, I would not be a very efficient detective if I did not connect those aspects together.'

Ashto could not hide the surprise he felt: 'But Inspector you cannot possibly think that I had anything at all to do with those dreadful events. I abhor violence of any sort! At the time they took place I was in my guesthouse room with my wife, Margot.'

'Mr Ashton, you have to realise that we, as the guardians of public safety in this city, must follow up all the leads that we have in order to catch this criminal who may or may not refer to himself as Jack the Ripper. You are of course free to go on your way although we would like you to give Sergeant Thick your address so that we can confirm the details of your explanation with your wife.'

Ashto breathed a sigh of relief as he stood up from his chair. He had had a horrible feeling that he was going to have to spend a great deal of time locked in a dismal police cell in the damp basement of the police station while his alibi was checked out. He smiled at the Inspector, 'Of course, Inspector, I fully understand. I will be only too happy to supply any details you wish – I am pleased to be of assistance.'

'Thank you, Mr Ashton, you are most helpful.' And then just as Ashto was about to leave the room with the Sergeant, Inspector Reid said, 'I was lucky enough to spend some time in New York City two years ago on police liaison business. I stayed in a district of the city called Kings. Do you know it at all?'

Ashto, feeling relieved that he was being released, answered before bothering to check his neural implant: 'Yes Inspector, I do, it's a very pleasant part of the city.'

Reid watched as Ashto and the Sergeant left the room and walked down the corridor. Under his breath he said to himself, 'American my arse!'

My greetings and utmost felicitations to the esteemed members of the Sub-Committee.

The area of London in which we have chosen to reside called Whitechapel has been rocked to its core by the recent terrible murders. Apprentice Commander Atia and myself have decided, as part of our mission to observe and assess the inhabitants of the Earth, to take a particular interest in these murders to try and ascertain what motivates a certain human to commit such atrocities and also to monitor the efforts of the local policing authorities and how efficiently they go about investigating the crimes and eventually, hopefully, apprehending the individual responsible. The data Apprentice Commander Atia and I compile on these aspects will, we believe, be very important when we come to make our recommendations to the Sub-Committee with regard to future missions to this planet and the potential attitude of Earth humans to their first contact with Federation diplomatic experts.

The perpetrator of these quite horrific killings has been given a new sobriquet by the local printed media. They are now calling him 'Jack the Ripper' a name that came about following a number of written missives that were purportedly sent by the killer himself. Whether or not these communications were actually sent by the murderer or are some sort of sensationalist hoax concocted by the proprietors and editors of newspapers in order to create even more interest in the crimes than already exists and therefore sell more of their products is a matter of some debate in police and public circles. Whatever the case the episode highlights a number of interesting aspects that helps to inform Apprentice Commander Atia and myself about the attitude to adversity shown by the Earth humans of the area. The policing authorities seem to be trying their best to catch the perpetrator but so far have failed to track the killer down. They have questioned over two thousand individuals recently and a number of arrests have taken place, mainly of foreigners, itinerants and vagrants, but so far all it seems have been subsequently released without charge.

Remarkably, the police have also questioned me after I attempted to investigate the sites of the most recent murders in an attempt to gather any organic or other forensic evidence that may have been left at the scenes of the killings. Apparently my guise as a writer from the United States of America caused me to attract the suspicions of the local law enforcement authorities, which were carefully guarding the murder sites. I was questioned, albeit briefly, by a police official called Inspector Reid, a perspicacious individual who it was very useful for me to observe as part of my field study of Earth humans. He would seem to be the type of individual any future Federation mission on this planet would be wise to approach and to earn the trust of. My interview with this human went quite well and I believe that

I allayed any suspicions about my motives that he may have originally harboured.

Our computer scans of the Whitechapel police records have generally only highlighted the rather haphazard and unscientific way the authorities have generally gone about the investigation of the murders so far, despite the best intentions of certain officials. We have discovered at least one example of a highly placed individual in the policing structure purposely destroying possibly important evidence. In a street very close to where Atia and I reside the murderer may well have written a message in chalk in the alleyway entrance to a building on the same morning as two murders took place. This message was erased on the orders of the Metropolitan Police Commissioner, a human male called Sir Charles Warren, before the message could be visually recorded. The message was found directly above a piece of blood-soaked clothing belonging to one of the murder victims causing most to assumes that the two pieces of evidence were connected. What the message actually said could not be uncovered by our computer scans in police records and my attempt to make a visual recording of the site proved unsatisfactory.

The interest in the Whitechapel murders has now become worldwide. Our computer scans have shown that newspapers all over the planet are informing their readerships about the events in this relatively small and seemingly unimportant part of the city of London. We have also noticed that many of the more wealthy states of the Earth such as the United States of America and some of those on the continent of Europe have begun to send journalists to Whitechapel to report on events. This has proved both a boon and a handicap to Apprentice Commander Atia who has been posing as a reporter for the New York Times newspaper in the United States and will now need to be on her constant guard in case she meets an actual journalist from that particular newspaper. In that guise the Apprentice Commander has been attending the inquest of the first of the two latest victims of the murderer and soon she will also be in the reporters' section at the inquest of the second victim. Part of her plan is to attempt to actually examine the body of this victim, a female called Catherine Eddowes, with a view to procuring some of the killer's DNA that may still exist on her body. Although forensic science on the planet Earth is in its infancy (even fingerprinting has not yet been effectively utilised by the law enforcing authorities) and therefore DNA recording is unknown, it may be possible for us to analyse any such samples we can obtain, via the ship's computer and track down the killer using the scanning equipment. It is a long shot certainly but one that could possibly yield fruit. In my next report to the Sub-Committee I will hopefully have more news about this particular strategy.

With my utmost loyalty, etcetera,
First Commander Treve Pacton Ashto.

13

Catherine Eddowes

The body of murdered Catherine Eddowes lay in the mortuary adjoining the City of London Coroner's Court, which was situated in Golden Lane. After the twelve men of the Jury had witnessed the corpse of the unfortunate woman the large number of press members present were also allowed to file through the mortuary to view the deceased victim. As the only woman in the group of journalists Apprentice Commander Atia was asked by the Coroner if she really wanted the witness the terrible and shocking mutilations that had been inflicted on the body of the poor woman. Atia had answered that she would and so followed on behind the rest of the reporters as they trooped through to the mortuary.

The reality of the injuries that were evident on the naked body of Catherine Eddowes was far worse than anything

Atia had expected. The Coroner had already explained that the woman had had her throat cut causing her to bleed to death very quickly. The murderer had therefore carried out the extensive mutilations to her body post mortem, the Coroner, Mr Langham, had explained. Atia thought that it was some comfort to know that the poor woman had died almost instantaneously and so was not aware of the indignities that were carried out on her body after her death.

The mutilations were horrific and the Apprentice Commander could easily understand why some individuals would find the terrible sight very difficult to look at. The injuries to the woman's abdominal area were evident enough, despite having been sewn up and cleaned by Doctor Brown who during the inquest would report, in graphic detail, on the extent of the mutilations. Atia was to learn in the course of the inquest how various parts of the internal organs of the woman had been removed from her abdominal cavity. Much of her intestines and colon had been cut away by the killer and placed over the victim's right shoulder and her uterus and one of her kidneys had been removed and taken away by the murderer. Those injuries were bad enough, thought Atia, but the damage to the victim's face was even more grotesquely extensive and horrific. The sight of what was left of the woman's face caused one of the male reporters to gag, hold his hand in front of his mouth and quickly exit the mortuary in some distress.

Catherine Eddowes' face had been virtually destroyed by the killer, labelled Jack the Ripper by the newspapers. Atia could see the deep wound in the woman's throat that had caused her untimely death. Her nose had then been sliced off and her eyelids and upper lip had been cut across. There were cuts on both of her cheeks in the shape of triangles or arrows pointing towards her eyes, there was a large deep, diagonal cut across her face and part of her right ear had been removed. To Atia it was evident from the injuries to the body of the woman that no surgical skill had been required to inflict them. Indeed it was obvious to her as she peered at what was left of the poor dead woman's face that this was the work of a madman who in his frenzy had tried to erase the very identity of another human by slashing away at her face until she was unrecognizable. A madman with a very sharp knife, thought Atia – not a very attractive combination.

As the journalists finished writing in their notebooks and began to file out of the mortuary, Atia hung back on the pretense of making notes until she was the only person left in the cold, white tiled room that smelt of death and carbolic soap. Quickly she held up the victim's right hand and using a small nail file scraped under the fingernails of the dead woman. Atia had noticed that there was a certain amount of material that could possibly be skin, hair and blood under her nails where it was possible that Catherine Eddowes, in her death agony, had raked them down the killer's hand or arm even as he sliced through her throat and waited for her to expire as the blood gushed from her neck. Atia carefully transferred the substance into an envelope she had put ready in her bag. If this small sample proved to be organic substance belonging to the Ripper, Atia thought, it might just be possible to use it to apprehend this perverted individual and stop him from being the perpetrator of any more awful and unnecessary deaths.

Back in the Coroner's courtroom, once everyone had settled down, the inquest commenced. Atia listened carefully to the many witnesses that were called to testify by the Coroner and made detailed notes in her notebook. These witnesses included the victim's sister, Eliza Gold, who broke down in tears several times while testifying, and a man called John Kelly, who had been living with the deceased woman for the past seven years and who told the Court how she had often used his surname as though they were a married couple. Atia was interested in something in particular that the man Kelly said when he was asked by the Coroner to say what he meant by the words "walking the streets" a phrase Kelly had used to describe what he and Catherine Eddowes did from time to time when they had no money to pay for a bed for the night. He obviously meant that they would walk around the streets until they found a sheltered spot somewhere out of the wind, cold and rain where they could settle down for the night. However, the Coroner, Atia suspected, as well as the representatives of the press and the members of the Jury interpreted the words "walking the streets" as meaning that the murder victim was willing to prostitute herself for a few small denomination coins, as many other women of her class were forced to do. Atia thought that this implication was a slight on the poor dead woman who may not have had anything to do with casual prostitution at all.

Another witness to speak was Edward Watkin the heavily bearded police constable whose beat took in Mitre Square every 15 minutes or so on the night of the murder. At 1.30 a.m. he had passed through the Square and there was no sign of a body but at 1.44 a.m. when visiting the Square again Catherine Eddowes was lying there with all of her injuries apparent. He did not see anyone leave the Square at this time nor was he aware of anyone concealed in the shadows. If the police constable was accurate in his evidence it would seem, thought Atia, that yet again the person everyone had begun to call Jack the Ripper had vanished into the night, unseen or unheard after performing his dreadful deed in the very limited amount of time he had between the visits of the officer.

A little later the Coroner's Court heard the evidence of Dr Frederick Gordon Brown, the man who had performed the extensive examination of the deceased woman's body at the mortuary. He described the injuries in great and graphic detail and Atia listened particularly carefully to the doctor's evidence regarding the removal of the woman's kidney. Although most of the injuries inflicted on the body showed no anatomical skill, according to the doctor, finding and removing the kidney did perhaps require some knowledge of how the internal organs of the human body were arranged. The Coroner specifically asked Dr Brown if someone used to cutting up animals would have the skills needed to locate the kidney and the medical man had said yes they would.

At the end of Dr Brown's long and detailed evidence it was announced that the Lord Mayor of London had offered a reward of £500 for the capture of the Whitechapel killer, the news being greeted by applause from those present in the public gallery. The inquest was then adjourned by the Coroner until the following Thursday.

Apprentice Commander Atia packed her pencil and notebook away as she waited for the crowds to leave the room. As she did so a familiar individual walked up to her.

'Mrs Ashton, how nice to see you again,' said Mr Rogers of the Evening Standard, tipping his bowler hat and smiling.

'Mr Rogers,' answered Atia shaking the tall, young reporter's outstretched hand.

'I would have spoken to you earlier, Mrs Ashton, but you seemed so busy making notes that I didn't wanted to disturb you.'

'Well, Mr Rogers, there is such a great deal of information to take in about this dreadful killing and I do want to make sure that my readers back in New York are able to read about the events in the most detailed way.'

'Yes of course, Mrs Ashton, you must be congratulated on your diligence,' Mr Rogers smiled briefly and then his face took on a more serious aspect. 'Mrs Ashton, I need to tell you something. Er ... could we walk together for a while to allow me to impart to you some important information?'

'Yes of course, Mr Rogers.'

Atia and Rogers walked out of the courtroom and out into the rather dull early October afternoon.

'What is this piece of important information you wish to tell me about, Mr Rogers?' Atia said as the couple walked slowly down Golden Lane and on to Beech Street in the direction of Whitechapel.

'Well, Mrs Ashton, I was speaking to another journalist earlier today, a countryman of yours in fact. He too represents the New York Times newspaper and has been sent across the pond, as it were, to report on the Whitechapel homicides, as he terms them.'

'Really, Mr Rogers, how interesting.' Atia needed some time to think. She knew that her story about herself being a reporter from that particular newspaper was in a certain amount of jeopardy.

'The thing is, Mrs Ashton, he was present in the courtroom today, but when I pointed you out to him, an unnecessary thing to do really as you were the only female in the press gallery, I'm afraid he did not recognise you nor indeed had he heard of your name. I thought this most curious in the light of your claim also to represent that newspaper.'

'Again, Mr Rogers, how interesting, and what exactly is the point you are making?'

'My point would be, Mrs Ashton, is that you are not who you say you are and do not represent the New York Times newspaper or indeed any other such journal.'

Atia stopped, delved into her bag and pulled out her press pass, which she passed to Rogers to examine. 'I think that you will find my accreditation fully in order, Mr Rogers, the local police authorities seem to be fully accepting of it.'

Rogers smiled as he handed the pass back to Atia having briefly examined it. 'It is a very good forgery I'll give you that, Mrs Ashton but a forgery it is nevertheless. Please tell me who you are in reality.'

Atia smiled resignedly; she realised she had been discovered telling untruths. 'Very well Mr Rogers, I admit that I am not in fact a reporter with the New York Times newspaper as I had previously stated. I am in this country, from America, with my husband, who is in the process of writing a book about Great Britain, which will give advice to future travellers from the United States eager to learn about Britain and be guided around its most interesting features, history and recent affairs. We are staying in London and so he asked me, as his assistant, to find out as much about the terrible recent murders as I can in order that he can include full details about them in his book. I felt that having a press pass would allow me access to places I would otherwise not have.' Atia's two hearts were beating rapidly but she was hopeful that her outward demeanour did not reveal any of the nervousness she was feeling to Mr Rogers who, she noticed, was watching her closely.

'I see Mrs Ashton. That explains things very well indeed. I thank you for being so candid with me and I apologise for any offence I may have given you. There is one other thing, however.'

'And what would that be, Mr Rogers?'

'I would like you to have dinner with me on Saturday evening.'

'That would, I am afraid, be impossible. My husband would be most upset if I went out to dinner without him, particularly if I were accompanied by someone whom he had never met.' Atia smiled at the Evening Standard reporter in a way that she hoped would appeal to his sense of fairness.

'That is indeed most unfortunate, Mrs Ashton, as your refusal to have dinner with me will almost certainly cause me to mention to someone in authority that you have obtained a press pass in a somewhat dubious and unorthodox fashion. That would doubtless have certain ramifications and consequences that might lead to you and your husband being asked to leave the country and force him to abandon the writing of his book.'

Atia stared at the young reporter to try and ascertain if his threat was a serious one. She decided it was. 'Very well, Mr Rogers, I will accompany you for dinner on this coming Saturday evening. Where and when shall we meet for this great event?' Atia couldn't help but include a note of sarcasm in her question. She had successfully managed to master that particular trait in human speech in the short time she had been on the planet.

'I will be at your place of residence in a hansom cab at 7 o'clock sharp on Saturday, Mrs Ashton. If you could write down your address for me I would be most grateful.'

Atia somewhat annoyed that she hadn't got around to having business cards printed, took the notebook and pencil from her bag, tore out a page, quickly wrote down the address of Mrs Smith's Select Guesthouse and passed the piece of paper to Rogers.

The young newspaperman looked somewhat askance at the information Atia had provided. 'You are actually residing in Whitechapel? Wasn't that something of a rash decision?'

'On the contrary, Mr Rogers, it puts myself and my husband right in the very heart of the place where events are happening that seem to have interested people from all over the planet.'

'Well rather you than me, Mrs Ashton,' said Rogers puffing out his cheeks. 'In any case please be ready at 7 o'clock on Saturday, I will be looking forward to seeing you again with great anticipation.' Rogers held on to Atia's hand for just a little too long before he turned and walked away.

'I wish I could say the same,' said Atia under her breath. She watched Rogers take a pipe from his pocket, fill it with tobacco, light it with a practised technique and walk down the street, an obvious spring in his step.

'You have agreed to go to out for a meal with this individual?' said Ashto back in their room later on that day.

'I had no choice Trevor. Rogers used what Earth humans call *blackmail* to force me to comply with his wishes.'

'So, Margot, what is it this human male wants?

'I believe,' said Atia, blushing slightly, 'that he finds me attractive and wishes to spend time in my company. It is a feeling, however, that I do not in any way reciprocate.'

'I would hope not,' said Ashto huffily.

Atia was secretly pleased that First Commander Ashto gave every indication that he was jealous and was not even attempting to cover the fact up.

'Where is this individual planning to take you for this dinner?' Ashto turned back to the portable replicator with which he had been busy, prior to Atia's return to the guesthouse, producing a number of gold sovereigns.

'I do not know, Trevor. He plans to call at this address at 7 o'clock on Saturday evening in a hansom cab. I will of course be carrying a communicator and disrupter weapon about my person should a problem occur with which I am unable to deal,' said Atia, trying hard to placate the obviously upset First Commander.

'Hmm,' said Ashto pointedly concentrating on using the replicator.

Atia smiled. 'Trevor,' she said, 'would it be fair to assume that having accomplished our various tasks for the day that we can now consider ourselves off duty for a period of time? As she spoke she gently caressed Ashto's cheek. He turned and smiled at his Apprentice Commander.

'Margot,' he replied holding her hand and squeezing it gently, 'I do believe you are correct in your assumption.'

Ashto stood up, kissed Atia and the Jaran couple moved swiftly across the room to the bed.

14

The Fly in the Restaurant

Fortescues' Restaurant, situated in the Strand, was one of the capital's up and coming eating establishments in this year of 1888. Originally a smoking room and then a coffee house it had become the first restaurant in London where large joints of roast meats were wheeled out on silver trolleys to be carved next to the diners' table so creating a fashion soon copied by other such establishments.

Atia was actually quite impressed with the comfortable chairs, the silverware, linen tablecloths and napkins and by the standards of cleanliness evident throughout the restaurant. It was much removed from the earthy coffee shops, cookshops and chophouses she and Ashto tended to visit in the East End. Occasionally they had ventured further afield to eat and had been to a number of West End ordinaries, as they were called, small establishments that provided a limited menu at fixed prices. Those had been a cut above Whitechapel eateries but had not been so grand as Fortescues where, Atia was later to discover, Victorian celebrities like Charles Dickens, William Gladstone and Benjamin Disraeli, had been in the habit of frequenting on a regular basis in the past.

Before coming to planet Earth Atia, like all inhabitants of Jara Prime, had eaten meat, but only that produced in lab-farms where animal protein had been grown in laboratory conditions using stem cells and where no actual animals needed to be killed to provide it. Since living in Whitechapel, however, Atia and Ashto had occasionally eaten meat like beef, lamb and pork although they mainly consumed fish. Atia had to admit though that the large piece of roast beef, currently being carved by the side of the table at which she sat looked and smelt wonderful. As the thick slices of meat were transferred to her plate, along with roast potatoes and green vegetables, her mouth was watering at the prospect of eating the delicious looking meal.

Over the soup course Mr Rogers, who it turned out had the first name of William, had extolled the virtues of Fortescues'. 'I do not come here too often,' he explained, 'my meagre salary from the Evening Standard sadly does not allow such extravagance on a regular basis. However, I have an arrangement with the manager, Mr Simpson, that as long as my newspaper is prepared to publish extensive reviews of my dining experiences here I am, on occasions, allowed to dine gratis.'

'So, Mr Rogers, you are saying that you are not prepared to spend money in taking me out for such a meal?' Atia, after a few sips of a very nice red wine, something she had not tasted before and had been surprised how pleasant it was, was now feeling relaxed and had started to enjoy this new experience. Tolerance to alcohol was obviously something, she reasoned, that even for Jaran physiology improved after exposure to the substance, but she was determined to be careful and not to overdo things. She wanted to stay sharply focused while around Mr Rogers, the tall, perceptive and quite attractive human newspaper reporter who appeared quite charming but who yet might, she believed, prove to be a threat to her, First Commander Ashto and their entire mission.

Rogers nodded in Atia's direction; 'I would spend a vast amount of money on you Mrs Ashton, if I had a vast amount to spend that is.' He smiled and started to tuck into his large plate of food with gusto, occasionally swatting around at a fly that had taken to buzzing around his head.

'That is gratifying to know, Mr Rogers, but why, can I inquire, were you so determined to ask me to accompany you to this restaurant this evening?' said Atia also beginning to eat her beef.

'Well, Mrs Ashton, as a poor newspaper reporter it is not very often one gets to share a meal with possibly the most beautiful woman in London, if not in the whole of the British Isles.' Rogers put more of his beef into his mouth and again had an ineffective swat at the fly, which had returned to hover around his head.

Atia watched the flying insect carefully as it flew silently around and then realised it would be a good idea to deflect Rogers' attention away from it and back to herself.

'Mr Rogers, may I remind you that I am a happily married woman who is hoping to hold you to your promise not to inform the authorities of my little deception with regard to my press pass.'

'You should have no worries in that regard, Mrs Ashton. Unlike many newspaper reporters with whom I am acquainted I am a man of my word. As for you being married I would have to say that, even though I have never met him, your husband sounds a very interesting chap and is also a very lucky one to have such a desirable wife as yourself.' At that very moment the bothersome flying insect chose to dive down from the ceiling, where it had temporarily been perched, and fly straight into Mr Rogers' left ear. Rogers' gave a yelp, stood up and furiously rubbed his ear, causing diners on nearby tables to stare and tut reproachfully at him.

''Are you quite all right, Mr Rogers?' Atia seeing what had happened could not stop herself from smiling as Rogers sat back down again still rubbing his ear. 'I believe I saw the fly travel out of your ear and it is currently situated on the ceiling above where we are sitting,' Atia added. Rogers, flustered, returned to eating his way through his meal and occasionally casting nervous glances upwards to the ceiling as he regained his equilibrium.

'Mrs Ashton, perhaps we could take this opportunity to discuss the Whitechapel murders and your views as to what sort of person is responsible for such heinous crimes?'

'Very simply, Mr Rogers I believe him to be a madman and one who for some unfathomable reason despises women of a certain sort. Moreover this Jack the Ripper, as he has been nicknamed, does not want just to kill these women but seeks to destroy their bodies, their very identities even, as much as possible.'

'Ah, I knew that you, Mrs Ashton, would be able to sum up the situation in a thoroughly cogent way. By the way, the Jack the Ripper epithet along with the "Dear Boss" letters that he is supposed to have sent were, I believe, fabricated by a reporter working for the Star who wanted to, how can I put it, spice up the stories surrounding the killings.'

'If you are correct in that thesis, Mr Rogers, then I fear for the future of news reporting in this country. Surely it is the role of a newspaper journalist to report the truth to the public and not make up or generate erroneous accounts in order to sell more newspapers.'

'I couldn't agree with you more, Mrs Ashton. Your analysis is "spot on" to utilise a little piece of journalese that has been doing the rounds recently in the Fleet Street news offices. I have to admit the more I converse with you Mrs Ashton – or can I call you Margot? – the more I realise that you are not only very beautiful but you also have a highly developed intellect of the sort that one rarely finds in a member of the gentler sex.'

Before Atia could reply Mr Rogers had leapt up out of his seat in the process tipping over his glass of red wine and gave another loud cry as he clutched his nose. Nearby diners, normally used to dining in virtual silence, again tutted loudly to show their displeasure.

'Mr Rogers, what *is* the matter?' said a concerned sounding Atia.

'That blasted fly!' shouted Rogers to an increased chorus of tutting and even a few heartfelt harrumphs from the other restaurant customers, scandalized that he should be using such language in their presence, 'it has flown straight up my nose! I'm sure that it remains there.'

'Please let me see, Mr Rogers,' said Atia, getting up out of her seat and standing in front of the reporter peering into his left nostril. 'I can perceive no fly ensconced in your nasal passage,' said Atia, trying hard to stop herself from grinning.

Back at Mrs Smith's Select Guesthouse First Commander Ashto sat at the writing desk and giggled. The drone, disguised as a fly, which he controlled using keys on his computer terminal, had momentarily flown in and out of Rogers' nose and was now concealed in a chandelier hanging from the ceiling of Fortescue's restaurant. The fly's camera and microphone relayed the ensuing sight and sounds to the small screen on Ashto's computer. The First Commander had watched with great enjoyment as the miniature drone had zoomed down from the ceiling to the reporter's head and entered his left nostril, squeezed through his frontal sinuses and shot out of his right nostril causing the human to jump up, shout out and clutch his nose in what was, for Ashto, a very satisfying display. The overtures that Rogers had been blatantly making to Apprentice Commander Atia had been beyond the pale and the First Commander was so pleased that he had dispatched the drone to follow the hansom cab in which this odious Rogers individual had whisked Atia away to visit the smart looking restaurant in the West End.

Jealousy was not a trait that the Jaran First Commander was overly prone to. Jaran emotional attachments to the opposite sex were, generally speaking, fairly fluid and flexible. It wasn't unknown for a pair to stay in a monogamous relationship for many years, but it was an arrangement that was generally seen as somewhat quaintly old-fashioned and a trifle aberrant. In recent times on Jara Prime it had become the norm for males and females to have several concurrent relationships on the go at any one time and for any resultant children to be looked after in a communal crèche system instead of the more traditional nuclear family of bygone days. Ashto however, who had always considered himself a more traditional type of Jaran male, had had his views confirmed during the time he had known Apprentice Commander Atia. In the two years plus since their mission had commenced Ashto had become far closer to Atia than he had to any other individual ever before. Yes he had had many sexual relationships with both males and females in the past but never before would he have described those as anything other than indulgences designed to satisfy biological and physical urges. With Atia it had been different. Their rapport had developed slowly from a purely recreational sexual one to one that exhibited caring, closeness and yes – love. When Atia had accepted Rogers' offer to take her for dinner Ashto began to worry that his own feelings towards her were perhaps not being reciprocated in the way he had assumed and so he felt jealous for the first time in his life. It was a strange feeling Ashto had to admit but at the present time it had taken over the whole of his thought processes. As he watched the young newspaper reporter standing up convinced that the drone fly was still in situ somewhere in his nasal passageways with Atia peering intently into his nose obviously trying to stifle a laugh, the First Commander felt gratified that Rogers' plans for a convivial evening had been spoiled.

Back in Fortescues' Restaurant matters had calmed down somewhat and Atia and Rogers had sat down and were able to finish their meal although the newspaper reporter could not help occasionally holding his nose and attempting to clear it in such a noisy fashion that still more tutting was emitted from diners on adjacent tables.

'I am almost totally convinced, Mr Rogers, that the errant insect did fly out of your nose and headed for the large chandelier over our heads. Could we continue our analysis of the recent murders that was so quickly curtailed by your indisposition?'

'Of course, Mrs Ashton,' replied the still flustered and red-faced Rogers, 'I would like to hear more from you about the possible motivation of the so-called Jack the Ripper. Or perhaps the perpetrator is a Jill the Ripper?'

'No, Mr Rogers, the murderer is definitely a male. Everything so far that we know about the murderer's profile points to that fact. Whoever is responsible has a deep and fundamental hatred for women that have, perhaps for no fault of their own, fallen on hard times. I believe that he has a particular loathing for those women who have turned to street prostitution in order to scrape together the means to survive, although it has not yet been proven that all the murdered females had been engaged in that particular trade. The man responsible for the killings knows Whitechapel very well. Only someone with a great familiarity for the area would be able to slip away so stealthily without being seen and disappear so quickly without a trace.'

'And what do you think, Mrs Ashton, of the oft repeated accusation that only someone with medical or anatomical skill could have eviscerated two of the bodies, post mortem, in such a comprehensive fashion?'

'Well, Mr Rogers, you saw the body of the unfortunate Catherine Eddowes. Do you believe that any anatomical knowledge would have been needed to carve up her face in such an extensive way?'

'Indeed, Mrs Ashton, but what about the removal of certain organs from her body, the missing kidney for example? Here was the murderer operating in virtual darkness and yet he was able to locate one of the woman's kidneys before cutting it out and taking off with it. Surely that presupposes some knowledge of human anatomy?'

'More likely, Mr Rogers, that the perpetrator of the murders has knowledge of the internal workings of animals. There are very many slaughterers and butchers in the Whitechapel and Spitlefields districts and each one of them would be able to recognise and locate the various organs of sheep, cows and pigs as part of their daily work. These men too are a common sight in the East End as they walk the streets in aprons and clothes that still bear the gory traces of their chosen employment. The spattered bloodstains of animals appear quite indistinguishable from that of humans and people of Whitechapel would not look twice at such a tradesman marked in such a way. Neither would they comment at the sight of someone carrying around the sharp knives necessary for their profession.'

'That is indeed what the doctor giving evidence at the Eddowes inquest seemed to imply, Mrs Ashton. You have summed up the situation very well although the general feeling out on the streets of the East End I believe is still that the murderer may well be a West End toff used to spending his leisure hours in the less salubrious areas of the city in search of poor unfortunates to slaughter. One theory I have heard expressed recently is that Jack the Ripper is a well to do society medical man out to avenge himself on certain ladies of the night who were responsible for infecting his son with some terrible intimate disease that led to his demise.'

'That is a somewhat fanciful theory in my humble opinion, Mr Rogers. While not beyond the realms of possibility it would surely be far more difficult for such a person to negotiate the streets of Whitechapel with such a high degree of anonymity as would be necessary to disappear with such acumen and stealth. I know from comments made about Mr Ashton and myself that anyone who appears to be better attired than is the norm can be subject to some comment and scrutiny. A toff walking the streets late at night carrying anything looking like a bag full of medical paraphernalia and with possible bloodstains on his clothes, whether from the West End or indeed from the London Hospital on the Whitechapel Road, would be instantly considered unusual enough to be arrested by the police or quickly apprehended by concerned residents.'

'But, Mrs Ashton, what if the toff had a temporary residence in the East End that allowed him to disappear to after each killing. If a man like that spent his weekends say living in Whitechapel surely he would be able to get to know the local area with its narrow streets and alleyways well enough to navigate his way around just like someone born and bred in the region. I know of a well-to-do artist, for example, who divides his time between living in his well-appointed studio in Chelsea and also in a rented room in Whitechapel. Your husband, to use another example, whilst not a West End toff, but whatever the American equivalent would be, must surely know the area as well as any local by now. If, for the sake of argument, Mr Ashton were Jack the Ripper, then he would be more than adept at avoiding capture by retreating to the rather rundown guesthouse from where I collected you this evening.'

By now Atia and Rogers had selected some cheese and savory biscuits from a trolley wheeled to their table and were working their way through some exceptionally tasty cheeses and sipping coffee.

'I hope, Mr Rogers, that you were not accusing my husband of being Jack the Ripper. I would be very unhappy if you were. He would not even harm the fly that was so bothering you a short while ago.'

Right on cue the fly-drone that had been secreted on the chandelier busy transmitting the visuals and conversation between Atia and Rogers took off, dropped down to where the Evening Standard man sat and flew straight into his mouth that was open to receive a piece of camembert and biscuit. Rogers leapt up for the third time, gagging and spitting out bits of food along with the drone. Again the nearby diners, also attempting to enjoy their cheese course, tutted and even in some cases expressed phrases such as 'good lord,' 'disgraceful' and 'what on earth?'

Back in his guesthouse room First Commander Ashto smiled with satisfaction. He doubted whether the human newspaper reporter who had been casting lascivious looks at Margot for most of the evening would be allowed back into the restaurant where he had taken her. Ashto had to admit that the food the two had been served had appeared extremely palatable. He had witnessed the whole of their meal via the ultra high definition camera in the fly-drone and the beef they had eaten as well as the cheese with which they had been served looked very appetising. While watching Atia and Rogers eat their meal Ashto had had to make do with some of the desiccated food they had brought with them from the ship and now he felt hungry again. Tomorrow he would experiment with the replicator and see if he could get it to produce facsimiles of the cheeses that Atia had been offered at the restaurant. Ashto had attempted in the past to get the replicator to reproduce Earth foodstuffs but his efforts had always ended in extremely bland tasting results. He speculated that the replicator would need to have more relevant data inputted into its memory before it could produce Earth food that tasted, as well as looked, the way it should.

Ashto's attention returned to the scene in the restaurant where the Apprentice Commander and Rogers had finished their meal, suffered the pointed looks of their fellow diners and some of the waiting staff and were now leaving the dining room. As they collected their coats from the cloakroom attendant Ashto carefully followed them with the fly-drone, watching them and listening to their conversation.

'Well thank you for an interesting evening, Mr Rogers.'

The newspaper reporter, still a little red in the face, smiled somewhat self-consciously and said, 'we must do this again, Mrs Ashton, although I doubt if I will be allowed to set foot in this particular establishment in the future.'

'That would be unfortunate, Mr Rogers. If it is any solace to you that was by far the nicest meal I have had since arriving in London.'

'That is most gratifying Mrs Ashton … Margot. Will you allow me to accompany you back to Whitechapel?'

'That will not be necessary, Mr Rogers, I am very used to riding in a hansom cab on my own.'

'Of course, Mrs Ashton, in that case I will probably see you again at day two of the Catherine Eddowes inquest this coming Thursday.'

'You will indeed, Mr Rogers, just as long as my press pass still allows me entrance to the reporters' gallery.'

Mr Rogers smiled at Atia before taking her hand and kissing it. 'Until then, Mrs Ashton.'

Watching the actions of Rogers fawning on the Apprentice Commander, First Commander Ashto was tempted to again send the fly-drone into action. This time he considered directing it up one of Rogers's trouser legs before dismissing the idea. He did not want Atia to receive any more public attention than she had already and so decided to let the newspaper reporter go on his way unmolested. Ashto used the fly-drone to follow the hansom that Atia hailed and as she approached Whitechapel he directed it to fly inside the cab and land on Atia's hand.

'That was very unnecessary, Trevor. I did not need your protection from the likes of Mr Rogers,' said Atia raising her hand in front of her face and speaking directly to the fly-drone. However, your remote intervention made for a very entertaining and amusing evening indeed. We must reserve a table at Fortescues' at some time in the future, you will, I believe appreciate the food there, which was delicious. In the meantime, as you can see I will soon return to the guesthouse and from that time I will consider myself off duty if you perceive my full meaning.'

Back in their guesthouse room Ashto smiled fondly at the computer screen where an image of Atia was displayed.

He couldn't reply to her comment as the fly-drone had no internal speaker but he knew that Atia could visualize him in her mind's eye and simply blew her a kiss, yet another earth trait to which he had recently taken a liking.

My greetings and utmost felicitations to the esteemed members of the Sub-Committee.

Our mission to the planet Earth continues in a satisfactory way. As I stated in my last report some of our time and energies are now focused on finding the perpetrator of the Whitechapel murders, events that have caused much consternation among the population of the local area in which Apprentice Commander Atia and I are based. We remain convinced that fully understanding the reactions of the humans in this area to these tragic events, as well as observing how the authorities go about tracking down the killer, will shed a great amount of illumination on how Earth humans comport themselves both individually and as a group.

Over the last few days we have been striving hard to ascertain whether we can utilise some organic material the Apprentice Commander was able to recover from the dead body of the latest of the victims of the so-called Jack the Ripper. The material, some skin and hair was found under the fingernails of the dead female who, Atia believes, was able to scratch the killer's hand or arm even as he wielded the knife that murdered her. We have analysed the substance and transferred the resultant DNA data to the ship's computer and then instructed it to utilise the satellites, which have now been recalibrated, to scan for possible DNA matches throughout the London area. We are hoping that the computer via its scans will be able to compare the DNA held in its database with any trace elements left around the city and so enable us to identify the killer and lead the police to apprehend him. At the moment Atia and I do not even know if this procedure is possible. It has, to my knowledge, never been achieved before, but we are prepared to try it in order to stop this merciless killer before he kills again. So far there has not been another murder for 9 days but everyone expects this 'Jack the Ripper' to strike again sooner rather than later.

The Apprentice Commander and I were puzzled for a while by the antipathy local humans tended to show towards the police and their collective efforts in finding the murderer. After some further scanning of police records we have, we believe, discovered the reason for this seeming anomalous behaviour. Last year there had been a gathering of some ten thousand people in a place called Trafalgar Square, which is a large meeting place in the middle of London. These humans were protesting against unemployment and the government's handling of the situation in Ireland, which is a part of this state where a separatist movement has recently been growing in importance and adherents. These demonstrators were addressed by a number of important individuals who are locally very well known, such as a female political activist called Annie Besant and a male poet and designer by the name of William Morris. The police and the armed military were brought in to disperse the gathering, resulting in one person dying and some 75 individuals suffering serious injuries. The man held to be responsible for this 'Bloody Sunday', as the press soon labeled it, was the Metropolitan Police Commissioner, Sir Charles Warren, the very same individual who now bears overall responsibility for the police force's attempts to find the Whitechapel murderer. So the policing authorities started off being unpopular and, because of their signal lack of success in finding the Whitechapel killer, their popularity, particularly among the people of Whitechapel, has fallen still further. The general lack of confidence in the police has manifested itself in a number of ways. Foremost among these have been the setting up of local so-called vigilance committees in the Whitechapel and Spitlefields areas. These organisations have so far confined themselves to writing letters to the press and urging the authorities to offer incentives for the capture of the Whitechapel murderer in the form of monetary rewards. It is quite possible to assume that if the murders continue and the police fail in their attempts to apprehend the killer then these 'committees' might resort to more direct forms of vigilantism.

What all of this tells us about the humans living in this city is manifold but fundamentally it indicates that unless the people of planet Earth are treated in a very careful and equitable fashion they can quickly turn on any governing authorities they perceive as being inefficient or unfair. This obviously has lessons for any possible Jaran Federation incursion into the life of this planet particularly in terms of how the local populace perceives that intervention in the first instance. A soft touch will be needed by Jaran officials when or if the time comes but obviously I will elucidate further on this matter when I present my final report to the Sub-Committee at the culmination of our five-year orientation mission.

In two days' time Apprentice Commander Atia hopes to attend the second day of the inquest on the last murder victim. There she will probably meet again the newspaper reporter who has recently been paying her some unwanted attention even to the extent of asking her to accompany him for a meal, an invitation that, here on Earth, usually means that the interest shown is rather more than transitory. Atia did attend the meal with this Mr Rogers, as he calls himself, but the event did not go quite as well as he intended. The story of how I caused the human male some mild discomfiture during the meal is one that I am sure I will tell many times in the future at social gatherings back on Jara Prime.

With my utmost loyalty, etcetera,
First Commander Treve Pacton Ashto.

15

Inspector Reid

Inspector Edmund Reid was one of the most remarkable men in London. An ex-sailor, ex-pastry-cook, actor, magician and singer who also held the record at the time for the highest ascent in a balloon and who was the first person in England to make a parachute jump. He was a policeman of tenacious reputation despite being, at 5 feet 6 inches tall, 2 inches shorter than the normal requisite height for entry into the Metropolitan Police Service. Above all, as Head of CID in Whitechapel, he was the scourge of criminals throughout the East End of London.

On this morning of Wednesday 10th October Reid interrupted his otherwise purposeful walk up Goulston Street by stopping outside one of the entrances to the building known as Wentworth Model Dwellings. It was here that Sir Charles Warren, the Metropolitan Police Commissioner, had ordered Reid's officers to erase the words that had been chalked on the black painted wall just inside the entrance. They had been scrawled there soon after the double murder of the 30th September, almost certainly by the murderer, as they were written just above the spot where part of Catherine Eddowes' apron, torn and bloody, had been deliberately dropped. This Ripper, thought Reid, was leaving clues for the police to find as part of the game he was playing. The chalked message should have been photographed as evidence but Warren had ordered that it was to be sponged off the wall with immediate effect. Luckily one of Reid's uniformed men had scribbled down the words in his notebook and this remained the only rendering of the message, which had read: *The Juwes are the men that will not be blamed for nothing.* The meaning of these strange words remained as unclear to Reid as it was to everyone else and perhaps it did not really mean anything but was just simply another move in Jack's little game; misdirection for the police to follow blindly. But getting rid of the words seemed to show a complete disregard for the rules of evidence as far as Reid was concerned. Commissioner Warren had believed that the reference to the Juwes – although the word was obviously spelt wrongly – would have immediately led to riots and possibly the lynching of some of the many Jewish people who resided in the Whitechapel district. Reid had agreed that the words could have been incendiary in an already volatile atmosphere but he could not understand why the chalked graffito could not have been covered up and guarded by uniformed officers while the police photographer was sent for.

Reid stepped away from the entrance, sighed and continued the short walk up Goulston Street, where market traders were already doing brisk business and into Bell Lane, the ultimate objective of his early morning walk. He could have sent the upright Bill Thick, his trusted sergeant to call on Mr Trevor Ashton and his wife but there was something about the so-called American writer that Reid wanted to check out for himself. He wanted to look into the eyes of both of the Ashtons and see what made them tick.

Reid knocked on the door of Mrs Smith's Select Guesthouse and was quickly confronted by the eponymous lady herself. After a brief explanation Reid was led to the room in which the Ashtons were staying and Mrs Smith, dressed in black and looking particularly excited that this burly, short but impressive looking Detective Inspector in a loud check suit was taking such an interest in two of her residents, did all that she could to enter the room along with him. However, one glance from the formidable looking Reid in her direction was enough to send her scurrying away.

'I apologise for having to call on you so early in the morning, Mr Ashton, but there were a number of aspects I would like to clarify with you,' said Inspector Reid removing his bowler hat as he walked into the room.

'That is quite all right Inspector,' said Ashto somewhat nervously for he had just noticed he had left his computer device on the writing desk and quickly moved to put himself between it and Inspector Reid. 'This is my wife Margot.'

Reid nodded at Atia, 'Mrs Ashton, I am pleased to meet you.'

'Likewise, Inspector,' said Atia holding out her hand for the Inspector to shake.

'Well, Inspector how can I be of further help to you?' said Ashto turning slightly towards the window and slipping the computer into his coat pocket.

'Thank you Mr Ashton, but really my question is aimed at both of you. You are, or you claim to be, from the United States and are visiting London in order to write a book about the many interesting sights you come across in the city. The book's purpose is for the education of your fellow Americans who might one day visit our city?'

'That is correct Inspector.'

'And am I also correct in saying that Mrs Ashton is acting as an assistant helping you to compile this volume?'

'That is also correct Inspector,' said Ashto.

'In that case would it be possible to see the notes that you have so far made in relation to your book. I am not an author myself, although at some point in the future I hope to rectify that fact, but I would assume that the research needed to generate such a tome must be voluminous in the extreme.'

Ashto was momentarily lost for a reply but luckily Atia was able to continue the conversation with the senior police officer. 'It is an unusual request, Inspector, but one that if pressed I will comply with but first can I ask you why you would want to see the notes we have made in the process of researching my husband's proposed book?'

'You can, Mrs Ashton. I am one of the officers to have been charged with apprehending the Whitechapel murderer, lately known as Jack the Ripper. We have certain information that has led us to the belief that the perpetrator of the recent murders could be an American and so, as I intimated to your husband recently, we are interviewing all those individuals who appear to have some affiliation with the United States of America and who are currently present in London. I would therefore like to examine your notes simply to confirm that you are who you say you are and that you are truly involved in the planning of a book about our city. We can then eliminate the pair of you from our inquiries'

'I understand, Inspector. It is part of my function as an assistant to my husband to write and organise, in various distinct sections, notes that he will one day refer to in order to help him to write his planned book.' Atia walked across to the desk where Ashto still stood, pleased that he was able to have secreted the computer away from the sight of this intelligent human who would doubtless have had a myriad of questions to ask about the small digital device. Atia picked up a thick black folder from one of the drawers in the desk and walked over to Inspector and handed it to him. The Inspector had a perfunctory rifle through the pages held neatly together in the folder. Even with such a brief examination he could see that these notes were the result of someone who was painstaking and organised and who also had beautifully legible handwriting.

'Mrs Ashton I would congratulate you on the orderliness and your diligence of your note making. I am sure that Mr Ashton will be very grateful to be able to use such well ordered, neatly written and comprehensive notes when he finally comes to write his book.' Reid smiled at Atia. "Mrs Ashton, if ever you have any spare time in your doubtless busy life perhaps you could come along to Leman Street Police Station and teach my fellow officers about the importance of keeping records and notes in such a meticulous and tidy fashion.' Reid handed the folder back to Atia who smiled at him in return.

'Well Inspector is there any other way in which we can be of service to you?' said Ashto, feeling slightly smug.

'There is one thing, Mr Ashton. Can you tell me why you lied to me the other day when I asked you about New York?'

'I'm sorry, Inspector, I do not understand.'

'Mr Ashton, when I asked you about an area of New York City called Kings you said that you knew of it. As I mentioned to you when we spoke before I have spent time in that city and nowhere is there a place called Kings.'

Ashto looked at the Police Inspector quizzically. 'Did you really say Kings, Inspector? I was under the obviously mistaken belief that you said Queens. Unfortunately my hearing has not fully recovered from the long sea voyage we took back in July when, to my great embarrassment, I spent most of my time suffering from sea sickness and a doctor has since informed me that that particular affliction occasionally results in temporary damage to the inner ear which takes some while to heal.'

Inspector Reid, widely known in the London police force for his taciturn nature and poker face, could not help but betray his skepticism a little at the First Commander's reply. He did, however, shrug his shoulders slightly in a gesture that implied he had bigger fish to fry than the Ashtons and headed towards the door. Just before he opened the door to leave he turned to the Jaran pair saying: 'Well goodbye, Mr and Mrs Ashton. By the way in the course of your researches about our city you ought to visit a certain Mr Merrick who resides at the London Hospital in Whitechapel Road. He and his experiences would, I guarantee you, lead to a very interesting chapter in your proposed book.' With that Inspector Reid placed his bowler hat back on his head, nodded to the Ashtons and left.

First Commander Ashto breathed a sigh of relief. "How on Jara did you manage to produce those handwritten notes? I thought you were entering all our data directly into the ship's computer."

The Apprentice Commander smiled broadly. 'When you told me about your encounter with the human law officer called Reid I took the precaution of instructing the ship's computer to send copies of all my notes, all codified and in my handwriting, to our portable replicator. I had an intuition that the Inspector might decide to show up and ask for some sort of proof of who we are and I was obviously correct in my assumption.'

'If there is anyone else quite so resourceful as yourself in the whole of the Jaran Explorer Executive I would be extremely surprised,' said Ashto smiling with admiration at his Apprentice Commander.

Atia beamed with pleasure at the First Commander's words. In spite of the fact that they now acted as monogamous lovers and were, to all intents, in Earth terms at least, a married couple, Ashto was still her commanding officer and such a comment from him was immensely valuable in terms of her future promotion prospects. 'Thank you very much Trevor I will always do my best. What do make of the Inspector's comment about visiting this Mr Merrick at the London Hospital?'

'I do believe that he was testing us, Margot. I have heard of this Joseph Merrick who became well known two years ago when his story first emerged. I think that a visit to see the individual in question would be prudent if we are to maintain our cover story of writing a book about London that will be useful to travellers from the United States. Such visitors would, I believe, be quite fascinated to hear about Mr Merrick, and I am sure that Inspector Reid will be checking up that we have indeed paid a visit to the residence of the so-called 'Elephant Man'.

16

The Elephant Man

The day after Inspector Reid's visit was the day on which the inquest into the death of Catherine Eddowes was due to reopen. However, Atia had decided that there was a good chance that Reid, or one of his subordinates, would also attend the event and so felt it would not be safe for her to again take on the guise of a New York City newspaper reporter, utilise her forged press pass and reignite Reid's suspicions. Anyway she believed that she had probably learned all there was to know about the poor woman's death and a brief scan of police records would almost certainly fill in any gaps in her knowledge. No doubt Mr Rogers of the Evening Standard would be extremely upset that she wouldn't be present at the inquest thought Atia, smiling to herself.

To comply with Inspector Reid's suggestion First Commander Ashto and Apprentice Commander Atia arranged to visit Mr Merrick at the London Hospital on Friday 12th October. Ashto dropped a request in at the hospital later on that Wednesday afternoon and had received an immediate response from Frederick Treves, Merrick's doctor and friend, who said that Mr Merrick would be only too pleased to receive Mr and Mrs Ashton in his rooms at the hospital.

The London Hospital had been situated in the Whitechapel Road since 1757 and was one of the first in the country to have a medical school attached to it. When it had been built the hospital stood very much on its own, with that part of East London sparsely built upon. By 1888, however, the imposing facade of the hospital loomed large over the narrow streets, slums and rookeries of Whitechapel. As Ashto and Atia entered the hospital's impressive entrance they were very aware that a plain-clothes policeman was following them who was, Ashto considered, remarkably unsubtle in his surveillance techniques.

'Well we were certainly correct in our assumption that Inspector Reid will be kept informed of our movements. I can only hope that he and his fellow officers are just as diligent in looking for the Ripper,' said Ashto quietly to his Apprentice Commander.

At the reception desk Mr Treves was sent for and the Jaran couple did not have to wait long before the slightly built doctor appeared, greeted them in a friendly fashion and led them down to the basement of the hospital. Joseph Merrick, always for some reason referred to as John by the doctor, lived permanently in two rooms that had been specially adapted for him in the bowels of the hospital.

Before knocking on the door Treves turned to Atia and Ashto, a serious look on his mustachioed face.

'I must warn you, especially you Mrs Ashton, that John's appearance can be somewhat shocking to those who meet him for the first time. While saying that, I would also mention that if you can possibly overlook the grotesque nature of his facial and bodily deformities you will find him to be a person of great charm and of no little intelligence. When I first met him I assumed that he was an imbecile incapable of any significant thought processes, but I soon had my assumption disproved. Perhaps tragically, under the circumstances, John has a quick mind and a gregarious nature that means he greatly appreciates any social interaction that may come his way. Since being rescued from his previous life as a freak show exhibit and coming to live at the hospital John has received many visitors from the higher echelons of society including Her Royal Highness the Princess of Wales and he has invariably charmed them all.' Treves smiled nervously at the pair and then rapped gently on the door.

'Come in,' shouted a thin and reedy voice.

The door was opened by Treves who ushered the Jaran pair into the room.

'John, may I introduce Mr and Mrs Trevor Ashton, who hail from the United States of America and are in our country to write a book about London for the benefit of those of their countrymen who may follow in their stead?'

Joseph Merrick stood at a table in the centre of the room he referred to as his drawing room. He had been engrossed in constructing a cardboard model of a church, or cathedral, which stood half complete on the table. As he looked up both Ashto and Atia managed to stifle a gasp as they could see the full horror of the human male's disfigurements.

Merrick shuffled across to the Jaran pair and held out his left hand, the only part of his body that appeared to be normal. Ashto and Atia shook hands with Merrick also using their left hands and managed to smile at the poor man whose story of his suffering prior to meeting Frederick Treves had become well known to the public in the newspapers of two years ago.

'I am so very pleased to meet you. You are the first people from the United States of America I have ever met in the entirety of my life so far,' said Merrick in his strangely piping voice that was accompanied by odd slurring and unintended whistling sounds.

'We are also very pleased to meet you, Mr Merrick,' said Ashto still amazed as to the extent of the deformities of the slightly built man who faced him. The most remarkable and perhaps horrifying aspect of the so-called Elephant Man was the size of his head, which seemed to take up a large proportion of his overall body. Most of the individual features on his face were virtually unrecognisable as those of an actual human being. The dome of Merrick's head was massively enlarged and misshapen with great swellings of protuberant lumpy skin evident on the right side of his face. His eyes looked normal but appeared small and sunken in the great head that dwarfed all of his features. His nose was broad and flat without any discernable form and his lips were so large and shapeless that it seemed remarkable that he could speak as well as he could. Sparse strips of lank dark hair had been carefully arranged neatly on the top and back of his bulbous head. His right hand was so enlarged and malformed that it looked like it should have belonged to an entirely different type of life form. Ashto had once seen the bipedal humanoid inhabitants of Iainm, one of the moons in orbit about a gas giant in the Jaran planetary system, who he thought until now, to have had the strangest appearance of any sapient creature he had ever come into contact with. However, this human called Joseph Merrick was by far the oddest-looking person he had ever seen on any of his visits to alien planets. To think that this poor individual had been fending for himself in a cruel and unsympathetic world before he had been taken under the caring wing of Frederick Treves was nothing more than tragic, thought Ashto.

'It is a great pleasure to me,' said Merrick in his wispy voice, 'that people such as yourselves come to visit me here at the London Hospital. As you will understand it is very difficult for me to leave the confines of my rooms to see other people. I used to wander freely around the hospital in the past but I believe I had an unsettling effect on many of the patients so I was advised by Doctor Treves to desist that particular activity. So now I solely stay in my rooms, which have been so beautifully arranged and decorated for me by the staff here at the hospital – and the nurses and cleaners here look after me to such a wonderful extent that I consider myself to be the most fortunate individual in London.'

The Jaran pair dutifully looked around the small room crowded with many photographs and mementoes that had obviously been given to the young man by his many upper-class visitors. It occurred to both Ashto and Atia at the same time that in many ways Mr Merrick was still being displayed to certain members of the public who had come to gawp in amazement at the poor man's disabilities. Even in such comfortable surroundings with a fire roaring away in the fireplace and with velvet curtains draped by the window Merrick was still the Elephant Man exhibited in a veritable freak show.

Treves noticed that Atia had a solitary tear running down her cheek. 'I am sure that John is extremely impressed by your ability to understand what he is saying. I have to admit that when I first encountered him it was difficult for me to discern everything he vocalised, but you, Mr and Mrs Ashton, seem very adept in that area.'

'Indeed,' said Atia, desperately trying to overcome the lump that seemed to have developed in her throat, 'I think that Mr Merrick annunciates his words very well and his speech is as conducive to understanding as anyone Mr Ashton and I have encountered so far in our visit to London.' Atia smiled to cover up the great sadness she felt in regard to this young man who was so burdened by disfigurement and yet still managed to maintain a friendly disposition to others.

'Is this all your own work?' said Ashto walking across to the table and bending down to examine the half finished model of the church.

'It is,' said Merrick. 'I am very fortunate in having a number of activities to pass my time here in my rooms. It is very rare for me to leave the hospital although recently I was taken to the theatre for the very first time. It was a wonderful and exciting experience that I will cherish for my entire life and I think that Doctor Treves will attest to the fact that I could not be stopped from talking about it at length for days afterwards. However, I do tire rather easily, as Doctor Treves will confirm and so I have to moderate my activities and rest as often as I need.' Merrick pointed to a door that led into his bedroom. He was obviously keen to show his visitors the full extent of the rooms in which he lived and so gently guided the Jaran couple into his sleeping quarters.

'What a charming room,' said Atia looking around at the small bedroom that contained a bed, a bedside cabinet, a table with a washbowl and jug and many framed pictures on the wall. These included a print of a stern looking Queen Victoria and one of Alexandra, the Princess of Wales to which was attached a paper red rose. Merrick saw Atia admiring the picture and was keen to tell her about it. 'That beautiful portrait was given to me by Her Royal Highness herself when she visited me in these very rooms. She stood exactly where you are now standing, Mrs Ashton, as I had to be in my bed on that particular day due to my feeling somewhat out of sorts. She was even more beautiful in real life than in the picture,' he said, admiration in his voice. 'I made the paper rose on the same day in her honour.'

'I notice that your bed is arranged in an unusual fashion,' said Ashto looking at Merrick's pillows and blankets, which were carefully propped up against the headboard and wall.

Merrick replied to Ashto with a great sadness in his reedy voice. 'Unfortunately it is necessary for me to sleep sitting up, Mr Ashton. The great weight of my head you see would, if I lay down in the normal fashion, cause me to experience breathing difficulties as well as a great pain in the region of my neck and throat. It is the one thing in my life that I would like to change for the better. I would love to spend just one night lying down to sleep in the same fashion as the rest of God's children. It is a prayer I make every evening. Sometimes, you understand, I find it very uncomfortable sitting up with my head resting on my knees but it is sadly the only safe way that I can sleep.' Merrick spoke with a quaver in his thin voice and as he spoke tears ran freely down Atia's face. Instinctively the Jaran Apprentice Commander stepped towards Merrick, threw her arms about the small young man she towered above and hugged him to her bosom. It was a gesture that while not unusual back on Jara Prime was one that was usually reserved for close friends and family members who were likely to be absent for an extended period of time, or who had recently returned from a long journey to an outlying planetary system. In this reserved Victorian London of 1888 it was something that few people did in the everyday course of their lives especially when faced with someone who looked so out of the ordinary as Joseph Merrick. Merrick responded to Atia's heartfelt hug by burying his great misshapen head into her shoulder and wetting her jacket with his tears. Ashto and Frederick Treves looked on. Neither Earth bound doctor of medicine or Jaran space explorer, had ever witnessed anything quite so touchingly emotional or so utterly tear provoking as the scene before them in that small bedroom in the basement of the London Hospital.

Sometime later, in the corridor outside Merrick's rooms, Frederick Treves turned and spoke to the Jaran couple. 'Mrs Ashton your heartwarming gesture towards John was, I think, perhaps the greatest example of human empathy I have ever witnessed in my entire career as a medical man. I thank you with all my heart for your kind action.' Atia smiled, partly at the irony of Doctor Treves' statement and partly because she felt, under the circumstances that it was a fairly insignificant response in relation to the daily problems faced by the young, disfigured human male.

'Doctor Treves, has it been discovered what medical affliction has caused Mr Merrick's extreme deformities? Presumably he was born that way?' said Ashto.

'We do not know how or why the affliction came about, Mr Ashton. John apparently was completely normal until the age of five when he started to display a thickening of the skin and the growth of the boney protuberances one can see all too readily now. He tells a fanciful story of how his mother, while expecting him, was knocked to the ground by a runaway circus elephant. It was a long held but erroneous belief by some that traumatic experiences suffered by expectant mothers could affect the child she carried in ways that only might transpire in later years. Modern science has disproved this theory, of course, as no more than an old wives' tale. What really caused the grotesque deformities in John's body we do not know but perhaps at some point in the future when we understand rather more about such matters we will be able to prevent such aberrations occurring.'

'What is the prognosis for Mr Merrick's future health, doctor?' said Atia still trying hard to stop the flow of tears. There were few times in her life when she had felt quite so sad. She was at that moment almost on the verge of telling Doctor Treves that she would consult the ship's computer and get it to analyse and then diagnose the complaint from which the young Joseph Merrick suffered but her professionalism ultimately prevented her from doing so.

'Mrs Ashton, when I first came across John being displayed in a freak show on the other side of the Whitechapel Road I fully expected him to expire within two or so years due to the serious heart and lung conditions he was suffering from. However, since he moved into the hospital his health has improved somewhat and it is now uncertain how long he will be with us. All we can do is provide John with as much care and attention as we can. The nurses who look after him at first were frightened by his appearance but since they have come to know him and the gentleness of his nature they simply view him as another of God's creatures who is need of their care.'

Ashto and Atia stood on the steps of the London Hospital in the autumn sunshine. They had said thank you and farewell to Frederick Treves who, moments before, had assured them that in spite of the many mutual tears shed their visit will have raised Mr Merrick's spirits greatly and will have provided him with many hours of conversation with his nurses about the very beautiful American angel who had visited him on this day.

'Do you know, Trevor, this meeting with Joseph Merrick has made me all the more determined to track down the man they call Jack the Ripper as quickly as possible.'

'Please explain, Margot.'

"It is so very simple, Trevor. While good people like Joseph suffer daily through no fault of their own, in a fashion that is almost beyond understanding, I feel that we should harness all of our efforts in the tracking down of evil in the shape of the so-called Ripper who appears to stalk the streets of Whitechapel with seeming impunity. I vow on this day to waste no time at all in linking up with the ship's computer and searching for the DNA of the killer. And when we find him I believe, Trevor, that we should offer no mercy to the execrable Earth human who has perpetrated the murders and who has caused Whitechapel to feel fear on such a widespread scale.'

Ashto nodded. He had never seen any Jaran exhibit the sort of determination and restrained anger than he saw in Atia now. Jarans were invariably measured, dispassionate and calm under duress but Atia had not only harnessed all of those traits she had also developed a 'fire in her belly' to use an Earth phrase, that Ashto had never seen in any of his race before. More in love with her than ever he placed her arm into his and the two walked silently and resolutely back to their room at Mrs Smith's Select Guesthouse.

He was beginning to feel impatient. God had not spoken to him for many days now and he was starting to worry that He had abandoned him. The newspapers had christened him 'Jack the Ripper', a nickname he liked and one that he was happy to adopt. It was a good name. It was a name he hoped would instill terror into the hearts of those whores who still walked the streets and conducted their filthy business.

In the meantime he planned and waited. He already knew that the next time he sent a harlot to hell things would be different. Next time he would complete his God-given work inside the unholy room of a whore. He would get her to invite him in after finding a suitable slut in a pub. He had already marked out one of that godless breed in the Ten Bells; a place where he sometimes drank alone after work. He would talk to her. He would cajole her, make jokes, look into her eyes and charm her; he was good at that. His mother used to say he had the gift of the gab and could charm the birds out of the trees if he had a mind to.

His mother. When she had died he found himself alone for the first time in his life. Whoever had been his father had left before he could recall and all the rest of his mother's children were dead, all six of them taken by the colic, cholera or diphtheria. His mother then had gone out onto the streets in order, she said, to earn money to put food on the table. She would give herself to strangers in the dark alleys and grimy backyards of Whitechapel and sometimes she would even return home with them. He would lie awake listening to the sounds that came *from his mother's room and then cry himself to sleep. It was after his mother passed away that God started to talk to him and told him in no uncertain terms to rid the city of its whores. It would, of course, take him a very long time, there were so many of them; monstrous hoards of them, but he was prepared for that. However, for the moment God remained silent to him and the whores still plied their vile trade on the streets. He must wait, even though it was painful for him to do so. He must not go against God by anticipating His instructions and so, in the meantime, he must carry on performing his daily work and wait for His divine instruction to come his way.*

He picked up his long, sharp knife and chose the next young pig. He shoved it out of the pen and into the yard. The pig squealed in alarm as he grabbed it and propelled it awkwardly forward, its back legs hobbled by a short piece of rope. Animals always knew when death was near; they could smell the blood. That was, he had noticed, one of the differences between people and beasts. People never saw the blackness of death approach; it was always a surprise to them. Animals on the other hand sensed what was about to happen and this was the reason why this pig was trying, in its desperation, to slip from his grasp as its ear-piercing squeals and shrieks became even louder. His grasp was strong though; it had been honed since the age of fourteen. He straddled the pig, grabbed its head and forced it back, keeping his gloved hand well away from its mouth with its teeth that could easily take out a neat crescent of flesh. And then he drew his knife smoothly across the pig's throat and watched, fascinated, as the blood gushed out, the creature's eyes bulging with pain and shock. It was a sight that had always fascinated him. Within seconds he felt the animal go limp between his legs and then he hoisted it up by its hobbled back legs and attached in to the hook so that the rest of the blood could drain away. He stood watching the bright red blood create a viscous pool on the floor of the yard, before it slowly ran into the drain. He took off his thick leather gloves and briefly rubbed the puckered pink scar on the back of his hand where a deep scratch had been inflicted by the last of the whores he had dispatched. He put his gloves back on, took up his knife again and began to butcher the pig in his usual, practised way.

17

Deoxyribonucleic Acid

'Any tangible progress yet, Margot?' said First Commander Ashto.

Apprentice Commander Atia had sat at the desk with one of the small computer terminals in front of her since the early hours of the morning. Every now and again she pressed a key and ended up looking frustrated. 'I'm afraid there has been no progress as yet, Trevor. The ship's computer has analysed many millions of trace elements that have been secreted by Earth humans on clothes or left in public places throughout this vast city, smears of such things as blood, saliva, urine, semen and skin cells for example. I have programmed it to keep searching but it is a mammoth task even for the ship's computer to manage. We can only hope that it will be successful soon and we can track down the man responsible for the murders before he can commit any more atrocities.'

'I believe you have achieved all you can for the time being, Margot. I would suggest that we leave the computer link for now and go for our daily walk around the area. We must remember to have with us our notebooks and writing implements due to the very real risk that one of Inspector Reid's men is still observing our movements. We must look as though we take notes on paper rather than simply relying on our visual and audio equipment to record our experiences.'

'Yes, Trevor, you are correct although I would have remembered in any case,' said Atia a little sharply. It was evident to Ashto that the frustration felt by Atia was making her more and more impatient as each day passed, so intent was she on tracking down the man known as the Ripper.

Atia looked up at Ashto realising that she must have sounded rather terse in her reply. 'I apologise, Trevor. I must not let my frustration with our lack of progress regarding the DNA search make me somewhat short tempered.'

'That is quite all right, Margot. Your feelings in regard to the matter are completely understandable. Shall we leave? The weather outside looks clement enough at the moment and the morning will soon be over. A dense fog is forecast for later in the day across the whole of the city.

'Of course, Trevor,' said Atia standing up and slipping on her brown worsted jacket, placing her small brimmed hat on her head and picking up her shoulder bag.

Outside the guesthouse the Jaran couple turned left and walked up Bell Lane, into Crispin Street and past Dorset Street before stopping at Spitlefields Market on their right. As usual when crossing the roads in this city they had to carefully avoid stepping into the many large piles of horse dung lying in the street, an all too common feature of the busy main thoroughfares of London.

The frontage of Spitalfields Market, newly built in the previous year, looked bright and modern against the adjacent smoke-blackened brickwork of the houses and the many nearby commercial properties. The busy indoor market, with its impressively high glass and metal roof, was open seven days a week and was the place where many East End residents shopped for fruit, vegetables and meat. Atia and Ashto often on their daily walks enjoyed strolling through the market listening to the loud, inventive cries of the traders selling their produce and overhearing the cockney accents of the locals mingling in with the Yiddish language spoken by the many recent Jewish migrants to the area.

Ashto occasionally looked around to see if the pair was still being shadowed by one of Reid's officers. He decided that on this occasion they were not but he was careful to keep a notebook in his hand and occasionally wrote in it with his pencil. Over the previous few weeks Ashto had altered the type of clothes he wore during the day. He would still be identified as a toff by most of the residents of the local area but rather than wearing the silken top hat and dark formal clothes in which he had arrived in London he was now dressed, as was Atia, in attire more suited to everyday life in the city. He still found the garments unnecessarily heavy and bulky but he had begun to grow quite fond of the greenish-brown cape, tweed jacket, matching trousers and yellow waistcoat with its fashionable pocket watch that he had taken to wearing during his and Atia's daily walks. On his head he sported a soft deerstalker cap, an affectation he had adopted since he had first read about Sherlock Holmes in the novel *A Study in Scarlet,* which along with illustrations of the detective had first appeared in Beeton's Annual magazine earlier in the year. Around his neck he still wore a pointless long narrow piece of cloth tied in a knot but at least its orange colour was bright and cheerful looking.

Ashto and Atia stopped at a few of the market stalls and Atia, also with her notebook in full sight, made notes about any unfamiliar foodstuff she noticed or any interesting phrases or words she heard being spoken aloud by individuals. Occasionally she had to put up with suggestive remarks made by young market workers or youthful shoppers but she was well used to such comments by now and simply responded by smiling in her usual way. If she had been in her Maggie disguise she would have given the young men a suitably saucy and colourful mouthful of invective. She smiled at the thought and in some ways wished she could have another adventure in the role of the poor, homeless but feisty young woman again. Playing the part of Maggie had given her a marvelous sense of freedom in what she was allowed to do and say. That freedom contrasted greatly with her role of the much more conventional Margot Ashton, who had to conform to the rigid norms of middle class Victorian society. Atia sighed and put the thought to the back of her mind.

At a fruit stall Ashto purchased two apples and gave one to Atia to eat as they walked around the market. The apples reminded them both of the day they first arrived in London, just over two months ago, when everything they encountered was new and very alien to them. Since then they had learned a lot about this part of the planet Earth and like all members of the well-trained Jaran Explorer Executive they had adapted extremely quickly to their new surroundings. Even though they were considerably better off than the majority of the people that lived in the Whitechapel area they felt that they had successfully integrated into East End society and had very much grown to like the place and the majority of the humans they encountered there. Yes, certainly there was a great deal of poverty and many petty criminals in the area as well as more serious ones, like the Old Nichol Gang, that tended to blight the community, but generally speaking the average East End residents were straightforward individuals who just wanted to get on with their lives in circumstances that all found to be extremely exacting.

It was just as Ashto was finishing his apple, that he noticed the man who was following them. Without looking at the individual directly Ashto was able to discern that the he was young, tall for a human, wore a dark overcoat and bowler hat and sported a sparse ginger mustache. He looked extremely familiar but it took a few seconds for the First Commander to realise who the man actually was. Ashto moved closer to Atia and informed her of what he had just seen and was not surprised when the Apprentice Commander turned and looking directly at the man, smiled and beckoned him over. Rather sheepishly he walked up to Ashto and Atia, an embarrassed smile on his face.

'Trevor may I introduce Mr William Rogers of the Evening Standard. You may remember Mr Rogers was kind enough to treat me to dinner recently.'

'I am pleased to make your acquaintance, Mr Rogers,' said Ashto, a smile on his face as he shook the newspaper reporter's hand and fondly remembered the man's discomfiture when attacked by the fly-drone.

'I am very pleased to meet you, Mr Ashton. Your wife has told me a great deal about you and the book you are currently working on. It sounds extremely interesting. I trust it is progressing well,' said Rogers.

'It is, Mr Rogers, I thank you for inquiring. As you can see my wife and I are out this morning continuing to observe the people and places of this area of London as much as possible and collecting useful information for my book.'

'Indeed, Mr Ashton and are you intending to explore the rest of the city in the same amount of depth as you are currently doing in the Whitechapel and Spitlefields areas?'

'We intend to do exactly that, Mr Rogers. Mrs Ashton and myself have given ourselves the next five years to complete the task as comprehensively as possible.' Ashto couldn't help but notice that when Mr Rogers spoke he did so with a slight but discernable ugly twist to his mouth, what the Earth humans called a sneer.

'And during that time will Mrs Ashton take on any extra roles as well as that of your assistant?' Again the young reporter smiled in a way what he obviously intended to be interpreted as warm and friendly. To Ashto though there was something else behind those seemingly benign looking eyes, something less congenial than that which showed on the surface.

'I do believe, Mr Rogers, that I can answer for myself in that regard,' said Atia. 'I do not intend to take on any more roles other than the one I am currently involved in. Being a wife and assistant to my husband will be good enough for me in the future,' said Atia, who also had picked up the peripheral sense of threat in the young newspaperman's words.

'I am very glad to hear that, Mrs Ashton. My professional integrity would not allow me to ignore any further secret and untoward forays you were planning to make into the world of newspaper journalism'.

'There is no danger of that I assure you, Mr Rogers. But can I ask you why is it that you follow us in such a surreptitious way on this particular morning?' said Atia.

Rogers looked rather shamefaced again. This was a person who found his emotions hard to conceal, thought Ashto.

'It is a fair question, Mrs Ashton. I didn't actually set out to pursue you this morning but as I was walking along Dorset Street on newspaper business I noticed the two of you taking a constitutional walk and decided to follow you into the market. I would have made myself known to both of you eventually but, I have to admit, I was interested to see how Mr Ashton and his Assistant went about their business of research for this promised tome about which I have heard so much. After all you are alien visitors to this country and you may approach things differently than is the accepted norm when it comes to the gathering of information.'

Ashto again bridled at the slightly skeptical tone in the man's voice. What game was this human playing? What did he suspect? Was this Rogers someone that he and the Apprentice Commander ought to be concerned about? Rogers' use of the word 'alien' worried Ashto somewhat. Was it a word loaded with some sort of significance or was he reading more than he should have into the newspaperman's off the cuff phrasing?'

Atia still managed to smile at the young man as she spoke to him. 'Mr Rogers, you ought to be commended on your efforts by the editor of your newspaper, but I think that you would be much better employed perhaps, in terms of your chosen profession, if you spent a little more time looking for news items that your readers would find interesting rather than dogging the paths of two unremarkable people who are simply engaged in garnering information about the sights and sounds of this city.'

'Ha! You are doubtless correct in your analysis, Mrs Ashton. How someone can be so perceptive as well as so beautiful will remain a great mystery to me,' said Rogers smiling as he touched the brim of his bowler hat.

Inside Ashto felt his anger rising at the young man's over-enthusiastic blandishments aimed at the Apprentice Commander. Rogers was being deliberately provocative almost as if he was goading the Jaran First Commander into some sort of response. In his mind's eye Ashto imagined dealing a quick and sharp blow to Rogers' smug face that would render the newspaper reporter senseless for some time but there were far too many witnesses about to risk such an attack. However justified Ashto's potential bellicose actions might have been he did not want to be arrested by the police and have to deal with the likes of Inspector Reid again.

'Well, Mr Rogers, I think that Mrs Ashton and I will now take our leave of you and continue with our researches. I doubt very much that we will meet again,' said Ashto pointedly as he shook the hand of the young man and uncharacteristically patted him on the back of his right shoulder. Atia also shook hands with the young reporter before the Jaran pair turned and walked away arm-in-arm.

Rogers watched them as he took out his pipe from his pocket, placed it between his lips and lit it. He had only picked up the pipe-smoking habit recently; he had come to believe that breathing in the fragrant tobacco fumes enabled him to think problems through with increased clarity.

Ashto and Atia left the market hall and crossed over the road into Hanbury Street. This was the street where the Ripper had murdered Annie Chapman over a month ago. The pair passed number 29 and the passageway that the woman and the murderer must have walked down, either together or separately, before the hideous crime had taken place in the building's back yard. Ashto and Atia paused for a moment and looked at the building. They both felt sad and concerned that so far they done little to bring about an end to these terrible murders. Atia in particular had wracked her brain to think of other ways in which she could supply the ship's computer with more relevant data to assist it in the search for the murderer's DNA. The Jarans had a saying that related to the inherent extreme difficulty there was in locating a piece of information among many other similar items of data: 'It was like looking for a particular full stop in a library full of books,' they would say. The ship's computer endeavouring to find one tiny sample of DNA in a densely populated city of many millions of people was, she reasoned an even more difficult task with an equally unlikely outcome. Atia sighed at the thought, causing Ashto to look at her. He nodded as if he too had been thinking along much the same lines.

After Hanbury Street Ashto and Atia soon found themselves in Bucks Row and the site of the murder of Polly Nichols in August. That seemed a long time ago now and was another reminder of how the murderer was still free to stalk the streets and terrorise the local community. The First Commander and Apprentice Commander were pleased to leave the gloomy and narrow Bucks Row, pass Whitechapel underground railway station and cross over the Whitechapel Road in order to walk down the long and narrow Sidney Street. Soon they found themselves in Commercial Road and turned right where they eventually passed the corner of Berner Street, the road where Elizabeth Stride had met her grisly fate.

During their journey from Spitalfields market both Ashto and Atia had occasionally checked behind them to see if they were being tracked by Mr Rogers or by one of Reid's plain-clothes officers. The Jaran pair reasoned that anyone following them now was either extremely skilled at surveillance, which, on past experience, seemed unlikely, or that on this occasion both the Evening Standard newspaper reporter or the police of Inspector Reid's H Division had given up shadowing their every movement quite so assiduously.

At the end of Commercial Road the Jaran pair turned into Whitechapel High Street and passed by Aldgate railway station on the right. Ashto and Atia had travelled on the underground railway on one occasion only and hadn't enjoyed the experience at all. The smoke, ash and grit produced by the steam locomotives had been extremely unpleasant especially when it had been confined in the underground tunnels and it was impossible not to breathe some of it into their lungs. It had caused the Jaran pair to spend much of the next day coughing. Ashto and Atia had no doubt that the railway, currently in the business of expanding, was a good idea and would one day enable Londoners to move around the whole of the London conurbation at relatively high speeds. In its own way, considering the primitive technology available to construct the railway, it was an impressive achievement but in Ashto and Atia's opinion the underground network would never be totally user-friendly until the system was electrified, an improvement that was obviously some years away.

A short distance on from Aldgate station was Mitre Square; the place where Ashto had visited the day after Catherine Eddowes had been murdered in the hope that he might examine the exact spot where her death had taken place. Now it was unguarded by the police Ashto and Atia were able to enter the small square that was surrounded on all four sides by three or four storey warehouse buildings and by a number of private dwellings. All traces of the scene of the killing had by now been washed away and not even a slight shadow of a bloodstain remained. Ashto was convinced that had he been allowed to examine the site soon after the murder he would have found some physical evidence that the police had missed, perhaps some microscopic organic clue that would tie a certain person, now walking the streets, to the scene of the murder. The police were operating under a primitive system, however, where very few forms of forensic science had yet been discovered. Even the knowledge that all humans had a unique set of fingerprint patterns, information about which could be collected, codified and used to apprehend the perpetrators of crimes, had yet to be utilised by the Earth humans. Ashto made a mental note to somehow guide the local police into discovering the uses of fingerprinting in their future investigations. Such an intervention was completely against the rules of the Explorer Executive of course but Ashto could not see how the gift of such a small technological advance in forensic science would be harmful in any way to human society.

As the couple walked back to Bell Lane the promised fog started to descend on the city. By the time they had arrived back at Mrs Smith's Select Guesthouse the day had become dark and gloomy, as the thick, grey mixture of fog and smoke engulfed the area like a shroud. The October of this year of 1888 would turn out to be a very bad month for 'London Particulars' as the dense fogs came to be known. The smoke-laden atmosphere that glowed pus yellow as the gas lamps were lit, seemed so thick that one might be able to cut through it with a sharp butcher's knife. Black sooty specks could be seen floating in the relentless gloom and it was impossible for those going about their everyday business not to breathe the cough inducing particles into their lungs. In later years Londoners would refer to the fogs as 'Peasoupers' in that understated, comic way that Londoners had when faced with great city-wide unremitting problems, but that levity disguised the seriousness of such aberrant and death-dealing weather conditions. Not only did the fog cause many to die with respiratory diseases but the deeply opaque atmospheric conditions would lead to many individuals being killed or badly injured by the busily ubiquitous horse drawn traffic. In some cases individuals walking from familiar place to another familiar place would lose their sense of direction entirely and end up in the Thames where they often drowned in the cold, filthy black water, unseen and anonymous.

Ashto peered out the window of the Jaran couple's room at the guesthouse; he was not able even to make out the outline of the buildings opposite in the narrow lane. He looked and sounded downcast as he spoke to Atia. 'This dreadful weather situation is even worse than that which was forecast. There will be many worried individuals out there this evening particularly those many poor women without refuge who will be forced to spend the night on the street,' he said.

'It is true, Trevor. These current weather conditions will be ideal for the Whitechapel murderer to operate in and they are also likely to continue for many days according to today's newspaper. Some people will be very scared, there is no doubt.'

Atia had been working her way through that day's Times newspaper checking on the latest hoped-for developments in the police's search for Jack the Ripper. She sighed loudly when she concluded that there hadn't been any. Putting the paper to one side she took out the small computer terminal from the drawer of the writing desk and turned on its link to the ship.

As it continued to orbit around the planet Earth linked to its many scanning satellites, the Jaran spacecraft used its powerful computer to continue the search for any traces of human DNA that matched that small sample left inadvertently by the killer under the fingernails of Catherine Eddowes. It was a massive task that required virtually all of the machine's computing power. The computer, had it been sentient and equipped with human feelings, which it wasn't, might have given up on the task seeing it as a pointless exercise in blind optimism over rational expectation. There were simply too many people and too many places in this vast city of London many miles below the unseen space vehicle. Painstakingly and methodically the computer scanned every public place, every nook and cranny, every door handle on every door, the inside of every hansom cab and omnibus, every horse's rein, every sweaty palm, every item of attire worn by everyone, every blood, saliva, urine and semen stain, every dead and discarded human skin cell, even those left by the old Queen ensconced in Buckingham Palace. It was, of course, a totally stupid, completely impossible and never-ending task. And then one of the computer's metaphorical lights lit up. It had found something.

Report Number 0008 to the Glorious and Munificent Jaran Galactic Federation High Council (Planetary Exploration and Viable Exo-Planet Evaluation Committee – Sector 2007 Sub-Committee) by First Commander Treve Pacton Ashto.

My greetings and utmost felicitations to the esteemed members of the Sub-Committee.

Our orientation mission here on the planet Earth continues apace. Both Apprentice Commander Atia and I feel that we are developing a much greater understanding and insight into the indigenous human population as each day passes.

As I indicated in my last report both the Apprentice Commander and myself have thrown ourselves (an Earth idiom!) into the task of helping the local police authorities find the killer who has become universally known as Jack the Ripper. Our efforts in endeavouring to find trace elements of the murderer's DNA, as I have previously indicated, was a long shot (another Earth idiom!) and one that we couldn't be very confident would actually work. However, late yesterday the ship's computer alerted us to the promising news that it had found a possible match. We set about analyzing the result and indeed the computer had discovered a trace element that conformed to the DNA fingerprint we already had in our possession. This, Apprentice Commander Atia and I believe, is a great breakthrough even though it only informs us of a location where the Ripper has been recently and doesn't yet enable us to track his movement about the area, which of course is hopefully going to be our next task. It does mean, however, that we are one step nearer to finding the killer, apprehending him and handing him over to the authorities. How we are going to explain all of this to the police when we actually present the murderer to them we haven't as yet quite decided.

The police themselves seem to have made little progress in catching the Ripper since my last report, hampered as they are by the lack of any forensic science to speak of. Despite the definite personal qualities of police officers like the impressive Inspector Reid they know no more about the killer than they did a few weeks ago. Disturbingly it seems I am still under surveillance by the local police force. As well as having another interview with Inspector Reid, Atia and I have been followed on at least one occasion by his officers. I believe, however, that we have not done or said anything that could arouse further suspicion into our identities by Inspector Reid or his subordinates.

The occasion a policeman followed us was when we were visiting the London Hospital, the place of residence of a local celebrity called Joseph Merrick. Mr Merrick spent much of his early life, due to his extensive physical deformities, displayed for the private financial profit of others, in what the Earth humans call a 'freak show'. There is really nothing that could be considered analogous with this type of distasteful 'entertainment' in any part of the Jaran Federation, thank goodness, but it is to the credit of Earth humans that most now seem to deplore such displays and endeavour to prevent them from taking place. Being introduced to Mr Merrick with his extreme disfigurements, which can be quite shocking at first sight, was somewhat of a cathartic experience for

Apprentice Commander Atia. After meeting him Atia, extremely impressed with his friendliness, fortitude and good humour in spite of his life-limiting disabilities, vowed not to rest until the Ripper has been caught. This determined and focused attitude shown by the Apprentice Commander is something to which I have grown used and typifies her approach to all aspects of her work.

The newspaper reporter by the name of Rogers who has displayed some admiration for Apprentice Commander Atia continues to show an interest in our activities to the extent that on at least one occasion he was caught following us on one of our data-gathering walks around the local area. We are distrustful of this particular individual who appears to have his own agenda that is only partially explained by his declared appreciation for the physical appearance of the Apprentice Commander. We are now able to monitor the movements of this Rogers as, on our most recent encounter with him, I was able to attach a micro tracking device to the back of his overcoat. With the weather in this part of the planet becoming colder as the northern hemisphere moves into its winter season I feel sure that Rogers' coat will be experiencing a great deal of usage, as will our tracker.

On the subject of the weather, a topic of conversation that is always extremely common amongst humans, London has been experiencing a thick fog for the last 24 hours. Because of the ubiquitous burning of fossil fuels such as coal by private residences as well as large and small manufacturing concerns this has quickly become a somewhat toxic mixture of naturally occurring water vapour based fog and large amounts of smoke issuing from chimneys that cannot escape into the upper atmosphere due to the overarching weather conditions. Atia has come up with a portmanteau word to describe this unpleasant admixture of elements – *smog*. It is a word I believe that will soon be universally adopted by Earth humans in London and elsewhere. So thick is this *smog* that it is sometimes impossible to see more than an arm's length in front of oneself. This obviously becomes even more difficult during the hours of darkness when the primitive lighting system of gas lamps used in London hardly penetrates the intense gloom of the night. Many local people are worried, as are Atia and myself that the Ripper will use these impenetrable nighttime hours to carry out yet another one of his murderous rampages.

On a lighter note I would like to say something about the food that is available to us here on Earth with a view of offering some advice to those Jarans who may eventually follow in our footsteps in future times. Apprentice Commander Atia and I have sampled a number of local edible delicacies during our time here in London. Perhaps our favourite food so far had been deep fried white fish accompanied by a fried chopped root vegetable known locally as potato. In the local vernacular this dish is called 'fish and chips' and is consumed after it has been sprinkled with sodium chloride and something called vinegar, an aqueous solution of acetic acid. No doubt this sounds extremely odd to Jaran ears back home but believe me it is totally delicious.

That is all I have to report for now. In my next report I hope to be able to announce that the activities of the man they call Jack the Ripper will have ended.

With my utmost loyalty, etcetera,
First Commander Treve Pacton Ashto

18

The Ten Bells

'Where is Rogers located now,' Margot?'

'He still appears to be in his Fleet Street office. It is a cold day so he is unlikely to be in the outdoors without his overcoat,' replied Atia peering at her computer screen.

It was the morning of Wednesday 17th October and the two Jaran explorers were intent on knowing where the newspaperman was before they began to put into action their plan to track down the Whitechapel murderer. They certainly did not want Rogers 'bumping' into them again particularly once Atia had gone under cover as Maggie. If he followed them and somehow saw Atia in her guise as the destitute and homeless young woman he would doubtless be even less accepting of her and Ashto's antecedents and supposed place of origin than he was already.

During the previous evening, after Ashto had sent off

his latest report to the Sub-committee, the two Jarans had decided what their action plan should entail and now they were ready to set it in motion. Ashto was dressed in his tweed suit and cape and had already placed his deerstalker cap on his head ready to venture into the still foggy and chilled atmosphere outside.

'I am ready to leave, Margot. I have on my person the disruptor, a computer terminal, a fly-drone to use if necessary and of course the communicator. It is vital that we will stay in contact with each other throughout the day as we agreed. If we are to have any hope of catching this Ripper criminal it is important that we work in unison.'

Atia smiled. She was attired in the malodorous and very grubby clothes that constituted her Maggie disguise. 'You are quite correct to remind me of the situation, Trevor. I will of course ensure that my microphone and earpiece are turned on at all times. I don't know how long I will need to be in the Ten Bells public house but if I require your assistance at any time I will quickly be in touch with you.'

'Thank you for reassuring me, Margot ... or Maggie as I should refer to you in your present somewhat dishevelled state.'

Ashto looked fondly at his Apprentice Commander. Even with frizzy, dirty looking hair down to her shoulders and dressed in the threadbare and none too pleasant smelling attire that would, to the outside world, mark her out as a homeless, penniless street woman of dubious virtue, she still looked beautiful as far as he was concerned. Ashto had a momentary unbidden urge to go over to Atia and propose that she take off her ragged clothes and spend some time with him in the bed but quickly dispelled such thoughts as unprofessional and counter to their task in hand. It was important that they proceeded with their plan without further delay. The information supplied by the computer that a match had been found with the DNA of the killer found on the body of Catherine Eddowes had surprised and delighted Ashto and Atia the day before. The trace element, probably of the murderer's saliva, had been located on a drinking glass in the Ten Bells, which meant that the killer had almost certainly been inside the pub sometime during the previous day. Today Atia was going to spend much of her time in the Ten Bells in her undercover disguise as Maggie in the hope that somehow she might spot the man who was Jack the Ripper. She didn't harbour any illusions that it would be simple; the killer would not make himself obvious. In fact, according to her profile of the sort of person the Ripper probably was, his most prominent feature was likely to be his anonymity. He would almost certainly be totally unremarkable and ordinary, someone who, by his very nature, could blend into the background and remain unseen and unregarded; the type of individual that others would have trouble remembering. In any case for all she knew the man they called the Ripper might not go into the Ten Bells today; perhaps he divided his time between the many public houses of Whitechapel always on the lookout for new victims. But she had to be ready just in case. The ship's computer had focused all of its scanning capacity on the Ten Bells and the area adjacent to it. If any trace of the Ripper's DNA showed up again the computer would pinpoint the individual and alert Atia to his exact position.

Ashto, all romantic and carnal thoughts reluctantly pushed aside, gave Atia a chaste kiss on her deliberately soot-smeared cheek, wished her well and left the room. His part in the day's plan was to act as a decoy, drawing away from Bell Lane any plain-clothes police officer sent by Reid to watch the guesthouse and his and Atia' comings and goings. With any policeman lured away from Mrs Smith's establishment Atia would be free to slip out and carry on with her part of the plan. Ashto, notebook and pencil in hand would continue to carry out mundane research activities around and about the local area before gradually moving West to where he would continue to monitor the movements of Mr Rogers. Ashto smiled to himself at the thought that he might have to utilise the fly-drone again on the Fleet Street journalist in order to stop him meddling in their affairs. All the time he would be in constant touch with Atia and could move to assist her if she needed help in any way.

'Margot, I'm just testing the communications. I'm in Whitechapel High Street making descriptive notes on the market activities going on around me. There is no sign that I'm being followed so either Inspector Reid has finally decided we're not worth surveilling or he has sent a more skillful exponent of the art to undertake the task in these foggy conditions.'

Atia smiled. 'I have just set out for the Ten Bells, Trevor. I will of course keep my communicator switched on so you can hear what goes on in the public house. If we have another positive DNA result from the computer then I will try to stay close to the subject. I will endeavour to imbibe as little alcohol as I can.'

'Of course, Margot, good luck.' Not without some misgivings about Atia's plan to locate the Ripper and the possible danger she might be putting herself in glanced again at the foggy thoroughfare behind him to see if there was any sign of a police officer in the damp and murky street.

The Ten Bells public house was, like all of the pubs in the East End, a popular meeting place for the local inhabitants of the area. For the many who toiled in the markets, slaughterhouses, haulage and transport firms, factories, foundries, boot makers, blacksmiths and butcher's shops of Whitechapel it was a place they could visit for a quick after-work pint of beer or two before going home to their families. For others, however, the pub was a refuge where a large portion of the day could be wiled away letting the false joy of an alcoholic haze mitigate the despair that they felt at the harshness of a life spent in the day to day business of abject survival in a cold and unsympathetic world. Whatever money these individuals had been able to scrape together was invariably and swiftly transformed into beer or gin. Often, those men and women of no-fixed abode, who, at best, relied on sleeping on a stained and flea-ridden mattress at a common lodging house, would find that the few pennies they had set aside for their bed had disappeared and yet again they would face another fitful and uncomfortable night in some cold, dank corner of a back yard or shop doorway. The more desperately enterprising females, as well as some males, could earn money through street prostitution; the swift servicing of any willing individual making his way home from the pub while, at the same time, they fervently hoped they hadn't inadvertently met up with the Ripper and his sharp knife.

As Atia approached the Ten Bells in Commercial Street she swayed from one side of the foggy pavement to the other in her, by now, well-practised 'drunken' fashion.

Occasionally she purposely bumped into men and asked them to treat her to a drink or to 'lend' her some money. As before some ignored her, others swore and pushed her away and one suggested they could go down one of the dark alleyways for a 'bit o' fun' but she was able to disabuse him of that idea before he got too seriously excited.

Entering the crowded and loud pub she marched to the bar and ordered a gin, producing a few coins from the depths of her skirt pocket. Ignoring the lewd comments from some of the men at the bar she looked around the pub's large room. Yesterday the Ripper had been in this very place and had probably sat in one of the quiet corners with a pint of beer, speaking to no one but observing all those present. Doubtless he would have looked particularly carefully at each of the women in the pub and considered which one of them could be his next victim. He targeted street prostitutes, of that there was no doubt, but none of the women in the Ten Bells wore a sign around their necks marking them out as such. Of course there were the unwritten signals; Atia knew about those: the lack of a hat or bonnet, the skirts pulled up higher than would be the norm among more respectable types, the wink of an eye, the forced friendliness, the drunken desperation. He would pick out one of these 'unfortunates' as the newspapers called them and either engage them in conversation inside the pub or simply follow them out into the street. He would be silver-tongued when he spoke, he could be charming perhaps; he might well have developed a friendly demeanour for those very situations. Above all he would seem to be ordinary and trustworthy, certainly not someone a woman would ever suspect of being the monster, Jack the Ripper – until it was too late.

Perhaps he was here now, looking at her with hungry eyes. If he was and if he had again left enough saliva on the glass he was drinking from, saliva that could be matched up with the DNA data they already had, then the computer would issue her with an alert. Surreptitiously she took the small computer terminal from her pocket and quickly glanced at it. No alert from the ship's computer as yet, so probably the Ripper wasn't here at the moment but Atia realised that the search for the killer wasn't going to be that simple. She would have to be patient and wait – maybe for a considerable time.

As she stood slouching with her back to the bar surveying those present a woman appeared next to her and ordered a glass of beer paying for it with some coins taken from a small reticule that hung from her shoulder. Atia looked at the woman and nodded to her. She was young, with dark, almost black hair and surprisingly attractive for a female frequenting the Ten Bells at this time of day. She was tall for a human female, like Atia wore no hat and was dressed in a white blouse, white apron, black skirt, bodice and jacket, clothes that certainly were not new but looked neat, clean and well cared for. When the woman smiled at Atia, a smile that seemed both warm and genuine, she displayed an even, full set of teeth, something that immediately set her apart from the majority of women in Whitechapel who invariably had at least one of their incisors missing. Atia liked the woman's smile and smiled back.

'Pleased to meet you,' said the woman taking a large gulp of her beer, and then holding out her hand to shake that of Atia's, 'I'm Marie.'

'Likewise I'm sure,' said Atia, 'I'm Maggie.'

'I haven't seen you in here before, Maggie. Would you be new to the area?'

'Bin 'ere a few weeks now, but first time I've come into this place. Seems friendly enough.'

'It's not at all bad, considering the rough and ready types that gather in here.'

The woman called Marie spoke in a slightly lilting accent that was unfamiliar to Atia. She made a mental note to consult her neural implant later so she could analyse it properly. For now though she wanted to concentrate on the job in hand and look out for any sign of the Ripper's whereabouts. However, as she was likely to be in the pub for the rest of the day striking up a conversation with the young woman who called herself Marie might be a good way to pass the time.

'So Maggie, do you live round here?'

Atia looked into the large dark eyes of the woman. She estimated her age to be about middle twenties and she was probably the most attractive young woman she'd seen so far in the whole of the Whitechapel area.

'I stay where I can as long as I ain't spent all me money on gin by the end of the night. If I can't afford a doss 'ouse I 'ave to find somewhere safe to kip – ain't too bad usually but the nights are gettin' a bit chilled now. What about yourself?'

'Oh I reside in a beautiful mansion up West and only come here to see how the other half live,' she said in a mock-refined accent laughing and then taking a large swig of her beer. Her laugh was as attractive as its owner, thought Atia. 'No, Maggie, in truth I live across the street in one very small room that I share with my fella, Joe – costs us 4 shillings and 6 pennies each week – bloody exorbitant if you ask me – and the landlord's a bully to boot. Been there since March. Don't think we'll stay much longer – we're behind with our rent so we'll probably have to do a moonlight flit some time soon,' said Marie in her almost musical accent, before laughing loudly. It was a laugh that seemed to illustrate the fun-loving nature of the young woman who displayed it. And yet her general bonhomie and lack of seriousness seemed to Atia to be a well-designed front that concealed her true nature; there was more than a hint of sadness behind those dark eyes.

'Hey Mary, give us one of yer Irish songs why dontcha?' shouted a man sitting at one of the tables, several empty beer glasses in front of him.

'Not yet me boyo – I ain't nearly drunk enough yet!' replied Marie. The man at the table laughed.

'What's your fella like Marie?' asked Atia.

'He's nice enough when we aren't having a drunken barny and he ends up thumping me and giving me a shiner. He's fair haired and big and handsome and he used to work at Billingsgate Market so he always smelled of fish until he was sacked in the summer.' Marie laughed again, finished her beer and banged her glass down on the bar waiting for it to be filled again. When it was she again retrieved a few coins from her bag and paid for the drink. 'So what about you Maggie, a lovely looker like yourself must have a nice fella to care for you and see to all your needs?'

'Did 'ave,' replied Atia taking a sip of her gin, 'but he buggered off just after we arrived in Whitechapel. Ain't seen 'ide nor 'air of 'im for the last month. Not that 'ee 'ad much 'air in the first place!' Atia laughed almost as raucously as Marie had done and the other woman joined in, the two of them holding on to each other, shaking with laughter as they leaned against the bar.

Atia was surprised to find, when she went to take another sip from her gin glass, that she had finished the drink. Better be careful she thought, that gin disappeared far quicker than I'd intended it to.

'Let me get you another,' said Marie noticing Atia's empty glass, 'I insist.'

'That's very kind of you,' said Atia smiling and thinking that she should play the part of the penniless Maggie as much as she could.

Marie fished around in her bag again for some money and came up with the correct number of pennies needed to pay for Atia's glass of gin.

'Ta very much Marie,' said Atia taking a sip of gin.'

'Do not in any way mention it – it is just, when all is said and done, merely money. Easy come, easy go!' said the young woman who then took another large swallow of her beer. 'So, Maggie – Margaret, I think I will call you as you remind me a lot of someone by that name I used to know many years ago – what do you do to earn your daily bread?' As she spoke Marie had led Atia over to a recently vacated table and the two women sat down at it.

'Oh anything I can turn me 'and to – a bit o' cleanin' 'ere and there – sold a few flowers an' matches from time to time.'

'Have you tried your luck up West at all?' Marie gulped down some more of her beer.

'Sold a few flowers around Covent Garden once. Didn't much like it though – too many toffs for comfort',' replied Atia, who had quickly consulted her neural implant to ascertain what sort of paid activity someone like Maggie might have done in the West End.

'I lived in the West End for a while at a gay house in Brompton. Had plenty of money too – rich pickings there of course. Plenty of rich young toffs eager to learn the ways of the world and some old ones too who often knew too much for my liking.' Marie paused in her story to take a drink of her beer giving Atia chance to consult her neural implant yet again to find out what a 'gay house' actually was. She wasn't that surprised to find that the phrase was a piece of upper class slang for a brothel. Atia could imagine that the dark haired, young and attractive Marie would indeed have been in very great demand by the upper class men who visited such places in the West End of London.

'Eventually I fell out with a few people, got drunk too many times and threatened to use a razor to castrate some bloke who wanted to use me in a particular manner I was not happy with.' Marie smiled resignedly and shrugged – there was that a hint of sadness in her dark eyes again, noticed Atia. 'And then, Margaret my dear, I went off to Paris – Oo la la!' she said in a mock French accent and then she grinned widely showing her white teeth and finished her pint of beer. 'It was in France when I became Marie Jeanette instead of plain old Mary Jane which was the idea of the particular Monsieur I was residing with at the time.'

'I'll get you another beer,' said Atia, noting that the young woman's glass was empty and interested to hear more of her story. At the bar Atia asked for a pint of bitter ale and for some water to be put in her gin glass reasoning that the busy waistcoated and aproned barman couldn't have cared less and Marie was by now too drunk to notice whether or not Atia was still drinking alcohol. Atia had already drunk two gins much quicker than she had planned and was starting to feel the alcohol's effects. When she returned to the table Marie was taking a large swig from a hip flask she had removed from her bag.

'Brandy,' she said to Atia holding up the flask, 'helps to lubricate my throat!' At which point she smiled, stood, hoisted up her skirt and somewhat unsteadily stepped up onto the chair. A few of those nearby let out a cheer as Marie started to sing in a clear and surprisingly melodious voice:

'Scenes of my childhood arise before my gaze,
Bringing recollections of bygone happy days
When down in the meadow in childhood I would roam.
No one's left to cheer me now within that good old home,
Father and Mother, they have pass'd away;
Sister and brother now lay beneath the clay,
But while life does remain to cheer me, I'll retain,
This small violet I pluck'd from Mother's grave.' …

Ashto listened in to the clear but mournful sounding voice of the human female now seemingly entertaining the drinkers in the Ten Bells pub as he sat on a public bench close to St Paul's Cathedral. The large structure, one that Ashto often admired, was only just about visible to him on this third day of London's thick fog. He had been listening carefully to the conversation that Atia was having with the strangely accented young woman to see if there was a chance he could ask his Apprentice Commander if there was yet any indication as the Ripper's location. Now that Atia's newly acquired friend, seemingly called Marie, was performing a song it seemed to be a propitious time to ask a question.

'Margot, how is your quest progressing? Any computer alert yet?'

Atia thought it was safe to speak to her First Commander as everyone's attention seemed to be firmly on the darkly attractive young woman who was putting all her effort into a song that she had obviously sung many times before but still found highly emotional as Atia noticed that a small tear was rolling down her cheek.

'No alert as yet, Trevor,' said Atia speaking quietly into the bracelet on her right wrist. ' It is likely that the Ripper has not yet entered the public house but I am hopeful that the ship's computer will let me know if he does and orders a drink. How are you getting on with our Mr Rogers?'

'He's still in his office according to the information from the tracker – hasn't been out at all today. I am planning to send the drone to observe him soon just to make sure he is where we think he is.'

'Well, good luck Trevor, I must now stop speaking as the human female has finished her song. I'll speak later.'

People in the pub clapped and cheered as Marie bowed extravagantly in response. Atia helped her down and immediately the young woman picked up her pint of beer and drank a good deal of it before slumping back onto the chair.

'That was a beautiful song, said Atia.

'Yes it is, it's one of my favourites. It reminds me of my childhood in Limerick and it always brings a tear to my eye in true Irish fashion, don't you know, Margaret my lovely.'

Atia quickly checked her neural implant for the location of Limerick. 'You're a very long way from 'ome, Marie,' Atia said smiling at the young woman and suddenly feeling that she had something in common with her. Both of us, she thought, so very far away from where we originate – both of us missing our homes in our different ways.

'A long, long way from home – in more ways than one,' said Marie, another teardrop forming in her eye. She finished off her beer and then sniffed loudly. 'From my Ma's home in Limerick – to Cardiff – to the West End of London – and then to Paris and now to the East End. Can't help thinking sometimes I might have been better off staying where I was born – the place where my happy childhood memories linger still. Oh well! Time for another beer I think,' she said, wiping the tear away on the sleeve of her jacket'

Atia watched her as she weaved her way to the bar, stopping occasionally to speak to a few men on the way and accepting a kiss on the cheek from one of them. Atia looked around the room again to see if any new men had entered the Ten Bells while she had been talking to Marie.

First Commander Ashto found a quiet spot overlooking the Thames where he could launch the fly-drone and control its flight to the Fleet Street Office of Mr William Rogers without being seen by others. He had checked his tracker and found that the newspaperman's overcoat was still situated in the same place. Either Rogers was far more sedentary in his habits than the impression he had given the two Jarans, or else he had left his coat off on this chilly day while venturing outside. Both explanations seemed somewhat unlikely and Ashto was keen to find out.

Ashto watched the small computer screen as he sent the drone in the direction of Fleet Street. He glanced around occasionally to ensure that no one was seeing what he was engaged in doing. The fly-drone's camera sent back images of the foggy byways as it flew about twenty or so feet above the city streets. As it got to Fleet Street Ashto located the office of the Evening Standard and carefully propelled the drone through its front door after waiting for it to be opened by someone coming out of the building. Homing the drone into the signal emitted by the tracking device he easily found the office where Rogers had seemingly been since the start of the day and carefully landed the fly onto the reporter's desk. Rogers was nowhere to be seen and as Ashto peered at his screen and the picture sent back by the drone he could see the black overcoat hanging on a hook on the wall behind the newspaperman's desk. So Rogers was probably still in the building in that case, thought Ashto as he suddenly heard footsteps behind him and a familiar voice start speaking to him.

'What a coincidence, Mr Ashton, who would have thought that we would meet up again quite so soon.'

Ashto quickly turned at the same time as he slipped his computer terminal into his pocket. There before him was the tall human known as Mr Rogers wearing a completely different coat to the one Ashto had just been looking at on the screen of his computer.

Back in Mr Rogers' office the lady bringing the young journalist a cup of tea noticed a fly sitting in the middle of the reporter's desk. Using a rolled up newspaper she crushed the insect and swept its remains into a nearby waste bin.

Very unusual to see flies around in such cold weather as this she thought as she then went on her way wheeling her tea trolley to the next recipient of her liquid bounty.

19

Marie Jeanette

'So what did you say to Mr Rogers, Trevor?'

'Well after I had recovered from my surprise at seeing him I merely said that I was continuing my researches and compiling notes pertaining to the River Thames. After exchanging some polite pleasantries, with Rogers' face continuing to wear that annoying smile of his, we both went our separate ways.'

'How do you think Rogers was able to end up in the same place as yourself?'

'Coincidence I suppose. He said he was going to interview a member of the Thames Marine Police about a body that had been found in the river. As I said before he was wearing a different topcoat, a grey one rather than the black one on which I had placed the tracker. He seemed very pleased to see me, almost as though he believed he'd deliberately outwitted me, which of course is not true at all. I think he just likes to annoy us.'

'And you lost contact with the drone?'

'Yes, that is somewhat of a mystery. It is lucky we have another but I do not like the thought that a piece of Jaran technology is unaccounted for and is out there somewhere. Hopefully any humans coming across it will not appreciate the drone's true nature. I think that I will not mention the loss in my next report to the Sub-Committee, misplacing technology on any orientation mission is of course somewhat frowned upon.'

'Very wise,' said Atia, smiling in a supportive way.

Atia was in her Maggie attire ready to visit the Ten Bells for the second time. The day before there had been no alert from the computer telling her that the Ripper was in the public house and so she was ready to do the same thing all over again. The two glasses of gin she had imbibed had left her with a slight ache behind her eyes when she had awoken this Thursday morning and so she had, secretly, taken a couple of analgesic capsules to help her get rid of it. She didn't want the First Commander to worry so she hadn't mentioned her headache. Ashto, she noticed, if anything was even more concerned about her safety than he had been yesterday. Today he had insisted that he would stay in their guesthouse room and monitor Atia throughout the day via her communication devices as well as keeping a check, if possible on the elusive Mr Rogers. If there was any danger at all to the Apprentice Commander in the Ten Bells Ashto reckoned that it would take him less than three minutes to make the journey from Bell Lane to the public house on the corner of Commercial Street and Church Street in order to go to her aid. As an extra precaution he had attached a tracker to her skirt just in the unlikely event the communicator she wore should malfunction in some way. Having eaten some bread, cheese and an apple obtained from Spitalfields market for her lunch Atia was ready to venture out and head for the Ten Bells where she would again spend the day waiting for any sign that the Ripper was in the vicinity.

'Take the greatest care please, Margot,' said Ashto, still feeling he should have insisted that it was he and not Atia going undercover in this way.

'I will, of course, Trevor,' said Atia kissing Ashto on the lips and smiling in what she hoped was a supremely confident and reassuring way. She didn't much relish the idea of spending the whole day in the pub again but realised that if they were to identify the Ripper this 'stakeout', as humans might one day call this type of operation, was necessary. Atia would slip out as surreptitiously as possible and hope that any of Reid's policemen, if they hadn't already given up watching the guesthouse, would not recognise her anyway. Outside the thick, yellowy fog still swirled about four days after arriving in the capital city with no sign yet of a relieving wind to blow the murk and smoke away. The sounds of the streets – the clip clop of hooves, the crunch of wagons on damp and gritty roads, the cries of the street hawkers – all were muffled by the damp, opaque gloom.

Atia got to the Ten Bells after her usual mock-drunken serpentining through the nearby streets. At the bar of the pub, which was even more crowded than it had been the day before, Atia decided to order a pint of beer as she reasoned that it would take her longer to drink and as a result she would not be quite so affected by its alcoholic content as she had been by yesterday's gin. Again Atia stood with her back to the bar and surveyed the room. A man drinking alone in the corner attracted her attention for a while, but he was soon joined by a fellow drinker who sat down beside him and the pair started chatting amiably to each other. She was convinced that the Ripper was going to be alone, at least until he homed in on a potential female victim. Then he might talk to the woman, charm her, promise her some easy money, suggest they go out and find a dark alleyway for quick sex. Or maybe he would simply follow a potential victim out of the door, wait his moment and then draw his knife and … On these fog-ridden days where the transition between night and day hardly existed, Atia knew that the Ripper could strike at any time. While the thick fogs lasted, no longer could the murderer simply be classed as a fiend of the night, preying on women in the darkness. These days he could carry out his evil business at any time, day or night.

At the bar of the Ten Bells Atia again had to put up with a number of men making bawdy suggestions to her. These she was able to ignore, sneering at them or, on occasions, issuing some choice expletive to send the Earth males on their way. However, one man who had decided that squeezing her left buttock was an enjoyable thing to do was quickly shown that it was not such a sensible idea as he received a sharp kick to his shin followed by a 'don't mess with me' look.

After seeing the buttock grabber off Atia secretly checked her computer terminal for any alerts from the ship and then headed to the far side of the room and sat down at the table where there was a clear view of those entering the pub by its main door. She intended to look out for any male who fitted her criminal profile of the Ripper and then observe him carefully. Apart from one time when a drunken man briefly sat down next to her and suggested unsuccessfully that she might want to go with him into the back yard of the pub to earn some beer-money as he put it, she sat alone looking at those around her and occasionally, for form's sake, sipping her beer although she did not like its taste one little bit.

Atia had been in the pub for about two hours when Ashto contacted her and asked her how events were progressing.

'Nothing to report as yet, Trevor,' said Atia covering her mouth with her hand and pretending to yawn as she spoke into her bracelet microphone. 'I am completely safe and simply sitting at a table in the pub watching the comings and goings. There is no sign yet of anyone who fits the Ripper's profile and there has been no computer alert. I am trying to make my pint of bitter beer last for as long as I can because I do not like it.'

'It is definitely an acquired taste, Margot, I can attest to that. Good luck. I will contact you again when I judge the timing to be appropriate.'

'Thank you, Trevor, I will look forward to it.'

A elderly drunken man with a white beard sitting at a table nearby looked at her strangely having noticed her talking to her hand and then shrugged as if, after all, talking to oneself was not something so out of the ordinary in this place of alcohol, inebriation and despair.

Atia continued sipping her beer and visually scanning the denizens of the drinking establishment. Most of those in the pub looked jolly enough as they drank their beer and gin and smoked their pipes and cigarettes. The majority of those present were male and most of those were dressed in clothes that had seen much better days. Atia had become aware that very few people in the East End owned more than two sets of clothes. They had everyday attire that they worked in, if they were lucky enough to have a job, and if they were very lucky indeed, a Sunday-best suit they might put on for the Sabbath day, as the Earth humans called it, or wear when attending weddings, or more probably funerals in this time of high mortality rates. The females in the Ten Bells wore equally shabby looking and down at heel clothes. Atia smiled at the ignorance both she and First Commander Ashto had displayed when first preparing to travel to the Earth when they had found it difficult to believe that humans could so easily assess each others' social standing by the clothes they were attired in. It was so obvious to her now. Virtually everyone in this pub at this time were members of the lowest class of society all leading a hand-to-mouth, day-to-day existence. What little money they had often went on cheap alcohol as they searched for the insensibility it bought. Only those begging and starving on the streets, the underclass of society, were in a worse position. Atia sighed and took another sip of her beer. She was finding the experience of her extended visits to the Ten Bells wholly dispiriting and was even beginning to wish she enjoyed alcohol and could join in with the false sense of well-being and bonhomie it seemed to engender in the Earth humans. It was at this point that the appearance of a familiar face put an end to her somewhat depressive musings.

Through the front door of the pub walked Marie arm-in-arm with a middle-aged man who looked extremely pleased to be linked, however temporarily, with such a good looking young woman. When Atia had last seen Marie the day before she had been unsteadily crossing Commercial Street, dodging piles of horse dung as she headed home to 'see her Joe and give him a good time,' she had said.

Marie and the man walked to the bar and he appeared to buy them both some beer. Marie grabbed her pint glass and drank greedily from it. Various other men were soon gathered around her and it was clear to Atia that the young woman probably would not need to buy a drink for herself in the near future. The small huddle involving Marie and the men – Atia counted seven at one stage – stood at the bar conversing and laughing loudly at each other's jokes. There was no doubt in Atia's mind that Marie's physical attractiveness was not the only reason for her popularity with the men, although of course that was a large part of it. It was also very obvious to her that the young Earth woman had a definite charisma that would have made her the centre of attention in whatever social circle she found herself in. Atia imagined what she would have looked like a few years ago when she worked at the high-class brothel in the West End, dressed in fine clothes, the plaything of rich men. Now she was in an East End pub entertaining much poorer males, flirting with them and when in need of some money no doubt taking one of them back to her small room just across Commercial Street where she would again become the sexual plaything of others. It was at this point with Atia feeling depressed again that Marie noticed her sitting at the table and, squeezing the shoulder of the man she had entered the pub with, sidled drunkenly over to sit with her.

'Top of the day to you my lovely, lovely Margaret,' said Marie loudly, hugging Atia and kissing her on the cheek before sitting down and banging her glass of beer drunkenly on the table.

'Yer look in a good mood today, Marie. Who was the bloke yer came in with?'

'Oh him? No one in particular – I just let him have a grope o' my tits earlier if he promised to buy me a drink, which he did. You see I'm all out o' money at present and the rent is due tomorrow. Joe hasn't got a penny to his name either so he hasn't. It looks like the landlord Mr, bloody, McCarthy is going to have to whistle for his rent again this week.' Marie laughed a little too manically for Atia's liking. Although drunk and seemingly jolly there was no doubt that beneath her jovial demeanour Marie was in a depressed state of mind. Atia briefly considered giving the young woman enough money to clear the debt with her landlord, something that was undoubtedly worrying her. It would be simple to give her one or two of the sovereigns produced by the replicator but how could she do so without disclosing the undercover nature of her current guise? The action would raise many more problems than it would solve and so Atia decided her best strategy would be to talk to Marie and try to raise her spirits while still keeping a look out for the Ripper.

'Your Joe, 'as 'ee bin able to find 'imself a job?'

'No, he hasn't as yet. Tried to get some work at a slaughterhouse in Aldgate High Street today but they didn't want the poor love and he was sent away with a flea in his ear. Said he almost punched the self-righteous fella that sent him on his way. He ended up traipsing around the area looking for work but there was nothing going on so he came home and we got drunk together,' laughed Marie.

'So where did yer get the money to buy drink?'

Marie laughed again, this time somewhat sheepishly. 'Well, I needed to get the rent money somehow so while Joe was out looking for work I found a chap outside the pub here who seemed a little lonely and who was all too willing to come back home with me to my room and pay me well for certain services I performed for him.'

Atia was so shocked she momentarily forgot to use Maggie's normal mode of speech. 'You took an enormous chance, Marie. How did you know that this man you met was not in fact the Ripper?'

Marie looked confused for a few seconds but then smiled. 'Have no worries there; I reckon I could spot that murdering bastard a mile off, Margaret me darlin' girl,' she said in a broad and comic Irish accent. However, Atia could see in Marie's eyes that she had not once considered, in her drunkenly depressed state, that she might have invited Jack the Ripper into her bed and now she felt fear at what might have occurred.

'Yer need to be more careful, Marie; in the future yer may not be so lucky,' said Atia reverting to her Maggie mode of speech.

'Oh there is no need to fret yourself darlin'. Anyway the Ripper operates on the street, I doubt very much that he would accompany any woman inside a room,' she said more in hope than in any real expectation.

Was there any point disagreeing with this young woman, thought Atia? Putting Marie's mock dismissive attitude to one side for a moment she said, 'Well Marie, since you're not takin' anything too serious at the moment would yer like me to get yer another drink?'

'Yes my darlin' girl – a gin this time I think – I've had my fill of beer for now I believe,' said Marie with a small belch, her dark, sad eyes brightening a little.

Back in Mrs Smith's guesthouse Ashto had been listening intently to the conversation going on between the two women. Now that Atia was standing at the bar he was able to speak to her. 'How is everything progressing, Margot?'

Atia looked around to see if anyone was observing her. 'No sign of the Ripper as yet Trevor. As you probably know I am now with Marie, the woman I met here yesterday. I was briefly trying to work out how I could supply her with the wherewithal to pay her monetary debt she has incurred with her landlord but have decided it would be an unwise course of action.'

Atia had to pause her conversation with Ashto as a burly man came to stand next to her at the bar demanding to be served. The barman though had noticed that Atia had been standing there for longer and so served her first much to the man's obvious displeasure.

On the way back to where Marie was sitting Atia managed to lift her right wrist to her mouth and give a brief message to Ashto.

'Must be quiet now – going back to Marie.'

'I understand, Margot. Get back in touch when you can.'

Ashto, full of nervous, pent up energy stood up and stalked around the room. If only he could think of some way to help Atia in her quest for the Ripper in the Ten Bells but nothing came to his mind and so he sat back down at the writing desk and listened again to Atia's conversation with the young woman known as Marie.

"There yer are, Marie,' said Atia putting the glass of gin down on the table. As she had approached Atia had noticed the young woman had been putting her hip flask back into her bag. While Atia had been away at the bar Marie had obviously been drinking from her supply of brandy and now she picked up the gin and swallowed that down in one gulp. There was no doubt, Atia thought, that as well as being in a general state of depression Marie was also suffering from an addiction to alcohol that would one day lead to serious illness and probable premature death. Atia felt sad for the attractive young Irish woman with the dark eyes and bubbly personality. As she watched, Marie closed her eyes and slumped forward seemingly about to put her head down on the table and fall into a drunken sleep. Atia made a swift decision. Standing up she lifted the drunken Marie to her feet, her strong arms supporting the young woman under her armpits and led her to the front door of the pub.

'C'mon Marie let me take yer 'ome and put yer to bed – you look exhausted. Where is it you live exactly?' Atia had decided that she had to look after the young woman, as there was no one else around that would. It meant leaving her station in the Ten Bells but the computer would still alert her to any appearance made by the Ripper and she would be able to rush back to the pub if she needed to.

In the foggy street outside, Marie stumbling and slumped against Atia who held her firmly, pointed across Commercial Street towards Dorset Street to the right. 'Mind the horse muck,' mumbled Marie as the two women crossed the busy thoroughfare with its carters' wagons, hansom cabs and omnibuses half concealed in the murky, misty atmosphere. On the opposite side of the road was the

Britannia public house, crowded and noisy, with some of its patrons spilling drunkenly out onto the pavement. Atia half expected Marie to insist on going into the pub but was far too insensible to have even noticed the crowded drinking establishment. The pair turned into Dorset Street and two thirds of the way down the cobblestoned street on the right, Marie mumbled some incoherent sounds and twisted her body indicating that they should turn down a narrow and gloomy alleyway. A sign high up on the alley's entrance read Miller's Court.

'What number is yer room, Marie?'

'It'd be number 13 so it would,' Marie gave a small chuckle and a belch, 'the luck o' the Irish,' she said.

Atia delved around in Marie's bag for a key and opened the door to her rented room. She maneuvered the young woman in and laid her down on the bed. Almost instantly Marie began to breathe heavily and fall into a deep sleep. Atia took off the young woman's boots and then moved her onto her side to prevent her from choking in the likely event that she vomited in her sleep.

Atia looked around the extremely small and dingy room. Apart from the bed itself the only other furniture consisted of a small bedside table and an upright wooden chair at the foot of the bed. In a fireplace that was full of cold ashes there was a kettle hanging from a hook. Attached to the wall over the fireplace were two ancient looking smoke-dried framed prints showing faded and indeterminate pastoral scenes. A small set of shelves held a few dusty items of crockery, cheap ornaments and general nick-nacks. The only form of lighting Atia could see in the room was a single candle in a candlestick on the table. One window, covered by curtains apparently made from sacking material, looked out into the enclosed yard letting a dim light into the room. The ceiling was low, the walls were whitewashed and grubby and Atia could see that this room had been created by the construction of a wooden partition separating it off from the rest of the building – a house in Dorset Street. The same was obviously true of the building next door, which was also owned by Marie's landlord, John McCarthy, the front of which served as his Chandler's shop. Above Marie's room was another of similar dimensions. The back yard of the two houses thus formed Miller's Court, a small and fetid space into which even the brightest sunshine would rarely find its way. At the end of the yard stood a small wooden shed that contained an earth-closet lavatory and was there to serve all of the tenants living in the cramped rooms of the Court.

Atia was amazed that anyone could exist in such a tiny, bleak space and then she remembered that this was Whitechapel where even this miniscule living area was preferable to spending the night outside in the cold and damp. But Atia realised she now had something of a problem. She needed to return to the pub to watch out for the Ripper but she couldn't leave Marie's door unlocked and Marie herself was currently in no fit state to lock the door behind her. And so, not able to think of anything else to do she took off her own boots and lay down on the bed next to Marie.

'Trevor, I seem to be detained for a while in the room of the young woman called Marie. I can't lock the door without then walking off with the key and I can't leave the door unlocked as Marie is in a deep, intoxicated sleep.'

'I understand, Margot. I can see from the tracking

device where you are currently situated. Shall I come to your assistance?'

'That will not be necessary or advisable, Trevor. If anyone sees us together our undercover operation will become untenable in the future. No I will wait here until Marie wakes and then I will return to the Ten Bells.'

'If you are sure, I personally can think of no acceptable alternative to your plan I'm afraid, but if there is anything you need please let me know.'

'I will, Trevor. Thank you.'

Atia was herself just drifting off to sleep when she heard the door to the room open. Instantly awake and on her guard she sat up and saw a man standing in the doorway. He looked a little surprised.

'Bloody 'ell, is she bringing 'ome some of 'er fellow bobtails now?'

'Who are you?' Atia stood up from the bed ready to defend herself and Marie physically if the situation called for it.

'Don't worry love,' said the man, immediately sounding friendlier, taking off his peaked cap, closing the door and sitting down on the chair, 'I live 'ere with 'er, she's probably told you about me.'

'You're Joe?'

'That's right. Is she drunk again?'

Atia looked closely at the man. He was slightly above average height for a human male with short fairish hair and a well-trimmed gingery mustache. The dark suit and waistcoat he wore were of the typically shabby Whitechapel norm. He was a youngish man, late twenties or early thirties estimated Atia and with his deep blue eyes looked handsome enough at the moment although despair and drink were already beginning to take a toll on his features with a few wrinkly lines starting to appear around his eyes and a with distinct reddening of his nose.

'Marie's just 'avin' a bit of a rest,' said Atia somewhat defensively and keeping to her Maggie accent.

'So she's callin' herself Marie again is she? Oh well I s'pose sleepin' is better for her than whorin'. Trouble is when we ain't got no money comin' in she 'as to go on the streets so as we can pay the rent, but I don't like it one bit. Keep tellin' 'er but she don't listen. An' anyway when she gets some money she goes an' spends it all on drink – although I sometimes do 'elp 'er out in that respect I 'ave to admit.' The man chuckled in a melancholy and resigned way.

'Well, now that yer 'ere I can take me leave. Only stayed 'cause I didn't want to leave the door unlocked so any Tom, Dick or 'arry could walk in.'

'Right love, I'll let Mary know you stayed with 'er 'til I came 'ome – she'll be grateful. She's not a bad girl y'know,' he said with some emotion in his voice, 'but she does 'ave a tendency to spin a yarn or two when she's 'ad too much to drink which is most times.' Joe stood with his cap in his hand and with his blue eyes shining in the semi-darkened room. Atia had the impression that he knew Marie needed help in some way but didn't know who to turn to in for that help. Again, momentarily, Atia thought that she might stealthily leave some money behind in the room and then remembered that Marie and her man Joe would almost certainly just go to the pub and spend it all making their problems even worse.

Atia put on her elastic sided boots, nodded to Joe, looked again at the sleeping Marie and left the room. Walking back down Dorset Street, crossing over Commercial Street, carefully avoiding the traffic, she made her way back to the Ten Bells stopping outside of the pub to speak into her bracelet.

'I will soon be back in the public house Trevor having left the room that Marie calls home. I assume that you heard my conversation with Joe, her man friend?'

'I did, Margot. What do you make of the human male?'

'It is difficult to say on such a brief meeting, Trevor. He appears to care for Marie but is obviously exasperated by her lifestyle choices. However, he, like her, is also somewhat dependent on alcohol and tends to spend whatever money he has on drink. I will perhaps visit Marie tomorrow and see how she is. In the meantime I am going back inside the Ten Bells and am hoping that the Ripper will make an appearance soon.'

'Very well, Margot, take especial care.'

'I will, Trevor.'

Atia entered the Ten Bells, as usual marched purposefully to the bar and ordered a pint of bitter beer inwardly thinking that she would have much rather preferred some tea served in a nice china cup and saucer, another Earth trait that she had recently grown to enjoy.

20

Tracking the Ripper.

The chilly autumnal days and nights of 1888 passed slowly and the seemingly unending series of dense fogs finally lifted. The Ripper murders appeared to have ceased as suddenly as they had begun; not one killing had occurred in the whole of the month of October. The population of Whitechapel and Spitalfields seemed to breathe a collective sigh of relief and slowly got back to some sort of normality. People speculated. Perhaps the Ripper had taken his own life, ultimately horrified at the bloody atrocities he had committed? There were plenty of drowned bodies of suicide victims found in the Thames and dragged into police boats or washed up on the river's stony foreshore. Perhaps he had moved away from London, travelled to the continent of Europe or to the United States to wreak his havoc in foreign parts? Perhaps he had been committed to an asylum his mind finally addled into lunacy by the horrors he had inflicted on defenceless women? Perhaps he had simply sated his bloodlust and would kill no more? Perhaps he was an important West End toff the police were protecting – fearful of a scandal that would shake the very foundations of polite society?

The letters to the police did continue, however. Usually signed 'Jack the Ripper,' most were considered by the authorities to be hoaxes and filed away for future investigators to argue over. Some, however, were truly disturbing. George Lusk, President of the self-styled Whitechapel Vigilance Committee, received a small parcel through the post which when opened was found to contain half a human kidney. An accompanying letter, which purportedly came 'From Hell,' informed Mr Lusk that the kidney had been taken from the eviscerated body of Catherine Eddowes and that the letter writer had fried and eaten the other half.

The police continued their enquiries. Their latest approach was to attempt to question all of the butchers and slaughtermen of the area – there were very many of them. Police officers did not enjoy these early morning trips to abattoirs and butcher's bloody back yards and cellars where chickens, geese, pigs, lambs and calves were given over to the knife and where carcasses dripping with gore were hung prior to being carved up for sale in the meat markets and shops of the East End. Most individual officers could only manage a few brief words with the individuals working in such places, their mouths and noses covered against the appalling smell of blood, offal and animal faeces. Many a young police constable felt the sudden need to run out into the street and vomit on the pavement much to the amusement of the hardened slaughterhouse workers.

The police, in their desperation, were forced to try other more unorthodox methods in their attempts to snare the Ripper. Sir Charles Warren in his role of Metropolitan Police Commissioner insisted on bloodhounds being used to sniff out the killer. No one seemed willing to explain to him that sniffing the bloodied clothes and meagre belongings of the murdered women would in any way enable even the most skillful of dogs to track down the elusive killer. An even more speculative method was tried by a number of detectives who dressed up as female prostitutes and then wandered around the streets of Whitechapel at night no doubt attempting to appear alluring to the murderous Jack the Ripper and then arrest him with his knife poised ready in his hand.

Ashto and Atia continued to monitor assiduously their computer's search for the killer's DNA. However, apart from the one alert they had received about the Ripper leaving a saliva trace in the Ten Bells pub there were no other indications that he had returned to that particular place. Consequently the Jaran Explorers widened the scope of the scans to include the whole of Whitechapel and Spitlefields and hoped that again the computer would alert them to the Ripper's location, perhaps in another of the crowded pubs of the area.

Atia had checked up on Marie as she had promised. The day after her abortive visit to the Ten Bells she had, wearing her Maggie disguise, called at number 13, Miller's Court early in the morning. After knocking on the door three times it was eventually opened by a sleepy looking and bedraggled Marie holding her hand to her head.

'Oh me darlin' Margaret, please come in.'

Marie looked careworn and dishevelled, obviously suffering from a hangover, no doubt a malady that she was all too often accustomed to, thought Atia. The young Earth female slumped back down on the bed and motioned Atia to sit in the chair.

'As you can readily see, Margaret, my drinking excesses of yesterday have somewhat caught up with me this morning.'

Atia took two analgesic capsules she had brought with her out of her skirt pocket and handed them over to Marie.

'Take these, Marie, they'll get rid of yer 'eadache.'

The young Earth woman looked at the two dark green capsules lying in her hand; she had obviously never seen anything like them. Atia was taking a chance bringing them from the Jaran medikit lying concealed in their guesthouse room, particularly as she had taken them without the express permission of First Commander Ashto. But she had accurately anticipated Marie's alcohol induced hangover and thought that the very least she could do was offer to alleviate the young woman's symptoms.

'Swallow 'em with some water – they'll quickly make yer feel better – woman I know gave 'em me.'

'Well, if you say so me darlin' girl.'

Marie walked slowly over to the fireplace picking up a chipped cup with a faded rose pattern on its side from the shelf and poured some water from the kettle into it. She put both capsules in her mouth after giving them one final curious look and took a gulp of the water from the cup, grimacing as she swallowed the pills.

'They'll cure yer 'eadache in no time at all,' said Atia.

'Well Maggie, you're a lifesaver and no mistake. Tell me what did you think of my chap, Joe, when you met him yesterday,' said Marie, pushing loose hair from her eyes and smiling at Atia in a careworn way.

'Joe seemed very concerned about yer wellbeing, Marie. Perhaps 'e an' you could lay off the drink for a bit,' Atia said hopefully.

Marie smiled but remained silent at the suggestion.

Atia had not seen Marie since. As far as she knew the young Irish woman continued to go into the Ten Bells each day, continued to get drunk and continued to pick up men and take them back to 13, Miller's Court where she had sex with them for money which then would enable her to go back to a pub and continue drinking. It was the perfect vicious circle, thought Atia, that one day would end in Marie becoming sick with some alcohol induced illness, after first being ejected from her squalid room due to her non-payment of the rent. It was a hopeless state of affairs that Atia tried to put to the back of her mind. After all, she rationalised, she and First Commander Ashto had much bigger problems to worry about. True the Ripper had not struck for the whole of the month of October but Atia knew that one day soon the crazed killer would strike again unless they could stop him. And so Atia turned her full attention back to the problem in hand. She visited the Ten Bells on three more consecutive days without any tangible result before deciding that the Ripper must have either left London completely or had decided to visit pubs outside the Whitechapel and Spitlefields area.

And then on Thursday 1st November the ship's computer, in its continued scanning of the area, came up with two new alerts.

It was on the evening of that first day of the new month. Atia and Ashto had just returned in a hansom cab from Fortescue's restaurant in the Strand. This had been the first time Atia had been back to the plush eating establishment since Mr Rogers had taken her there. Atia had suggested to Ashto that they should go for a meal at Fortescue's as a special treat. She felt that they had needed to alleviate in some way the feeling of failure that both felt in regard to their lack of success in trying to catch the Whitechapel killer. They had known that the task would not be easy but neither had they thought they would achieve such limited results. In the whole of October they had only one lead in their quest to track down the Ripper by linking his DNA trace to that of the material Atia had found under the fingernails of the dead Catherine Eddowes and then there had been silence from the computer. It was continuing to scan everywhere in Whitechapel and Spitlefields everyday but apart from that one occasion the killer's DNA had not been found in any pub, chop house, coffee shop, door handle, piece of clothing, alleyway or gutter of the area.

Ashto and Atia felt full of fine food and both were in a lighthearted mood as they climbed the stairs to their room at Mrs Smith's Bell Lane guesthouse. They had dined on soup, roast beef and French cheeses and felt very satisfied. They had even indulged in a glass each of red wine to go with their food, a libation both agreed was definitely superior to the gin and beer they had imbibed in East End public houses. In the room Atia decided to make her usual routine check of the computer terminal to see if the ship's computer had managed to make a match with the Ripper's DNA fingerprint it held in its data bank. Suddenly Atia let out a triumphant sound – a mixture of surprise and delight – for there on the screen was the alert they had been waiting for since halfway through October.

Ashto quickly joined her to peer at the small screen. 'Earlier this evening,' said Atia, 'in the Britannia Public House. Another DNA trace, again most probably his saliva on a beer or spirits' glass and then another trace found in an alleyway in Goulston Street – almost certainly his urine where he stopped to relieve himself.' Suddenly Atia turned to look at Ashto a shocked expression on her face. 'Trevor, he must have walked down Bell Lane on his way from the Britannia. He will have passed by this very building. We must go out there and see if we can identify him.'

'No Margot, look at the time of the alert – just after 7 o'clock this evening in the pub and 30 minutes afterwards in Goulston Street – that's over 3 hours ago. He won't be anywhere nearby any more. He was most probably either going home from his work or going to work at the start of a night shift, I'm afraid his trail will by now have gone cold.'

That night in bed Atia found it difficult to sleep and instead formulated her plan for the next day. This was the time they had been waiting for and they must not let this opportunity slip through their fingers. Tomorrow, dressed as Maggie, she would go to the Britannia pub and this time would not sit quietly in a corner just watching and observing. This time she would, in mock-drunken fashion, circulate around the pub chatting, flirting, accepting drinks off men she conversed with, making herself an obvious target for the Ripper. She would rely on the computer terminal to alert her if the Ripper was in the pub and if he was she would do her utmost to walk out with him, promising him cheap sex in a nearby alley and then disable him when he was just about to strike. She would need to be careful; she knew the man was skillful and dangerous but she was confident that she would be able to disarm and overpower him. And when she had she would take him to the nearest beat policeman and her part of the action would be over and she would be able to relax and get back to her mission. It was all very simple. She was looking forward to it.

Next to her in the bed Ashto was also lying awake making plans. Leaving Atia to carry out all the work herself would not be something that would happen again. Tomorrow they would begin to work together to catch Jack the Ripper.

'Is that wise, Trevor?'

'Yes, Margot I think it is. I have been thinking it all through very carefully and it is much safer than you going undercover alone.'

'But Trevor, are you really confident that you can converse with the customers of the Britannia in the manner of a fellow member of the East End working class?'

'Yes Margot I believe I can,' said Ashto a little hurt that his Apprentice Commander did not believe he could be as successful in an undercover role as she had been. 'I am going to adopt the role of a dockworker; there are, of course, many in this area of London. If questioned about any inaccuracies of my speech I will claim to originate from the country called Germany, a recently formed state situated in the centre of the European continent. My researches have indicated that there are many nationalities working in the East End docks and therefore I will not seem out of place.

What this means is that I can be on hand to work with you and so pursue the Ripper if we identify him as one of the customers in the Britannia pub.'

Atia looked down at the clothes that Ashto had purchased that morning from the same pawnshop where she had obtained her 'Maggie' outfit. She looked carefully at the thick but worn trousers, stained blue-striped collarless shirt, dusty dark grey jacket, grubby deep red patterned waistcoat, greasy flat peaked cap and large lace up boots with iron toecaps. She nodded her acceptance of the clothes but still wasn't convinced that the First Commander would be able to carry out a convincingly correct impersonation of an East End dockworker.

'Trevor, have you settled on what we might term the back-story of this German dockworker you are planning to portray?'

For a moment Ashto looked quizzically at Atia and then realising what she meant said: 'I understand, Margot, you mean my origins and how I have come to be living and working in the East End of London. I have decided that my name is Johann Schmitt and I have lived in London for the last ten years and therefore my use of English is good but not perfect. I will therefore have an excuse if I do not immediately recognise a particular English idiom or colloquialism that is used by someone with whom I am conversing. I have been studying the language information on my neural implant for some useful informal phrases that I will be able to employ in my speech to convince others that I have been working in the East End for a relatively long period of time.'

'I see, Trevor. If you are certain that you can be convincing in this role then of course you must follow through with your plan,' said Atia, still not wholly convinced that the First Commander's plan was a sound one. 'How do you propose we should comport ourselves in the public house?'

'What do you suggest, Margot? You are now far more used to such places than I am.'

Atia was pleased that Ashto was letting her put forward her ideas of what their strategy should be once they were inside the Britannia. 'Trevor, it is my opinion that we should take a more dynamic approach to the situation than both of us merely observing the Earth humans in the pub. I will play an active role by circulating among the customers in the drinking establishment and talking to as many of the men in the pub that fit with the criminal profile of the Ripper I have formulated. In other words I am going to make myself an obvious target for him and hope that he then walks out with me onto the street and then, when I have proof of his intentions, I will overpower him and deliver him to the nearest police officer.'

'And what should I be doing while you are performing in such a way?' Ashto sounded skeptical. How could he let Atia place herself in so much danger while he did so very little?

'Well, Trevor it will be your role, if of course you agree, to observe matters while I go about talking to men in the pub and then if I leave with one of them you will follow me, at a discrete distance hopefully, and act accordingly when the man attempts to attack me.'

'Margot, that seems extraordinarily dangerous. What if the man strikes before you can react? We know that he must be skillful and adept in his murderous intent. I could not bear it if you were harmed in any way.'

Atia smiled, grabbed Ashto's hand and held it to her face. 'Please do not worry, Trevor. We will both be there to protect each other and together we will be more than a match for this lone, psychotic killer.'

Unconvinced, Ashto smiled back at Atia, leaned forward and kissed her. He had never felt more protective towards anyone than he did at this moment.

'Well, Trevor I think it is about time you got dressed in your Johann Schmitt outfit,' she said picking up the clothes from the bed where Ashto had laid them and giving them a shake in the vain hope that some of the lice that undoubtedly inhabited them might be shaken off.

He stood in his room staring out of the window to the street below. He could see the people scurrying about – mere ants carrying out their ordinary everyday mundane matters. Street sellers shouting about the goods they had piled on their barrows; small, vulnerable looking match girls; people peering at, handling and buying fruit, vegetables and other goods; others coming and going from Aldgate underground railway station, all with their important business to attend to no doubt. As he observed the outside world he drew his knife along a whetstone – first one side then the other – mechanical, rhythmic, practised. Every so often he would feel with his thumb the sharpness, the keenness of his knife's edge, but still he carried on as though ending the process would somehow make his actions up until now meaningless and pointless. His knife had to be sharp and ready for the moment God instructed him when his next act of holy work would take place. He felt it would happen soon. It had been a long time since he had last been called on to do God's bidding; so long ago that his headaches had returned – keen, isolated, throbbing pains right behind his eyes. Sometimes they were so bad that he had to lie down on his bed and close his eyes against the bright stabbing lights that assailed them and which seemed to bounce around inside his skull. The headaches came more often now but he knew they would stop once God had told him it was time for him to act. 'It wouldn't be long now,' he told himself out loud. Soon his knife would again feel the softness of a tart's neck. Then her blood would gush out, not onto the street this time but onto the stained linen sheets of her bed. He had seen the one he wanted. He had followed her to her room down that dark alleyway. He had peered through her window. He had seen her bed where she carried out her filthy business – the bed on which she would die. He was looking forward to it and could hardly contain his impatience. All he needed now was a signal from God. Last month he had thought for a while that the thick fog smothering the area had been the sign he had patiently waited for. On one occasion he had been ready but then his headache had started, so painfully he had felt like screaming. He had to leave the pub where he had been watching her and return home to lie down with the curtains drawn. Since then he had observed her on several more occasions – drunk, loud, singing, luring men into her foul embrace. He had seen her up close yesterday, her dark eyes and long white neck, but he had missed his chance. It was in the pub nearest to where she lived. He had drunk a pint of beer while he watched her leave with another man. He had followed them across the busy street just in case the man abandoned her before she took him to her room. But they had both disappeared inside. Through the window he had seen her on the bed, legs wide apart with the man, trousers around his ankles, lying on top of her. He watched for a while and then, realising he badly needed to relieve himself, walked back down the alley into Dorset Street, turned left down Bell Lane and into Goulston Street, where unable to hold on any longer, he emptied his bladder in one of the entrances of the Jew building. As he did so he issued a sigh of relief and then smiled at the realisation that this was the very same entry way where he had left part of the last whore's bloodied apron on which he had wiped his hands; the same place where he had chalked his clever, cryptic message to the police.

21

A Return to the Britannia

The Britannia Public House was noisy, smoky and warm, a contrast to the cold and rain soaked streets outside. First Commander Ashto, wearing his newly acquired suit of clothes and black peaked cap, had entered the pub on his own, somewhat reluctantly bought himself a pint of bitter beer from the bearded, waistcoated barman and then found a seat in the corner beneath the orange glow of a gas mantle where he could observe carefully the clientele in the room. Only one person had spoken to him so far, a drunken human male who uttered something unintelligible to him at the bar and then seemed quite satisfied with the grunt and the nod that Ashto gave him in return. Looking around Ashto noticed that the customers were the same sort of mix as on his previous visit to the pub. Workingmen who had called in on their way home from their labours made up most of those present, many still carrying evidence of their trade on their clothes, hands and faces. Butchers and slaughtermen displayed bloodstains on their trousers and boots; blacksmiths and foundry workers had numerous burn holes in their attire along with soot traces on their faces. Mixing with the workmen were those more feckless individuals who had managed to spend most of the day in the Britannia having scrounged money off their friends, acquaintances or wives or by spending their rent money before it could end up in the hands of their landlords. Alongside the men Ashto estimated that about 20 per cent of those present in the pub were women. There were flower sellers and market workers as well as a fair smattering of what the newspapers called 'unfortunates' – prostitutes, some casual others inveterate – the sort of women that the Ripper had homed in on and who were at greatest risk of being slaughtered in some lonely alleyway, dark court or deserted square. Ashto recognised one of the men he had spoken with on his first visit to the Britannia and hoped that his disguise as a foreign dockworker was good enough to fool those with whom he had drunk a large amount of beer and whisky on that occasion. He was sure that his torn, rank and ragged clothes plus the dirt he wore on his face would fool even his favourite crèche mother, in the extremely unlikely event that she was to walk into the Britannia public house and begin a conversation with him. Ashto smiled and sitting back in his chair, sipped his beer and waited for Atia to appear.

Even though the First Commander was used to seeing Atia in her undercover disguise as one of the destitute women of Whitechapel her arrival into the pub still surprised him. She looked so convincing as she threw open the door and staggered in, bumping into chairs and people and gruffly apologising as she did so. Swaying her way to the bar she banged on the counter demanding to be served while exchanging friendly jibes with the men already standing there.

'Ain't yer 'ad enough already?' said the barman as he responded to Atia's slurred demand for a pint of beer.

'Not yet nearly enough, me ole cock,' replied Atia smiling and winking at the man behind the bar.

Atia turned and looked round the room, pint of beer in her hand. She saw First Commander Ashto sitting in the corner to her right but did not acknowledge him. What she was looking for were the men in the public house who would fit her profile of Jack the Ripper. She had estimated that he would probably be in his thirties or early forties – unmarried, a loner who would almost certainly be sitting on his own. He would probably be a workingman and a local who knew the Whitechapel area intimately – knew all the alleyways, byways, shortcuts, back-yards, courts and dark corners. He was someone who was very aware of the beat schedules of the police constables who patrolled the area and the time it took them to complete their rounds; a man who was nerveless, ingenious and driven by some illogical but powerful force that compelled him to kill women of a certain type and then savagely mutilate their bodies. What that force was Atia didn't know but she was convinced that she would recognise it if or when she came into contact with the Ripper.

As Atia looked around an elderly white bearded man standing next to her at the bar turned and spoke to her.

'Are yer lookin' for someone in particular love, or will I do?'

Atia looked disdainfully at the man who was much too old to fit her profile.

'Lookin' for someone a bit younger than you old man – someone with a bit o' go in 'im who isn't at death's door already.'

The man chuckled. 'There's life in the ole dog yet me dear. Let me take you round the back an' I'll soon show you there's plenty o' lead in this ole pencil.' He grabbed his crotch area as if to prove the point.

'Well if I ever get desperate I'll let yer know, yer dirty ole goat!' said Atia winking at the man, giving him a friendly punch in the shoulder, laughing loudly and moving away from the bar. She had just seen a man sitting at a table on his own by one of the large windows of the pub. He was staring into his half drunk pint of beer and had a pensive expression on his face. He fitted Atia's Ripper profile to a tee and it was time she spoke to him.

As she weaved in and out of the tables, chairs and people in the crowded room, Ashto watched his Apprentice Commander intently as she then sat down next to a man. He quickly got out his computer terminal and checked whether the ship's computer had issued an alert about this particular male Atia was now sitting by and speaking to. It hadn't, but that was not a reason Ashto should stop worrying. Perhaps the man, if he were the Ripper, had not yet left enough of his DNA on the pint glass he was drinking from to register with the scans that were being carried out by the ship's computer many miles above where he now sat.

Atia was finding it difficult to get a conversation going with the morose man she had decided to speak to. He had merely grunted when she had asked him how he was keeping. 'An' what is it yer do darlin?' persisted Atia.

'What's it to you what I do?' said the man.

'Only askin' dearie, that's all. Yer were lookin' a bit lemoncholy so I thought I might come an' cheer yer up a bit.'

'Yer not goin' to cheer me up any – me missus 'as just run off with our bleedin' lodger – so be off with you, whore, an' go an' bother somebody else – I jus' want to sit 'ere on me own an' be left in peace.' The man looked even more morose as he peered again into his beer glass with sad, forlorn eyes.

Atia didn't quite know what to say in response. She doubted that this man could be the Ripper. According to her criminal profile the Whitechapel killer most probably lived alone and had developed a hatred for woman based on something that had happened to him in the past. This depressed man had been married until recently when his wife had left him for pastures anew and he was obviously upset at what had occurred. She glanced at his hands. They belonged to someone who wielded a pen rather than a knife; they were soft and uncalloused. He was most probably a poorly paid clerk in a local business and certainly not someone used to manual work in a cobblers, blacksmiths, foundry, butchers or market. The type of occupation Atia believed was carried out by the Ripper would require a man with strong hands, one probably used to wielding sharp knives as part of his everyday work and who would have an easy charm about himself that would disguise the deep darkness of his evil intent. Atia patted the man on his shoulder in a consoling fashion and stood up and left him to his own doleful thoughts. He didn't even look up as Atia departed.

Atia walked over to another man in his mid to late 30s who sat on his own, an altogether more cheerful seeming individual who smiled at her and beckoned her over to sit on his knee. She sat down in his lap immediately aware of his pungent smell – the strong mixture of tobacco and beer on his breath and the almost overpowering odour of sweat exuding from his clothes. He gave her a kiss on her cheek. 'I ain't seen yer 'ere before – I know most o' the street girls an' I'd 'ave recognised someone as tall and fetchin' as yerself an' no mistake.'

'Oh I've bin in in 'ere many times – yer've just bin too elephant's trunk to notice me.' The man laughed. Atia looked closely at him – his outdoor florid complexion, his dark drooping mustache, his pale blue eyes in which she could perceive no obvious malevolence.

'Perhaps me an' you could leave 'ere for five minutes and find a dark alleyway somewhere?' said the man giving Atia another kiss on the cheek and moving his right hand up to her right breast and squeezing.

'Not yet, maybe later – I 'aven't 'ad enough beer yet 'andsome.' Atia moved his large, work-hardened hand from where it had strayed, stood up from the man's lap and winked at him before taking a large gulp of her beer. The man looked a little disappointed but seemed happy enough as he exchanged ribald comments with three other men at the next table. Atia was convinced that this individual was not the Ripper despite his suggestion that they should leave the pub to engage in an act of casual sex. The man they called Jack the Ripper was going to be someone who would be more cunningly charming and less direct in his entreaties. Someone who might simply be content to follow a potential victim out of the pub, catch her up, make a suggestion and then accompany her down a dark deserted alleyway where he would be able to take her life, giving her no more thought than he would to an ant he had just stepped on. Added to this Atia, while sitting on the man's lap, had felt around for any evidence of him carrying a concealed knife on his person. She had also looked for a bag or package on the floor beneath where the man sat which would, if he were the Ripper, contain the tools of his trade. Besides it was probably too early in the evening for the Ripper to strike. His normal pattern was to kill his victims late at night or during the very early hours of the morning when there were few people about to interrupt him in his work. Atia was convinced that she and Ashto, who she could see was still sitting on his own in the corner pretending to read a newspaper, would be in the Britannia until late on in the day, observing all the obvious Ripper candidates. Even then the chances were that the murderer would not make an appearance at all on this particular evening.

Ashto had picked up a day old newspaper from the floor near to where he sat and pretended to read it whilst he watched out of the corner of his eye Atia sit down on the knee of a man over on the far side of the room. He was ready to leap up and deal with any attempt to harm Atia but was careful to restrain himself for the time being despite seeing the man caress Atia in a somewhat intimate fashion. Ashto knew that for their plan to succeed he would have to let Atia expose herself to certain indignities at the hands of Earth humans as he watched the man squeeze Atia's right breast. However, he was pleased when she stood up from the man's knee, exchanged pleasantries with him and then walked to the bar where she asked for her beer glass to be refilled. Ashto thought about joining her at the bar but decided to let the Apprentice Commander carry on having conversations with all and sundry while he would keep a close eye on her as she did so.

Atia started to chat to a man who stood alone at the bar.

"Ow are you me ol' china?' said Atia, winking at the man.

'I'm very well my dear. Can I buy you a drink?' said the man smiling back at Atia; his intelligent looking eyes examining her up and down.

'Course you can ducky, that's very decent o' yer – I'm 'avin' a pint o' ale.'

'Certainly – it will be my pleasure to buy a lady a pint. By the way 'as anyone ever commented on the fact that you are uncommonly tall?' said the man taking out some coins from his pocket and paying for Atia's beer. The human male wore a long black overcoat with a fur collar and must have been about 5 feet 8 inches tall in Earth measurement – Atia was three inches taller.

'Yeah, me dad used to call me a beanpole before 'e went an' kicked the bucket. Kept growin' an' growin' I did – cost me ma a fortune in clothes afor she sent me out on the street to fend for meself.'

The man looked down at the torn and shabby clothes Atia was wearing and smiled at her again. Atia thought he had a pleasant appearance, handsome with an attractive smile that lit up his whole face. She guessed was in his early thirties and had large, dark eyes, brown hair and a fashionable well-trimmed fairish mustache, slightly turned up at the ends. She looked down at his hands and saw that although they were clearly the strong hands of a manual worker, but they were well cared for with unmarked, well-shaped fingernails. He was obviously someone who liked to keep himself clean and tidy and who washed regularly – his unusual lack of a strong body odour, which was almost universally prevalent among the inhabitants of this part of London, was something else Atia noticed as she stood a little closer to the man.

'Well, my dear you are no longer a mere beanpole but, if I might say so, you are a very beautiful young lady. Here's to your health,' said the man as he took a large mouthful of his beer and, peering over the top of his glass, watched Atia as she did the same.

Atia looked back into the man's eyes, which creased together in an attractive way when he smiled. But was there something else in those eyes, thought Atia – something deep, liquid and impenetrable. She found herself staring unable to shift her gaze from them even though she tried. She gradually felt herself floating – a pleasantly detached feeling that she had never experienced before. She stood transfixed as she stared into the depths of his dark brown, almost black eyes and felt as though she had begun to fall headlong into a bottomless pit – down and further down – and she felt inordinately happy as she did so.

Suddenly someone speaking to her, seemingly from a far-off, distant place, interrupted her thoughts. With great difficulty and with a strange reluctance she tore herself away from the man's eyes and turned to look at the person who had spoken to her and persistently tapped on her shoulder. There was the white bearded, aged individual who had exchanged words with her when she had first entered the pub and stood at the bar.

'I said, 'ave yer changed yer mind yet? I bet you a quid to a bloater yer money will soon run out and yer'll be lookin' for someone to treat yer to a few beers in return for a bit of a fumble round the back o' the pub.'

Atia, jolted back to reality, smiled cheekily at the man. "As I said afore I like me fellas to 'ave a bit of life in 'em. Yer'd drop dead with exhaustion afore yer got yer money's worth!'

A number of men at the bar overhearing Atia's comments laughed loudly and poked and pointed at the old man in friendly fashion. The white bearded man himself guffawed deeply and loudly and raised his glass to this spirited young woman. Atia smiled back and also gulped down some of her beer.

She turned back ready to carry on her conversation with the charismatic young man with the mesmeric eyes only to find that he had gone, his glass of beer standing unfinished on the bar's counter. Her first reaction was disappointment. She had been looking forward to conversing further with the attractive, quite charming and seemingly intelligent human male. At that very moment both Atia and Ashto's computer terminals in their respective pockets gently vibrated. Both Jarans secretly glanced at their small computer screens. The ship's computer had issued another alert. The Ripper's DNA had been left on the pint glass which stood on the bar near to Atia. With shocked looks on their faces the Jaran deep space explorers, for a few crucial seconds momentarily numb, stared at each other across the smoky room realising that only a minute or so before Atia had been talking to, admiring and looking deeply into the eyes of the man the world called, Jack the Ripper.

22

Chasing the Ripper

Ashto and Atia ran to the front door of the Britannia public house and dashed outside. They stood in the pouring rain looking up and down Commercial Street, quizzical concern etched on their faces. They peered to no avail down the dark and narrow Dorset Street. Which way had the man gone? They could see no sign of him. And then Ashto exclaimed, 'Goulston Street, that was the way he went before!'

The Jarans set off at a run down Dorset Street, turning left into Crispin Street and then into Bell Lane past gas-lamps with their yellow light reflected dimly in the glistening pavement. Running at speed, occasionally bumping into individuals and issuing quick apologies that were invariably greeted with swear words and curses, they dashed past Mrs Smith's guesthouse and on into Goulston Street where the Ripper's DNA had been identified by the computer sensor scan the day before. At the end of Goulston Street they stopped. Whitechapel High Street was as busy as usual and in the twilight with the rain still teeming down it was well nigh impossible to make out any particular individual among those coming and going along the crowded thoroughfare. Thinking quickly and knowing it was a gamble Ashto said, 'let's go right – we know that the Ripper had once headed in that direction when he murdered Catherine Eddowes in Mitre Square.'

The Jaran pair tore down the busy pavement as fast as the crowded conditions allowed. As they approached Aldgate Street Atia stopped and pointed. 'There,' she shouted, 'I'm sure I've just observed him entering Aldgate station.'

Dripping wet Ashto and Atia ran into the entrance hall of the station just in time to see the back of the Ripper descending the stairs down to the station's platforms. They began to run after him but were stopped by the outstretched arm of a burly, blue uniformed ticket collector who wore huge mutton chop whiskers and who glared at them sternly. 'Let's see your tickets,' he said gruffly, looking with distain at the shabbily dressed pair.

Atia grunted with impatience. She considered grabbing the ticket collector by the arm and throwing him to the floor before running down the stairs in pursuit of the Ripper but thought better of it and turned to see where they could purchase tickets.

There were two ticket booths. One was labelled District Inner Circle and the other Metropolitan Outer Circle. There were no customers at the latter window and so Atia, quickly grabbing coins from her pocket, moved swiftly across to the booth's window and asked for and paid for two tickets.

After showing them to the smug looking bewhiskered ticket collector Atia and Ashto dashed down the stairs and turned onto the Outer Circle platform where they saw a train waiting, doors to the carriages in the process of being closed by the several station porters. Luckily for the Jaran pair the underground trains waited for a longer period of time at Aldgate station than at any of the other stops along the recently completed Metropolitan and District Circle lines in order to enable the water tanks of the steam locomotives to be topped up ready to complete the 13 mile round circuit of the city. Having no idea if the Ripper was already on this train or had boarded another going in the opposite direction, all Atia and Ashto could do was to quickly enter the last of the train carriages and hope for the best.

Inside the compartment a number of people were already sat; unfortunately the Ripper was not among them. Soon afterwards the door to the compartment was slammed shut, a guard blew a loud blast on a whistle and the train, with a great whooshing of smoke and steam moved off and entered the dark tunnel.

Ashto looked around at those others in the compartment quickly realising he and Atia, in their pawnshop purchased clothes, were by far the most badly turned out individuals present. A well-dressed elderly lady looked rather disdainfully down her nose at them as though she soon expected to be asked for money or even robbed by the disreputable looking pair with dirty faces and torn clothes. The other three in the compartment, studiously ignoring the Jarans, were all male, all youngish and appeared by the look their clothes to work as junior clerks, probably in East End offices. All were puffing on cigarettes and reading newspapers.

Atia looked out of the window as the train travelled through the tunnel. She considered it was a somewhat of an ironic situation for her to find herself in – travelling through an alien subterranean tunnel in a primitive, noisy, hissing, steam driven vehicle at, she estimated, something just over 20 miles per hour. When she and Ashto had travelled through deep space from Jara to this small and insignificant planet situated on the far side of the galaxy their ship had travelled at an unimaginably fast speed and still the journey had taken two Earth years to complete. Travelling the 13-mile underground circuit with its 27 station stops took 70 or 80 minutes as she and Ashto had discovered several weeks before when, as part of their researches, they had first been passengers on the underground railway. They had not liked the journey at that time and had not been keen to repeat the experience. But now here they were again, rattling along in the train, their nasal passages assailed not only by the tobacco smoke of the passengers but by the mixture of sulpher and coal dust that seeped into the compartment and also by the fumes of the oil lamp which provided a modicum of illumination as the train trundled through the pitch black tunnels.

As the train arrived at the first station, Trinity Square, the Jaran pair both stepped out onto the platform to see if the Ripper was leaving one of the carriages, ready to pursue and apprehend him if he did. However, there was no sign of him so Ashto and Atia could do nothing else but re-enter the compartment at the insistent urging of the station porters and sit back down again, much to the sniffy annoyance of the elderly woman who leant on her walking stick and tutted loudly at their apparent indecision.

At each subsequent station, Mansion House, St James Park, Sloane Square, Earls Court, Kensington High Street and Edgware Road, Ashto and Atia repeated their routine of getting out of the compartment, checking whether they could see the Ripper leave the train or not, and then climbing back aboard to be greeted by further loud tutting noises from the well attired lady. And then at Baker Street station, as the train drew to a halt, the elderly woman herself got up and leaning heavily on her walking cane began to exit the carriage after the porters on the platform had thrown open the door of the compartment. Much to her obvious surprise Ashto stood up and gallantly steadying the woman by her arm assisted her slow and deliberate progress backward out of the carriage. She was noticed by one of the porters who started to shove her back into the compartment saying, 'Hurry up ma'am, train's about to leave.'

'Excuse me young man I am in the process of leaving your infernal contraption not getting back into it. Now help me down.'

As the elderly woman was negotiating her slow egress from the carriage, helped by Ashto and the porter, Atia was keeping her eye open for any sign of the Ripper leaving the train and heading for the stairs at the end of the station platform with its crimson and gold tiled walls and numerous advertising hoardings.

Eventually with the woman safely departed and the doors closed again the train began to move with the usual accompanying cascade of smoke, steam and noise. Ashto looked at Atia. 'Margot, It's looking more and more likely that our man is not on this particular train and must have caught one of those going in the opposite direction,' he said in a whisper.

'It does Trevor and we were so close to apprehending him,' replied Atia looking disappointed. 'All we can do is continue to check at each station as we have been doing and hope for the best. Do you think he knows we are following him?'

'It seems unlikely Margot. We were only alerted to his presence by the computer's sensor scan after he had left the Britannia and it was only a matter of chance that we saw him when we did.'

Atia looked concerned as she thought back to her conversation with the man at the bar of the Britannia, the man they now knew was Jack the Ripper. 'Trevor, there was something strange about the man's eyes, something I have never seen before in the eyes of any Earth human or for that matter any Jaran I have conversed with.'

'What was it you saw in his eyes, Margot?'

'I'm afraid I do not know Trevor. There was a strange power there – magnetic almost – as well as a raw, terrifying and evil intelligence that somehow belied his looks and something else … I cannot explain … ' Atia looked puzzled. It was the first time that Ashto had seen his Apprentice Commander lost for words and floundering over something she could not explain nor fully understand.

The train pulled into the next station and as usual the Jaran pair stood up from their seats to observe those leaving the train. By now the compartment was empty save for the two of them, the three junior clerks having departed at various stops along the way. The stations came and went – Portland Street, Gower Street and Kings Cross. As Ashto stepped out of the carriage observing those leaving the train he made a last-second decision to run down the long platform and look into as many of the grimy carriage windows as he could in an attempt to ascertain if the Ripper was on the train. Porters were already closing the compartment doors when he reached the carriage closest to the steaming and hissing locomotive. And then peering through the greasy, ash smeared carriage window he saw him seated on the far side of the compartment. Their eyes met and for a brief moment Ashto thought he saw the Ripper's mouth break into a thin smile of surprise.

Ashto grabbed the door handle just as a porter behind him shouted something loud and unintelligible at him. As the train began to pull away from King's Cross station Ashto desperately but unavailingly tried to open the door as the train began to enter the dark, forbidding tunnel. All the Jaran First Commander could do was to flatten himself as much as possible against the grimy and oil splattered carriage, hold on to the door handle and try to find a solid purchase for his feet. Ashto felt his jacket brushing against the bricks of the tunnel wall as the train picked up speed.

First Commander Ashto didn't know it but he had found himself clinging to the outside of one of London's underground trains on the section of the Metropolitan Line that was the straightest and fastest part of the line that circled the city. On this section, between Kings Cross and Farringdon Street, the engine drivers looked forward to virtually doubling the speed of their trains and usually reached close to 40 miles per hour.

Ashto, who had flown through deep space where there was never any actual sensation of speed now found himself clinging for his very life to a primitive, clanking, steam driven vehicle moving rapidly below the ground level of an alien city. The First Commander's peaked cap flew from his head, his hands began to ache and cramp and his arms felt as though they were being torn from their sockets. His vision began to be obscured as smoke, coal dust and hot pieces of ash assailed his eyes and flew into his nose and mouth causing him to gag and cough.

Inside the compartment its occupants stared in disbelief at the rough looking man who grimaced with effort as he tried to hold on to the fast moving train in the darkness, his face and hair growing increasingly covered in grime and with bright orange shards of burning ash constantly flying past his head.

Atia, who had climbed back aboard the train before it started to move, assumed that Ashto had been able to gain entry into another of the train carriages as she had not seen him standing on the station platform as the train pulled away. Had he found the Ripper? Was he, at this very moment, confronting the man with the hypnotic eyes and restraining him in some way ready to hand him over to the authorities at the next stop? However, one thing she did know was that the train had recently gained a lot more speed and now seemed to be positively racing through the dark of the tunnel.

Ashto was certain that he was soon going to slide from his position on the side of this train as it moved swiftly through the blackness of the tunnel. In his mind's eye he saw himself, unable to hold on any longer, falling from his precarious perch, smashing his head against the tunnel wall and plunging unconsciously beneath the wheels of the train. He winced as he imagined what his mangled body would look like after the entire train had run over it. Even advanced Jaran medicine would not be able to repair the injuries he would doubtless sustain. How ironic, he thought to have come all this way across trillions of kilometres of deep space only to die ignominiously in the dust, filth, and grime of a rat-infested underground tunnel on some strange planet far from home.

Inside the compartment the Ripper smiled again. This unknown man who had obviously followed him, along with the tall woman from the pub, might well be an undercover policeman but whoever he was the prospect of him still being in one piece by the time the train reached the next station was extremely unlikely. Perhaps it would be merciful to hasten the process, he thought. He moved over to the door. 'I must help this poor man,' he said to the group of individuals with whom he shared the train compartment. Grabbing the handle he moved it downwards and attempted to push open the door.

'No, you can't do that, you'll kill him!' shouted a young man in a billycock hat.

The Ripper turned and gave him such a withering and menacing look with his dark, piercing eyes that the young man could do nothing else but sit down again in his seat and be quiet. The Ripper, with his strong hands waggled the door handle and using his shoulder tried again to open the door to which the Jaran First Commander still clung, desperation in his eyes.

Ashto could hardly see, so full of dust and soot were his eyes. He could just make out the inside of the compartment with its dim light from the single oil lamp on the wall illuminating the face of the Ripper smiling malevolently at him through the grime covered glass. He felt his hands, numb and icy cold, gradually slipping from the door handle as it repeatedly and quickly turned. He also felt the door on which he hung so desperately begin to open. Ashto tried to look ahead where the end of the carriage he clung to was attached to the locomotive that pulled it. He could just make out a few features through his ash filled eyes that smarted terribly; he would so like to rub them clean. Could he possibly gain enough purchase with his feet at the bottom of the virtually smooth wood of the carriage to move himself a few feet forward and enable him to grab the brass coloured rail at the rear of the locomotive. He decided to give it a try as his only hope to come out of the situation he found himself in with his life and body intact. Reluctantly moving his right hand from the still waggling door handle he clutched the frame of the last window in the carriage. Locking the very ends of his index finger and thumb around the narrow, wooden window frame as tightly as he could he slowly moved his right foot along until he was in a spread-eagled position almost at the very end of the carriage. Now was the tricky bit he thought. He had to let go the door handle with his left hand and move his left foot at the same time and hope that his grip on the window frame was strong enough to support his entire body. After a brief moment's hesitation his left hand released the jiggling door handle and in one movement fastened it onto the window frame and shifted his left foot at the same time. Just as he moved, the door to which he had been clinging flew open, scraped against the tunnel wall and slammed shut again. Quickly, Ashto with his grip on the thin window frame slowly slipping made a desperate leap and just managed to grab hold of the brass rail that formed part of the back of the tender of the railway locomotive. Pulling himself on the small platform that lay between the front carriage and the locomotive he breathed a deep sigh of relief and allowed himself a brief moment of comparative calm before he considered what he should do next.

Back in her compartment, Atia felt concerned about Ashto's safety. What if he had confronted the Ripper and had been injured, or worse, in the process? She now wished that she had accompanied the First Commander in actively looking for the murderer rather than simply waiting for him to appear at some point. She paced about in the empty compartment and wished that the train would soon slow down and stop at the next station.

"Ere what do you think yer doin'?'
The train driver had just noticed Ashto standing in the gap between the back of the locomotive and the first carriage and shouted at Ashto above the clanks and hisses of the engine.

'Apologies. Almost missed the train. Couldn't open a door – so jumped on here,' Ashto shouted back. He smiled at the driver in the hope it would show he was not threatening in any way.

The driver shook his head in resigned fashion. He was constantly surprised at just how idiotic some people could be. He looked at his fireman standing next to him on the footplate and shrugged his shoulders. He turned back to his controls; now was the time to apply the brakes and slow the train down ready for the next stop.

As the train pulled into Farringdon Street station the Ripper sat back in his seat. He had weighed the pros and cons of leaving the carriage at this stop but had decided against it. He was convinced that the scruffy individual who had followed him and had clung to the side of the train carriage was now lying on the railway track, some distance back, his body satisfyingly twisted and mangled. He considered that it was now safe for him to remain on the train until it returned to Aldgate with only the tall, good looking bitch to deal with if she attempted in some way to detain him. He felt his knife that was tucked into the waistband of his trousers and hidden beneath his coat. If necessary he could quickly deal with that woman and disappear into the maw of Whitechapel's backstreets and alleyways – something he had done so many times before.

He was then hugely surprised at the sight of a seemingly fully fit Ashto entering the carriage after the door of the compartment had been flung open to let out two of its occupants, both of whom still looked shocked at what had transpired during the previous few minutes. The scruffy man now seemed to be even more dirtied and dishevelled than when the Ripper had first noticed him. His torn clothes were more tattered with loose strips of cloth hanging from his oily trousers and jacket. His face was almost entirely blackened save for the area immediately around his eyes from which Ashto had partially managed to scrape away some of the grease and grime.

Ashto stepped into the carriage, determination on his face. He was about to approach the Ripper and apprehend him when he felt a firm hand clamped upon his shoulder.

'Hey you – get out o' there – you're coming with me.'

Ashto turned to see a police constable, truncheon poised in a threatening manner, standing behind him with the train driver at his side.

'That's the man constable,' said the driver, 'endangered the safety of the train with 'is shenanigans.'

The police constable gripped Ashto's shoulder even tighter. Ashto could have disarmed the policeman and rendered him insensible but decided not to. If he did so then in the ensuing chaos that followed, with probably many more policemen being called for, the Ripper could easily slip away unnoticed. Ashto had seen Atia standing on the platform nearby and with his eyes managed to indicate that the Ripper was in the carriage he had just been ejected from and hoped that Atia would know what to do.

Atia watched and considered what was the best policy she should adopt. She could see that Ashto could have easily dealt with the uniformed police officer if he had so desired and so had obviously decided not to. Therefore, she reasoned, what he wanted her to do was to continue to monitor the movements of the Ripper. If the killer stayed on the train so should she and if he left and headed for the staircase up to street level she should follow him.

The engine driver got back onto his footplate, satisfied that justice would be meted out to the man who had encroached onto his locomotive and began to prepare for the train to leave the station. Compartment doors were closed and a whistle was blown. Atia seeing that the

Ripper stayed where he was also got back onto the train and made eye contact with Ashto through the window as he was manhandled toward the stairs by the burly looking policeman who had a firm grip on his collar.

Ashto was led up the stairs by the policeman and began looking for a suitable place where he could free himself from the constable's grip. At the top of the stairs were a large number of people buying tickets, presenting them to ticket collectors as well as those just standing inside the station building sheltering from the heavy rain, which still poured down making the pavements outside wet and slick. The policeman ushered Ashto to the street outside and led him down Cowcross Street. Away from the crowded station Ashto saw his chance as he was led past a dark, deserted alleyway. He quickly turned, releasing himself from the police officer's grip. The constable lulled by Ashto's quiet compliance so far was taken by surprise. He aimed his truncheon at Ashto's head but the Jaran First Commander was too quick for him and avoided the blow. Ashto forced the policeman back to a wall, quickly located a pressure point in the human's lower neck and using his strong, practised fingers rendered the man unconscious. He sat the policeman up against the wall and, worried about what might happen to him if the insensible, uniformed law officer was found by disreputable characters, took the man's whistle out of his pocket and gave three loud blasts on it. He knew that this was the signal that indicated an officer needed assistance and was sure that in less than a minute or two some of the unconscious man's colleagues would be there to look after him.

Atia stood in the train compartment impatiently tapping her foot. After checking that the Ripper hadn't left the train at Moorgate Street she returned to the compartment and sat down. She had thought about walking along the platform and getting into the same compartment that the Ripper occupied but had decided against it. When he leaves the train, Atia thought, her best strategy would be to carefully follow the murderer and see where he ended up. With luck he would lead her straight to where he lived. After that it would be a simple matter to inform the police where he resided and let them do the rest.

At Bishopsgate Street station Atia made sure that the Ripper did not exit the train before she stepped back inside the compartment where two men had entered. One of the men made a lewd suggestion to her as she sat down and it was all Atia could do to stop herself from angrily taking his head and bashing it against the carriage floor. As it was she just decided to ignore his comments.

As the train pulled into Aldgate station having completed the entire circuit of the Metropolitan Line and Atia stood up ready to leave she felt a hand reach round her, grab her by her waist and pull her backwards onto the seat again.

'George,' said one of the men, 'stand by the door so no one else gets in. We'll 'ave a bit 'o fun with this 'ere tart.'

Atia said nothing but swiftly flew into action. Within no more than thirty seconds both men lay on the floor groaning loudly and nursing their broken arms and Atia was able to leave the carriage. However, she had lost valuable time and couldn't see the Ripper in the group of passengers that had left the train and were now walking up the wooden staircase. She ran down to the front of the train, the water tanks of which were in the process of being filled, and peered into the open door of the compartment the Ripper had occupied. It was empty; he had left. Atia bolted up the stairs hoping that she hadn't lost him touch with the killer who had caused so much pain and mayhem in the area to which he had now returned.

At the top of the somewhat rickety wooden staircase a queue had formed as the newly arrived passengers presented their tickets to the ticket collector. That was when Atia saw the Ripper again. He was ahead of her in the queue and was just about to hand over his ticket to the whiskery uniformed station official who had stopped Ashto and Atia before.

Atia held back and ducked her head a little behind a man who stood in front of her. She didn't want to take the chance that the Ripper might look back and see her. The queue of people handing over their tickets grew shorter and Atia would soon be ready to follow the killer who she saw was pulling the fur collar of his coat up around his neck against the rain and cold of the night before stepping out of the station booking hall and onto Aldgate High Street.

Atia was only two people away from the ticket inspector when she reached into her skirt pocket to retrieve her ticket ready to hand it over only to find that it was gone. The struggle with those two men, Atia thought, it must have dropped out of my pocket.

'Ticket,' said the man, again looking with complete distain at Atia in her shabby attire.

'I'm very sorry but I'm afraid I seem to have mislaid it,' said Atia sounding as apologetic as she could.

The ticket collector, baffled a little by the correct English used by this dirty and shabby looking woman, still smiled in a triumphant fashion. 'You don't expect me to believe that old story do you?' he said as he grabbed Atia's arm. 'We'll see what the coppers say when they 'ear you're trying to defraud the railway company.' He tightened his grip on the Apprentice Commander's arm and started to pull her to one side. 'In the meantime you can kick your 'eels while you're locked in our office. Bill, get out 'ere and go and lock this tart in the office until the police arrive to take 'er away.'

Atia was losing her patience. Aware that the Ripper was escaping and that she would lose him if she didn't act soon she grabbed the lapels of the man's jacket and swung him over her right shoulder onto the floor. She issued a swift warning look to Bill, the young man who had emerged from the ticket office, who backed away warily from this tall, mad looking woman with dark frizzy hair who had just thrown a large muscular looking man over her shoulder with apparent ease.

Atia dashed out onto the street where the rain still hosed down from the night sky. She had noticed that the Ripper had turned left as he had exited the station and so set off after him in that direction. Looking up Whitechapel High Street she could see no sign of her quarry. At this time of night there were not as many people about in the street as there had been earlier but there were still a few but none of those ahead looked anything like the man she had spoken to in the Britannia.

As Atia walked up the road peering into the distance, to her left was a narrow side street called Bull Yard that Atia knew led to a series of joined up dark, unlit alleys that formed one of the many rookeries of Whitechapel. If the Ripper had fled into the mazelike network of small courts and alleyways there would be no way that she would be able to find him. She stopped. It was hopeless. She felt as though she had again failed to apprehend the Ripper and present him to the authorities. Behind her she could hear the blowing of whistles and a general confused buzz of noise as the police, who had been called to the station to deal with the fracas she had caused, were already writing down the description of the deranged woman who had assaulted one of the station officials. Gathering her rain-soaked jacket around her against the cold and wet of the night she quickly headed off up Whitechapel High Street and then turned into Goulston Street making her way back to Mrs Smith's guesthouse.

Across the street, in a dark doorway, unseen and sheltered against the pouring rain, the man who was known as Jack the Ripper watched the tall woman who had followed him all over London as she walked along the pavement and disappeared into Goulston Street. Who she was and who the even taller man she had been with on the train was, he did not know. What he did know was that if he ever came into contact with the woman again he would greatly enjoy watching his sharp knife slice through her long, elegant looking neck.

Back in his room he sat lovingly sharpening his knife again. Tonight had been his closest call since that time in Berner Street when the driver of the cart had almost spotted him. Who the tall man and woman who followed him on the underground train were he knew not. He had first noticed them in the Britannia. He prided himself on noticing things that no one else did. He had seen them exchanging swift and secretive glances from the very moment the tall, good-looking bitch had first entered the pub. He had deliberately gone to stand with her at the bar in order to talk to her – to find out who she and her friend really were. She looked like a street whore but he knew she was only acting out a role. Her disguise might fool most people but not him; he knew more about disguises than anyone else he was sure about that. He had lived in a disguised state for much of his life pretending to be someone he wasn't. He was, he believed, more skillful than anyone on the Earth at covering up his true nature but deep down he was always aware of who he really was. Ever since his mother died he had known exactly that he was God's holy weapon – combatting the foulness and filth he found all around him. When he had realised that his own mother was one of those disgusting creatures who sold herself for the pleasure of others he had no alternative but to dispatch her and end the misery she had endured. She had pleaded with him – tried to make him understand. She said that she had done those things to pay the rent so they wouldn't be thrown out to starve on the street or have to crawl shamefully into the workhouse. It didn't matter. How could she go on living after what she had done – the men she had brought back into their home –THEIR HOME – the things they had done to her – his mother. To kill her was a mercy really – he had saved her from the indignities she would have had to further endure. He had left her on the blood soaked bed, her throat cut, her eyes open in shock and he had packed his few belongings into a battered old case and headed off to end up in this benighted place where he now lived. He hadn't been in Whitechapel long before God told him there was work for him to do – God's holy work to rid the area of the whores who were to be found on every street corner, in every pub, in every dark alleyway. He had waited so patiently for a new sign from God – a clear sign that would indicate to him that it was time to begin his labours again. And now those that had followed him around London had provided him with that sign. The woman in the pub who had looked into his eyes and peered into his soul; the man who had clung to the outside of the train and survived – somehow they knew who he was. He didn't know how they knew, but they did and the fact that others now knew was obviously a clear sign from God that he needed to begin his work again soon because he might not have much more time. He felt sad that he would never be able to fully complete the task that God had ordered him to carry out but he was proud to have made a start. There would be others to follow in his footsteps for he had set the benchmark that many would strive to emulate in the future. He would forever be remembered. He was certain that no one would ever forget the name of Jack the Ripper.

23

Strange Meetings

Friday 9th November 1888 was an important date in the social calendar of London for it was the day of the Lord Mayor's Show. Every year the newly elected Lord Mayor of the City of London would be paraded through the streets of the capital escorted by cavalry, and a holiday atmosphere would be engendered as crowds gathered along the route of the parade. Early morning heavy rain had not dampened people's spirits and when the skies finally cleared at 10 o'clock a watery sun shone on the banners, flags and flowers that decorated the streets. The route was lined with police and in the area in front of the Mansion House, where the lavish Mayoral banquet would take place for the benefit of the wealthy and the privileged, mounted police were conspicuously deployed. The Commissioner of the Metropolitan Police, Sir Charles Warren, who had suddenly resigned from his role the day before, had been so concerned that another 'Bloody Sunday' style riot might occur that he had ordered many more mounted police officers to stand ready around Trafalgar Square in order to crack a few skulls with their truncheons and billy clubs should the gathering crowds become too boisterous or threatening. However, as it turned out it was not Charles Warren or the Lord Mayor of London who would make the biggest headlines in the newspapers of the following day. By the time the Mayor's parade began at 12.30 in the afternoon news was spreading rapidly throughout the city that Jack the Ripper had struck again.

On the morning of Thursday 8th November, the day before the Lord Mayor's Show, First Commander Ashto and Apprentice Commander Atia had sat in their guesthouse room still brooding over the events on the London underground several days before. Both of the Jaran explorers had returned to the Britannia every day since then and in their disguises had waited for the Ripper to reappear while not really expecting him to show his face. They had also visited a number of other public houses in the district again to no avail. The Ripper had seemingly gone to ground and it was unlikely that he would be visiting any of the local pubs in the near future.

'Do you think it is worth our while turning up at the Britannia again today?' said Atia as she checked her computer terminal for the umpteenth time in case the ship's sensor scans had identified the Ripper's DNA and therefore his location again. So far there had been no positive result since the computer alert the Jarans had received on the 2nd November prior to their unsuccessful chase around the underground system. Ashto and Atia felt dejected. Had they missed their one and only opportunity to snare Jack the Ripper?

'I am not sure what but we must do something having come so far,' said Ashto.

'Perhaps we should split up and tour the pubs singly this evening and keep in touch with each other in the event we spot him,' replied Atia.

Ashto had no alternative plan to offer and so just nodded in a resigned way. 'I suppose the only good thing is that the Ripper has still not struck again and it is possible we may have frightened him off.'

'It is a nice thought, Trevor but I doubt very much that it is the case. If anything the fact that he was able to avoid capture has probably emboldened him and made him feel more invincible than ever. He will murder again soon I'm sure of it.' Atia looked back at her computer screen almost willing an alert to pop up giving them the current location of the Ripper.

The Jaran pair changed into their ragged disguises without speaking. They felt that they were going through the motions to a large extent with no great hope of success. Tonight's foray into the world of East End pubs would most likely end in exactly the same way as their search of the last few days had done – with no positive result. Things probably wouldn't change until the Ripper struck again and perhaps left some sort of clue for them to follow. As Atia and Ashto helped each other smear their faces with soot and ensured their communication devices were functioning correctly they looked with sadness into each other's eyes. This great adventure of theirs where they had crossed the galaxy to discover all that they could about this small, intriguing blue planet had turned out to be a disappointment. Instead of controlling events as Jarans were used to doing, events perpetrated by a psychotic Earth human were controlling their actions and so far their efforts to stop him doing so had been found wanting.

Ashto checked that the pair had everything they needed. Disguises in place, computer terminals tucked away in their respective pockets and communication equipment working perfectly. As a last-second thought Ashto picked up their one remaining fly drone and dropped it into his pocket. 'Just in case it could be of some use,' he said not sounding very convinced that they would be successful in any way this evening.

'Where shall we begin tonight, Trevor?' Atia said as the pair walked up Bell Lane.

'If you start in the Horn of Plenty I'll go to the Britannia,' said Ashto wearily. He was beginning to wish he'd never set eyes on crowded, noisy and grubby East End public houses and cheap eateries. Over the last week he and Atia had visited so many such places and in the process had drunk many pints of the sour drink the locals called bitter ale and eaten some poor, badly cooked food. He longed to be able to visit a fine eating place like Fortescue's again. He longed for the rich, delicious and wholesome food they served up in that restaurant and even missed the occasional glass of red wine the Jaran pair had lately grown to appreciate.

Atia agreed to Ashto's plan and when they arrived at Dorset Street they looked at each other with fondness in their eyes before bidding farewell and reluctantly entering the respective pubs in that street.

The Horn of Plenty was a small dingy pub on the corner of Dorset Street and Crispin Street. As Atia walked into the gloomy, crowded room, which was, as usual, pungent with the smell of tobacco and stale beer she immediately discerned the loud and clear tones of a voice she knew well. Over in the corner, at a table with her man friend Joe and another female, sat Marie the young Irish woman. Atia smiled as she approached the table in her by now well-practised 'drunken' fashion.

'Marie,' Atia shouted.

'Margaret, me darlin',' shouted Marie in return as she stood up and hugged Atia. 'Let me go and buy you some beer,'

'No ta,' replied Atia, 'already 'ad a belly full tonight – I'm goin' to giv' it a rest for a bit.'

'Oh me darlin girl I hope you're not comin' down with some malady or other,' said Marie looking concerned.

'I'll be right as rain soon,' said Atia sitting down at the table nodding to Joe Barnett as she did so.

'Of course you already know Joe and this is my good friend the lovely Julia,' said Marie ruffling the straggly blonde hair of the woman who looked up at Marie and smiled.

Julia looked to be in her twenties and had the usual unkempt and slightly weary appearance of those who lived in the Whitechapel area. 'I am very pleased to meet with you,' said the woman in an accent that told Atia that she most probably had originated somewhere in the central or eastern part of the continent of Europe.

'Julia lived with me for a short while but now has got her own place nearby,' said Marie. As she spoke she looked across to Joe Barnett who looked a little embarrassed and to seemingly cover his discomfort picked up his beer glass and drained its contents.

'Well, I'll be off then Mary, I may come and see yer tomorrow if I 'ave the time,' said Joe somewhat sheepishly as he picked up his cap from the table, nodded to Atia and left.

Marie watched him leave, sadness in her eyes.

'Are things with Joe all right?' said Atia tentatively.

'No I'm afraid they're not, my dear Margaret. He upped and left me last week although, as you have witnessed, he comes to see me most days and check that I've got enough money to buy food and drink.'

'But why Marie, you two 'ave bin together for a long time?'

Marie turned to Julia and gave her a handful of coins she took from her little bag she had hanging from her shoulder. 'Go and get us a round of beer me darlin' girl while I speak to my old friend Margaret here.'

Julia got up and pushed her way to the crowded bar while Marie leaned in closer to Atia. 'He left me after I had let Julia stay in my bed for a few days – she had nowhere else to go. Joe said he could put up with me going whoring around the streets, although he didn't like it much, but he couldn't abide our room becoming a doss house for all the tarts of the district to sleep in. He was very vociferous on the subject so he was.' Marie rubbed her left eye, which Atia could see still looked somewhat discoloured; Joe had evidently aimed a punch there.

Atia grabbed Marie's hand and squeezed gently.

'And so Joe's living at Mrs Buller's boarding house and I'm on my own again with the darlin' boy coming to see me whenever the fancy takes him.' A tear ran out of Marie's injured eye and rolled down her cheek. She wiped it away as Julia returned with three glasses of beer. Marie picked hers up and smiling a forced smile said: 'Cheers my two lovelies,' and drank down half of the contents of her glass.

At the Britannia Ashto had carefully scanned the faces of those present and had not seen the man he now knew was the Whitechapel murderer. He wasn't surprised of course, the Ripper was far too canny; the fact that he hadn't been caught up to now proved as much.

Somewhat reluctantly Ashto bought himself a pint of bitter ale and sat down at a nearby table. The pub as usual was crowded and it wasn't very long before another man sat down at the same table. The man lit a cigarette and then offered one to Ashto.

'No thank you, I do not smoke.'

'Don't blame yer mate, filthy 'abit,' said the man blowing a plume of smoke in Ashto's direction. 'You ain't from roun' 'ere are yer?' continued the man.

'No, I am not. I originally came here from Germany,' replied Ashto quite pleased that his deliberately slightly accented speech had been noticed by the stranger.

'Workin'?' said the man.

'Yes I do work, at Shadwell docks.'

The man looked Ashto up and down.

'A docker eh. Dirty work?'

'Yes, and hard work too but it means I can eat and drink everyday.'

The man nodded and drank some of his beer. Out of the corner of his eye Ashto did a quick assessment of him. A manual worker obviously, the state of his clothes told him that. He had a pale face and fairish hair and drooping mustache made him look rather older than his chronological age that Ashto guessed to be late twenties or early thirties.

'So, my friend what's yer name? I'm Danny,' said the man holding out his hand.

Ashto shook his hand, which he thought was surprisingly soft and uncalloused and also showed distinct traces of ink on his fingers causing the Jaran First Commander to reassess the occupational activity of the man.

'My name is Johann,' replied Ashto.

'Is that a Jewish name?'

'No, just a German one, although there are many Jews living and working in Shadwell.'

'A lot roun' 'ere as well. Like rats scurrying about all secretive like — keepin' theirselves to theirselves — queerin' the pitch as it were.'

Ashto knew there was a great deal of anti-Jewish prejudice in the East End. Many Jews had migrated to London in recent years often from Russia where government inspired pogroms had forced them out of that country. However, Ashto was not going in any way to agree with the man's racially based disparaging comments about people he regarded as his fellow residents of Whitechapel, whatever their philosophical or religious beliefs.

'I cannot criticise other migrants as I am one myself,' said Ashto, 'and in my experience the vast majority of people in this area are decent, hard-working folk who are trying their best to survive in extremely difficult circumstances.'

'Well that's one point of view I s'pose,' said the man a look of skepticism having crossed his face. 'But anyway don't yer think Jack the Ripper is a Jew? Most o' those on the streets reckon 'ee is.'

'Who knows whether he is or not,' said Ashto, 'but in any case one person can never represent or stand for an entire race of people. If the Ripper is Jewish it does not mean that we should paint the whole of his community with the same brush.'

The man who had called himself Danny sneered and drank more of his beer. Ashto suddenly realised that he hadn't touched his and so to keep in character he took a large gulp of beer too. As he had found before the strange taste of the bitter ale was not quite as bad as he had anticipated.

'Gor blimey, mate' said the man putting down his glass, 'yer've got a way with words an' no mistake. Yer speak the Queen's English better than I do! 'Ow long 'ave yer been 'ere from … Germany, did you say.'

Ashto hoped that he hadn't been using English too properly. He drank some more of his beer to give him time to think.

'I have been in your country for ten years …' said Ashto as, out of the corner of his eye, he noticed that a familiar figure had just walked into the Britannia and quite suddenly the whole atmosphere inside the pub had changed.

Back in the Horn of Plenty Atia listened to Marie as she related more about her life. '… And then I married a man in Wales. John Davis his name was. Fine lookin' too – big, strong and dark – a coalminer he was. We were only together for a year and then one day in the village where we lived the hooters started hooting and the bells started ringin' and news spread around that there had been a collapse in one of the mine's tunnels. John and four others never got out. The poor boys never even had funerals.' Marie dabbed her eyes with a handkerchief she pulled from her bag and then took a large swig of her beer. 'And that's when I came to London and to its streets paved with gold.' She smiled at the thought and dabbed her eyes again.

Atia could see that despite Marie's smiles there was no doubt that the young woman was severely depressed. Getting drunk every night was obviously not helping her mental state one little bit. As Marie drained her pint glass and began sorting in her bag for money to pay for another Atia felt it necessary to make a suggestion.

'Tell yer what Marie shall we go back to yer place an' 'ave a nice cuppa tea? What do yer say Julia?'

Julia nodded and Marie, after making an initial protest, also agreed and rose unsteadily from her chair. There were one or two men who made comments directly to the young Irish woman as she swayed and staggered out of the pub and out onto the rain swept Dorset Street. 'Actually me darlin' girls,' slurred Marie as she walked with difficulty along the street, 'I am all out of funds for beer anyway as it turns out. What I have been spending tonight was my rent money for tomorrow that Joe gave me earlier.' She started to laugh, hiccupped, looked surprised and then vomited into the gutter. Julia held Marie's dark hair out of the way while she did so.

Atia and Julia guided the very drunken Marie down the alleyway to her room in Miller's Court and Julia retrieved the key to the door from Marie's bag. Inside the room they lay her down on the bed and Julia set about lighting a fire in the dark and cold room. Atia lit the only candle that stood in an old, wax-encrusted candlestick on the small table next to the bed.

Atia then discovered the reason why the room was so cold. One of the panes of glass in the window that faced out onto the court was broken and the piece of cloth that had been shoved in the hole in a halfhearted fashion only partially kept out the rain and cold blustery wind.

'Julia, do you know 'ow this 'appened?' said Atia pointing at the broken pane.

'I am afraid that happened because one day when Joe returned and found that I was still here he got very angry and he and Marie started shouting at each other. He hit her with his fist and she told him to get out and she threw something at him – a pottery figure I think – and instead of striking him it hit the window and broke it.'

Atia looked at Marie lying on the bed now peacefully asleep and breathing deeply and rhythmically. The Jaran Apprentice Commander deplored the fact that Joe had hit Marie and if she had been here when he had done that she would have laid him out unconscious in a moment but she also saw Joe Barnett's point of view and was not surprised that he had ended his and Marie's relationship. The fact that he had given money to Marie for food and the rent and had returned to see her on most days showed that he still cared for her in his own way. Marie, on the other hand, incorrigible as ever, had squandered her rent money on drink and would inevitably soon be prostituting herself again in order to obtain more money for beer and gin – and so it went on. Atia inwardly shrugged and decided to get back to the Horn of Plenty to look out for the Ripper. She was sure that Julia would stay to look after Marie until she woke up again –

the young foreign woman seemed capable and trustworthy enough. And then as Atia was preparing to leave Marie's room she received an urgent sounding, whispered message from Ashto via her hidden earphone. The First Commander was in trouble.

When Detective Inspector Reid along with Sergeant Thick entered the Britannia the noise and chatter in the pub immediately stopped. East End residents it was said could smell a policeman at a great distance and those inside the public house weren't afraid to give vent to their feelings about the police in the form of sneered comments delivered as stage whispers as the two detectives looked around the room.

Ashto kept his head down and was horrified when he realised the two police officers were heading towards the table he was sat at. Inspector Reid seemed to wave his hand in dismissal at the man Ashto had previously been speaking to who got up and quickly left the pub, his beer unfinished in his glass.

Inspector Reid sat down in the vacated chair and Sergeant Thick stood in a somewhat threatening fashion immediately behind the Jaran First Commander. 'So what are you calling yourself today Mr Ashton?'

For a moment Ashto thought he might stay in the character of the German docker, Johann Schmitt, and attempt to bluff his way out of the situation but then realised it was hopeless. It was obvious that the police Inspector had somehow already seen through his disguise and so he remained silent.

'Well then, Mr Ashton would you like to explain what it is you are doing here in your very unfamiliar garb?'

continued the Detective Inspector his steely gaze fixed on Ashto.

'I would have thought it was obvious Inspector Reid,' answered Ashto trying to sound as confident as possible, 'I am continuing to gather information for my book which, as you know, I have been researching since arriving in your country in the summer. Adopting this disguise is one way I can get to meet individuals and talk to them without in any way intimidating them.'

'That is very interesting, Mr Ashton. Can you therefore explain why you, along with your wife, have been seen on many occasions to have been frequenting various public houses in the area and acting in an extremely suspicious fashion.'

'Suspicious, Inspector – please explain what you mean by that?'

'What I mean by that Mr Ashton is that you have been followed for the past week by one of my undercover men, the very one you were speaking to when we arrived in fact. He has previously told me that you have been observed going into local pubs and doing nothing but sitting down talking to no one, while your wife, if indeed she is actually your wife, drunkenly cavorted around the said pubs attempting to solicit business. At the very least it looks as though you may have been living off her immoral earnings; at the worst it could be that you are the man they call Jack the Ripper.'

Ashto was horrified at what Reid had said. He tried to speak but nothing intelligible seemed to emerge from his mouth and he gasped as he felt the strong hand of Sergeant Thick grip his shoulder.

'I think,' said Inspector Reid, 'that, under the circumstances, and for the second time, I am going to ask you to accompany myself and the Sergeant to Leman Street police station for questioning.'

As the three men walked down Commercial Street Ashto put his hand up to his mouth and hurriedly said: 'Excuse me Inspector but I badly need to vomit.'

Edmund Reid nodded to his sergeant, whose hand had rested on the Jaran First Commander's shoulder all the way from the Britannia, to watch over Ashto as he bent over the gutter.

'Margot,' Ashto whispered into his microphone that was attached to the inside of his jacket's lapel, 'I've been arrested – Leman Street police station.' Ashto coughed, pretended to gag before standing up straight and rubbing his stomach.

'I think I am all right again now Inspector, thank you.'

Inspector Reid looked skeptical. He could have sworn that the disguised so-called American writer had been quietly speaking rather than throwing up but for now all he wanted to do was to get the suspect back to Leman Street, place him in one of the cells, sit down and have a nice cup of tea. It had been another long day.

Atia knew what she needed to do. After making certain that Julia was going to stay with Marie until she awoke she dashed back to Bell Lane changed into her Mrs Ashton clothes, quickly wiped her face clean of soot and set out for Leman Street.

Arriving at the police station she marched up to the desk sergeant gave him her sweetest smile and asked to see Inspector Reid. Although she didn't know who had arrested First Commander Ashto she suspected Reid would have had a hand in it and in any case the Inspector was the only police officer she knew by name.

After Atia had waited for about fifteen minutes the Inspector emerged from his office and invited Atia in.

'You've missed a little bit,' Reid said as he pointed at the side of Atia's face.

Atia took a handkerchief from her reticule and used it to wipe away the smear of soot from just below her left ear.

'Please sit down, Mrs Ashton,' said the Inspector.

'Thank you, Inspector,' said Atia, 'can you tell me why you have arrested my husband?'

'Yes, Mrs Ashton, I can. I have arrested your husband on suspicion of carrying out the recent Whitechapel murders.'

Atia was genuinely shocked. 'What? That is ridiculous. You must know that is impossible, Inspector.'

'Impossible, Mrs Ashton? I think not. The murders began at the same time that you and your husband arrived in London. There are indications that the letters sent to the Central News Agency and signed Jack the Ripper were written by an American. And finally your husband and indeed yourself have been observed on many occasions recently disguised as poorer members of the community and mingling with the customers of various public houses in the area and continuing to act in an extremely suspicious manner. That is certainly enough reason to hold your husband for questioning in the present circumstances and you can consider yourself quite fortunate, Mrs Ashton that you have not been arrested as well.'

'Is it possible for me to speak to my husband, Inspector Reid?' Atia was a little stunned at Reid's summing up of the evidence against Ashto and needed to discuss with her First

Commander what they should do to extricate him the from parlous situation he found himself in.

'It is certainly possible, Mrs Ashton, but first I would like you to answer me one question.'

'And what is that question, Inspector?'

Detective Inspector Edmund Reid opened a drawer in his desk, took something from it and placed it in front of where Atia was sitting. 'The question is, Mrs Ashton, what on Earth is this?'

Atia tried hard not to look shocked when she saw the object that she had last seen when the First Commander had put it in his jacket pocket. On the desk in front of her was one of the small, silver coloured computer terminals that she and Ashto had been using to receive scanning updates from the ship's computer as well as inputting data for the ship's database.

'So what did you say to Inspector Reid, Margot?'

'Well Trevor, I told him that it was a new type of clock that had recently been developed in the United States by a certain Mr Thomas Edison who is a prolific inventor and well known in that country.'

Ashto and Atia were sitting in a dark holding cell that smelt strongly of urine and was situated in the basement of Leman Street police station. A drunk in another cell was singing a popular ballad loudly and badly out of tune.

'And did he believe you, Margot?'

'Well I displayed a digital clock on the screen which seemed to impress him greatly but he held on to the computer and I'm rather worried that if he fiddles about with it or tries to take it apart he will discover that it contains technology far in advance of anything they have on Earth at the present moment.'

'Is there a possibility of getting it back do you think, Margot?'

'Only when they eventually choose to release you, Trevor. In the meantime I fervently hope that it will stay locked in Inspector Reid's desk drawer away from the prying eyes of other inquisitive humans. Fortunately I still have mine and have checked it constantly for any alerts the ship's computer may have issued.'

'Can you think of any strategy that could persuade the police to free me, Margot?' Ashto looked tired and dejected. He knew that he would probably have to spend the entire weekend in the police cell. He was aware that the Metropolitan police resources were fully stretched at the moment with not only the Ripper murders to investigate but with the security surrounding the Lord Mayor's Show, that it was their job, at least in part, to organise.

'I'm afraid not, Trevor,' said Atia who then had a thought. What if she were to enlist the support of Mr Rogers in attempting to persuade the police to free the First Commander. Surely the police would not welcome the Evening Standard reporter poking his nose into affairs at Leman Street and highlighting the ridiculous lengths the police were going to in order to find unlikely suspects to blame for the Ripper murders? Atia decided not to raise the First Commander's hopes too much by mentioning her idea but would, as soon as she left Leman Street, go straight to Mr Rogers' office in Fleet Street and inform him of the situation. Knowing that the newspaperman thought highly of her she was sure that he would agree to use his powers of investigative journalism to encourage Inspector Reid to let Ashto go.

'Time for you to leave Miss,' the policeman in charge of the cells said.

Atia looked at Ashto, sadness in her eyes. For one of the few times in her life she was on the verge of shedding tears. The Jaran pair embraced and kissed before Atia was ushered out of the cell, glancing back at the forlorn looking First Commander before walking back up the stairs from the basement.

Outside the police station and in the dark of the evening where it was still raining heavily, Atia hailed a hansom cab and told the driver to proceed with all haste to Fleet Street. It was late but Atia was hopeful that she would still find Mr Rogers hard at work in his office.

Arriving in Fleet Street and entering the Evening Standard offices Atia asked the woman behind the reception desk as to the whereabouts of Mr Rogers and was informed he had left the building some thirty minutes before. With a knowing glint in her eye the receptionist told Atia that she would almost certainly find the newspaperman in the Cheshire Cheese public house a short walk away further down Fleet Street.

Ye Olde Cheshire Cheese pub was a favourite meeting place for the journalist fraternity of Fleet Street. Although not quite as dark and squalid as many of the East End pubs Atia was now familiar with, it was still crowded, smoky and redolent with the aroma of beer and tobacco smoke.

Atia attracted a lot of attention as she peered into the many small rooms, nooks and crannies of the Cheshire Cheese looking for Mr Rogers. Although it was not unknown for certain ladies of the night to find their way into the pub it was generally considered to be the domain of males and not usually frequented by well-to-do women in expensive looking attire. The Apprentice Commander was just about to give up her search when Mr Rogers appeared from the outside where the pub's privies were located.

'Mrs Ashton,' said Mr Rogers obviously very surprised to see Atia.

'Mr Rogers, is it possible for us to speak outside?'

'Certainly,' said Rogers as he quickly unhooked his overcoat from a peg on which he had hung it. As he did so he was the butt of many ribald comments from the men he had been drinking with prior to Atia's arrival.

Outside the pub the pair stood in the pouring rain while Atia explained the predicament Ashto found himself in, stuck in a cell in Leman Street police station.

Mr Rogers listened intently to Atia's story and had just agreed to return with her to the police station when Atia felt a vibration in the small bag she carried. Leaving the computer in her bag and on the pretence of searching for a handkerchief in order to dry her eyes she peered at the small screen and her heart skipped a beat. The ship's computer scans had identified another DNA trace belonging to the Ripper. This time the DNA had not been left in a pub or in a dark alleyway. This time the location on the screen was given as 13, Miller's Court and Atia's blood felt as though it had been flash-frozen in her veins.

He had waited for a long time observing the comings and goings at the Britannia. While he lingered there he had sheltered from the rain in a narrow doorway across the street and every so often droplets of water pattered down onto his hat from the doorframe above. He had decided not to risk going inside the pub even though he had earlier seen the tall, scruffy man being taken away by the police for some reason but he didn't know whether the tall bitch was in there. He was waiting for someone in particular – the whore he had for a long time marked down to be his next job to carry out. She was a bit different to the others – younger, prettier, not yet so badly beaten down by her life of sin. He had often seen her solicit men outside the Britannia and then take them back to her room in Miller's Court. It would be good to be inside on such an inclement night – he wouldn't end up being drenched while he carried out his God given work and he would have much more time to do it. He waited. He looked at his watch. It was late. It was a good job that he was the patient sort and didn't rush into things. Everything he did had to be carefully considered, planned and practised – that had been the reason why the police had not caught him yet – that and the fact that they were a bunch of clodhopping idiots. He smiled. He shook his head so that a few more drops of water fell from the brim of his hat and plopped onto the ground. He could wait all night if necessary – he didn't mind. He took out his pipe and lit it keeping the match out of the rain as he did so.

And then he saw her as she crossed Commercial Street. She looked dishevelled and had a shawl wrapped tightly around her against the rain. 'Now is the time,' he whispered and crossed the street so as to intercept her before she went into the pub.

'Good evening, my dear, how are you?' The whore had looked at him obviously trying to remember if he was someone she knew. Her face looked pale, her eyes were red and bleary.

'I'm very well sir. Would you be willing to treat a lady to a drink at all?' she had replied.

'I would,' he said, 'but only after we have conducted a little business. Do you have a room nearby I could dry off in?' The whore looked as though she was in two minds but then reluctantly agreed.

The two crossed back over Commercial Street and in Dorset Street turned into the alley that led to number 13, Miller's Court. Inside, she lit the single candle, closed the sacking curtains that just about covered the window and then built up the fire, which soon began to warm up the small room. He took off his overcoat and hung it up on a peg next to a shelf on which there were a few pieces of cheap, chipped crockery. He took out two half-crown coins from his pocket – showed them to her and placed them on the shelf. She smiled and began to take off her clothes, folding them and placing them carefully on the chair. As she did so she sang a song – something about a violet picked from her mother's grave. The whore had a good voice he thought as he listened and watched her disrobe. When all she was wearing was a skimpy white chemise he told her to lie on the bed and close her eyes.

He stood over her. She looked peaceful – he would now give her peace forever. He took his knife from the waistband of his trousers. He would bring the knife to her soft white neck and then he would have plenty of time to complete his work. But then she had opened her eyes. She looked at the knife and opened *her mouth ready to scream. She was able to shout 'murder!' before he covered her mouth with his left hand. She grabbed his hand that held his knife and as he used his strength to bring it down to her neck she managed to deflect the knife away from her throat so that it made contact with his hand that lay over her mouth and muffled her screams. The knife slashed across the back of his hand and immediately bright red blood started to seep from the long cut and onto her face. He was angry now. He was not supposed to be hurt in any way – that was not part of the plan. He redoubled his effort as the whore's strength faltered. Her large, dark eyes widened still further as he brought the cold, sharp knife to her neck and felt it begin to slice into her throat. He smiled. He removed his hand from her mouth; the only sound coming from her now was a quiet gurgling as the blood gushed from her throat and onto the bed. He tore off a piece of her chemise and wrapped it around his injured and still bleeding hand and then watched as the life seeped out of the body of the pretty, young woman lying on the bed.*

24

13, Miller's Court

Atia told Mr Rogers that she would be very grateful if he would go to Leman Street police station and ask about her husband who now languished in the cells. She hoped he would do so on the pretext that he would like to write an article about how the police were so bereft of ideas they were now arresting all and sundry, including innocent foreign writers, and accusing them of committing the Whitechapel murders irrespective of the fact that they had little or no evidence to support their accusations. Atia hoped that the mere thought of the story appearing in the Evening Standard newspaper would be enough to ensure that Inspector Reid would release the First Commander.

'You will not be coming with me?' said Rogers.

'No, I believe that it would be a less effective strategy if Inspector Reid suspected that we were acting in unison,

Mr Rogers,' said Atia quickly, desperate to leave and travel as quickly as she could to Marie's room in Miller's Court. She flagged down a passing hansom cab and waved a brief farewell to Mr Rogers who stood outside the Fleet Street pub looking slightly baffled and confused.

Atia sat on the edge of the cab seat mentally willing the cabby to go faster. Would she be there in time to save Marie from the clutches of the Ripper? She felt a great sense of foreboding and dread with regard to the young Irish woman, someone she had grown fond of lately. The Ripper did not need very much time to kill his victims. Normally he did so outside. Why on this occasion did he appear to be inside a prostitute's room? There was a small sliver of hope in that anomaly. Perhaps the Ripper had given in to his sexual urges and planned to spend time with Marie in her role of a prostitute before taking her outside in order to kill her. Or perhaps he planned to leave Marie unscathed before going out and killing some other unfortunate woman. She did not know. The time until she arrived was almost unbearably tense but eventually the hansom cab pulled up in Dorset Street and Atia quickly paid the driver before hoisting up her skirts and dashing down the alleyway that led to Marie's room.

Outside the room Atia paused. There were no sounds coming from the inside. Atia went round to the window. From behind the sacking curtains there was light in the room and Atia could perceive some shadowy movement. There was nothing else for it but to force her way in. She carefully tried the door handle fully expecting to have to use her considerable strength to batter it open but there was no resistance as she slowly opened the door to the room. What she found inside was a sight so horrific that it would forever be graphically imprinted on her memory and would cause her to suffer recurrent nightmares for the rest of her life.

The Ripper stood next to the bed in the process of putting on his long overcoat that would cover up his blood soaked jacket, waistcoat and trousers. He first looked surprised at the sudden appearance of Atia and then smiled and picked up his long knife that had been lying on the bed. His hands and clothes were red with gore and blood dripped from his knife onto the floor. Atia dragged her eyes from the Ripper to the figure that lay on the bed. A short time ago it had been a fully functioning human being, capable of laughter, tears, happiness and sadness, with dreams for the future and regrets about the past – a person Atia had met and talked with, sympathised with, and liked. What lay on the bed in a pool of viscous red with its legs spread wide apart was now no longer a person. Beside the eviscerated body, between its feet and on the nearby table lay piles of bloody flesh and internal organs in what looked like some perverted and hideous butcher's stall in a hellish meat market. But what was worse, worse even than the horror of that which had happened to the body that was in some places completely denuded of flesh with bones clearly visible, was the face. The 'face' – it could now no longer be called as such for the features had all but disappeared from it. The nose, ears, lips, eyebrows and the cheeks had all been hacked away and great irregular gashes ran from the forehead to the chin and from one side to the other. Only one dark eye remained untouched, open and staring out as if surveying the damage that had been done to the rest of its body, a clear look of horror permanently fixed upon it.

Atia stood open mouthed unable to move her eyes away from the unmitigated horror that lay on the bed, unable to fully take in the grim magnitude of the sight before her. Never had she imagined a scene so horribly alien as that which she now gazed upon. After what seemed to be an age she managed again to look at the Ripper standing there, half of his body illuminated red and orange by the blaze that roared in the fireplace. He continued to smile at Atia as if pleased with what he had done and gratified that there was another to witness his great achievement at first hand. This was the culmination of his work; this was what it had all been leading up to. He had not only killed the whore but had been able to eradicate her completely – to send her to hell without a face – an anonymous entity that no one ever again would recognise in this world or the next. And now he would have to kill another – kill this finely dressed woman who stood before him – the woman whose eyes were wide and whose mouth was open in a look of shock and disbelief. Who was she? Why was she here? He would probably never know for in a few short minutes she would also lie on the bed with her delicate throat slit from ear to ear. It would be a fine memorial for him – two dead in one room. In a way it was a pity this woman had to die for she obviously was not a whore although she did strongly remind him of someone else he had seen recently. Who was it? No matter; it wasn't important. He approached her, his knife at the ready. It would be easy – she seemed frozen to the spot – shocked into immobility.

Atia felt numb. It took her a second or two for her mind to refocus away from the hideous sight she had witnessed. The Ripper was approaching her – moving towards her as though in slowed down motion – long, red knife in his right hand, demonic eyes blazing. The Apprentice Commander's fine features suddenly twisted into a grimace and she snarled like a trapped animal as the Ripper struck – his knife aiming straight for her throat. She grabbed his arm – he looked confused as she forced him backwards and twisted his hand to an unnatural position. There was a loud popping crack as his wrist dislocated – he screamed and dropped the knife but was able to lash out with his angry left fist and catch Atia with a heavy blow on her cheekbone, forcing her to take a step backwards. That gave him time to pick up the knife with his uninjured hand and lunge at Atia again. Atia, momentarily stunned by the blow to her face, was slow to get out of the way and the Ripper's knife plunged deep into her right side burying itself up to its hilt.

The Ripper, his face just inches away from Atia's, grinned. He would pay her back for hurting his wrist, which now hung limply by his side. When she was dead he would strip her of her fine clothes and carve great slices from her tall body and place bits of her next to those of the whore on the bed. He pulled the knife from the woman's side and drew it back. No messing about this time – he would stab it into her throat and let her bleed out like a calf in the butcher's yard.

Atia ignored the extreme pain in her side and looked into the Ripper's eyes. She now knew what it was she had seen in his eyes in the pub a few days before. She already had known that the Ripper would have to have been mentally unbalanced to do what he had done but she had never before witnessed absolute and total madness reflected in someone's eyes in such a way. It was as though all of his inner mania had been deeply and secretively contained within them – kept locked away from the world – piercing and dark as they were – in order to keep his evil secret safe from the rest of humanity. It would have enabled him to live as an ordinary person so far as the rest of the world was concerned but would have caused him, every so often to commit actions of such unspeakable violence and barbarity that most would have found it beyond impossible to comprehend. Now these eyes were focused on her – on her throat – as she heard a strange sucking noise as the Ripper withdrew his knife from her side and prepare to deal her a final blow. Mustering all her strength she lifted her right leg – a sharp excruciating pain shot down her side as she did so – and kicked out – catching the Ripper in his midriff and propelling him backwards against the wooden partition wall of the room.

The Ripper looked surprised and stopped smiling. He began to move towards her again. Atia reached for her bag that had fallen onto the floor, with a shaking hand she found the disrupter that nestled inside and withdrew it. She pointed it at the Ripper who first looked confused and then smiled again. He raised his knife. Atia could see that there was no way that he was going to allow himself to be apprehended and taken to the police. He was obviously intent on killing her but she would have to give him a chance to surrender himself.

'This is a powerful weapon,' she said raising the disrupter and pointing it at him, 'drop your knife and come quietly with me in order to find the nearest police officer.'

The Ripper grinned now despite the pain in his right wrist. Who is this woman? Who does she think she is? That weapon – what is it? It doesn't look like a revolver or any other pistol he had ever seen before – why would a small piece of silvery metal cause him to give himself up to this woman? He grinned and lunged forward again with his knife

So be it thought Atia who fired the disrupter at the advancing, hideously bloody figure of the Ripper. A bright beam of light surrounded the killer who stopped, opened his mouth in a scream that never emerged and disappeared as every atom in his body and the knife he held were forced apart leaving only a fine mist momentarily suspended in the air, which was soon dissipated into nothingness by the heat radiating from the fire and the cold draught from the broken window.

Atia remained frozen in her position; eyes open wide, unblinking, her face pale as death and the disrupter now pointing at nothing in particular except the back wall of the room. He was gone – she had killed him – she had taken a life – something she had never done before. She felt stunned and then she slowly moved her head to look again at the sight of the carnage that lay on the bed. She peered again at the bloody and desecrated remains of poor Marie that were scattered at random around the room. She sobbed. Tears rolled down the Apprentice Commander's face as she slowly took in the full panoply of horror that lay before her and the violent events that had just happened. And then she realised she must quickly leave this hellish room. She couldn't afford to be found here – she would have to answer far too many questions. With difficulty she moved again suddenly becoming aware of the painful throb in her side. She dropped the disrupter back into her bag and left the room, closing the door quietly, almost reverentially, behind her. She held her side from which blood still poured and which caused her a pain like she had never felt before, walked up the alleyway that led to Dorset Street and slowly made her slow and difficult way back to Mrs Smith's guesthouse.

My greetings and utmost felicitations to the esteemed members of the Sub-Committee.

I am very pleased to be able to inform the Sub-committee that the killer known almost universally on the Earth as 'Jack the Ripper' is no more. The murderer was stopped in his tracks by Apprentice Commander Atia who was able to dispatch him by using her disrupter and ensuring that the 'Ripper' will never be heard of again. Unfortunately, before the Apprentice Commander could deal with him, he had succeeded in killing again, another unfortunate female of the Whitechapel area who had become known to Atia. The Apprentice Commander also suffered a serious injury in the process of her struggle with the murderer. When I returned to our lodgings I discovered her lying on the bed with a deep puncture wound in her side from which she had lost a large amount of blood. Luckily I was able to treat her injury using the supplies present in our medikit and did not have to risk taking her into one the rather primitively equipped buildings the Earth humans have designated as medical facilities. I am pleased to report that after a short period of rest and recuperation the Apprentice

Commander will be fit and well and ready to resume her duties and our mission.

Whilst Atia was dealing with the Whitechapel murderer I had been spending time being incarcerated by the local policing authorities. Inspector Reid, who I have mentioned before in my reports, had taken me into police custody because he suspected me, of all people, to be Jack the Ripper. An acquaintance of ours, a journalist called Rogers – again I have referred to this human in past reports – was able to intervene on my behalf and convince the police that I was innocent of all their accusations. His help eventually proved to be superfluous as it turned out for as soon as Reid and the rest of the Whitechapel police force realised that another 'Ripper' murder had taken place, one which it was patently obvious could not have been committed by me, I was released.

It will be good to get back to the main substance of our orientation mission here on planet Earth again, after the anguish and chaos caused by the recent murders. Apprentice Commander Atia and I now intend to range far and wide over the London area. Whether we will do so from our base in Whitechapel or not we will need to discuss between ourselves over the next few weeks. What is certain, however, is that we will continue to send detailed data to the Sub-committee regarding conditions here on Earth and also continue to file reports about our general findings over the next four or so years. As planned we will eventually be able to give our substantive recommendations as to the viability or not for the planet Earth's peaceful inclusion into the Glorious Jaran Galactic Federation of planets.

Therefore, as usual, I will continue to report back to the Sub-Committee on our future observations with reference to the planet and would be fully prepared to answer any questions about our progress so far that any member of the Sub-Committee would care to ask.

With my utmost loyalty, etcetera,
First Commander Treve Pacton Ashto.

25

Aftermath

'I wonder what his name was?' said Atia.

'We'll probably never know,' replied Ashto. 'I'm sure that the police could find out if they wanted to but I think that they will be satisfied when they realise that the murders have ceased and that life in the East End can return to some sort of normality.'

The Jarans were sitting on a bench in Hyde Park. They were wrapped up warmly against the November cold but they were enjoying the sunshine that had, unseasonably, descended upon the city of London.

'Hmm, a return to normality,' said Atia. 'I suppose that will mean that the poor of Whitechapel will remain poor; the rich will remain rich; the exploited will stay exploited; husbands will beat their wives with impunity and the homeless will continue to starve and freeze to death on the streets.'

'I'm afraid so Margot, but at least the Ripper has gone and women all over Whitechapel will no longer have to fear for their very lives each night.'

'Trevor, we should at the very least anonymously inform Inspector Reid that the Ripper has now disappeared for good. Perhaps if we pen a letter to him and say that Jack the Ripper is no more.'

'That is certainly possible, Margot, but whether any credence would be given to such a letter is debatable – the police have received many hundreds of letters of one sort or another in recent times. I have a feeling that the police and the public will argue for many years as to the Ripper's true identity and why the murders suddenly stopped.'

Atia sighed. She felt tired and the strain of her encounter with the Ripper and the injury she received at his hands was still evident on her face. The last few months, since the Jaran pair had first arrived on the Earth, seemed to have been going on for far longer. For the first time since joining the Explorer Executive Atia had begun to wonder if she was actually suited to the task she had been sent to tackle. Since first speaking to Marie, or Mary Jane Kelly as the newspapers were now referring to her, she had, for the first time in her life, felt homesick. Poor Marie had missed her childhood home in Ireland. Had she stayed there she would not have become the final victim of the man known as Jack the Ripper. Instead she had ended up in a small, squalid room in the East End of London brutally murdered, her body then mutilated in a hideous fashion. Atia had wept for Marie and all the women whose lives had been taken from them in such a horrific manner. In her grief Atia had felt a strong urge to see her friends and family back on Jara and talk face to face with them.

Of course she had no intention of giving up the exploration of space, something she had wanted to do since she was a small child. She knew that it was her job to stay on the planet Earth for the next 4 years and 8 months or so and complete the task she had been set. All that had happened in the short time they had been on the Earth had convinced her that exploration was something she enjoyed and was something that she wanted to continue doing. Her relationship with Ashto was an added bonus and was something that made her feel happy and went some way to dispel the sheer horror of the incident with the Ripper. She still felt a twinge of pain in her side when she moved around and she found that she needed to rest rather more than before but she had the First Commander to thank for the fact that she had recovered from her injury relatively quickly. Luckily the Ripper's long knife, that he had plunged into her, had not damaged any internal organs and Ashto had been able to clean and close up the wound easily enough using their emergency medikit. If only he could take away her memory of seeing what was left of the body of poor Marie after the Ripper's frenzied attack.

The Jaran pair had decided not to inform the authorities about the Ripper's demise – to have done so directly would have certainly caused the police, in the form of Inspector Reid, to have bombarded them with questions the answers to which would probably have compromised their mission. No, Reid and the police force would have to solve the conundrum of the Ripper on their own. Of course the police had found the body of Mary Jane Kelly later that morning and the whole of London, if not the entire planet, had been utterly horrified at the details of the killing that had emerged at the inquest that had been held shortly afterwards. Marie's funeral had taken place at Leytonstone Roman Catholic cemetery on the 19th November. Atia had donned her Maggie disguise one more time in order to attend – it was her first trip out following her injury. Also present were Joe Barnett and Julia along with a number of other local women who had known Marie. Despite the worldwide publicity that had surrounded the murder not one single member of Marie's family was present to watch her coffin being committed to the ground. Afterwards Atia had stood at the graveside for a long time, tears running freely down her cheeks.

Coming away from the cemetery Atia fervently hoped that the public would soon forget the name of Jack the Ripper and focus on those of the poor, destitute women who had died so horribly. Perhaps, because of the murders, society here in London might one day improve and become a fairer and more equitable place but she very much doubted that anything substantial would change all that soon. If and when the Jaran Federation became involved in the affairs of the planet Earth then maybe, at some point in the future, the people of the planet might experience progressive improvements that would lead to a greater opening up of opportunities for all and a fairer distribution of wealth and resources. She would look forward to that day when the residents of the East End of London could begin to lead lives that were as free from poverty and privation as were those of the West End 'toffs'.

It was while Atia was deep in thought that she became aware that a familiar voice had spoken. Standing in front of the Jaran pair's Hyde Park bench doffing his bowler hat was the figure of William Rogers

'Well what a coincidence that I should bump into you both again so quickly after our recent exploits,' said Rogers.

The Jaran pair got up from the bench and shook the newspaperman's hand.

'Can I thank you again Mr Rogers for helping obtain the release of my husband from the Leman Street police cell,' said Atia.

'I'll add my thanks again also, Mr Rogers,' said Ashto.

'Think nothing of it. It was one of my most exciting days. A famous American writer in gaol disguised as a manual labourer on the very night another Ripper murder took place. I have to admit I got very little sleep that evening.'

'Well thank you again in any case,' said Ashto, 'and also for not revealing in your newspaper that I was in disguise. As I explained at the time that little deception did allow me to venture into places in Whitechapel that would otherwise have been closed to me and I was able to learn a great deal about the local area and its people.'

'I fully understand,' said Rogers smiling, 'think nothing of it Mr Ashton. I hope that we can consider each other to be friends in the future.'

Ashto smiled back, not quite sure whether Rogers' friendly demeanour and comment were totally genuine. 'I am certain that we will, Mr Rogers. And now we must take our leave and continue our researches. Good day Mr Rogers, I am sure that we will meet again soon.'

Rogers smiled again, doffed his hat and watched the pair walk away a wry and slightly quizzical look on his face.

As the Jaran pair continued along the park path Atia mused aloud: 'I wonder how it is Mr Rogers continues to find us in all sorts of places?'

'Hmm, it seems to happen all too frequently to be mere coincidence, Margot.'

'I have a feeling that we haven't seen the last of that individual, Trevor.'

'You are almost certainly correct, Margot.'

Atia looked at Ashto who had suddenly sighed deeply. He looked rather sad and careworn.

'What is the matter, Trevor?'

'I was just thinking, Margot that I have now sent off several reports to the Sub-Committee along with a great deal of data detailing our work here on this planet and I have not, as yet, received any sort of response or indeed any acknowledgement from any of the members of the Sub-Committee. I wonder at times if anyone back on Jara ever bothers to even read my reports.'

Atia was surprised at the First Commander's comments. He had never before expressed any doubts at all about the Sub-Committee in their supervisory role.

'I'm sure that they have been studying your reports with great interest, Trevor.'

'I sincerely hope that you are correct, Margot, but I have recently had a feeling that this planet, this Earth is so unimportant in their eyes that the reports are simply filed away unread and that the minds of the members of the Sub-Committee are focused on the ongoing missions on planets nearer to Jara that are seen to be more profitable or are places that seem easier for the ideals of the Federation to take root. Explorer-class ships with only two personnel aboard like ours are only ever sent to the most distant or less strategically important planets in the galaxy. Those places the Committee deem to be more vital locations are visited by bigger and more sophisticated vessels containing a larger and more specialist crew to complete the initial study of the planet in question. Aboard those ships would be exo-planet experts – biologists, geologists, chemists, sociologists, anthropologists, historians, computer technicians – some ships even have dedicated artists and writers to help assess the planet's viability in more esoteric ways. In our case however, there is just the two of us to carry out all those disparate roles and I have begun to wonder whether the Federation would be the slightest bit interested in taking a planet like the Earth under its wing at all. Oh well,' Ashto sighed, 'I'm sure that, as you say, I am completely mistaken and that the Sub-Committee is taking our work here completely seriously. I certainly hope that is the case.'

And then First Commander Ashto suddenly stopped in his tracks, a look of deep concern on his face. 'Oh no! I've just remembered something, Margot.'

'What is it, Trevor?'

'The computer terminal that Inspector Reid took from me at Leman Street police station – he still has it!'

Historical Notes

Most of the details in this story are historically accurate and are the result of a good deal of research about London during that fascinating late-Victorian period when it was undoubtedly the richest and most important city in the world. Despite the wealth of London, built upon the profits of an Empire 'on which the sun never set', extremes of poverty existed in areas like Whitechapel that is hard for us to comprehend. Like Ashto and Atia we would find the unfair and unequal society and lack of opportunity for the vast amount of people there quite alien compared to today's world.

The main books I used for my research, all of which are excellent, were:

The Jack the Ripper A-Z – Paul Begg, Martin Fido and Keith Skinner

Jack the Ripper, The Definitive History – Paul Begg

Jack the Ripper, Scotland Yard Investigates – Stewart P. Evans and Donald Rumbelow

The Five – Hallie Rubenhold

Walks Around London No. 2, Jack the Ripper's London – Leonard James

The Subterranean Railway – Christian Wolmar

The Victorian Dictionary of Slang and Phrase – J. Redding Ware

All of the pubs mentioned in the book actually existed and some, like the Ten Bells are still serving beer (and gin) to this day. Fortescue's restaurant in the Strand was an invention, however, as was Mrs Smith's Select Guesthouse in Bell Lane.

Most of the people mentioned in the novel by name were real. Joseph Merrick did have rooms at the London Hospital, Inspector Reid and Sergeant Thick did investigate some of the murders from their base at Leman Street Police Station, Joe Barnett was Mary Kelly's man friend and Squibby (possible real name George Cullen) was a violent East End Criminal. Mrs Smith and the journalist Mr Rogers were pure inventions, however.

As we all know Jack the Ripper, the perpetrator of the hideous crimes against perfectly innocent women in the East End of London, was never caught and after the terrible killing of Mary Jane Kelly seemed to disappear without trace. My solution as to who he was is only one of many that have been put forward over the years. It has always seemed likely to me that the Ripper was a butcher, slaughtermen or market worker local to Whitechapel, anonymous and on the surface quite ordinary. Secretly, however, he would have had deep psychopathic tendencies along with, for some perverted reason, a violent hatred of women.

First Commander Ashto and Apprentice Commander Atia are, of course, also fictional characters and London – as far as I know – was not visited by aliens in 1888. The Jaran explorers will return for further adventures in the future and now they have developed a taste for sleuthing and tracking down highly dangerous criminals who knows what they might get up to in the future?

Neil Coley